Commuters

Patrick S. Lafferty

For Bridget

Acknowledgments

In addition to my ridiculously supportive wife, I want to thank everyone who had a hand in getting this story out there. To my boys, Aidan and Conor, thanks for pumping me up when things looked grim. Thanks to Deb and Phil Harris at *All Things That Matter Press* for their vision and guidance. Thanks to Chris Bartholf, Katie Boyle Earle, Dan Lafferty and Jean Todd, as well as Rob Riley, Eric Lanke and the other members of the MWW Novel Group who helped me fine-tune this manuscript. And a special thanks to Bev & Clay Lafferty for their decades of unwavering love.

PART ONE

He's Gone

CHAPTER 1

Twenty-eight years ago Mitchell Treadwell witnessed his first murder. In just a few hours he'd witness his last.

He sat in his BMW waiting at the red light, his phone held to his ear, the man on the other end assuring him that the changes Mitchell wanted made to the China contracts were in place and approved by all parties. Just then, from the corner of his eye, he noticed a young man who looked an awful lot like his youngest son, Davis, standing on the corner of the busy intersection. He rolled down the passenger window of his black sedan, leaned across the middle console and said, "What are *you* doing here?"

The young man jumped, frightened by the intrusion.

"Dad?" He looked around as if expecting to see a hidden film crew.

"Hey, I thought you didn't work on Tuesdays."

"I usually don't. But they needed me to cover for someone."

"So what are you doing out here?"

As they were talking, the light turned green and Mitchell felt the pressure from his fellow drivers to move his vehicle. He motioned to his son to meet him a little ways down on the cross street. Mitchell turned right and pulled up to the curb about fifty feet from the corner. He continued on the phone and watched his son make his way to where the sedan now idled next to the curb. Davis crouched down, folded his arms, rested them on the door and listened to the window hum all the way down into its weather-sealed slot as Mitchell held out a finger to indicate he was one minute from finishing his call. Mitchell noticed Davis stand back up, in apparent disbelief that his call would only take a few more seconds. He quickly said good-bye and hung up. "So, you're working, huh?"

"Yeah."

"If they're paying people to stand around outside, maybe I'll apply."

They both smiled and forced a small laugh.

"Nah, I *was* working, filling in for someone." Then, looking as though he were searching for something just out of sight, he added, "But he showed up and they told me I could leave."

"So what are you doing now?"

"I never really get a chance to see what's going on out here at night so I thought I'd just kick around for a while and then head home."

The downtown area had changed recently, not in appearance but in its feel, its vibe. It was not the kind of place any father wanted to see his son after dark on a cold, autumnal night. "I don't want to sound like an old fart but you shouldn't be hanging around these street corners at night."

"Yeah, I suppose. There's really not much for me to do around here anyway, at least not 'til I start drinking coffee or I turn twenty-one."

"Coffee'll kill you. And alcohol, well," Mitchell smiled wide and rubbed his stomach, "alcohol will only slow you down."

Again, they both forced a small laugh.

"Do you need a ride home?"

"Nah, I got mom's car back behind the Unique Boutique."

"So, I'll see you at home?"

"I'll be just a few minutes behind you."

Mitchell rolled up the window and pulled away from the curb, anticipating his final meeting of the day, his most important meeting of the year, with mild apprehension.

* * *

Davis watched his father pull away. He pulled his keys from his pants pocket, swirled them on his index finger and crossed the street, the whole time thinking about the ridiculousness of the evening's misadventures. He entered the alleyway leading to the small parking lot behind the Unique Boutique. The single street light on the alley was out, but the moonlight cast a soft glow across the twenty-or-so cars that filled the lot as well as its lone inhabitant: a short gentleman walking toward him. Davis noticed as they passed that the man seemed to be staring at him as if studying his face. Then the man spoke.

"Were you just standing out on the corner?"

He stopped and turned to face the man. "Yeah." He nervously chuckled at his own embarrassment while looking down at the ground.

"I was just coming to talk to you."

He chuckled again, "Really?"

"Yeah, I was wondering if you and me could have a little party together."

CHAPTER 2

The woman was near hysterics as she yelled into the receiver. "Connie, it's me, Prudy. I think something's happened to Davis. No, I know something's happened to Davis. You have to come over right now."

Sitting at her desk in the stationhouse, Officer Constance Wysczyzewski replied in a soothing tone, "Prudy, calm down. I'm right in the middle of my shift. I can't just—"

"Your nephew is missing, Connie. For Christ's sake! You have to come over now!"

Connie debated about which face to put on: the concerned police officer who knew it was probably another teenage kid who just stayed out a little too late, or the supportive sister who could be relied upon to see her older sibling through any difficulty, real or perceived. Connie hoped Prudy would take the pregnant pause as an opportunity to relax. "Take a few deep breaths and tell me what you mean by missing."

"Missing!"

Before her sister could go any further, Connie interrupted, "Deep breaths first."

Connie heard her sister on the other end of the line inhale and exhale with audible bursts from her lips. She did this once more before continuing, only slightly less agitated than before. "Mitchell was coming home from work when he saw Davis in front of the Ridgeway Theater. They talked for a bit and then Davis said he'd be home right after his father. Mitchell saw him cross the street and go into the alley where he parks, but he never made it home. That was over an hour ago."

Connie looked at the clock on the wall. It was 10:33 p.m. She then cycled through the thoughts in her head to come up with a non-committal response that would satisfy her sister. "Kids Davis's age are always coming home late, you know that. Chances are he's just out with some friends."

"Then why would he tell Mitchell he'd be right home? That's just a lie he couldn't possibly wiggle out of. It doesn't make sense."

Connie could see Prudy's point, but it still wasn't enough to convince her that Davis wouldn't walk through the door later that evening. Connie had to reassure Prudy that this was typical teenage behavior, nothing more. Connie had to reassure Prudy on hundreds of issues, some as inconsequential as what dessert to bring to the neighborhood association's annual pot luck dinner and some as imperative as checking into alcohol rehabilitation after laying in a pool of her own blood, gashed by the broken vodka bottle on which she had fallen.

Prudy pressed on. "Connie, this isn't some hysterical melodrama. Something's happened to Davis and I need you to find out what. Right now, before I go insane with worry."

And with that, Connie acquiesced: she went into detective mode. "You said something about an alley before."

"Yes, oh, yes, the Unique Boutique, across the street from the Ridgeway. It has a little parking lot in the back. That's where Davis parks when he's working."

"And he was at work?"

"He usually doesn't work Tuesdays, but he got a call this afternoon to come in. No, wait, he called them. Does that matter?"

Connie attempted to hear Prudy's words as impartially as she could and what she heard was a son lying to his mother.

"Was he driving the Volvo?"

"No, my Audi. Lowell had the Volvo."

"Is Lowell home?"

"Yes, and when I asked him if he knew anything about what Davis was doing this evening, he said he didn't know anything."

Connie knew brothers conspired against their parents, just as she and her sister had done when they were growing up. Prudy's translation of Lowell's comments did nothing to support her case.

"Did you call any of his friends?"

"Why would I do that? Mitchell had just spoken to him and he said he'd come right home. Damn it, Connie."

"Prudy, look." All pretenses of hiding her annoyance were gone from Connie's voice. "I've gotten hundreds of calls just like this from frantic parents just like you and they all end up the same: the kid was just out with his friends." She paused to collect herself. "Now, you said Mitchell's home. What does he think about all this?"

Prudy didn't say anything for a long while. Then, with defeat in her voice, she said, "He thinks the same thing you do."

Connie waited before speaking, this time hoping her sister would accept the situation's most logical conclusion. "I'll tell you what, my partner and I will check out the parking lot and be at your place as soon as we can. My guess is that Davis will be home by the time I get there, but even if he's not, please promise me you'll try to relax. It's not so late that you can't start calling his friends to see if their parents are waiting up for their kids, too."

"All right, Connie. That's a good idea. I'll get something to calm my nerves and make some calls. But I'm telling you, I know something's happened to him."

"Prudy?" Connie hesitated.

"Hmm?"

Connie tried to be tactful. "Why don't you put on some tea for aroma and try meditating to relax." Then, unconcerned with whether she was being tactful or not, Connie said, "Stay away from the liquor and don't take any pills. They'll just make things worse."

"Thank you for your concern, Connie, but I know exactly what two things I don't need: babying from you and poison in my system."

They both hung up angry.

CHAPTER 3

Prudence Treadwell pulled out the phone book from under the kitchen desk, looked up under Stevenson the number for Michael and Christine. She dialed and looked at the clock above her stovetop. It read 10:39.

"Hi, Michael, this is Prudy Treadwell, Davis's mother. I'm sorry for calling so late, but Davis hasn't come home from work yet and I was wondering if maybe he and Tom were out together."

"No, Tom's right here watching something on his phone, but let me ask him if he knows anything."

Prudy could hear the muffled sounds of voices beyond Michael's hand as it covered the mouthpiece.

"No, Prudy, I'm sorry. Tom says he doesn't know what Davis was doing tonight."

"Well, thanks, Michael."

"No problem. Talk to you soon."

"Good night."

Prudy made a half dozen more calls with similar results, leaving her feeling more and more anxious each time she hung up. Scared and alone in the kitchen, the panic that had been building all evening reached near-critical levels. She sought the company of her husband for support and reassurance only to find him in the shower.

"What are you doing in the shower, sweetheart?"

"I've got a conference call with China at midnight. Then I'm working through the night and taking tomorrow off. I told you that this morning, remember?"

She didn't and wondered if he had actually told her anything about it that morning. She sat on the toilet and pleaded, "But you can't leave now, with Davis still out there."

"It's an important call. I can't just not go."

"Your son is important, too, Mitchell."

"Yes, he is, as are Lowell and you and everyone else in my life. But what can I do? Sit around and wait?"

"You could help me," she blurted out. Her tone was more needy than she intended. She composed herself and continued. "I'm a nervous wreck, Mitchell. It'd be nice if you could put your career on the back burner for once instead of placing me and the boys second."

"You and the boys are always first, you know that. Everything I do is for you. I'm sure Connie agreed with me, that he's probably just staying out late." He seemed to wait for her reply, and when none came, he

6

stated with an unnatural confidence, "I'm sure he's just fine, sweetheart. My being here isn't going to help matters. If you need someone, Lowell's home. And I'll bet your sister said she was coming over, too."

This time she replied angrily. "What if she did?"

"Good. She's a cop. She knows more about this stuff than I do and she's much more, I don't know, maternal, soothing."

"You mean Connie's more caring?" Prudy prodded. "More loving?" And with that she stood up and walked out.

Prudy could still hear Mitchell trying in vain to navigate the conversational hot water in which he placed himself as she hurried down the hall and into Davis's room. It was clean but cluttered, which made scavenging the top of his desk that much more difficult. She quickly scanned his bulletin board covered with various pictures and newspaper clippings and business card-sized notes. She looked for a name or a number, some tidbit of information that might indicate where he might be, but nothing stood out.

She grabbed the pull for the desk's lap drawer and hesitated. The boys' rooms were always their own and she never violated what she perceived as their privacy. The most time she ever spent in their rooms was to vacuum the floor or to drop off clean clothes, which the boys were expected to fold and put away themselves. The top of his desk and the bulletin board were out in the open and subject to inspection, according to Prudy's sensibilities. Looking through his drawers, on the other hand, was an invasion. The hesitation from her moral standards gave way to her fright and she pulled the drawer open.

She rummaged through the pens and pencils, paperclips and tacks, finding nothing that she believed of any use. She opened the next drawer and it, too, offered no help. In the next drawer, beneath a handful of sports magazines and clothes catalogs, was a curious magazine called *Going Down*. Upon reading its title and seeing its cover—the front half of a pretty young blonde looking over her shoulder and beaming a wide smile at the camera as the large, erect penis held in her hand splashed one last dollop of semen on her already-glazed face—Prudy flushed.

"What are you doing?"

Prudy seized wildly as every muscle in her body contracted in reflexive response to the interruption. She threw the magazine into the drawer, shut it and turned around in one quick yet utterly awkward motion. Standing there in the doorway was her oldest child.

"Jesus Christ, Lowell. You scared me half to death."

He chuckled. "Sorry."

"Don't you ever sneak up on me like that," she said loudly, analyzing whether she said it out of shock from the jolt or the embarrassment of holding the magazine.

"I said sorry. And I didn't sneak up on you. I was just walking by and asked you what you were doing."

She finally gained control of her body and her senses and backtracked. "You're right, you're right. I know you didn't do anything wrong. It's just that I'm so worried about Davis."

"Is that why you were rifling through his drawers?"

"I wasn't rifling through his drawers. For heaven's sake, Lowell, you know I don't just randomly go through your stuff. I was looking for something that might tell me where he is."

"Did you find anything?"

Her face had lost some of its color but it came rushing back when she blushed again at the thought of what she found in the drawer. "I found lots of things, but nothing that will help."

"You should call Aunt Connie."

"I did. She'll be here in a while. And I'd appreciate it if you'd wait until she gets here before you sail off to bed."

"It's getting kinda late," he said and looked at his wrist as if checking the time on his watch, though he never wore one.

Perturbed by his self-centeredness, Prudy wallowed in her own. "Your father is leaving for the office in a few minutes and I have no idea when Connie will be here. Is it too much to ask for some support around here?"

"Fine," he said, leaning away from the door jamb. "I'll be in my room *not* sleeping if you need me."

Prudy heard him walk into the bathroom and the door shut without latching. Then, with what must have been another shove from Lowell, the door latched. She got up, considered returning to the drawer to remove *Going Down* so she could confront Davis with it when he finally returned home, but continued out the door, letting that sleeping dog lie.

CHAPTER 4

She was fixing herself a strawberry yogurt smoothie in the blender. The whine from the small motor died down as she set about pouring its contents into a glass. Mitchell entered the kitchen wearing a torn shirt and jeans. Prudy thought it was exceedingly casual, particularly for the office and particularly for her husband. She looked up at the clock and saw that it was a few minutes after eleven o'clock. "Off to the office?"

"I am. But in an effort to support my all-important wife and mother of my children, I will be home immediately following the call rather than spending the rest of the night at the office."

She flashed him a smirk.

"Too little too late?" he asked.

Wiping the smoothie from the curls of her lips, she said, "I just don't understand how you can be so calm when our son has either lied to your face or gone missing. You should be angry or worried or something, not traipsing off to some international conference call to make a few bucks."

She noted a clumsy shift in his posture as he responded. "That's what I do, make calls that make money. But, here's my prediction: a few short moments after I leave, Davis will come walking through the door with some sob story that you will care nothing about; you'll refocus the discussion as to the worry he's put you through; he'll follow with profuse apologies; and, you will take away all driving privileges for, hmmmm, two weeks. I will then walk back into the house, play good cop to your bad cop and commute his sentence to one week without television, thereby winning the adoration of my son and the wrath of my wife."

He walked over and hugged her. Prudy took it for what it was: a gesture of caring. She reciprocated, reluctantly. Then she thought about what he said and replied into the crux of his shoulder, "You better not undermine my authority like that."

Smiling, Mitchell played along. "Okay, I'll play worse cop to your bad cop and extend his sentence to three weeks, thereby winning the adoration of my wife and the mild perturbation of my son."

The side of her head was against his chest as she looked out the kitchen window at absolutely nothing in particular. "So it doesn't bother you if he lies as long as he's punished for making me worry?"

"Look, sweetheart, I was sixteen once. So were you. We all lied to our parents. Sometimes a little, sometimes a lot. He's a really good boy. As long as he's safe, right?"

Still mulling over the inconsistencies, she asked, "But where would he go in his uniform?"

"He wasn't wearing his uniform when I saw him." Prudy contemplated this and then Mitchell continued, "You see, it was premeditated: he brought clothes to change into. That just makes me feel more strongly that he's just fine. Until he comes home, anyway. Then he'll have to deal with you."

She thought about it, all of it: the unnecessary and illogical lies; the network of elaborate schemes; her usual habit of jumping to conclusions. It all pointed to a single, most logical conclusion.

"You're probably right." She pushed away from Mitchell and looked up at him. "Connie'll be here pretty soon and Lowell said he'd stay up until she got here. Go on, get to your call."

He walked toward the door to the garage, grabbed a windbreaker from the closet on the way and slipped it on. Then he pulled his keys from the pegboard on the wall and eased out the door without saying a word.

Prudy stood in the kitchen, alone, looking at the door through which her husband just exited. She listened to the car's starter, the initial vroom of the engine, the low idling of the car backing out of the garage and the slow rumbling of the automatic door opener as it closed. Her eyes were fixed on the recessed panels of the door. She was strangely afraid that her eyes were playing tricks on her as the panels appeared to be raised rather than recessed as she knew they were. She took one step toward the door and breathed a sigh of relief when her eyes refocused and perceived them as recessed once again.

"What is going on tonight?" she muttered and returned to her smoothie. She sat in her chair in the family room, quickly got comfortable and turned on the television. She was watching, with intense interest and horror, a woman undergoing reconstructive knee surgery.

* * *

Waves of guilt rushed over him as he backed out of the garage. His wife was never one to fully relax, not even when everything was going well. With something she could actually worry about, something as monumental as her son's so-called "disappearance," Mitchell needed to remind himself that what he was doing was for her and for their sons. He continued trying to convince himself of these things and many others as he reached the end of the long, winding driveway and turned toward the city.

He didn't have to convince himself that his son was all right. His analytical mind had already calculated that there was maybe a five percent chance that his son was in any kind of real trouble. The other ninety-five percent of the scenarios he concocted ended with his son tucked in bed, sound asleep, when he got back home. But, like any parent, his mind was eaten away by the possibilities of that remaining five percent as it conjured up disturbing images and unpleasant conclusions.

He made his way through the affluent roadways that comprised his gated community until they spit him out onto the heavily traveled surface street that connected him and his neighbors to the less-fortunate citizens of the suburban hamlet. All the while, the disturbing images and unpleasant conclusions continued to poke at his mind. Several attempts were made to change his train of thought, but he inevitably returned to pulling back a sheet at the hospital morgue or receiving a finger in the mail wrapped in a ransom note.

In an effort to rid his mind of these unpleasantries, Mitchell thought about his friend, Natalie Belling. Had it already been a year since she died? He still had her obituary, nestled in his desk's lap drawer, and read it often. So often, in fact, he'd memorized it. He read her obituary not in fond remembrance, but rather in scornful loathing; a contempt so deep, perpetual and unyielding, that reading it became salutary, reciting it became therapeutic. To keep his mind off Davis, he recited it aloud as he drove. *Activist, Former Lieutenant Governor Belling Dies; the byline, by Alexander de Large; the location and date, KOROVA CITY – (Friday, September 12th).* He delivered the first paragraph with reverent tones. *Former Lieutenant Governor Natalie Belling, the impassioned and persuasive victim's rights activist and founder of the Belling Foundation for Victims of Violent Crimes, died Thursday. She was fifty-five years old.* He lingered on the unabridged quote he wrote for the piece. *"A shining star has gone dim before its time. Natalie Belling was a great leader and a great friend to a great number of people. She will be sorely missed, by me and by many."* He continued reciting, word-for-word, to the very end, emphasizing various phrases as if applying a salve to emotional scars.

When he finished, he thought, a woman's life summarized in a dozen paragraphs.

He questioned whether he had anything to do with her death. It had never dawned on him to consider such a thing, not until that very moment. The potential answer to that question disturbed him and he shuddered. He shook his head to rid himself of the misplaced guilt he suddenly felt for the death of his friend and colleague. His mood turned sour with his inability to focus on something joyful. He looked around the car to find something else on which to focus. He looked at the passenger seat and realized his briefcase was missing. Instead, sitting in the space his briefcase normally occupied, were two carefully folded lengths of cloth, one woolen and one linen, a pair of hand-crafted, red leather sandals, a bright, gold-colored rope with long tasseled knots on each end and a clear plastic mask.

The missing briefcase was a small, unfortunate detail he had overlooked while trying to quickly get out of the house, but it provided him with something else to distract his cluttered mind and eventually bring it around to what lay ahead of him. Mitchell thought about his meeting, the one at Gambel's. He had to go over what he would say. He had to focus. Even had he wanted to dwell on his son or his briefcase or his dead friend, he couldn't. Not now.

CHAPTER 5

The full moon, shining brightly through the trees' empty patches where their leaves had already fallen away, was nearly enough illumination to navigate the empty streets. It was creeping up on 2:00 a.m. Wednesday morning when Mitchell, returning home from his meeting, noticed from a block away that all the lights in the downstairs were turned on. He slowly rolled his BMW up the street and into the driveway. The boys' Volvo rested in its usual space tucked into the thick line of hemlocks that edged the property. As the garage door retracted, the space reserved for his wife's Audi stood vacant. He pulled his car all the way in just as the automatic door stopped its strained creaking. Mitchell turned off the engine and the lights and got out. When he shut the door and turned to walk around his vehicle to enter his home, he was instantly met with both the shrill voice and ghostly face of his wife.

"You said he'd be home by now," Prudy screamed. "You said he'd be fine. You said everything would be fine."

He made his way over to the door, confused. "Davis isn't home yet?"

"No," she screeched. Her shrill voice made the hair on Mitchell's neck prickle.

Mitchell moved past her, hitting the garage door button as he walked into the kitchen. In the adjoining den, Connie sat in her police uniform sipping tea. When the look of concern on her face confirmed his wife's outbursts, a swell of panic rose up in him and he went directly to his sister-in-law for answers.

"What happened? What's going on?"

Connie put her tea cup on the tray and stood. "There's no easy way around this. We found his keys on the ground next to the car, and some blood about a foot away from the keys. It looks like—"

"The police think Davis was kidnapped," Prudy screamed.

"Kidnapped?" Mitchell asked. "Someone wants a ransom?"

"Not kidnapped," Connie corrected, seemingly annoyed that her sister had not yet calmed down. "Abducted. We think he's been abducted."

"Abducted, kidnapped, what's the difference?" Prudy said, flopping into an overstuffed chair. Then, low and soft, "I told you something was not right and no one listened to me."

Looking at his wife, Mitchell pleaded, "Honey, please, let Connie explain this to me, okay?"

Prudy said and did nothing.

Connie took her cue. "A couple of police officers saw you talking to Davis on the corner tonight. They thought you were trying to solicit him for prostitution."

Mitchell moved as though he was going to say something, but Connie cut him off before he could speak. "The corner was tagged by the Highland police a few weeks back as a pick-up spot. They were there for other reasons, which I'll get to later, but it looks like after talking to you, when Davis went to his car in the parking lot across the street, someone grabbed him and took off."

The corner of High Ridge Road and Summit Avenue instantly came to his mind. "That bastard," he said to himself.

"What?" Connie asked.

Realizing he must have mumbled it aloud, he snapped back to the moment, "Nothing. Please, go on."

"This works best," Connie began, "if you let me do all the talking and you mostly listen."

Mitchell grabbed a chair from the den's game table and set it next to the ottoman on which sat a fully prepared tea set. Prudy to his left, slumped in her chair, and Connie to his right.

Connie took a deep breath and sighed. "Okay. The theater where Davis works, the Ridgeway, is on the corner of High Ridge Road and Summit Avenue. It's downtown suburbia, right? It's not a bad corner with drug dealers or gangs or any of the other stuff you find in the city, but it's a busy corner: lots of people passing by at every hour of the day and night, right?"

Mitchell was impatient. "Yes it is. So what?" He needed specifics, not background.

"Well, two Korova City detectives, Brown and Watts, told me that the Highland police have been picking up young male prostitutes on that corner.

"Listen," Connie continued, "I know Davis is not a prostitute and so does everyone else. I assured them of it coming over here."

"Them?" Mitchell yelled.

"We tried calling you a thousand times, but since you wouldn't answer …" She trailed off. "They, the two detectives, Brown and Watts, were there collecting information. Anyway, they were at that corner tonight and saw Davis standing there by himself. And when they saw him they immediately thought he might have been, you know, soliciting."

Prudy let out a whimper.

"They said he was only at the corner for a minute or two before you arrived. They thought you were soliciting Davis but now they know better. Remember, this is all background to help you understand the whole picture."

"The whole picture?" Mitchell asked. "What whole picture?"

"Two other boys were also last seen on that corner: one each the last couple of Tuesdays. The detectives think this might be related to those boys because they've each been abducted on a Tuesday."

"Abducted," Prudy exploded. "Jesus H. Christ, Connie."

Prudy stood and paced in the small space of the den like a caged tiger. Her frail fingers tugging at her gaunt cheeks, covering the quivering lips of her mouth.

"Dammit, Prudy," Connie yelled. "You're making me dizzy. Sit down and shut up."

Once Prudy sat, Mitchell let Connie proceed uninterrupted, listening intently to every word. According to the detectives, High-Sum, the corner of High Ridge Road and Summit Avenue, had become a solicitation hot spot almost overnight. Within a few weeks of one another, a number of new shops had opened less than a block from the corner: Ink, Inc., a tattoo parlor; Spanky's custom leather accessories shop; Square Wheelz, a clothing and sporting gear shop for skaters; boarders and extreme sport enthusiasts; Welders, a high-end gizmo and gadget retailer; and a Jittery Joe's coffee shop. Innocuous individually, the convergence of these stores' unique and divergent clientele and staff seemed to propagate a promiscuous atmosphere. Adventurous young men and wealthy older men went about their business almost unnoticed by one another. Then, they noticed one another. Fetish-laden men saw nubile boys willing to pleasure them for a pittance. Money-strapped teens saw tired cash cows willing to part with hundreds of dollars just to watch them do relatively benign activities: defecate on a glass table; urinate into a specimen cup; masturbate. The police had only recently been made aware of the situation and made only two arrests, though the defendants involved, a lawyer and a corporate executive, were thoroughly embarrassed when it made the local paper and when it was picked up by the *Korova City Bugle Gazette*. The boys were saved such blatant embarrassment due to their status as minors, but their families were fully aware.

As for the abductions, Connie retold the story told to her by Brown and Watts. The first boy reported missing was a Highland High School junior, William Cross. He was a sales clerk at Square Wheelz who, when strapped for cash, would occasionally step out onto the corner and wait. He was reported missing by his father when William didn't come home for dinner after work. When told of the corner's recent activities, the boy's father, Charles Cross, an ophthalmologist, insisted his son was not a prostitute. The other clerks at the store insinuated otherwise.

The second boy reported missing, and the first one abducted, was a runaway living on the streets of the city's downtown area. He heard about the Sum-High corner in the affluent suburb of Highland from another runaway. The two of them went there together expecting to make some easy money only to find the clientele was far more particular than on the downtown street corners; they sought clean-cut, fresh-faced boys-next-door. After a few hours of standing, the friend went to buy some coffee and when he returned he found the corner empty. After more than a week with no communication between the two street walkers, an anonymous phone call was placed to the Highland Police Department. They filed a Missing Persons report with very few details.

As Connie recited the same details she had provided Prudy an hour earlier, Mitchell concentrated on every word offered, seemingly holding each one in his mind for far longer than it took to say it, as if they were strands of fiber and he were weaving them into a story unto themselves.

Finally, there was Davis Treadwell, son of Korova City's most influential business tycoon, missing. Presumably it was his blood, found next to his keys, that stained the asphalt in the parking lot across the street from the theater where the teenager worked.

"If two boys were already taken, why wasn't there a policeman there tonight to prevent it from happening again?"

"A couple things. First, Brown and Watts *were* there. Second, there's an old saying: 'One's an accident; two's a coincidence; three's a trend.' I'm not sure the Highland detectives put the other boys' abdu ...," She paused and they both looked at Prudy who made no reaction to the word that almost slipped from Connie's mouth. "I don't think anyone thought these were related except for Brown and Watts, and they're working a couple of old cold cases. They were strictly observing. They got your license number, along with a few others they're running through the system. They had a wait-and-see approach because they didn't know what or who to chase after. There's something else." Connie looked into Mitchell's eyes and continued, gently. "Those two city detectives? They're from Homicide. The two boys who were abducted, their bodies were found in dumpsters: one last Wednesday out in the suburbs and one the Wednesday before in Salem's Lot, Detective Brown's previous division. They being investigated by different departments, which is another reason no one put two and two together. Brown and Watts, they think it might be the same person."

"Why?" Mitchell said.

"Why what?"

"Why do they think the same person killed these two boys?"

Connie thought a moment. "I guess because they were," she looked at her sister out of the corner of her eye, "abducted from the same spot."

Mitchell sat in silence a moment and stared thoughtfully at the tea set sitting on the ottoman in front of him. His facial features shifting slightly as he reflected upon everything Connie had said. Then, he abruptly stood up and vomited.

* * *

"Oh, God," Prudy gasped, clutching her face with both hands.

Connie ran to the kitchen to grab a wad of paper towels. By the time she returned, Mitchell had vanished, leaving Connie alone to scrub the carpet to avoid any staining. As she scrubbed she heard more vomiting in the bathroom off the den.

A few minutes later, the mess nearly cleaned, Mitchell came out of the bathroom with the same determined look he had worn since arriving, only his face was paler and the hair above his forehead dripped with water. He walked over to Connie, knelt close to her and whispered, "We have to get down to that corner, Connie."

"There's nothing we can do down there. The police—"

"You and me," he whispered forcibly. "Right now."

Connie took one look at Mitchell and knew he was going with or without her.

"What about Prudy?" Connie asked.

Mitchell stood up. "Prudy. Connie and I are heading down to the parking lot to see if there's something the police missed. You stay here in case anyone calls, all right?"

Connie rose as Mitchell pulled her up off her knees and away from the wet spot on the carpet. They headed toward the door, Mitchell pulling her along. Prudy remained in the chair. The distraught woman rocked gently, closed her eyes and mumbled so softly that Connie could barely hear as the door closed, "How could this have happened? How could this have happened?"

PART TWO

Going to Gambel's

CHAPTER 6

It all started with a simple conversation between Mitchell Treadwell and a woman named Natalie Belling. It was a hot summer day. They were attending a relatively inconsequential black tie reception at the prestigious Hoyt Art Museum downtown. Neither he nor Natalie knew anyone else in the room, but they found themselves at the bar simultaneously scoping out the city's VIPs. When he turned to order a gin and tonic, she quickly moved to stand directly next to him. "I'll have what he's having."

"Two, please," he said quietly to the bartender.

"So," she asked, "whose ass are you looking to kiss tonight?"

He looked her up and down. "I'm not looking to kiss anyone's ass. I'm looking for the most likely candidate to kiss mine. Are you interested?"

She looked at his hands. "You're married. I'll pass: too much red tape."

He laughed and extended his hand. "Mitchell Treadwell."

"Ahhh, you're a Treadwell," she sang.

"In so much as I'm the son of Edwin Treadwell, founder, president and CEO of Treadwell International, yes I am. And you are?"

"Natalie Belling, assistant district attorney."

"Ahhh, you're a lawyer," he mimicked.

"In so much as I passed the bar examine, yes I am."

She was far more than just a lawyer, as Mitchell soon found out. She was a politico guerilla, an ambitious woman determined to accelerate her career within the governmental machine by whatever means she could conceive.

"Is there anybody here worth talking to?" he asked.

"Everyone's worth talking to," she said. "Talk is cheap. Time ... time is money."

"I see. So, is there anybody here worth my time?"

"Well, there's me, for one," Natalie said without a hint of flirtation in her voice.

"You?" he laughed, a bit harder than he wanted to. "You're a civil servant."

"So is the President of the United States."

"You plan on being the next president?"

"You have to be thirty-five to run, so no, I'm not going to be the *next* president. But then who wants that job? Seriously? No, I'm focusing on the governor's mansion in about twenty years. And when that happens, won't you look like a complete jackass for thinking I wasn't worth your time?"

They bonded instantly: she was the civic-minded Yin to his corporate Yang. They met frequently for lunch, forming not a friendship, but an alliance in the inevitable event that they would one day walk into a black tie reception and have ambitious young men and women fawn over them as they approached the bar.

She immediately recognized his compelling desire to stretch beyond his father's shadow. That's how she convinced him he needed to become "that which you most desire to be," a phrase she continually stated until, by rote, it became his own mantra. It was a line she had learned the year before as part of her initiation into what she referred to as a highly selective group of forward-thinking leaders. And it wasn't long before she sponsored him for membership into the group, knowing full well that he would make an excellent addition and thrive, both personally and professionally, regardless of the spiritual and emotional costs.

After reviewing the intricacies and peculiarities of the group's bylaws, he was put through an extensive and unsettling interviewing process which disturbed him initially, but eventually grew on him like a melanoma. He slowly embraced these intricacies and peculiarities with the same unwavering passion he embraced his work. One of the bylaws asked each participant to internalize the phrase "that which you most desire to be." For Mitchell, that meant to be revered and respected by the multitudes. This, in turn, manifested itself into the personification of Marcus Ulpius Nerva Traianus, commonly referred to as Emperor Trajan, the second of the five good emperors of the Roman Empire.

And so it was that at nearly midnight, fourteen months after he'd first met Natalie Belling at that reception, Mitchell Treadwell, dressed in his toga picta and concealed behind his clear plastic mask, followed the assistant district attorney down into the bowels of a vacant subterranean print shop where he participated fully and enthusiastically in his inaugural ceremony.

It was a night like no other, one that he would never forget. It would haunt him in his unconscious nightmares and terrify him more resoundingly in his waking thoughts.

It was a night that had changed him forever.

That was twenty-eight years ago.

CHAPTER 7

Forty-two Simsbury Road. That's where Andy Walker lived, on a corner lot tucked away in Highland, the affluent suburb of Korova City. His was a small house compared to the others on the block, but it was as much house as he could provide for his wife and himself. As Andy escaped his domestic existence and entered into the morning chill, he softly closed the front door behind him, careful to lock it as his wife had demanded of him more times than he cared to remember, and headed toward his car parked in the driveway.

He opened the driver's side door, threw his brief case across the armrest and into the passenger seat, and then slid behind the wheel. Comfortably situated, he reached out, pulled the door closed and prepared himself for his morning recital: Andy was a vehicular performance artist.

He leaned slightly to his right so that he could guide the key into the ignition on the steering column. It slid in effortlessly. Turning the key, with its black vinyl enveloping its bulkiness and providing the auto manufacturer an additional opportunity to remind him just exactly who was responsible for the freedom he enjoyed through ownership of this modern marvel of engineering, he pumped the accelerator. The engine roared momentarily then subsided as it wound down to idle.

He moved his right arm across his body, grabbed the belt buckle, which almost filled his smaller-than-average hand, pulled so that the top portion of polyester webbing rested snugly against his sternum while the bottom spanned his waist, and inserted the metal tongue into the red-buttoned slot. At one time or another, he had chuckled at the sexual connotation of the procedure, but he'd performed the act so often that the idea passed him by without notice.

He turned on the wipers to remove the condensation left by the chill night air and while they swept the water aside he put on his costume: his sunglasses and driving gloves. He released the parking brake, locked his fingers around the knobby end of the stick shift and guided it into reverse. He scanned left, then right, and, seeing no oncoming traffic, revved the engine and released the clutch. His one-ton prop eased backwards onto the asphalt roadway. There was no need to apply the brake: he simply shifted into first and went, letting the clutch act as the go-between from backward to forward.

And so it was that on that Tuesday morning, some eighteen and a half hours before Connie would tell Mitchell that his son had been abducted, Andy was off to a day at the office. It would be his last.

Andy mused silently about that morning's particular performance. "You gotta grab 'em by the lapels and make 'em take notice." He believed, had there been a critic in the passenger seat, he would have most definitely received a rave review. But then, the first act was always routine, broken only by the theatrical flourishes he added for fun, or the ever so seldom driver who made him wait in the driveway before backing out. That day, there was no waiting and no theatrical flourish, merely a solid, straightforward interpretation of the material.

From his driveway, he headed north. His beige, vinyl-sided ranch home disappeared from his rearview mirror as he crested the rolling hill that seemed idyllically suburban, particularly in autumn, adorned by the colors of approaching dormancy above and the narrow ribbons of streaming rainwater below.

He worked, quite literally, on the opposite side of the city from where he lived. There were exactly thirteen miles of roadway between his driveway and 65th Street, consisting mostly of fast-paced highway driving, unless it was under construction, and exactly thirteen miles between 61st Street and the small parking lot outside his office, consisting mostly of well-paced urban traffic flow. It was the "Half-mile of Hell," as he referred to it, the portion of Club Road between 65th and 61st, with its four traffic lights, that made his daily trek to and from his office wholly unpleasant.

Once he crested the idyllic suburban hill, it was only a few blocks and a few quick turns before he was on High Ridge Road, a four lane divided capillary that shared a middle lane at major intersections. On High Ridge Road sat the upscale boutique shops and ubiquitous coffee houses that did a fair amount of business. Each of them owed a special thanks to the Ridgeway Theater, as it was the initial renovation project that transformed Highland's downtown area from a quaint village square to a chic, thriving suburban business district.

From there, it was a quick ride on the freeway, slithering between the various moving obstacles in his path, to the Club Road exit. He maneuvered himself in front of as many large trucks as possible until, at the bottom of the off-ramp, he turned right and headed east toward the Half-mile of Hell, some fifty blocks away.

They were an easy fifty blocks unless obstructed by nefarious interlopers to his daily constitution. To these amateurs, he'd mutter various disdainful comments, obscenities and vulgarities. He had a good two dozen patented outbursts fit for almost any occasion, as well as the gender-specific epithets. He also improvised verbal assaults whenever necessary. This was how he spent his mornings, particularly when navigating the Half-mile of Hell, which he passed through with a minimum of four or five colorful outbursts.

From 60th Street, it was a straight shot of appropriately placed and properly synchronized lights to 10th Street where he picked up Highway 18, another north-south thoroughfare, to Hope Street, the misnomer given to the roadway on which rested his place of employment. From the off-ramp, it was a hop, skip and a jump to the freshly sealed parking lot where his vehicle spent the remainder of the day awaiting his return.

His sunglasses, nestled in the sturdy protective case they came in, and his Italian leather driving gloves were meticulously placed between the front seats in the space left vacant by the engaged emergency brake. He got out of his car with as little flair as he got into it nearly fifty minutes prior and headed toward the building's front door.

He walked the two flights of stairs to avoid the crowded elevator and pushed through the glass doors of Hope Street Manufacturing.

"Morning, Andy," chimed Becky walking out the very door he opened. She was a small, plucky, flat-faced brunette with patches of freckles across her wide cheekbones. She, like him, was a marketing specialist. Her unofficial job as department welcomer was due in part to her proximity to the elevator and stairwell, but mostly to her abundance of cheer and her willingness to foist it upon others.

"Morning, Becky," he replied, quickly and coarsely.

He made his way to his cubicle much the same way he drove to work: aggressively and with little concern for the others who shared the convoluted, patchwork grid. He came to a cubicle with a small, black plaque with white, san-serif, capital letters that suggested the space it flanked was reserved for someone else; someone named ANDY WAKLER. However, it was Andy Walker's space, the typo notwithstanding, though by the look of it, one would be hard pressed to distinguish it from a vacant cubicle.

In addition to the company-requisite equipment, supplies and accoutrements, only two items sat on the pristine horizontal work surfaces that took up two full walls of the cubicle. The first was a picture of a baby, immediately following its delivery. In it, the baby is crying, its face and chest a peachy pink. The baby's face is framed by a blue, striped cap and matching blanket: the same outfit the hospitals provided all newborn boys.

The second item was another photo, this one of his wife, Chastity, on a lounge chair at the beach. It was taken the day he offered and she accepted his proposal of marriage some nine years earlier. "Never before, nor since, has she looked as beautiful as she did that day," he told himself every morning, and a lump would form in his throat as he confessed silently that he was a very lucky man.

Andy entered the cubicle. His ill-fitted business-casual attire hung loose on him, like skin on atrophied muscle. He dispassionately placed his briefcase next to his desk and took his seat, cycling through and prioritizing his "To Do" list in his mind. The list was very long and filled with many items he believed unnecessary. Some he even considered detrimental to the long-term success of his area's sales efforts. However, from 8:30 in the morning until he left his office, which was after 6:00 most nights, his beliefs and concerns were of little value. The list would be completed, and if not by him then by someone in his place.

Andy was an order-taker. He would continue to be an order-taker for the foreseeable future because neither his Area Sales Manager, nor her three Sales Associates, believed him capable of anything more. Nothing they asked of him was beyond his capabilities and he performed his duties accurately and on time, yet he offered no more than what was asked. He voiced no career ambitions, nor did he show any through his actions. He was exceedingly content in his position as Mountain States Marketing Specialist at Hope Street Manufacturing as it provided him with the opportunity to do what he enjoyed most: commute.

CHAPTER 8

When Andy sunk low and strapped in to the upholstered seat of the Green Menace—his wife's appellation for the vehicle, not his—he changed. He became what he couldn't be at his desk in the eyes of his superiors, or in the copy room in the eyes of his peers, or in the bedroom in the eyes of his wife. He became the supreme master of a defined and recognizable universe. He ruled the *Rules of the Road*: judge, jury and executioner to those who broke them. For an hour to and another fro, Andy was someone who commanded the respect of others.

From his first taste of empowerment at age sixteen, like most teenagers, Andy took to driving instantly. He ran every errand for his parents, however small, and drove aimlessly on the weekends, expanding the boundaries of his kingdom. It was a passion and an obsession. And when others his age grew tired of the intoxication, seeing their vehicle as a means to an end, Andy saw it as the end itself and his drive to drive continued to grow. He became a delivery boy for his father's rather successful tool and die shop while attending community college, but found driving for a paycheck different, somehow, from driving for himself. He found it oddly unpleasant. He also found it difficult to formalize why it was so unpleasant, though his best attempt was likening it to a prostitute making love to his boyfriend: too familiar to be intimate.

It was 5:45 and he was wrapping up the last item on his list. Rush hour would be winding down and, if all went well, he'd have an uneventful drive to the other side of town. Even the Half-mile of Hell, with its herky-jerky motion of traffic, would be relatively free of congestion. While others in his office daydreamed of getting home to their kids, happy hour cocktails with co-workers or simply veggin' out in front of the tube, the small, peculiar man in the cubicle marked ANDY WAKLER dreamed of his commute, of his reign over his individual universe and of dispensing street justice in a manner only he could.

It was late summer and the sun hung low. Andy figured by the time he pulled into his driveway the sky would fade into a deep purple, the graying clouds would turn a vibrant pink and the sun would dip below the horizon. As he approached his vehicle, he pulled his keys from his pocket and prepared to dazzle the world with the mastery of his craft.

It was show time.

"Break a leg," he said aloud with an evil smile.

He climbed into his car with little flair. He cracked open the pleather-wrapped, felt-lined glasses case and stared at the pair of sunglasses he'd purchased online from a retired Navy jet fighter. Then he stared at the gloves: a gift from his wife. He believed them the most thoughtful gift she'd ever given him. They were a dark camel color, open-backed and unlined with hook-and-loop wrist closures. *Soft, supple and comfortable, hand-crafted of buttery deerskin, these classic, full-fingered driving gloves feature vent holes, piping and outside stitching to ensure maximum comfort and superior performance,* he remembered from the olive green card that hung on the gloves by a black string when he opened the box.

He put them on, first his sunglasses and then his gloves, adjusted them quickly and got into character. He moved to his right, looked at himself in the rearview mirror, smiled widely and recoiled back into his seat.

"Let's go, my sweet chariot," came low and guttural as he gently caressed the dashboard, grabbed the knobby stick shift and thrust it into reverse.

Eight years earlier, while completing a seemingly arbitrary and useless task for his Area Sales Manager, Andy came across the Greek mythology of Helios, the sun-god.

He read:

As Eos threw open the gates of Helios's golden palace of the east, Helios mounted his golden chariot and drove out into the sky. The rays that encircled his head and his chariot lit up the darkness before him, and he was so bright only the gods were able to look straight at him without being blinded. Helios drove his chariot, pulled by four fiery steeds, up to the heavens. Although the path was steep and narrow, and the steeds were wild, Helios always held them on their course. At noon Helios would stop and look upon the world, for at the top of the sky nothing could escape his fiery gaze. He drove on, giving free rein to his steeds now able to see Helios's palace far to the west. Eager to reach their stable, they ran on faster and faster as shadows grew long and dusk settled over the world once again.

The symbolism was too much to ignore and his car would forever be known to him as his chariot. The image of him as Helios, the sun-god, was even more corrupting, so much so he used "Helios" as his password for nearly everything requiring one. He also personalized his license plate to reflect the devastating tragedy that both he and the sun god shared.

Andy drove a green, pre-owned Saturn SC2. It was a sturdy, economical, practical vehicle that performed the tasks necessary to get from Point A to Point B. It was, in all truth, an outstanding car in many respects, but for those attributes in which it excelled, he cared little. It did not command the respect afforded other, more prestigious vehicles and

Andy longed for the day his chariot would adequately reflect the judiciousness and skill with which he ruled the roads. He did not yet know if he was a vintage muscle car owner, a racy sports car owner, or a luxury sedan owner. But until he became "that which he most desired to be," he would counter the lack of respect his SC2 commanded with his virtuosity behind the wheel.

And he was a virtuoso. His skill and application of his trade was beyond reproach. His inspiration and aspiration for greatness was boundless. Since accepting the responsibilities required by the state to follow and obey any and all traffic regulations, rules, signs and signals, Andy gave flawless performance after flawless performance. Never once did he receive a speeding ticket or other moving citation, nor get into an accident. He had never so much as run up and over a curb or tapped a bumper while parallel parking: a true master of his craft.

He sat in the left lane at the most meaningless traffic light ever installed, the one on Club Road between 63rd and 64th Streets. It choked the flow of traffic to near death even late in the evening, long after rush hour. There were two brown sedans in front of him and a long line of cars he paid no attention to behind him and to his right. When the light in front of him turned green, nothing moved. It wasn't until the light at the intersection of 64th changed also that the masses moved westward to wait at the fourth and final light of the Half-mile of Hell at 65th Street.

At the intersection of 65th, the succession of cars waited patiently for the first sedan, a newer, rounder, cleaner vehicle, to turn left. When it did, the second sedan, older and more bronze than brown, moved a few feet forward and stopped in the middle of the intersection. The light cycled yellow and nothing happened. It turned red and there was still no movement, leaving both northbound lanes blocked.

The drivers on 65th Street traveling northbound were as perplexed as Andy. They crawled to within a few feet of the sedan but then stopped with nowhere to go. They honked politely and watched their southbound brethren move past. The light cycled green and there was still no movement from the bronze sedan in front of Andy. The cars traveling eastbound on Club Road crept forward until they could go no further, securing three links in an inevitable, nearly unbreakable chain. Andy felt the approaching gridlock. He also felt the right lane moving and checked his rear-view mirror feverishly for an opportunity to merge and bypass what was shaping up to be a long night of sitting in immoveable mayhem.

Andy saw a negligible gap in the right lane briefly appear in his rearview mirror. By sheer instinct, he put the car in gear, swiveled his head, glanced at his blind spot and gunned it for the gap before it could close. The foreign sound of shredding fiberglass, splintering glass and crumpling metal filled his ears. His body, restrained by the seat belt, was thrust awkwardly by the slow but mighty force of the impact. Panic and terror enhanced by adrenalin filled him quickly and dissipated.

He sat a moment, confused as the cars in the right lane passed him using the remainder of roadway reserved for bus and right-turn-only vehicles. His confusion continued. His brain quickly processed the information but concluded an improbability. The motion of the impact suggested the front driver's side was the source of the impact, yet he knew there was enough room between his chariot and the metallic bronze sedan to successfully maneuver into the next lane.

He looked over and saw that the sedan that was wholly in front of him was resting only somewhat in front of him. It had moved. Backwards. His mind scrambled, unable to process the input. The only scenario he could formulate was that the driver of the bronze sedan had backed up in the middle of the intersection even though there were a dozen or so blocks of barren roadway lying before him. It racked Andy's brain like a Zen koan. It was like trying to understand that three is the color of love or that the sky tastes like music.

The traffic light cycled again. Andy watched the southbound traffic flow until it came to rest amid the other immovable vehicles. Andy motioned to the driver of the sedan, who was paying no attention to him, that he was going to move his car out of harm's way, but he couldn't: the gridlock was complete as the southbound traffic halted, leaving all lanes at a standstill. The traffic light lost all purpose.

He turned off the ignition, pulled the parking brake and sat there a moment, perplexed, anxious and scared, scanning his mental hard drive for proper procedures in the event of an accident. His insurance card was in the glove compartment, along with a pen and a pad of paper, and his driver's license was in his wallet in his pocket. He collected these items, blocking out the horns blasting at him from all directions.

The door to Andy's car was too close to the gleaming metallic bronze sedan to open, forcing him to climb out the passenger door. He saw an annoyed woman sitting in the car to his right and she saw that he saw her. He was thankful for the remainder of road until she rolled down the window and emitted from her pudgy, ugly, pale-white face, "Nice goin', dumb-ass. We gonna be here all night cuz-a-you."

"Shut the fuck up," he snarled, surprised at the force behind his words. Then to himself he said, "He's the cock-knob who backed up in the middle of the intersection." He was still in character. That's when he removed his gloves and his glasses, threw them on the passenger seat and shut the door.

Sentiments similar to the one voiced by ugly woman were offered from other open windows as Andy circled around the front of his car and stood at the front of the bronze sedan where he waited for the driver and passenger to cease their arguing and emerge from their vehicle.

The sirens from two cruisers slowly rose above and cut through the din of horns and voices. He remembered the police had recently added a satellite station a few blocks away from the Half-mile of Hell. Lights flashed as the hope of restored order rolled up single-file eastbound in the almost empty westbound lanes. Over the top of the strobes, Andy watched the eastbound vehicles making u-turns to escape the madness. Then he turned in ninety-degree intervals to confirm his assumptions that everyone else was doing it, too. They were, even those behind him whom he thought would be forever locked behind the gates of traffic light hell with him.

The driver and passenger of the vintage sedan remained in the vehicle arguing. Andy wondered if they even realized that their car was in an accident.

"Are you okay?" asked the stocky female officer making her way toward him.

"Me? Yeah, I'm fine, I guess," Andy replied.

"What about them?"

"I don't know."

"Okay, I'll talk to them," she said as she walked up to him. Then, placing the palm of her hand on his chest and gently, but forcibly, moving him back toward his car she continued, "You need to stay by your vehicle. My partner will be with you in just a second."

Andy walked slowly backwards and looked over the line of cars at the cruisers, their sirens silent. A third cruiser was approaching as the officers from the second vehicle went in opposite directions, to direct traffic, he thought. A burly male officer with a notepad already opened and awaiting ink was walking slowly toward Andy using the same path between the cars his partner used. He looked at the front of Andy's car and then at the debris on the ground.

"Well, this doesn't look too bad. You hurt?" he asked in a surprisingly effeminate voice.

"A little shaken, maybe, but not hurt."

"I'm Officer Jenkins and I apologize up front for my bluntness, but you wanna get outta here, I wanna get outta here, so the less you talk the better, okay? Here's what's gonna happen. You're gonna tell me your story and they're gonna tell my partner their story," he said, nodding at the sedan and clicking his pen. He continued, "Then we'll compare notes, issue citations as warranted and send you on your merry way. Got it?"

"Yes, sir."

"Good." He smiled and changed to an even softer inflection, "So, what happened?"

CHAPTER 9

Uncle Max sat in his car waiting for Faith to drop off the vehicle and fill out the necessary forms. He busied himself by rubbing the long scar across the left side of his forehead, a scar he collected what seemed like a thousand years ago. It was an altercation over power and personal ideology, but then, he thought to himself, that's what all altercations are about.

Uncle Max was everybody's Uncle Max, a one-time community leader relegated to urban codger and, what some considered, an ornery ol' fool. His most unique trait was that he dealt entirely in trade. When he needed new tires, he went to the guy who asked him to get a pig on a spit and all the barbecue sauce he could drink for his oldest son's eighteenth birthday. When he needed an oil change, Uncle Max went to the guy who needed to be bailed out of jail at two in the morning on Christmas Eve. Trade kept Uncle Max's car, his whole life, for that matter, running smoothly. And when he needed someone to expedite an insurance claim through Midwestern Insurance, Uncle Max went to Faith.

And when Faith needed a ride to the car dealership Monday evening and back again Tuesday evening, she went to Uncle Max. Faith had told the old man her odometer read 90,345.7 miles and, dutifully, called her Ford-certified service center to make an appointment for Tuesday.

Uncle Max had followed her out to the dealership Monday evening where she dropped off her car to avoid the hectic hassle of morning rush hour traffic. She walked stiffly and without much purpose toward his car. When she got in, he immediately instigated, "You know them scheduled maintenances ain't nothin' but a scam, don't you?"

"Really?" she replied, knowing it would only encourage him.

"Yeah, girl. It was somethin' they made up in Detroit, Motor City i'self, back before you was born. Designed opulescence or obulescence or some stupid shit like that. Whatever it was, it was designed to part you from as much a yo money as pos'ble."

Uncle Max, like most of the people who surrounded him, dropped letters, sometimes entire syllables, when speaking. He would then string together these fractions of multiple words into mumbles of meaning. Like a heavy accent, it took some time to decipher, but once acclimated, it became a second language. Faith was fluent.

"It ain't enough-at-ay git yo money when you come through the door. Hell no! They gotta get yo money comin' in, go'n'out, go'n' goddam sideways, no'm'say'n? Do you know what I'm saying?"

He looked over at her and laughed. It was a deep, thick, raspy snicker that got caught between his tongue and cheek on the way out of his toothless smile.

"Hell, look at this car," he continued. "Ain't never once been to no dealership serviceman and she still purrin' like a kitten."

And just like everything Uncle Max said, it was almost true. Almost.

Faith smiled proudly. "Yeah, well, when I trade in my car for a new one, I want to make sure I get as much as I can. I don't get why people just drive their cars into the ground. Don't they realize how quickly they're depreciating their car's value?"

"Shee-it. Listen to you. Depreciating value. You couldn't get a dime more for that damn thing if you kept it in the garage and never drove it nowhere. It's a scam, girl. Listen to your Uncle Max. The way they sell cars, you can be damn sure the salesman gonna get his money. Every penny more he give you gonna come outta his pocket. So he gonna nickel and dime your ass down and down 'til he got you feelin' your car ain't worth shit. And then he give you a little something to make you feel like he doing you favor. But it still a helluva lot less than what it's worth. Then, he gonna turn around and sell it for a helluva lot more than what he paid you. Know that."

"So you don't think I should keep taking my car to the dealership?"

"Hell, your service calls are probably paying for the braces on some pretty little white girl riding horses out in the country." This time the snicker exploded out of his toothless smile and was followed by great bursts of laughter from both passengers.

* * *

They called it Salem's Lot, those who lived there. It sat on the corner of Club Road and 60th Street. It was once a grassy park. Now it was simply a square block of heaving asphalt adorned with the crumbling statue of a man few people knew. And it was where Uncle Max worked, using the hood of his car as a make-shift desk. Uncle Max didn't so much work as he traded favors with friends, acquaintances and near strangers. With his cell phone, a thick, leather-bound ledger and a wireless laptop, Uncle Max was only a coffee maker and a secretary away from a full office.

He guessed it was a little after five when the streets swelled with traffic and the scurrying rats raced from their confining workspaces to their equally confining homes. When he saw Faith, who worked just a few blocks away, walking toward him, the time was confirmed.

"How's business?" she asked.

"Ahhh, ya know, some days you up, some days you down."

"And today?"

"Li'l-a bofe. Speakin' of which, I hope you don't mind, but I got some things to do before we can head all the way out to your car."

"No problem. You want to pick me up at my place or should I ride along?"

"Well, you know, this here vehicle shines a little brighter on the outside when there a beautiful young lady on the inside." A soft snicker squeezed out and Faith replied with a bright smile. Uncle Max opened the passenger door, slipped his office equipment into the back seat and curtsied for her entry.

Standing in the vacancy of the open door Faith asked, "Can we stop by my place real quick and let the beast out?"

"You bet. How is old what's his name?"

Slipping into the car she replied, "Winston. His name's Winston and he's doing great."

Uncle Max drove the back roads and parked on the street in front of Faith's apartment, just a dozen or so blocks from Salem's Lot. He stayed in the car making call after call while Faith disappeared inside, emerging moments later with Winston, her splotchy black and white Boston Terrier. Winston was very amenable, doing his business almost on demand and then as quick as they came, they disappeared inside again. A short while later, Faith came out alone dressed in a pair of faux-designer jeans and a sweater she had picked up at the thrift shop. She climbed into the car, this time without any assistance from Uncle Max, who was engulfed in a phone conversation.

"Sure, sure, I know where it is. Couple blocks south of Ricky's."

Uncle Max motioned to her to climb on in and turned the key. "A'ight … yeah … A'ight … A'ight, fifteen, twenty minutes." He took the phone from his ear, turned it off and tossed it in the small plastic bin he had sitting in the middle of the front bench seat.

"Everything okay, Uncle Max?" Faith asked, guessing at the answer and hoping Uncle Max would offer to pick her up later.

"Ahhh, same old same old." He let out just a quick laugh and pulled away from the curb. "I gots to run over to Willie Spence's place and pick up a few boxes, is all. And then drop them off. How late's your car place open?"

"Eight o'clock. Are we gonna make it?"

"Shit yeah. We pick up a few boxes, make a few stops, do a little this-and-that and we be out there by seven."

"These *this-and-thats* you do for people, for Willie Spence. Are you doing anything you shouldn't be?"

"Sweetheart, if I stuck to only them things I should be doin' I'd be old and gray," he said pointing to his salt and pepper hair, smiling widely and snickering.

The old man's attempt at humor was lost. Instead of calming her, his non-answer made Faith even more anxious and Uncle Max instinctively picked up on it.

"Willie Spence is no one you need to be doing this-and-that for. He's—"

"He's a thug," he interrupted. "But I know he's a thug. And he know I'm an old man and the business I do for him, while maybe not always on the proper side of what's right, is what helps me do things for others that I couldn't do no other way. Now, I ain't never put anyone in harm's way and I ain't aiming to start now. This little bit of business here ain't no big thing. I pick up some things, take them somewheres else and that's all."

"I just wish you would have picked me up when you were done with all of it. I left that neighborhood for a reason."

"Sweetheart, this car shine more brightly when you in it."

"Yeah, yeah, save your sweet talkin' for someone else, Uncle Max."

They drove a dozen blocks south and then another dozen or so blocks east, moving closer and closer toward the neighborhood Faith tried to leave behind. The difference in locale was palpable. Tiny squares of grassy meadows extended from once loved homes that stood, worn and neglected, as rages against gravity. Faith's comfort level dwindled with every "Beware of Dog" sign they passed. While she might have thought from time to time that Salem's Lot was a bit unsafe, she knew this neighborhood was downright dangerous. She silently felt sorry for the kids she saw playing outside.

Uncle Max pulled up to a disheveled bungalow with half the shingles from the roof laying torn and scattered in the yard. On the small rotting porch steps were two young, strong men: guardians. They wore olive green pants, white tanks and black skull caps that covered their shaved heads. Both had several tattoos on their arms. The one sitting a step down from the other appeared to have a tattoo covering his entire left cheek, narrowing a bit at his jaw and tapering down his neck.

"A'ight, Faith, you stay here, I'll be just a minute. I'll go in, get them boxes and we be on our way." He reached into the small plastic bin on the bench seat and pulled out a bright red cell phone. "Here, this one got some games: two or three kinds of solitaires and some others. I'll be back before you done with the first game."

His continued attempts to make her feel at ease appeared to have the opposite effect. But to Uncle Max, she seemed to be playing along bravely.

"I don't know," she said, taking the phone. "I'm pretty bad at these kinds of things. You better hurry up if you plan on getting back here before my first game's over."

Uncle Max swung around the car, walked up the steps, slipped cautiously between the two men on the porch and vanished inside. Upon his return, Faith, appearing relieved to see him, put down the phone she didn't even pretend to play and motioned to get out of the car.

"Na, na, na, na," came the rapid fire dialog. "I got it, sweetheart. They ain't heavy. You stay where you is." Uncle Max propped one end of the boxes on the bumper of his car and rested the other in the crux of his hip as he bent to get the keys from his pocket. He popped the trunk, eased the boxes inside and closed the trunk in a fairly fluid motion before saddling up the driver's side of the metallic bronze car that looked surprisingly fresh in contrast to the backdrop of the discarded vehicles lining the neighborhood.

Before he even set foot in the car, Uncle Max was already working to make Faith feel secure. "What I tell ya? In and out," he said and followed it immediately with a smile.

With the window open, Faith spoke softly, "Yeah, well, the sooner we're out of here, the better."

Uncle Max turned the key, but all that happened was the starter whined and clicked and begged the engine to turn over. When it didn't, panic filled the car like an airbag. Uncle Max noticed Faith's eyes fixed on his frail, dry, right hand almost trying to will it, through telekinesis, to turn the key. He calmly pumped the gas once or twice and twisted the key. Again the starter whined and clicked.

Faith turned and looked out the window. The two men who had played their part as the stoic statues guarding the entrance of their master's castle turned their attention to the car. Uncle Max could almost feel Faith's tension as she looked out the window: an impala in the sights of two stalking tigers.

After a few failed attempts and what seemed a small eternity, the engine finally turned over and roared to life. Uncle Max released the clutch and edged forward. Then he leaned a bit and waved his hand as if to say, *Thanks fellas, I'm all set.* The two men turned again to one another and talked with the same disinterest they had shown before.

Uncle Max and Faith drove in relative silence as the neighborhoods that enveloped them became more vibrant. The streets where Faith had grown up lay far from the soft pastels of the affluent suburban homes owned by the businessmen who wear suits and park imported luxury sedans in their three car garages. But they were not quite as stark as the muted grays where Willie Spence and his associates chiseled out a hard existence amidst the domestic mid-size vehicles stripped to their bones on the curb.

Faith broke the silence. "So where you gotta drop these boxes off? A crack house?"

Uncle Max heard the disapproving tone. The deaf could have heard it. "We goin' to a place called Gambel's on the west side. Drop off a couple DVD players and some DVDs or CDs or whatever in the smaller boxes."

"You mean you *hope* that's all that's in them boxes. Probably money in them shoe boxes, drug money. Or maybe worse."

"Worse? Worse how, like a hand or something?"

"Eew, no. Damn, Uncle Max. What would make you say that?"

"I saw a movie the other night where a guy cut another guy's arm off with a chainsaw."

"Stop."

"And when you said worse than drug money—"

"Uncle Max!"

"Plus the size of the box—" he added just to get her really riled up.

"Enough! That's not what I was thinking at all. But you made my point. There could be anything in those boxes. Willie Spence would just as soon give you three boxes of hands as he would drug money, or drugs, or poisonous snakes."

"C'mon, now. This is your Uncle Max. I been people's go-between for years now and I almost never do nothing for Willie Spence. He stopped by Salem's Lot today while I was doin' my thing and told me he might need a little somethin' somethin' from me. I couldn't just flat out say no to him right there, being who he is and all, so I told him to call me. He did and he assured me this thing was no big deal and that—"

"No big deal? Uncle Max! He'd lie to Jesus Christ in heaven and think he was getting' away with it. Of course he's gonna say that."

Uncle Max paused. "Like I said, I almost never do—"

"You better start making it never *ever* do, and right now or you gonna find yourself in more trouble than any sweet, old, wrinkly gray-haired man has any business being in."

He looked at her softly and spoke equally soft, "Sweetheart?"

"What?"

"This car, it don't shine so much when the pretty thing in the front seat yells a-tcha."

He flashed his toothless smile. And when she smiled back, his toothless snicker broke through on both of them.

He drove a few blocks north to Club Road and turned left again, heading west toward the dealership. They drove a while in silence as they approached Salem's Lot and the erratic cluster of traffic lights. He noticed she'd been seething in her silence, waiting for an opening. "Damn it Uncle Max, you know Willie Spence ain't no one you should be gettin' involved with."

"You right. I know you right. But it's not as simple as that."

"Yeah, well nothing's simple. Doing right ain't simple. I gotta ...." She stopped before she began. She wrung her hands and looked out her window as they sat before the small building where she worked. She took a deep breath, smiled and said simply, "Neither of us know what's in them boxes, right? As far as we're concerned, they're birthday presents, right? But from now on, you do what you gotta do, Uncle Max, but you keep me the hell out of any business you got with Willie Spence. You hear me?" At that moment, the car stalled.

"Aw, now you see what you done?" he smiled. "All your yelling upset my car."

He turned the key and spoke quietly, "C'mon, sweetheart," and the starter caught. The bulk of traffic ebbed and flowed through the next few lights like one big cruise ship moving from one canal lock to the next with Uncle Max and Faith flowing with it.

"Time for you to see Mr. Fixit, ain't it?"

"Last night you were making fun of me for bringing my car in to the dealership for a tune-up. Bet you wish you'd-a done it too, now, huh?"

"Oh, this here car gets tuned-up regularly, just not by no thievin' dealership, is all."

"The dealership guarantees their work. Does your 'Mr. Fixit' guarantee what he does?"

It stalled again, this time in the middle of the intersection.

"See," she added.

He tried his gentle ways once more, "C'mon, sweetheart." But this time, the car was having none of it and the starter whined away and clicked with no response.

"The light's changing, Uncle Max," Faith muttered, her voice notched up an octave.

"It's a'ight," he said reassuring himself as much as his passenger. "Here we go."

The car whined and choked without effect and, as the traffic from his left approached slowly, the air became heavy with panic. Uncle Max's senses dulled on the peripheral, focusing only on the immediate: his eyes on his hands, hands on the key, ears on the choking starter which filtered through the audible pulses of his heartbeat. Faith sat and watched the traffic build to her left as the light cycled.

"Did you hear that?" asked Uncle Max.

"What?"

"Did the engine turn over? I don't want to flood it, but I can't tell if the engine turned over."

"Put it in gear and see if it moves," Faith offered.

He watched the cars moving eastbound inch up against the line of cars blocked by his stalled vehicle. He shifted into gear and whispered, "A'ight, let's try this."

The car bucked like a rodeo steer: first backward and then forward and Faith let out a quick, high pitched scream. Then the car gently rocked to a rest as Uncle Max stood on the brake pedal.

He looked to see if his passenger was okay. She was. Then he looked around and saw a green Saturn behind him and to his right. He saw the cars on all sides and felt their drivers looking and pointing at the old man in the old car. He grabbed the shift handle, put it into neutral and turned the key. Neither he nor Faith perceived the engine cut out.

"Uncle Max, you okay?"

He didn't respond.

"Uncle Max, are you okay? Are you hurt? Uncle Max? We were just in an accident. Can you hear me?"

But all he could do was look around in slow, sweeping motions: left to right, right to left. He peered out the front windshield and glanced into the rearview mirror but only as a distraction, not to gather input. He had spent forty years behind the wheel of his golden girl and, aside from a few fender benders when he was first learning to drive, he'd kept it protected, just as he had kept thousands of people in his inner circle protected for centuries.

Faith's voice finally penetrated his thoughts. "Uncle Max? Are you okay?"

"Yeah," he uttered. Coming to, he turned to Faith, "You? How you, girl?"

"Fine. We were in an accident. Do you know what happened?"

"I-I-I'm not sure. It was weird. I put the car in gear, released the clutch and all-a sudden we start shakin', hit from behind, I think."

Looking over her shoulder, Faith said, "Yeah, a little green car. A white guy, too. He looks like he's gonna try and pull over or something." Then, turning back to Uncle Max, "He's crazy if he thinks he's going anywhere in this mess."

Uncle Max turned deadly serious and said, "Faith?"

"Yeah, Uncle Max?"

He lowered his head until his chin touched his chest. "I shouldn't be driving."

"Uncle Max, come on now. This wasn't that bad an accident. You're a good driver. You shouldn't..."

"No, no, no," he spoke into his lap. "I mean I shouldn't be driving." He raised his head and met her eyes, "My license is suspended and I ain't got no insurance."

"Oh my God."

"You the insurance girl, what do I do?"

"Uncle Max." She paused, but only briefly. "Okay, it's stupid to drive without insurance but it ain't illegal in this state so long as you can prove you can pay the damages of the accident. This don't seem too bad, maybe a couple thousand. If you can scrape together that much in a few months, you should be fine. As for driving with a suspended license, I don't know anything about that."

Uncle Max sat still and silent. It wasn't until someone in dark clothes strode to his door, bent down and offered, "Excuse me, sir?" that he finally came back to his senses.

CHAPTER 10

Officer Wysczyzewski cautiously approached the bronze vehicle from the front. Her right hand rested on the butt of her pistol and her elbow pointed high in the air. Inside, she noticed the two occupants of the vehicle talking without much notice of her or the situation. She bent at the waist and felt the varying equipment attached to her belt sway in response to the gesture.

Peering in, she asked with an authoritative voice, "Excuse me, sir?"

When the man behind the wheel stared up at her with his vacant eyes, unresponsive and confused, she simply assumed he was on drugs. He was an old man sitting in a beat up mid-70's Dodge Dart stuck in the middle of an intersection on the fringes of urban blight. He had to be somehow impaired. Nearly everyone with whom she came in contact, other than her fellow officers, were either drunk, high, on their way to get drunk or high or recovering from being drunk or high. Why should this be any different?

Immediately, she recognized these thoughts for what they were: an acquired bigotry through the constant exposure to the city's criminal element. And it bothered her. She was thankful that it bothered her, though, as its irritation somehow verified that she was still sane, that she knew right from wrong. The fact that she defaulted to a prejudgment was immaterial. What was important was that she recognized it within herself. She mentally fought back the urge to assume the worst and continued to assess the situation with a slate wiped as clean as she was able to provide.

"Sir, could you please roll down your window?"

His gaunt face was loosely fitted with weathered skin that took on an appearance of poorly aged leather the longer she looked at him. He turned away from her as the passenger, a much younger woman, quite dark, quietly handsome and by Officer Wysczyzewski's estimations far too conservatively dressed for the neighborhood, told the driver he should roll down his window.

When he did so, the policewoman leaned in a bit closer and explained her presence. "Sir, there seems to have been an accident involving this vehicle. I'm here to find out what happened. But first, are either of you injured?"

"No, sir, officer," replied the female passenger, "Neither of us are injured but I think he's a little overwhelmed by all this."

"That's understandable." She stood, took her hand off the butt of her pistol, looked around at the gridlock surrounding the disabled vehicle, returned to her bent position, this time with both hands resting on the driver's door, and spoke. "Since traffic is already screwed up, I guess there's really no reason for you to move the vehicle. How 'bout you two get out and come around the back with me. Bring your license, registration, proof of insurance and whatever else you have and we can take a look at whatever damage there is together."

She remembered from her training to always stay calm, to make the person you're dealing with feel as though you're on their side and to use "we" and "us" as often as possible. These tidbits of human psychology were as vital to her training as target practice, perhaps more so considering she had never once discharged her weapon in the line of duty, yet had relied on the knowledge attained in her Effective Communications course on a daily basis.

The passenger was the first to get out. She was a pretty woman with an undoubtedly feminine figure, though Officer Wysczyzewski thought it too-well hidden behind a stiff swirl of hair and conservative attire, especially more conservative than most of the urban woman with whom the policewoman usually engaged. The woman wore baggy BLZ jeans and a simple red wool sweater. She slunk down the passenger side of the car toward the policewoman and sheepishly asked, "What happens if Uncle Max doesn't have his license?"

"Well, that all depends on what the problem is. If he forgot it at home, that's a twenty-dollar fine. If it's been revoked, well, that's a whole different story."

"How different?" asked Faith as Uncle Max exited the car.

Officer Wysczyzewski rolled her eyes and sighed, "Crap." She regretted saying it the moment it slipped from her tongue, but she couldn't help it. A typical traffic accident took about thirty minutes to resolve in the field and another forty-five minutes in the office filing the report. In Salem's Lot, traffic could add another thirty minutes in the field. A driver without a license could add as much as three hours in the field plus another hour filing an arrest report and processing the offender, if an arrest was warranted. And that was just the lost time. The emotional toll on all involved was even more costly.

"What'd you say his name was?" she said quietly to the young woman.

"His name's Sledge, Mike Sledge," she whispered back, "but everyone calls him Uncle Max."

"Uncle Max, eh?"

Uncle Max was a staple of the community. Somehow, she remembered that he was on the City Council at one time and held some sway over community matters. Looking at the man walking toward her, she found the image of distinguished civil leader unlikely, but continued with procedures as if he were just another offender because, to her, that's all he was.

"And your name?" she asked directly.

"Faith Underhill."

"Mr. Sledge, Ms. Underhill, my name is Officer Wysczyzewski. I know. It's a mouthful," she smiled. "So try to remember me as the drunken Polish cook: Whiskey Chef-ski. Got it? Now, Mr. Sledge, I'm told you don't have a license."

"That's right, officer. No insurance neither."

"What happened to the license?"

He was leaning against the trunk of the car with his hands clasped in front of him and his head looking down, dejected, taking in the debris scattered across the asphalt. "Well, couple things. First, I had some parking tickets, then I had a little fender bender with this young boy that stole a car and I got a ticket for driving with an expired license. And then I missed when I was supposed to show up in court so they sent a letter sayin' my license was no good no more, but I never got it."

Having been assigned to the Salem's Lot satellite station, Officer Wysczyzewski had heard variations on this same story a thousand times. And what amazed her most was that, without fail, the driver always asked her to look the other way. Every man, woman and child expected her to sympathize with their story and allow them to go on their merry way as if nothing had happened.

"I'm gonna need your full name and address and run you through the system to make sure there aren't any outstanding warrants. Is it Michael Sledge?"

"Yes, officer."

"And your address?"

"Well, right now I's stayin' at 2874 North 48th Street, apartment number 204."

"You with Manny?" Faith interrupted.

"Yeah. I been there a while. We get along good and he don't mind me sleepin' on the couch."

"All right, folks, I'm gonna call this in. I'll be back in a couple minutes to take your statements."

"Officer, um, Whiskey Chef-ski?" asked Uncle Max. "Is all that necessary? I mean, couldn't I just get the man's car fixed and be done with it without having to bother everyone and puttin' you through all this trouble?"

"I'm sorry, Mr. Sledge, it's not something I want to do. I have to. Everyone I stop has to get run through the system."

She thought he was a sweet, old man and had she stopped him for some minor moving violation, she might very well have cut him a break.

But there was damage to the other car, the traffic was so congested it had brought the news helicopters, her evening meal was bland, his name wasn't really Uncle Max. In the end, none of that mattered. What mattered was that it was procedure.

"I'll be right back. Please stay here behind the vehicle. Don't go in. Don't pop the trunk. Just stay right here and relax if you can."

"A'ight, then."

Constance Wysczyzewski had twenty years in as a cop and would probably spend another twenty years doing it if they let her. She was a stout, stocky woman who appeared to have more girth under her uniform than she possessed in actuality. Her round, pale face, particularly her cheeks, ran flush from the heat of summer as well as the chill of winter. She was a third generation cop, following her grandfather and her mother, who was both strict and loving. Her father was a public school teacher and together, Connie's parents provided the necessary tools to get along well in their tough-but-pleasant blue-collar neighborhood. Her younger sister, Prudence, was provided the same tools but ignored them, choosing instead to marry rich and, as she would say, rise above her upbringing. To Connie's sister, life was about attaining and retaining status. To Connie, it was about achieving contentment. And helping others made her happy.

As she turned to call in a Mr. Michael Sledge to have him checked through the system, she thought about his request to look the other way.

"Battin' a thousand," she whispered and smiled.

CHAPTER 11

A few moments after Officer Wysczyzewski called in Uncle Max's real name, Officer Jenkins returned to the passenger side of the cruiser to call in Andy Walker. He asked his partner how things were shaping up.

"Not good. No license or insurance."

"Yeah. Who didn't see that comin'?"

Unlike Connie, who tried to keep her acquired bigotry in check, Officer Jenkins made no such effort and it bothered her like a small rash, not so bad that it required a trip to the clinic, but bad enough to notice it when it flared. She did her part to show her disapproval of the comment. "Assumed innocent. Remember?"

"Yeah, well, look at my guy," he said, pointing to Andy. "He looks like a pain in the ass. Acts like a pain in the ass. And guess what? He is a pain in the ass. Going on and on about his perfect driving record. Never been in an accident. Blah, blah, blah. Like I care."

"Did you give him the speech about—"

"About 'the less you talk the better?' Hell yeah."

If her partner's apathy toward his own acquired bigotry was a small rash, then his constant habit of interrupting to finish someone else's thoughts was a full-body urticaria. It was uncontrollable and incessant.

"My point is," he continued, "Sometimes people are exactly what they seem to be."

"Maybe. But sometimes they're not."

On the screen of the in-dash computer she read, *Sledge, Michael T. Last known address: 2745 N. 59th Street. No warrants issued.*

She keyed in the address Uncle Max had given her and said, "Well, he says he lost his license due to parking tickets. What do you think? Should we—"

"Impound the vehicle?" he interrupted. "Abso-fuckin-lutely. You let him skate here and there's no lesson learned. What do I always say? People must be held accountable for their actions, right?"

She knew what his answer was going to be long before she tried to ask the question, but it helped to have someone else verify procedure. It allowed her to void the guilt she would invariably feel by inconveniencing someone's life for a couple days, particularly someone who seemed to be in desperate need of a break. But then, she thought, nearly everyone from Salem's Lot is in desperate need of a break.

"This is Unit 47. We're going to need a wrecker at 65th and Club to pick up an impounded vehicle. Officers on the scene: will direct on arrival. Over."

"Roger, Unit 47," came back in a broken hiss.

She looked at Jenkins, who had already run Walker, Andrew K., and sighed. Officer Jenkins interrupted before she even began. "If you want to make people happy all day long, become a clown or something. A good chunk of our job is to be bearers of bad news. If you let this get to you, man, you're gonna have a miserable career."

"You're all heart, Jenkins. How do you stay so chipper?"

"You took the same training I did. There's a tremendous amount of satisfaction in taking scum off the streets and making this a better place to live. Think about the little kids that didn't get run over because you got a drunk driver off the road. Last week, when we brought that kid back to his mom, nine out of ten days, she's bitchin' and moanin' about the police not being there when she needs them. But that day? She was in tears, thanking us for doing our job.

"That's how I stay so chipper."

"Jenkins, I thought you were a hard case. Now you're goin' soft on me? Are you menstruating?"

He laughed and muttered, "Fuck you!"

As she lifted herself out of the vehicle she noticed the traffic slowly dispersing. Only the cars caught in the heart of the gridlock remained. The wispy clouds that shone cottony white only a few moments ago had turned a faded, smoky gray, the sun a bright orange against the ever deepening sky. September, normally mild and pleasant, was unseasonably cold, a deep, unruly cold that made people hunch over and shuffle when they walked.

Officer Wyszczyzewski's blood was as thick as her Polish heritage. As someone who seemed to sweat through the simple act of breathing, she was thankful for the cooler temperatures. Anxiety, too, caused her to produce an uncommon amount of perspiration. It was a condition, hyperhidrosis, her doctor told her, that her peers noticed and about which they gleefully took every opportunity to rib her.

Her decision to call in the tow truck, even with Jenkins's authoritative stamp of approval, weighed on her conscience. She could feel her skin tingle as her sweat flowed. Her face, too, was affected by her decision, hued a brilliant crimson; her cheeks nearly bursting with blood.

When Faith and Uncle Max saw her, they seemed taken aback by the change in her complexion. Unsure of its meaning, Uncle Max spoke first.

"What's the good news, officer?" he said, smiling his toothless grin.

"I'm sorry to say, the news isn't good, Mr. Sledge. Those tickets you have outstanding—almost five hundred dollars—still need to be paid. And because you didn't pay them before, the city needs to make sure you pay them this time around. The only way that's going to happen is if we impound your car and make you settle up with the city before giving it back to you."

"You can't do that," Faith blurted.

"Yes, ma'am, I can." Then, trying to get back on their side, she continued, "It's really not up to me. If he had paid the tickets when he was supposed to, it'd be a different story. But he didn't. He has to settle up with the city and now it's not just the tickets but also the cost of towing the car to the city lot. As for the damages incurred in this accident, he's also going to need to work something out with the other driver's insurance company, some sort of good faith offer that he intends to pay for all the repairs."

The looks on their faces were almost too much to bear. She tried to think about the woman Jenkins mentioned, the mother of the prodigal son, but the woman's face was beyond her mind's grasp. Her efforts to let Faith and Uncle Max down softly were completely lost on them.

"He was taking me to pick up my car at the dealership. How the fuck am I gonna get out there, now?" Faith asked.

"Now, now, sweetheart, your Uncle Max is always good for a favor. I'll just make a few phone calls and get you out there before you know it."

The policewoman gently stated, "Mr. Sledge, Ms. Underhill, you're going to want to remove any personal items from your vehicle."

Faith pounced, "Personal items? Why, you gonna search it or something?"

Officer Wysczyzewski assumed the panic in Faith's voice was due to the annoyance and frustration of the situation. She had no reason to suspect an armload of items from Willie Spence, a name she would have undoubtedly recognized from the news briefs and reports that were required reading before each shift, rested within the trunk of the beaten down car that sat before her. She simply replied, "No, ma'am. We're just going to keep it in our impound lot until Mr. Sledge settles up with the city. You can keep whatever you want in there, but you won't have access to it until the vehicle is released."

Then, pulling a pamphlet from her notebook, she continued. "It's all outlined in this," she said as she handed the pamphlet to Uncle Max. "Where you need to go, what you need to bring. And if you have a question that isn't answered in this pamphlet, there's a number to call during regular business hours."

Their dejected looks didn't go away, causing Officer Wysczyzewski to ask, against her better judgment, "Where's your car, Ms. Underhill?"

"Carlson Ford out by 101."

Connie paused. "We're not supposed to do this, but since you're stuck here, I'll drive you out there and the two of you can figure out the best way to resolve this issue."

As hoped, the dejection slipped from Faith's face.

The intersection of 65th and Club leisurely buzzed back to life with some semblance of its previous chaotic order as the team of officers worked traffic control, Jenkins and Wysczyzewski procured the proper information from all involved parties, and Andy Walker went on his way with a moving violation, a busted headlight and some mangled fiberglass as his souvenirs. Even maneuvering the wrecker in and out of the busy intersection was quick and efficient. A few moments later a team from the Department of Public Works cleared the debris from the road's surface and one by one the police cruisers disappeared from the scene.

* * *

The ride out to the car dealership was an awkward one, with long pauses in conversations broken by blatantly forced small talk, stopping and starting abruptly.

"Got any plans?" Connie asked, looking at them through the rearview mirror.

"Who?" Faith responded.

"Either of you. What are you doing tonight?"

Staring out the window, she grunted, "Seeing a movie."

"Oh, yeah? Which one?"

"*Grey Matter*. The new one with Michael Stevens."

"Tonight? I thought that was opening tomorrow."

Faith didn't answer.

Officer Jenkins looked at his partner as if pleading with her to stop engaging their passengers, but she persisted.

"What kind of car do you have?"

"A Ford Focus."

"Oh yeah? What year?"

"I don't know."

It was nearly closing time at Carlson Ford by the time they got out there, but Officer Wysczyzewski had called ahead and asked that they keep the service window open a little while longer to accommodate Ms. Underhill. Officer Wysczyzewski got out from behind the wheel and opened Faith's door for her while Jenkins got out and followed his partner's lead, opening Uncle Max's door since the doors on the police cruiser only opened from the outside. By the time Uncle Max exited the vehicle Faith had circled around the cruiser and was leading the way to the service department entrance.

Uncle Max had emptied nearly everything out of the small bucket on the bench seat of his car as well as a few items from his back seat. These items he placed in several small plastic bags from the local supermarket which he pulled from various crevasses throughout the car. His wireless laptop stuck out of yet another bag, making it appear even more conspicuously out of place than when it sat in the disheveled rear seat. He wanted to grab a coat from the trunk but consciously left it so as to not reveal the boxes he had picked up at Willie Spence's place. Faith had only her purse, but carried Uncle Max's thick, heavy, leather-bound ledger under her arm.

Continuing her efforts to stay on their side, Officer Wysczyzewski called over the top of the cruiser, "I'll have everything pushed through by the end of the night and you can make arrangements to pick up your vehicle as soon as the lot opens tomorrow morning."

Faith did not say thank you. "Fine," was all that came out.

Both Jenkins and Wysczyzewski slipped back into the cruiser. She expected a lecture regarding breaking protocol by providing citizens with unofficial livery services. Jenkins obliged. "You do realize that we're not a taxi service, don't you?"

She ignored him.

During the fifty-block trek east along Club Road back to the satellite station the two officers remained silent. They eased into the police station parking lot and came to rest in one of the vacancies in the motor pool.

Jenkins broke the silence. "God, that guy was a prick."

"Your guy? Walker?"

"Yeah. I swear, he must have told me a dozen times he'd never been in an accident. Fuckin'a, you shoulda seen the look on his face when I gave him that ticket." Then he laughed, "He was so pissed, I seriously thought he was gonna take a swing at me. His eyes got all big and buggy; his face turned about sixteen shades of red. God, I love this job."

* * *

The full moon hung low and ghostly white in the deep blue sky of twilight. Only the brightest stars could be seen through the intensifying glare of the streetlights. The lights within the station flooded out the reinforced glass doors to greet the returning officers as they walked up the three long, gradual concrete steps. When Jenkins and Wysczyzewski entered the building, they quietly and dutifully went about processing their reports and filing their paperwork. Connie called the impound lot to ensure Uncle Max's car was placed close to the entrance to make its retrieval quick and easy. When she hung up the phone, she looked at the clock which read 10:26. She went to the break room for a cup of coffee and returned to her desk satisfied in knowing she had done all she could to make Faith's and Uncle Max's situation as unobtrusive and non-invasive as possible. Regardless of her efforts, she knew they wouldn't notice. But she knew what she did would make a difference, so she smiled.

From the intercom of her phone came, "Whiskey. Your sister's on line three."

"Thanks," she yelled at the phone.

Regardless of who she's told is calling, she answered her phone the same way every time. "This is Officer Wysczyzewski. How can I help you?"

Prudence Treadwell's voice, even more piercing than usual, came tumbling out of the ear piece. "Connie, it's me, Prudy. I think something's happened to Davis. No, I know something's happened to Davis. You have to come over right now."

CHAPTER 12

Detective Lonnie Brown was less than a block away sipping coffee with his partner and watching a young boy on the High-Sum corner stroll over to a black BMW that had pulled up to the curb. Brown raised the binoculars to his eyes and read the license plate out loud as his partner wrote it in his notebook. It was the only entry.

Fifteen minutes earlier, Brown was telling his partner about the last seven years of his professional career, explaining exactly why it was that they were out there; waiting in the cold autumn night for Brown's antagonist.

It was his very first homicide, the Winston Johnson case, the one that started it all, the reason he and his partner were in their car earlier that day driving back from the Highland morgue having just spoken to the medical examiner. He caught the Johnson case just a few weeks after being promoted to detective, almost seven years earlier to the day. He and his then-partner worked the case following standard procedure and came up with nothing significant other than that the victim had been killed elsewhere and his body was transferred to his girlfriend's neighborhood. They also found that he was a nice boy who everyone agreed didn't deserve to die.

It wasn't a high-profile case since the body was found in such close proximity to the site of several other open murder cases and everyone just assumed, that because of the neighborhood, he'd been mugged or mistaken for a rival gang member or some other unfortunate but extremely probable scenario. But Brown treated it like it was the most important case in the world because, to him, it was. It was his first. However, as was often the case with investigations in the heart of the inner city, false leads, dead ends and contradictory statements accumulated until a couple weeks and a few more-pressing cases slowly moved the file to the bottom of his stack and eventually into the cold case file drawer.

As he ascended the departmental ranks he became more intuitive and his investigative skills were more finely honed. He was transferred five years later to District 1, the downtown office. It came after too many years in the high-crime, low-rent neighborhoods of District 3. D3 had a way of eroding enthusiasm for solving cases and replacing it with apathy. Unlike so many before him, Brown used the rush he felt with his first case, the Winston Johnson case, as a point of reference for all future investigations. He treated each case like it was his first and viewed his promotion as validation of this practice.

Another case file bearing his name as the primary investigator, along with the name of his current partner, Detective Benjamin Watts, was a homeless man, John Doe. It had come in last year, six years after his other. It was officially a cold case but ran like hot lava through his mind. It exhibited many similarities to the Johnson case: the victim was eviscerated with a double-sided blade; there was a large, perfectly circular bruise around the wound; the crime was committed during the end of September; it was a dump and run; and, once the circle of family and friends were eliminated as suspects, the final similarity was its speedy and unceremonious rotation into the cold case drawer with no foreseeable conclusion.

Convinced that these cases were more than peripherally related, he cross-referenced what little data he had with the city's database of other open cases. While the city had officially gone digital in the late-1980's, the backlog of case files being added to the databank had only reached about a decade further back, giving him some forty years of searchable files. His search uncovered hundreds of open murder cases listing the cause of death as a single, fatal stab wound. This high volume disturbed him, not because of empathy for the hundreds of families who had lost a loved one, but because he'd have to read more reports than anticipated. Undeterred, he refined his search to murders committed in September, the same month as both his two cold case files, which culled his hits down to a manageable one-hundred seventy-two cases. He sifted through each file looking for further evidence that either tied it to the others or somehow indicated it was unrelated.

Noticing a wide geographical scattering of crime scenes, he expanded his search to the outlying suburbs, going through their databases. His expanded search resulted in an additional forty-six cases. For nearly a year, Brown scoured the metropolitan area for files that could be added to his already unwieldy stack. It was his hobby. It was his passion.

The gnawing issue he faced each and every time he dove into his files was that the cases showed far more differences than similarities. The victims were different ages, races, religions and genders and from the entire spectrum of socio-economic backgrounds. They lived, worked and socialized all over the greater metropolitan area and their crime scenes were equally dispersed. While each victim was killed around the same time of year, there were huge variances of dates from year to year. Certain elements of each case would occasionally overlap a few of the others but the stack of files lacked significant continuity as a whole.

He forced himself past any shadowy doubts of the cases' interrelatedness by focusing solely on their similarities. The times of death listed were all between 11 p.m. and 2 a.m. In each case the victim was killed in the same manner and dumped. Toxicology reports for most of the more recent cases showed the victims were drugged with sevoflourane, desflurane or some other generally used volatile anesthetic. He tagged all the files where the toxicology reports showed an indication of anesthetics, but was not able to use it to exclude all files that did not offer such findings. Still, he was unable to cull many of the files, leaving a stack of just over a hundred.

Brown knew that most people, murderers and victims alike, were animals of habit: that there were several threads of commonality woven through the stacks of files sitting in chronological order on his desk. Each criterion for his database search was an individual thread that had yet to reveal a discernible pattern. The fact that there was a disproportionate number of cases from September suggested the beginnings of a thread, but the scattered dates suggested otherwise.

He pored over the old case files hoping to find something that he'd missed, either while actually working the case or reviewing the case files left unsolved by others. Buried in a folder of one of the older files was a copy of a hand-written note from a patrol officer's initial interview with a witness:

Witness – Stephen Grafton
6347 North 107th Street
Walking dog about 11:30 –
After Letterman
Saw nothing in alley
Asked if sure - bright full moon
Could see everything,
Nothing in alley –
Positive

Brown quickly jumped online and typed *September, full moon* and the dates into the search engine. He got more than a half-million hits. He briskly scanned the titles and descriptions of the first couple hits and immediately noted the recurring phrase *Harvest Moon*. He clicked on the first Harvest Moon site listed.

The Harvest Moon is the name given to the full moon closest to the Autumnal Equinox, the moment when the earth stands perpendicular to the sun on its axis and a day consists of almost exactly 12 hours of sunlight and 12 hours of darkness, usually occurring on or about September 23rd. Two out of every three years, the Harvest Moon comes in September, but every third year it occurs in October.

Lonnie Brown's right hand, resting on the mouse, began to tremble with adrenaline. He read on.

Because of the earth's position, the time between full moon-rises on successive nights is shorter near the equinox than at any other time of year, so there is very little darkness between sunset and moonrise. The continuance of the moonlight after sunset has been used by farmers in northern latitudes for millennia to harvest their crops well into the evening: hence the name Harvest Moon.

"I'll be God-damned," he whispered.

His heart was pounding with excitement. Brown scrolled down the page hoping to find the dates of all the previous Harvest Moons. The site hadn't been updated in more than two years, but he did find the dates for five relatively recent years. Four of the five dates in the chart corresponded to a day before a body was reported found. He went to a second site that listed all the full moons from 1900 to 2099 and cross-checked the dates of the previous forty years against his files. He purged nearly three-quarters of his files, leaving him with twenty-six in total: one case each year for twenty of the previous twenty-nine years, including eight of the last nine.

Armed with the dates of the past Harvest Moons, Brown spent the next few weeks in the department's archives digging deep into those files not yet in the department database, searching for hard-copy case files that matched his profile. He pulled another eleven cases, most of them from the 1970's and one from as far back as 1946. These eleven new cases also included open files for seven of the eight most recent October dates noted on his list of Harvest Moons. Detective Lonnie Brown knew the subtle similarities were undeniable.

"A fucking serial killer."

In total, there were thirty-seven individual folders representing open cases, each one at least a half-inch thick and filled with copies of witnesses' statements, forensic files, autopsy reports and crime scene photos. Brown was the primary listed on only two of the folder jackets, but it seemed like more. Those two were by no means his only open cases, but they were the only cases that occupied his mind and his duties every time he had a few slow days to clear the backlog. Off-duty, he spent even more time on them. Eventually, he started calling the stack of files on his desk "my book." They were the foundation of what he hoped would be the first of his many successful novels.

This is what helped him treat each new case like it was his first. This is what helped him keep focused and stay excited. However, his focus and excitement remained internal because looming at every turn were his shadowy doubts: there were gaps, significant gaps if the hard-copy cases were included. His biggest fear was that the gaps were closed cases; ones with a conviction, meaning any attempt to package them with the open cases would be grounds for an immediate appeal by even the least capable defense attorney. High-profile lawsuits from innocent defendants serving life sentences were certain to factor into the department's decision to proceed with an all-out investigation. Also factoring into the department's decision were the hard-copy case files, particularly the file from seventy years earlier. Could there actually be someone out there who has been killing one person every year for seventy years? The suspect would be pushing ninety. Who in the DA's office wants to bring that to trial? And what kind of punishment is a life sentence to someone who's already beaten the actuarial tables?

Further compounding the difficulties of bringing his findings to the blue brass was the media's thirst for the kinds of splash headlines a serial killer would undoubtedly provide them. Brown was certain his superiors would keep it completely under wraps. But how long before the FBI started sniffing around to take over the remainder of the investigation?

Brown couldn't have that. Not any of it.

These are my cases, he told himself. They're going to be the exclamation point on my career and I'm going to make a fortune selling my novel.

Immediately following the assembly of his thirty-seven files he enlisted the help of an old friend from his youth, one of the community's elder statesman, so to speak, to help him review, organize, log and cross-reference all the evidence, statements and reports. Once he and the kindly old man finished the database from the files, Lonnie Brown spent the next nine months focused on writing. *Death by the Harvest Moonlight*, or *The Harvest Moon Killer*, or *The Harvester*. He hadn't settled on a title, but he had narrowed it down to those three. He delighted in the thought of turning in his badge, being on national television and hitching a ride on the celebrity express for as long as it would have him. He even wrote his dedication page: To Uncle Max for all your hard work, on this book and in my life.

It was for these reasons that Detective Brown did not share the information he had with anyone within the department, save one: his partner, Detective Watts, and only out of necessity. He didn't warn his superiors of the fatal possibilities the cold weather of fall would bring. He needed to work a fresh case with a fresh victim and a fresh crime scene.

He needed fresh blood.

CHAPTER 13

As the summer closed and September approached, Detective Lonnie Brown knew that there was no predicting where the next body would turn up, only when. He also recognized he was not going to be able to work the next case alone, so he provided his partner with the first draft of his novel. It was a more detailed summary of the research he collected to date than he could otherwise explain and it underscored exactly why he hadn't brought the case files to the attention of his superiors.

He was confident that there would be no movement on the case until after the Harvest Moon, Tuesday, September 28th, so he took off the entire week prior, holing up in a cabin deep in the rural woods upstate with his thirty-seven files. The days were spent silently fishing while the nights were consumed with the meticulous examination of the files, memorizing all that was in them so that when the call came in Wednesday morning, September 29th, he would have everything he needed at his immediate disposal.

Before leaving for vacation, however, Brown asked Watts to send a briefing bulletin to all stations in the metropolitan area asking to be contacted if anyone came across a dump and run stab victim. Unbeknownst to Brown, a body had turned up in the Highland morgue the Wednesday during his vacation that fit the parameters of his briefing bulletin. What's more, there was another body found in District 3 two Wednesdays prior which also fit Brown's scant parameters.

So, on Monday morning, immediately upon returning from vacation, Detective Lonnie Brown and his partner, Detective Benjamin Watts, met two detectives in the District 3 building. Except for the faces, little had changed since Brown was transferred from D3. It was just as dark and oppressive as he remembered.

Brown's plan was to share only a few details of the two previous cases that listed him as the primary, knowing full well that the two detectives from D3 would hold back information from him because nobody wants their cases solved by someone else, especially not a murder case. Brown and Watts went first, introducing themselves and then giving a shallow overview of their cases until it was time for the other detectives to reciprocate, which they did just as shallowly. Each side agreed there were substantial similarities, but Brown quickly dismissed them and did his best to thoroughly discourage any linking of the cases.

Brown and Watts then talked to the Coroner who performed the autopsy to verify there were no bruises on the sternum and that the knife was single-edged, as was indicated in the report. He double-checked various other details that either further differentiated the D3 case from Brown's thirty-seven files or brought it closer to a match. Most notable of these were the hundreds of tiny, red wounds found all over the body.

On Tuesday, the detectives skipped talking to the case detectives and went directly to the Highland medical examiner. They wanted a first-hand understanding of the most recent victim's autopsy report and all its various other accompanying reports. Again, Brown and Watts held their cards close to the vest when discussing their two open murder cases. The information imparted to them on the Highland case, as well as the case from District 3, did not sit well with Brown; he was visibly agitated by the volume of similarities between all the cases. Again, Brown mitigated the similarities and focused on the distinct differences, particularly the same red wounds that were found on the D3 body, hoping to nullify any thoughts that the Highland M.E. might have had concerning the possibility of her case and his two cases being related.

Watts drove the vehicle he'd taken from the motor pool across surface roads back toward the downtown office. His partner hadn't said a word since leaving the Highland morgue. He was still trying to wrap his mind around what he'd been exposed to the past two days. Nearly everything he'd heard since his return from vacation twisted and skewed everything he had been working on for the past year.

Unable to remain quiet, Watts broke the silence. "So what do you think, partner?"

Brown stared out the window pretending not to notice the interruption.

"C'mon," Watts insisted. "Time of death, dump and run, it looks like you were wrong about the Harvest Moon, chief."

Watts was a much shorter man than his partner. He talked quickly and with more than a hint of urban inflection and tone, which came in especially handy when dealing with informants and the worst of the city's criminal element. In his attempts to speak less colloquially, he developed the habit of adding a term of familiarization to all his comments: *How's it going, slugger?; You got that right, cowboy; I don't know, champ.* It was a habit that Brown found most annoying.

Brown turned and stared determinedly into the eyes of his partner. "There is no way that kid," he said pointing out the car's rear window, "is part of my book, CHIEF. The date is wrong, okay? Period. End of story."

"Maybe you're wrong," goaded Watts.

"Fuck you. I ain't wrong. Tonight's the night. The Harvest Moon. Not last Tuesday, not the Tuesday before. It happens tonight and the body gets found tomorrow. Just like all the others."

Then, trying to convince himself as much as his partner, he said, "I mean, what about the tattoos between the thumb and index fingers?" Brown pointed to the webbing on his left hand. "The kid last week had a '1'. This one in Highland had a '2'. My guy never did that. Hell, my guy would be up to, what, like," he fumbled for a number, "like, I don't know, seventy-two or something. I'm telling you, this ain't my guy."

"Well, your guy's almost ninety years old, right? Maybe he just forgot what number he was on."

"Not today, Watts" Brown warned. "Not now. I'm not in the mood."

Watts laughed loudly, ignoring his partner's idle threat as he pulled into the garage.

"These two cases," Brown resumed, "they were a week apart. My guy does one a year, not one a week. And he dumps the bodies within a few blocks of the vic's last known location. These two kids were picked up at the same spot, but dumped somewhere else and miles apart. Plus there was no bruise around the wound. And what about the leeches?"

"Don't even talk about no fucking leeches, home fry."

"Fine, but still, they've got nothing to do with my cases. Everything about these two cases is wrong."

"Not everything," Watts continued, verbally poking his partner while pulling into his parking slot.

Brown flexed and then relaxed, pondering the idea a moment. "Okay, fine, I'll grant you that yes, there are a lot of similarities. But these two? I ain't saying they weren't done by the same guy, just not my guy, is all."

They got out of the car and Watts slammed both his hands on the roof. "Hang on," he blasted. "Just stop for a second."

Brown looked back over the roof at his partner and waited. All he could see was a pair of arms up to the shoulders and the hair on the back of Watts' neck. Watts was looking down at the cement beneath him. When he raised his head, his eyes were closed and he brought his hands up to his temples as if he were keeping his brain from exploding.

"Look, I understand why you want this to be the way you want it to be. But just take a second to think about this from a different angle. What if this is your guy and he's focused on young boys, he's taken to numbering them, he's stepped it up to more than one a year, he…," Watts shivered and forced out, "uses leeches? What if all of this is something new and different after all these years? Aren't these patterns easier to figure out? Won't all these things make it easier to catch this guy?"

Brown stared blankly at his partner.

Watts didn't wait for an answer. "Maybe instead of telling yourself these aren't related and ignoring all these patterns, you should just forget the old patterns for now, follow these new ones to a suspect and then connect the dots to *your book* after the fact."

Watts slammed the car door shut and walked away toward the doorway leading to the stairwell. With his back to his partner, Watts kept speaking, "I say we hang out at the High-Sum corner where both these new vics were last seen. That's my two cents," he added, walking through the heavy steel door, leaving Brown to follow both his logic to its most obvious conclusion and his footsteps to their desks four flights up.

* * *

Brown and Watts watched as the young boy squatted down about fifty feet from the corner of High Ridge Road and Summit Avenue, talking to the driver of a black BMW.

"Get in the car, you little whore," Brown mumbled.

"C'mon, McNasty. That's some twisted shit. You can't possible want that kid to suffer the way those other kids did."

"Suffer? No. But we need a lead and that kid looks like our best shot."

The black Beamer drove away and left the young boy still standing on the corner.

"Damn it," Brown mumbled. He then watched the boy cross the street and disappear into the alley a half-block away. "Now where's he going?"

"What's your hurry?" Watts asked. "You got a date or something?"

"Shut up, Watts. I thought we had something."

CHAPTER 14

Young Davis Treadwell was lost in his own little world. He didn't pay much attention to the short, thin man as he approached until they were nearly face-to-face. That's when he noticed the man's soft, kind features.

When the man saw Davis looking down at him, he stopped and asked, "Were you just standing out on the corner?"

"Yeah," Davis said with nervous embarrassment.

"I was just coming to talk to you," the man said, moving a bit closer.

The nervousness continued. "Really?"

"Yeah, I was wondering if you and me could have a little party together."

A physical transformation came over Davis like a veil as his nervous embarrassment shifted to a confused blend of panic, curiosity, bewilderment and desire. Five minutes prior, he was frozen, struggling to simply walk to a street corner. He relaxed when he finally got there and contemplated what to do next. His panic returned when his father confronted him and it continued through his network of lies. And only a few footsteps had passed since he laughed at himself and his silly scheme. But, there he stood in the moonlit parking lot face-to-face with a well-dressed man who wanted to pay Davis to satisfy both their desires.

Davis had heard about the High-Sum corner. He thought about what he would have to do if he actually went through with it. In the theater, while others watched the movie, Davis imagined endless possibilities of how he'd be approached, what someone might say and how he would respond. Still, he was completely unprepared and, he determined in the time it took to walk from the doors of the theater to the street corner, completely unwilling.

"Nah, I need to—"

"C'mon," the man interrupted, "It'll be fun."

"No, really. I—"

"Look," the man continued, undeterred, pulling a money clip from his pocket, "I'll give you forty, no, fifty bucks."

The curiosity and desire quickly dissolved from Davis's mind, leaving only the confused blend of panic and bewilderment. His "fight or flight" instinct turned his body away from the man, sent impulses to his legs to walk toward his car and impulses to his mouth to blurt out, "I have to go home." When it came out, even he could hear the wavering panic.

As he strode, he heard the loose gravel crackle beneath two sets of footsteps walking in the same direction and his heart raced faster. With the key ring encircling his index finger, he squeezed the keys tight into the palm of his right hand until he could feel their jagged edges dig into his skin. When he was only a few paces from his mother's car, he felt the man's fingers wrap around his right elbow and he heard the man say under his breath, "Don't walk away from me." When he turned in response to the touch on his arm, his mind registered a shock of black and yellow, the sound of a dull, numbing thud and a blast of searing pain from behind his right ear.

Davis fell to his knees, dizzy and disoriented. He then put both his hands out in front of him to make contact with the ground as his whole body rocked further forward, drawn by gravity's pull. After gaining some semblance of stability, he put his empty right hand to the part of his head that was throbbing. Behind his ear, just below the base of the skull where his hairline began, he felt a slit in his skin and the warm blood flowing between the gaps of his fingers.

As Davis pulled his hand from his head and held it in front of his face to see the deep, dark liquid, the man walked around and stood directly in front of him. Davis could only see his feet set apart until he lifted his head. His tear-filled eyes followed the crease in the man's pants up to the belt that held them in place. The man stood akimbo, dominating and intimidating. Davis barely noticed something metallic clenched in the man's right hand which seemed to surround and encase each of his fingers.

"Oh, God," Davis whimpered. "Don't hurt me,"

"Shut the fuck up, whore," the man screamed quietly between his clenched teeth as he struck Davis on the left side of his head. This time, Davis' mind perceived nothing, it simply gave way to the force of the blow and his body slumped lifelessly to the ground.

* * *

The man surveyed the lot to ensure the privacy of his actions, gliding the brass knuckles into his right front pants pocket while simultaneously pulling from the same pocket a set of keys. He proceeded to lift the gangly teenager and sling him over his shoulder in a fireman's carry. The man's car was only a few spaces away from where the boy fell to the ground. He fumbled with the keys until he found the one that opened his trunk, slid it into the lock and turned it. When the trunk popped up, it took the keys with it, causing them to jingle. He clumsily lowered the boy into the deep trunk well, bound him quickly, but efficiently, with gray duct tape, and slammed the trunk shut, jingling the keys once more. He pulled them from the lock, edged along the side of the car, pulled his door open and slipped inside.

From between the two front seats, in the space beneath the emergency brake, the man gently removed his sunglasses case, set it aside, picked up his driving gloves and slipped one on each hand in slow, purposeful motions. Moments later, a green Saturn with a broken driver's side headlight pulled out from the parking lot behind the Unique Boutique and exited the alleyway onto Summit Avenue.

CHAPTER 15

Andy pulled into his driveway. It was dark; well into evening. He sat there hunched over the steering wheel for what seemed a long time unclear as to what transpired since leaving work. His glasses and gloves were still on the passenger seat, buried beneath two documents: an abbreviated, unofficial accident report with the information his insurance company would need to begin processing a claim; and, a moving citation for an Improper Lane Change.

Officer Jenkins, after conferring with his partner and a few of the other vehicle operators who stayed long enough to give their statements, was quite clear that the driver of the bronze sedan, a Mr. Michael Sledge, was completely and totally at fault for the accident by backing into the green sedan. However, Officer Jenkins, after seeing the bulk of the debris resting well beyond the pedestrian walkway, made it quite clear that the driver of the green coupe, a Mr. Andrew Walker, was completely and totally at fault for changing lanes in the middle of an intersection. Andy viewed the citation as a poor review of his evening performance and, like any vain performer who lives or dies by the printed word of critical review, he was devastated.

He collected his things from his wounded chariot and trudged up to the front door of his house. When he entered, the few lights that were on indicated his wife was watching TV in bed. He expected as much. His briefcase remained in the entryway as he shuffled to the kitchen.

"Where the hell have you been?" came a shout from the bedroom. Its tone was at once playfully sarcastic and inquisitively demanding.

"Hey, hon. I'm sorry I didn't call," he answered from the kitchen. "I got into a fender bender on the way home and—"

"Where?"

"I'm sorry, what?" he asked, unable to hear her over the rustling documents he placed in the very specific location she'd designated for all receipts and house expenses.

"Where was the accident?"

"65th and Club," he answered crouched in front of the kitchen sink. He opened the cupboard below and, from it, pulled out a garbage bag and shoved it in his pants pocket.

"65th and Club? It was on the nine o'clock news. You screwed things up good, huh?"

"Yeah, well, it's a mess to start with. I mean, whose idea was it to add another light?"

"How bad?"

He was walking toward the bedroom so they didn't have to shout. "I'm sorry, what?"

"How bad? How much do you think it will cost to get it fixed?"

He stopped in the doorway and leaned against the door jam. "I don't know. It shouldn't be too bad. If the guy had any insurance, it'd be a snap. But then, what do you expect."

When he entered her sightlines, she quickly turned to face him and just as quickly said, "No insurance. We can't pay for that."

"I know," he calmly replied.

He looked at her as he always did when he came home. In less time than it takes to fall in love, he compared her to the happy, beautiful, twenty-one-year-old bundle of love who sits on his desk and beams at him all day long from her lounge chair. She's older now and neither happy nor beautiful. It was difficult for him to determine if her lack of beauty came from being unhappy, her misery came from being unattractive, or if the two were unrelated. He longed for the days past, knowing he could never have them back except in his memories. But he knew he loved her and that that would never change.

"So, it was on the news, huh?" he asked.

"Yeah, along with the rapes, murders and missing children, the sports scores, the weather and, of course, some handicapped kid who got his fifteen minutes of fame for calling 911."

"I'm gonna take a shower and try to wash this day away. I might be a while."

"Okay. Don't wake me up when you come to bed." Then, noticing something on his hip, she pointed to it and added, "What's that?"

He looked down and saw what she was pointing at: a dark spot running across the top of his right pants leg about an inch long. "Hmmm. I must've got grease or something on me. I'll stain treat it before I throw it down the laundry chute."

"You better," she said in that familiar, playfully demanding tone.

He smiled. "Night, hon."

"G'night."

Andy went into the bathroom and ran the water for his shower. He pulled the garbage bag out of his pocket and watched himself undress in the mirror. The dark spot on his trousers appeared deep and penetrating, much too difficult to get out of the light khaki fabric. He stuffed the pants into the bag along with his briefs which were also stained. Then, noticing his dark blue shirt had similar but smaller stains, he stuffed it into the bag, along with his shoes and socks, and threw the bag on the floor. When he felt the first hint of steam on his skin, he pulled the shower curtain aside, stepped in and sealed the curtain behind him. He reached down, adjusted the water's temperature, and stepped into the cleansing spray. It felt good.

Facing the showerhead, the crown of his skull was fully in the descending water. The hair that matted to his head guided the runoff in tiny torrents. He opened his eyes and watched as the water obeyed gravity's pull down the tub drain, swirling at times with faint and transparent red-brown ribbons. He grabbed the soap and created a dirty lather rubbing it against the dry, caked-on patch of blood on his hip. There were other patches, particularly on the backs of his hands, but the one on his thigh was easily the biggest. Then he continued to scrub himself wholly with a soapy washcloth until all of his skin was pink from friction. He rinsed one last time and turned off the water.

Andy grabbed the soap and the washcloth and threw them in the bag. He pulled a big bottle of bleach and a spray bottle of glass cleaner from the bathroom closet and switched tops. He sprayed the tub surround with bleach until his eyes and nose couldn't stand it anymore, replaced the tops and put the two bottles back in the closet. He moved the showerhead in a methodical circular motion to rinse the shower. Once more from the bathroom closet he grabbed an old rag-of-a-towel, dried himself off, wiped down the tub surround, threw the towel in the bag and tied the corners.

Naked, he crept into the bedroom where his wife lay asleep and slipped on some old sweats, an old t-shirt, and an old pair of sneakers. Then, grabbing the plastic bag, he left the house, got into his car and drove to the corner gas station. The night was crisp and clear, the smell of gasoline overwhelming anything nature had to offer. He filled the car's empty tank, bought some chips and a soda and threw the plastic garbage bag into a dumpster.

Back home once again, he headed straight for the kitchen where he placed the gas station receipt on top of the other documents on the counter. He went back into the living room and sat in his favorite chair with his chips and soda in his lap. He turned on the TV, lowered the volume and watched Headline News coverage while tiny morsels of information crawled across the bottom of the screen. He couldn't get too comfortable; he had to be at Gambel's later.

CHAPTER 16

"Yeah?" he answered his cell phone.

From the other end came, "Hey there, it's me, Uncle Max."

"My boxes make it to Gambel's?" Willie Spence asked, smiling.

"Yeah, that's what I'm callin' about. See—"

"You did deliver them, right?"

"No, not yet. I can't. Not tonight. Tomorrow."

"Did you say tomorrow?" his tone turning angrier.

"We's in a accident and they towed my car."

"And the boxes?"

"See, we's hit from behind, and so, we didn't know if whatever was in them boxes was all over the place, and thought better safe than sorry, right? So we didn't open the trunk because the police was everywhere. And now the car's at the impound lot."

"Your car, with my boxes, is at the police impound lot?" he said, calmly rubbing his forehead and looking out the windows of the disheveled house he used as his base of operations. The brightness of the full moon touched the roofs of the other disheveled houses that lined the streets of the broken neighborhood, reminding him that he was running out of time.

"Yeah, but just until mornin'. The police lady, she said she'd get everything done tonight so's we can pick it up first thing tomorrow."

"What's in them boxes can't wait until tomorrow, old man. All them boxes need to be at Gambel's tonight. Right fuckin' now, to be exact."

"Well, the police lady said—"

"I don't give a mother fuckin' damn what the police lady said. You was supposed to deliver five boxes to Gambel's and now they're locked up in the impound lot 'til tomorrow. You fucked up *big* time, old man. You hear me? You've ruined everything." Then he took a moment. "Let me think," he muttered and took another moment. "You got an extra set of keys?"

"Yeah, back home."

"Where's home, old man? You still squattin' in that rat-hole with Manny on 48th Street?"

"Yeah."

"And where you at now?"

"Carlson Ford out by 101."

"Well you best be home in thirty minutes or you gonna be one sorry-ass mother fucker." He hung up without offering any opportunity for a response and slumped into his chair. He muttered to himself, looking around for help. The room he was in, upstairs in the back, was the largest of the three bedrooms in the house. It was one of the only rooms with any furniture and the lone room with unbroken glass in the windowpanes. It was appointed in a modest but comfortable fashion with overstuffed chairs and couches pushed up against all the walls. He leaned forward, letting his momentum bring him to his feet.

He walked out of the room and down the hallway, eventually descending the stairs to the house's main entryway. There, he grabbed a black and red herringbone sport coat that hung on a hanger in the meager closet and slipped it on, concealing his shoulder holster and gun. Together with his black mock turtleneck sweater, pressed black linen slacks and black Italian leather shoes, he looked surprisingly dashing and refined.

Willie Spence stood on the crumbling cement porch and spoke to the two young men sitting on the front steps while looking at neither. "Yo, fellas, Uncle Max fucked up. I need you two to help me make it right."

He moved down the front steps, slowly and purposefully, at a regal gait. He strode across the cracked and heaving slabs of cement which had once made up the sidewalk along the side of the house to the back door of the one-car garage facing the alley. Once there, he pressed the automatic garage door opener. The dim overhead light of the opener revealed the machine contained within: a Porsche Cayenne Turbo. It was completely decked out with underbody lights, custom wheels and rims capped with spinners. It had plasma screens for DVD viewing or X-Box plug-and-play capabilities and a several-hundred-watts-per-channel sound system. It was painted a brilliant purple and had the words "The Lord Is Thy Shepherd" airbrushed in black bubble script across the tailgate of the vehicle, as if it were the name of a boat.

This was more than transportation. This was accessorizing. And Willie Spence was an urban trend-setter.

He pressed the keychain remote for the alarm. The headlights, taillights and underbody lights flashed in unison. Moving over to the driver's side he said loudly, "He gotta go and fuck up my night like this. Goddamn it."

The two gentlemen from the front steps moved down the passenger side, each opening a door and sliding into a seat.

"Mark," Willie said to the man in the back seat, the one with a birthmark on his face that, from a distance, could have been mistaken for a tattoo. "I need you to meet us at Manny's place. But get some tools. You and Taj gotta break into the impound lot."

"You're kidding, right?" Mark yelled, getting out. "The impound lot? They got dogs there, man. I fuckin' hate dogs. That old man better pray his car is backed up to the fence."

Mark closed the door and walked out of the garage.

Taj turned to Willie and smiled. "Last time we dealt with dogs, one of them bit him right in the fuckin' ass. I damn near shit myself I was laughin' so hard."

As he turned to look out the back window for oncoming traffic, Willie Spence stopped to look Taj in the eye and replied, "Yeah, well no fuckin' around on this job, Taj. Hear me?" His voice was strong and thick, showing no reaction to Taj's story. Then, slowly backing out of the garage and into the darkening alleyway, he continued, "We gotta get them boxes outta that fuckin' trunk and over to Gambel's."

CHAPTER 17

It was a little before ten o'clock and just a narrow band of sky blue rested on the western horizon. The lone unbroken street lamp offered little more than metaphorical illumination on the dirty city street and its long line of four-family rental units. There was a large space between Willie Spence's purple Cayenne, which sat next to the curb pulsating to the sounds being emitted from its thunderous subwoofers, and the rusted and faded maroon Lincoln Continental with four flat tires in front of it. A red Ford Focus pulled into the open area between the vehicles and rested just long enough for Uncle Max to get out, retrieve his myriad belongings from the back seat and say a few words of gratitude to his driver. Then, as quickly as it had arrived, the car drove away, turned right at the next intersection and disappeared behind the corner building.

Uncle Max, wanting to reach his apartment before facing Willie Spence, shuffled his way up the front walk toward the building's poorly lit stoop. He was halfway there when the thumping vibrations from the obscenely ostentatious SUV stopped and the doors opened.

"Where you goin', old man?" shouted Taj.

"I was just goin' to put my things inside, is all," Uncle Max replied, not even turning around to see the younger man's reaction to his ambivalence.

Willie Spence simply stated, "You come on back with that extra key. You hear me?"

"Yeah, yeah, I hear you. I'll be back in just a minute."

The complexities of the situation apparently took hold in Taj's mind and he asked, "Yo, let me ask you something. Why the fuck you go-and-give them boxes to this old mother fucker in the first place? Why didn't you just take 'em?"

Calmly and without thought, Willie Spence recited what he had learned through his year of preparation. "Those who have seen their children's children ignore the blight and devastation within their midst must bear the heaviest burden, for it is they who did not teach the ones who followed the errors of their ways. The blood that stains their hands stains their lives until they deliver unto their people the tools by which their redemption can be claimed and their transgressions absolved."

Taj smiled a wide smile and laughed when he shouted, "Ho-ly shit." He continued to laugh and then asked, "What the fuck was that? You some church-goin' mother fucker quotin' the Bible now?"

Willie Spence ignored him, standing perfectly still, his hands clasped in front of him, his feet spread comfortably, body facing the very door the old man entered moments earlier.

Pulsing vibrations brought the two men's attention to another vehicle making its way down the street. Both turned and watched the silver Lexus pull into the vacant space recently abandoned by the red car. The engine cut out and the pulsations ceased. The young man with the birthmark on his face got out, shut the door and walked around the front of the car to join the two men. "So?" he asked.

"Yo, man, you missed the God-damnedest thing," Taj cackled.

Willie Spence cut him short, "Never you mind about that. Here's what I need from you."

He spent the next minute or so explaining to his bodyguards just how they were going to remove the boxes from Uncle Max's trunk. As if he were waiting for his cue, Uncle Max came out of the building as Taj and Mark were walking toward the Lexus, their shadows long and ghostly under the fully lit moon. Uncle Max held the key to his car out for Willie Spence to take, but he simply grabbed Uncle Max by his jacket shoulder and pushed him in the direction of the Porsche.

"You're comin' with me, old man."

Uncle Max turned to look over his shoulder and said, "I got some things I gotta—"

"Not no more, you don't. You was supposed to deliver them boxes to Gambel's and I'll be God-damned if you ain't gonna. Now get in."

The Lexus sedan roared to life and the pulsing vibrations filled the neighborhood once more while the vehicle's occupants bounced in rhythm of the thumping bass.

Uncle Max, feeling the vibrations as he walked to Willie Spence's vehicle, smiled and said quietly, "Dumb-asses are gonna go deaf before they reach thirty."

Willie Spence smiled, "If the worst thing that happens to them by the time they reach thirty is that they go deaf, they'll be a couple of lucky mother fuckers, wouldn't you say?"

Both he and Uncle Max crawled into the SUV. When Willie Spence turned the key, the music blared so loud Uncle Max winced and covered his ears. Willie Spence turned the music down and then off, filling the vehicle with an awkward silence in the wake of the din. Uncle Max had begun to explain how he got into the accident when Willie Spence broke through and said, "You know why I need you to come with me?"

"No, sir, I sure don't."

"You the past, old man: a relic of a lost generation. You, your friends, my mom, my dad, aunts and uncles, all of you just sitting on your fuckin' asses waiting for what you thought was owed to you to come and land, like manna from heaven, right on your fuckin' doorsteps instead of going out and getting it for yourselves. Well, I'll tell you what, relic, the days of waiting are over for me. I'm taking what's mine."

"You want it? Go ahead, take it. What's that got to do with me?"

"It's like this: I can't touch them boxes. Simple as that. I need you, a relic, to deliver them for me. Once you do that, you can go home and forget all about this."

Uncle Max nodded his head in understanding though it was clear from the look on his face that he had no idea what Willie Spence was talking about. Then he asked, "What's in the boxes?"

"On the phone you said you didn't want to open the trunk because you didn't know what was in them boxes in case something fell out. That's smart. Ignorance is bliss and curiosity killed the cat. You need to worry less about what's in them fuckin' boxes and more about what kind of shit you gonna be in if we don't get them to Gambel's before eleven-thirty."

He turned the music back on and listened for just a few moments before turning it back off. "Listen up, let me tell you what I need from you. We need to keep the dogs and the night guard away from your car so Taj and Mark can do what they got to do. When we get there, we gonna find your car and then you gonna pretend a car on the other side of the lot is yours, got it?

"Mm-hmm."

"We gonna tell him some sob story about how my daughter's birthday is tomorrow and you her grandfather and we need to get the gift outta the trunk of the car. We whine and pester and make a big damn deal."

"What if he says 'okay' and opens the gate and walks us to the car?"

"Never mind that. He ain't never gonna open that gate or let us near that car. He ain't gonna let us take one step inside that impound lot."

"How long we gotta do this for?"

"Fifteen minutes. The guard is gonna be some has-been beat-cop damn near retirement. He won't be nothin'. It's them damned dogs we gotta worry about. And no matter what, no matter fuckin' what, relic, you can't look at your car. You gotta stay focused on the bogus one we pick out, you understand?"

"Mm-hmm."

* * *

They drove past the impound lot located in the south central portion of the city's industrial district. Razor wire added another two feet to the already intimidating ten-foot-high chain-link fence. Uncle Max's bronze

Dodge Dart was close to the entrance: a few spaces from the entrance on the left, backed in so its trunk was a mere foot from the fence. The street light immediately in front of the chain-linked rolling gates shown like a spot light on the front of the impound lot and spilled into the parking lot of the muffler shop next to it. The muffler shop's parking lot was strewn with stacks of worn tires, discarded chassis and broken down vehicles in various stages of decomposition, offering Taj and Mark ample coverage from the glaring overhead light.

Willie Spence made a U-turn in the middle of the street and pulled up to the curb just short of the lot's entrance. He said, "Okay, old man, you see that blue Chevy Impala? Down on the right side, maybe seven cars in? That's your new car. That's the car you so desperately need to get into. Got it?"

"Mm-hmm. I got it."

"Which car is yours?"

"The blue Impala."

"A'ight. Let's go."

The two men got out of the flashy SUV and walked toward the gates. They were instantly met by the low, fierce, guttural growls of two very large, very menacing Rottweilers which, even with the fence, made both men take a step back.

"Them right there are a couple of mean-ass hell-hounds, wouldn't you say?" asked Willie Spence.

"Goddamn," was all Uncle Max could muster.

Willie Spence was going to rattle the fence, but as soon as he lifted his hand and took a step forward, both dogs began to bark, deep, resonant woofs.

From the darkened recesses of the impound lot, far from the bright cast of the street light, came another set of barks, deep and resonant, but this time, they were human. "Hans! Franz! End game!"

The barking ceased. Then, waddling out of the small wooden shed, presumably the lot's office, came a man in a security guard uniform stretched nearly to the point of tearing across his large frame. His leathery face and silvery hair made it obvious he was approaching seventy, if not already past it. His small steps made his traverse of the lot seem longer than it was and when he finally got to where the dogs stood awaiting his next command, he growled, "What do you want?"

Willie Spence answered while Uncle Max stared at the monstrous dogs before them. "My pops' car, that blue Impala," he pointed to it, "it's got my baby-girl's birthday presents in the trunk. We was hoping maybe we could just come on in, grab them and be on our way."

"Sorry, pal. Everything on this lot is impounded: the vehicles and everything inside. You'll have to come back tomorrow during office hours."

"Yeah, but you see, it's Vanessa's birthday tomorrow —"

"I don't care if it's Christmas tomorrow and you got a thirty pound turkey in the trunk, I can't open these gates for anyone. It's against procedures."

Both dogs quickly looked back into the moonlit lot, which looked darker than it was due to the excessively bright street light. Then, just as quickly, they turned back as the fat man bent down to give each of them a gruff rub on their thick necks. Involuntarily, Uncle Max's eyes darted toward his real car on the opposite side of the lot. Willie Spence knew without looking that Uncle Max was peeking at the fencing behind his car, so he interjected, "Oh, you got to be kidding, old timer."

"Old timer?" the guard rebuffed. And as Willie Spence planned, the guard droned on about his years of dedicated public service. "I'm probably ten years younger than your dad, here. Do you call your father old timer? I'll have you know I was protecting scum like you from scum worse than you since before you were born ...."

* * *

Taj and Mark heard the guard's ramblings followed by Uncle Max and Willie Spence pleading their case over and over while they worked on getting into the back of the Dodge Dart. First, they attached two metal bars, each about a foot long, to the links in the fence vertically about two feet from each other. Then they secured the bars to each other with cables, looping them through each horizontal line of links at the top and the bottom of the bars to maintain tension. Finally, they snipped the links between the bars one-by-one. This caused the dogs to turn. Had it not been for their master rubbing their necks, they would have most likely walked straight to the back end of Uncle Max's car and sunk their teeth deep into the fleshy part of Taj's forearms that stuck through the rectangular hole in the fence.

Taj inserted the key into the trunk's lock and waited. Mark quickly flashed a laser pointer at the guard's feet as the guard continued listing his long and distinguished record of public service. The dogs grew restless, Uncle Max remained confused and Willie Spence began to shout.

"Look, mother fucker, we gotta get into that Goddamn car. Right— fuckin' —now. Hear me?"

The dogs burst forth with their vicious barks and leapt, their paws shaking the fence and scaring Uncle Max back off the curb and into the street. The fence's clanging concealed the sound of the Dart's trunk being opened. The dogs paused, seeming to know something was happening somewhere else in the lot, but focused on the trouble before them and barked again.

Willie Spence stood his ground and continued to shout over the dogs. "I don't give a fuck about your service. I don't give a fuck about procedures. I don't give a fuck about you or your dogs. I need to get into my pops' car and get my baby-girl's present."

The guard barked out, "Hans! Franz. End game." They quickly sat at their master's feet as their barks turned to unnerving growls. "Now, you look here, shit-for-brains," said the guard as he unsnapped the strap that held his revolver in its holster. He continued very slowly, enunciating every syllable with biting anger. "I'm going to ask you nicely one more time to take your father, get back into that ridiculous purple piece of shit and get the fuck out of my sight. If you come back here again before tomorrow morning when this lot opens, I'm gonna empty my pistol into you. Then, I'm gonna reload and empty it into your pops over there. You got that?"

A long pause ensued as Willie Spence and the guard stared directly into one another's angry eyes. "Yeah, I got it," Willie Spence finally said. "You're a fuckin' racist. That's what I got."

He stepped backwards and continued, "If I was white you would have let me come in and get my daughter's shit." Then he vehemently spit on the ground, pushed Uncle Max toward the passenger door and walked toward the driver's side. Over the engine hood he shouted at the old man clutching the butt of his revolver, "Your supervisor's gonna hear about this. You can be sure of that."

The dogs stayed seated and continued to growl. Willie Spence got into the SUV and started the engine before Uncle Max shut his door. The guard and the dogs stayed still watching their every move until they pulled away from the curb at which point one of the dogs slowly lumbered toward the bronze Dodge Dart. The second dog followed a moment or two later. Neither barked.

As Willie Spence drove down the industrial street, he saw Taj and Mark off to his right carrying the boxes they had come to get. They were well beyond the muffler shop, passing the large-stone gravel entryway of a boarded-up factory with a beat-up car sitting in the driveway. He turned right at the next intersection, drove another half block before parking behind Mark's Lexus on the dimly lit street. Seconds later, Taj and Mark turned the corner carrying the boxes.

"Get out," Willie Spence said to Uncle Max. He got out of the vehicle, walked around back and addressed Taj. "Put the boxes down."

"Right here?" asked Taj.

"Right there. And you," he said, pointing to Mark, "Pop the trunk." Then, to Uncle Max, he said, "Now, old man, you put the boxes in the trunk. And when he's done, Mark, you let him drive to Gambel's."

"What?" Taj quipped turning the key to the trunk. "After he just got into an accident with his piece of shit? He fucked this whole thing up, not me. No fuckin' way he's drivin' my ride."

Willie Spence pulled his 10mm Auto Glock 20 from it holster and pressed it against Mark's left temple. "I ain't got time for this shit. Give him your keys."

"Yo, yo, Willie Spence, no need for all this," Mark laughed nervously. The keys dangled as Mark held the automatic lock fob high in the air. "No need for all this."

Willie Spence grabbed the keys and gave them to Uncle Max who was staring up into the off-white glow of the moon, rubbing the scar on his forehead.

"I love you and I respect you, Mark," Willie Spence explained, "but time is short, my patience is thin and we gotta go." He slid his pistol back into its holster and went back to his vehicle. "You can ride with him, but he's gotta drive."

"Whatever, man. No need for all this."

Willie Spence stood in the crux of his vehicle's open driver door and spoke, "And old man."

Uncle Max shifted uncomfortably to face Willie Spence.

"You best not get into another accident. I can *not* afford another fuck up."

As Uncle Max turned to get into the driver's seat, Willie Spence continued, loudly for effect, "And neither can you."

CHAPTER 18

The purple SUV followed the silver sedan through the mostly vacant streets of the city's industrial section. It was a long way to Gambel's, about twenty minutes, but, with the boxes gathered, they had plenty of time to get there. Willie Spence spent his time contemplating what he would do once he got to the night club. Willie Spence could see Taj was uncomfortable and restless in the vast silence inside his vehicle.

"It's a fuckin' crime to keep a bumpin' system like this dialed down."

Willie Spence heard his passenger, but continued staring forward silently.

Taj persisted. "Let me put on some soft R&B or some blues. I'll keep it low."

"No," was all Willie Spence said.

Taj sucked his teeth and went back to staring out the dark tinted window. Willie Spence focused on the car in front of him, almost willing it to make it safely to the night club. Tonight was his night at Gambel's and he wasn't going to let some miserable old man or a traffic accident or a police impound lot stand in his way.

Tonight, Willie Spence would question the status quo and determine his own perception of right and wrong. He would use the tools delivered to him by he who did not teach his children or his children's children the error of his ways. He would cleanse the stains on his elder's hands, the stain on their lives, with fresh blood. Willie Spence would take his rightful place in society.

Tonight, Willie Spence would commute.

* * *

The news network he was watching scrolled through the top stories of the evening once more. The flashing pixels from the television screen danced across the entire room and on Andy's eyelids as he slept in his favorite chair. The empty bag of chips lay on the floor while the nearly full bottle of soda sat open in his lap. Andy was one of those people who could fall asleep anywhere: on a plane, in a car, at work. He once fell asleep in the dentist's chair while having a filing replaced. He was a fairly sound sleeper as well.

This was a special night, like all the gatherings, and had he known he would fall asleep watching television he would have busied himself with some menial task to keep himself alert. But he didn't know and he didn't busy himself. Instead, he sunk, unconscious, into the chair and snored quietly while the evening passed him by.

Luckily, Andy shifted in his chair, knocking the soda bottle forward and causing its contents to empty into the seam between his leg and the seat cushion. The liquid was still fairly cold. He awoke, stunned, grabbed the bottle and stood up. He ran to the bathroom for a towel and quickly returned, blotting the wet spot in the cushion. Then he looked at his cable box and read 11:16. "Crap," he muttered, blotting the spot a few more times.

He grabbed the towel and the bottle and the empty chip bag and put them down on the coffee table as quickly and quietly as possible. His wife was still asleep and, though she was a very heavy sleeper, Andy felt no need to take any chances waking her. He could do a more thorough job of cleaning when he got home later. He grabbed his keys and his wallet and rushed out the door, again being quick and quiet.

He circled around the back of his damaged car, opened the trunk to double check its contents and, satisfied he had everything he needed, he hopped in. He pulled on his driving gloves, got into character and proceeded to make his way toward Gambel's.

* * *

On Friday nights it was nearly impossible to see any of the parquet flooring even from the narrow upper level that clung to every inch of the nightclub's external walls and seemed to hover above the masses. There, at Gambel's, people looking to relieve stress, have fun, get drunk or get laid, packed themselves together to create a human ocean of synchronized ebbing and flowing. It was one of the few nightclubs in town that catered to and was patronized by a diverse clientele. Its broad-minded DJs deftly blended rap, hip hop, industrial, rock, country and bluegrass into complex and surprisingly harmonious pulses of sound that required even those sitting at the long bar against the far wall to sway on their stools. On Saturdays, the club offered live music, drawing large and diverse groups of people simply wanting to be part of the "in" scene.

The club was closed Sundays for cleaning and Mondays for good measure. On Tuesdays, the club was open, but you could park a truck on the large dance floor. On that particular Tuesday, there were only a few handfuls of patrons scattered throughout. About half were regulars, while the others wanted a taste of the champagne atmosphere that crowds on Friday and Saturday consumed double-fisted. Unfortunately for them, on Tuesdays, the atmosphere was flat and anodyne.

Most of the patrons were either sitting at the long bar or secluding themselves in small groups of two or three on the upper level. The dance floor remained empty except for the two couples who were obviously together, intermittently dancing as a foursome to whatever the jukebox played low on the sound system. The bartender interrupted.

"Drink up, folks. We have a private party coming in at eleven-thirty, so you'll all have to clear out by eleven-twenty. That's in five minutes."

A murmur filled the air as a weathered African American gentleman made his way across the dance floor with a stack of boxes in his arms. He set the boxes on the bar and watched the bartender pour, mix and cash out the few people who charged their drinks.

"'Scuse me," the old man mumbled.

"How can I help you, sir?"

"These boxes here. They's for the party tonight," the weathered man babbled, seemingly trying to recall something important. "The, ah, Trajan? He said it'd be all right to leave them here for later."

"Yeah, sure. What's in 'em?" the bartender asked just to make small talk.

"I never looked inside. I was just told I needed to deliver these and that someone would set them aside for the party."

"You got it."

The bartender grabbed the boxes and set them further down the bar and out of the way. When he returned to his chores closing down the bar, he was surprised to see the weathered old man still standing there rubbing the scar on his forehead.

"Anything else I can do for you?" the bartender asked.

"Nah, I guess that's it, then."

"All right. Have a nice night."

The old man shuffled slowly back across the dance floor and out the front door. The bulk of the patrons soon followed until it was just the bartender and one of the waitresses in the cavernous space. He finalized receipts and closed up the bar while she cleared the tables. The bartender ran down to the basement, grabbed a couple of dirty drop cloths, brought them up and began covering the bar with them when what seemed to be someone dressed as a unicorn came through the door.

The man covering the bar smiled lightly to himself and looked at the clock. It read 11:37. But it was ten minutes fast: bar time. He shouted across the vast room, "Sir or ma'am, the place'll be ready for you in a couple minutes. If you don't mind, I'll need you to step outside while I lock up."

The figure stood at attention in the center of the dance floor, the intricate costume shimmering even in the low-level lighting. A male voice emanated from the costume, clearly and quietly, "We were told we could come in at eleven-thirty."

"You can, but it's not eleven-thirty, yet," the bartender answered. Then, pointing to the clock, "The bar clock's a little fast so we can get people out early on weekends. I just need to finish covering the bar then I'll be right out to let you in. But I need you to wait outside."

He finished covering the bar and escorted his co-worker toward the unicorn and the exit. The waitress walked past the equestrian statue toward the door and, before ducking out, said, "See ya, Doug."

"See ya, Sandy" he replied while standing next to the intruder. Then in a polite manner, Doug swept his arm toward the door and spoke softly to the man behind the mono-horned mask, "Again, sir, I apologize, but would you please come with me to the door. My boss told me I needed to do a few things first, like check invitations and—"

The horse-like figure held an envelope high in the air. "I have one."

Doug grizzled with frustration as the figure refused to be moved back toward the door. He caught himself before speaking and adjusted his intended inflection. "Sir, please," was all he said and maintained his pose directing the costumed figure to the door. Finally, the unicorn obliged.

They walked together until they came to the entrance where the unicorn pushed open the heavy wooden door and walked through. The bartender stayed behind, took his keys from his pocket and locked himself in. He took the night deposit bag from the small of his back, where he had hidden it prior to escorting the unicorn out, and walked down the stairs and into the office where he placed the deposit bag in the safe. He turned around, retraced his steps, returned to the door, unlocked it and went outside where he was met by a small circle of people in costumes.

Though he had been to a few comic book conventions with some of his college frat buddies, where Darth Vader, storm troopers and Goth outfits were the norm, never before had Doug seen such a mass of varied and intricate costumes in one place. It was almost overwhelming. He thought the chaos and pageantry was something only found backstage of a major Broadway production. Animals, both real and mythical, concepts and ideas, likenesses of historical and fictitious people were presented in painstakingly meticulous fashion.

Everyone had a mask. And everyone had an invitation lavishly hand-crafted by a highly skilled calligrapher. Doug smiled as he read each invitation. The formality of their generic copy was humorous enough, but it was the names and superfluous descriptions on the invitations that made him grin. The unicorn's invitation read:

His grace, Lord Spencerton
respectfully requests the attendance
of the honorable Physiologus,

a smart, brave and beautiful steed,
at the ceremony of his commuting
eleven-thirty in the evening
Tuesday, the twenty-eighth of September

At the very bottom of the invitation was a final note in the same beautiful calligraphic hand: *Admit one: no guest.* It was the same on all the invitations. All but two.

CHAPTER 19

After Mark and Taj left to bring Uncle Max back home, Willie Spence got into his vehicle, drove a few blocks away and pulled into the deserted parking lot of the Putnam Shoes building. He parked in the heavily vegetated shadowy darkness by the dumpsters behind the building. He got out, popped the rear hatch and pulled the door open. Nestled between the obnoxiously large speaker bases in the rear cargo area was the carpeted lid of an unseen compartment. Willie Spence reached down and opened it. On top lay an Elizabethan costume so lavish and colorful, it was rivaled only by the purple Porsche SUV.

The night was cold, but bright. Willie Spence stood naked next to his vehicle putting on the various pieces that made up his costume. First, he pulled on silk underwear of the period, cut very much like today's boxer shorts. They were tight against his skin but were comfortable and allowed for plenty of movement. Next, he pulled over his head a tight fitting linen undergarment with small box-pleated ruffles at the neck and wrists, trimmed with blackwork embroidery and embellished with gold thread and small beads. The clownish and colorful paned britches were pulled over his silk underpants. These were Kelly green, very fully puffed, mid-thigh in length, with several inner layers topped by strips of intricately decorated stiffened fabric of complimentary colors. Similarly clownish and colorful was his coat-like doublet, also Kelly green and triangular in shape from his shoulders to his waist, making his broad shoulders seem broader and his waistline narrower. Attached to the doublet were fine white linen sleeves that hung gracefully below his arms and bunched and gathered around his wrists. Long socks and uncomplicated flat-soled shoes added a touch of simplicity to the otherwise overstated outfit. About his head and neck he wore a hooded mask made of plush purple velvet that tucked into the ruffles around his neck and covered all but his tight, angular lower jaw, which showed in severe contrast to the soft flowing fabric from which it jutted. Atop his head was a floppy green hat which everyone who saw it remarked looked like something Henry VIII would wear. It was darker in hue than his jacket and pants and it had a long blue plume.

He glanced at himself in the side mirrors of the purple SUV. He was unable to gain a full appreciation of himself in all his regalia, but what he saw was enough to content him. He closed the lid on the compartment, shut the rear hatch and climbed delicately into the driver's seat, being careful not to damage his puffy pants, pleated ruffles or flowing plume.

The drive back to Gambel's was uncomfortable but, thankfully, short. Pulling into the driveway, he saw two people standing at the door. The first was a large man without a costume reviewing the handwritten invitation Willie Spence had paid a small fortune to prepare for each of the group's members. The second was Melusina, the short, two-tailed mermaid waiting to enter the building. Like many of the other guests, Willie Spence parked far away from the entrance so as to retain as much of his anonymity as was possible.

He walked toward the plain-clothed gentleman at the door, alone after having allowed Melusina to enter, and handed the gentleman his invitation.

His grace, Lord Spencerton,
Duke of Sahel
host and guest of distinction
is honored to present himself
at eleven-thirty in the evening
Tuesday, the twenty-eighth of September

The gentleman read it, noted the ubiquitous "admit one: no guest" message at the bottom, confirmed a single attendee and handed it back, jokingly adding, "Have a nice night, my lord."

Lord Spencerton paused, glowered and continued inside.

* * *

When Mitchell Treadwell pulled into the parking lot of Gambel's, there were a number of cars set apart from one another, their occupants trying to seclude themselves from the other masquerade attendees. Mitchell was no different. He noticed Arwen Undomiel, daughter of Elrond and Celebrian of Rivendell, shutting the door to her Pontiac Solaris convertible and making her way toward the front door of the club. She was not a Liv Tyler look-alike, but rather a wholly unique interpretation of the Elven princess created long before the Hollywood exploitation of Middle Earth. As she walked toward the entrance of the club, Mitchell parked next to her vehicle for some privacy of his own.

Mitchell took off his socks and shoes, his windbreaker, torn shirt and stained jeans he had thrown on prior to leaving the house as well as his briefs and white crew-neck undershirt. He stood barefoot on his loafers, avoiding the possibility of cutting himself on broken glass. The cold air nipped at his naked flesh until he meticulously wrapped his loins with a length of untreated silk and pulled a loose-fitting shirt, also made of untreated silk, over his head. He also pulled a long, linen, ochre-colored tunic over his head. It rested on his broad shoulders, hanging on him loosely and comfortably as the fabric flowed the length of his body until it reached just about the middle of his shins. On top of and around the tunic he swathed himself in a woolen toga.

The toga was a large, elongated, bright white semi-circle bordered by a plain, broad purple band. He draped one end of the semicircle over his left shoulder and let the fabric fall in front of him until it almost touched the asphalt. Then, with his right arm, he reached behind, grabbed the bunched fabric, pulled it around his waist, up across his chest and flung the remaining fabric over his left shoulder. He had done this so many times that the back end of the toga, which he had flung over his shoulder, rested only a few inches from the ground and required no adjustment. He pulled a satchel from under the passenger front seat and reached into the glove compartment for an unlabelled bottle of chloroform. He placed these items and his keys inside the satchel. Inserting his hand inside the material stretched across the chest, he created a pouch in the folds in which he placed his invitation.

He sat perpendicular to the car in the driver's seat, placed his foot inside his right mulleus and laced it up, its high leather strips intertwining well over his knee to the middle part of his thigh. He did the same with his left leg. Once tied, he secured it with a crescent-shaped buckle which, along with the purple band on his toga, distinguished him as a senator who held a curule magistracy. The gold rope he used as a belt had tassels dangling well below his knees. Finally, he placed a large iron ring on his hand before grabbing the clear plastic mask and the satchel.

Mitchell pulled the satchel under his flowing garments and ran the shoulder strap through the neck-hole and up, over his head. With the satchel nestled comfortably against his hip, he secured his mask and walked toward the door of the club. As he approached, Mitchell reached into the folds of his toga and withdrew his invitation.

"Good evening," Mitchell said, extending his invitation.

"Evening," Doug the bartender replied simply.

"A bit chilly tonight, eh?"

The bartender was engrossed in the language of the invitation and did not respond. He read the words "Emperor Trajan, Marcus Ulpius Nerva Traianus" aloud softly and read to himself "a compassionate, peaceful nobleman and one of the five good emperors." He noted "admit one: no guest," looked at the character before him, returned the invitation and offered, "Have a nice night," as he pushed the door open.

"Wait," the bartender hesitated. "You're the guy who needs to tell me everything's okay before I can go home."

"Is that right? Well, I'm sure everything is fine. Everyone should be here by midnight. Why don't you wait around until ten after to see if anyone else comes and then you can be on your way. Sound good?"

With that, Mitchell entered the bar, again reminding himself he was doing it all for his wife and kids.

CHAPTER 20

It was just before midnight when Andy pulled into Gambel's parking lot. Like many of the other attendees, he was not dressed in his costume when he arrived and would dress in the parking lot, away from the front door and secluded in a vacant part of the lot for privacy's sake. His was a simple costume; elegant and mysterious. He stripped off the sweats and the t-shirt to reveal his bright gold leotard. He changed into satin ballet slippers dyed, along with the satin leotard, to match his mysterious gold cloak.

The cloak itself was not mysterious in its construction or use, but rather in its appearance. It was made of several layers of fine satin hemmed at the neck with a small slit in the back secured with a button to accommodate placing it over his head. It skimmed just above the ground at all times and, when Andy moved, these satin layers worked with and against one another to create the illusion that he hovered. The cloak appeared to ruffle gently at the wind resistance as it moved through space but there was no noticeable "kick" from his feet to indicate that they had anything to do with his transport. The cloak's hemmed edges never dipped or rose, either, as would happen as a person strode forward. And when he spoke, the golden ruffles that covered his upper body appeared to remain still rather than moving with the in-and-out function of his lungs, giving the listener the impression that the voice they heard was being transmitted telepathically. There were two slits in the sides so that he could use his hands, though he found keeping his hands hidden added to the cloak's mysteriousness.

His mask was a simple continuation of the same shimmering fabric: a golden hood that tucked in under the hemmed neckline of the cloak. The hood jutted out from his forehead and from around his jaw, casting a deep shadow on the thin black fabric that covered his face, so anyone speaking to him would believe they were looking into an eclipse. Encircling his head was a thin, glowing halo that hung in the air as if by magic. Even upon close inspection it was difficult to determine how it stayed afloat, and yet it did without so much as the faintest jiggle when he walked.

He got back into his vehicle and drove it as close to the front door as he could. He stood by his car hoping to find someone to help him carry his guest into the bar. The first to pass was the Slipperman, in an awkward and bulbous costume.

"Excuse me, Slipperman."

The grotesque creature, his skin all covered in slimy lumps with lips that slid across each chin, stopped and offered a twisted rubber stump in a meager attempt at a slippery handshake. "Helios," he replied. "What can I do for you?"

Shaking the stump in salutation, Andy started, "Well." Then, fully taking in the utter awkwardness of the costume, he realized that the Slipperman would not be able to offer much assistance. "I'm sorry, Slipperman. I was going to ask you to help me bring my guest inside, but ..."

Clumsily looking at himself, Slipperman muttered, "Yeah. This costume was chosen for its significance, not its freedom of movement ... or lack thereof. Sorry."

Then, noticing another attendee approaching, Andy said, "Thank you anyway. Have a pleasant evening." As the Slipperman made his way to Doug at the door, Helios called out, "Excuse me, Queen of Hearts."

She stopped in her tracks, a bit startled. "Yes?" she asked.

"I need some help bringing my guest inside. Could you lend me a hand?"

With the initial wave of apprehension gone, she said, "Of course. I'd be delighted."

Her costume was colorful and stiff. It did, however, allow seemingly unfettered movement of all her appendages, making it easy for her to help. Andy opened the hatch door and pulled back a blanket coving a pile of rags. He reached in, grabbed a handful of the rags and withdrew a long, thick, weighty bundle. He continued to pull at the bundle until the rags solidified into the unmistakable form of a person wrapped in bandages; he was pulling a seemingly lifeless mummy by the arm.

"I got this arm," the Queen of Hearts offered, reaching in and grabbing another bundle of rags.

The mummy was small but weighty, and awkward. But the two were able to remove it from the vehicle with only minor difficulty. Andy shouldered the heavy load in a fireman's carry while the Queen of Hearts shut the hatch door.

Doug the bartender was mesmerized by the figure as it drifted down the sidewalk to the front door. Even with the load across his shoulders, Andy's costume still majestically shimmered and hovered. His concentration on the hypnotic movement was broken by the appearance of the Queen of Hearts as she quickly swung around in front.

"Evening folks," Doug grinned. "I need to see your invitations, please."

The Queen of Hearts presented Helios' invitation first. "This is his."

Doug read it thoroughly.

His grace, Lord Spencerton
respectfully requests the attendance
of the honorable Helios,
god of the sun and master of his steeds,
Pyrois, Eos, Aethon and Phlegon
at the ceremony of his commuting
eleven-thirty in the evening
Tuesday, the twenty-eighth of September

At the very bottom of the invitation Doug read "admit two." He was stunned. "Yours is only the second one to say 'admit two.'"

"Well, two is all there is," Andy answered. He waited for Doug to give him back his invitation and when it didn't come soon enough, he added, "This guy's heavy. Can I go in?"

Embarrassed, Doug fumbled for the door. "Sorry."

Then, the bartender asked the Queen of Hearts, "What's with the mummy?"

The Queen of Hearts took a step back, struck a defiant pose, pointed vehemently at Doug with her scepter and shouted, "Off with his head."

Doug seemed frozen in an uncomfortable fear tinged with disturbed amusement. A cracked smile rose on his face as he read the Queen of Heart's invitation, gave it back to her and opened the door for the lady.

PART THREE

The Dark Ages

CHAPTER 21

It was before Johannes Gutenberg and the advent of moveable type, when history passed from generation to generation through the spoken word. The Almoravids, a Negro Mohammedan people, established itself as a most glorious and spectacular empire, one that rivaled the Greeks and the Romans in its richness and culture. It was tumultuous. It was peaceful. It was the renaissance before the Renaissance.

The Almoravids began humbly around 1040 A.D. when a zealous Islamic missionary founded a monastery in the western Sahara. It was from these beginnings that this particular following of Islam aggressively spread and in less than half a century the Almoravids became the most powerful sect in all of Africa.

Led by military leader Abu Bakr ben Umar, they soon began to spread their power beyond the desert, moving northward toward the Mediterranean. They conquered the people of the northern regions as quickly as they subjugated the west. And in the final battle for Aoudaghost, completed by the slaying of the city's highest ranking chief, Abu Bakr took the slain chief's widow, Zainab ben Ishaq al-Nafzawiyya, as his wife.

Zainab was Helenian in appearance, captivating any man who gazed upon her. She was a young and willful woman of royal blood who drew many chiefs and emirs as her suitors. Her striking beauty and keen mind did not come through chance or happenstance, though. She, like her mother before her, was a sorceress able to control the jinn.

The jinn are a society of entities of the Islam faith made of smokeless fire, much like Adam was made of clay, which exist between the realms of angels and humans. It is said that while men are spirits breathed into shapes, the jinn are spirits breathed into winds. They are unruly and arrogant in nature and their hearts burn with the fire of malevolence. They are the subtle whispers heard when no one is near, the creaking floorboards of an empty house and the mystical force behind life's deepest mysteries.

It was in her role as a sorceress, her ability to manipulate the will of the jinn, that Zainab's legacy would be felt for a millennium.

Restless for battle, Abu Bakr made a division of the power he established within the Dark Continent and, handing over governing responsibilities of the more-settled parts of the empire to his cousin Yusuf ibn Tashufin, he set off on jihad to the unruly southern regions. Before doing so, however, Abu Bakr divorced Zainab and resigned her to his cousin.

Some argue Abu Bakr was unable to leave such a beautiful wife behind, uncertain if or when he would return. However, others suggest it was Zainab, using her control over the jinn, who orchestrated the divorce, as she had long admired the handsome Yusuf and saw in him a regal greatness and powerful spirit unparalleled in their world.

Yusuf was a tall man for his time with deep lines in his face, like eroded rivers across a vast landscape of dark earth. Generous and cunning, beguiling and respectful, Yusuf ibn Tashufin was loved by his people. And in a quiet and bloodless coup, the chief priests of the time, finding Yusuf a far nobler and judicious ruler than his cousin, seated the tall, dark man upon the empire's throne.

One year later, with his queen by his side, Yusuf began the arduous task of building a capital city worthy of his magnificence, with splendid homes, a glorious palace and beautiful gardens. To inspire the laborers, he showed his willingness to get his hands dirty by working alongside of them, founding the empire's capital: Marrakech.

Three centuries before the Almoravids ruled Northern Africa, the Moors had crossed into Spain in an attempt to conquer the Goths and Visigoths of the Iberian Peninsula and the southern regions of France. Their battles ebbed and flowed, constantly swaying the boundaries between the Islamic and Christian kingdoms. By the time Yusuf completed the construction of his capital city, the Christian king of Castile, Alphonso VI, had defeated the Moors so completely that all that remained were small pockets of Muslim worshippers scattered across the southern and western portions of Iberia. Those Moorish descendants, still hoping for a resurrection of Islamic power, looked to Yusuf ibn Tashufin, nearly eighty years old at the time, the champion of Islam, to come to their aid and reclaim the land they once called their own.

Yusuf heeded the battle call. He took the Almoravids across the Straits of Gibraltar, leading an army totaling fifteen thousand men. Three thousand of them rode atop camels while six thousand jet black Senegalese warriors, considered invincible by all who opposed them, rode on stark white Arabian stallions under the same flag. The scattered few left in Europe who had called Yusuf, able to raise only ten thousand men on their own, put themselves under Yusuf's command and marched northward, united in faith, in search of the Christians.

Alphonso's army consisted of more than seventy thousand soldiers, including two thousand French knights outfitted from head to toe in gleaming armor and considered the finest corps of combatants in all of Europe. They were well-trained and well-motivated, having been given assurances from the Vatican of eternal salvation as well as permission to collect all the riches they could plunder in exchange for their services.

On a cold day in early October, 1086, the Christians and Muslims faced each other on the field of battle in Zalacca. Though outnumbered nearly five to one, the Muslim army fought valiantly from dawn until dusk. Then, with the fiery sun sinking low on the western sky, Yusuf unleashed half of the Senegalese warriors he had kept fresh in reserve. They charged into battle, sweeping down on the Christians and passing through their ranks with fearful carnage. The stand-off became a massacre as pools of Christian blood stood stagnant on the saturated ground. Those who survived, including Alphonso, retreated back to the north and east in utter defeat.

Yusuf, fighting alongside his Muslim warriors, suffered only minor injuries, the most serious of which was a long, shallow gash over his left eye. The wound, though minor, bled profusely, spattering his entire face with blood and making it appear as though he wore a red mask. His intense white eyes peered forth from behind the blood.

It was surviving that battle with only minor scratches, outnumbered five to one, that Yusuf came to believe himself incapable of dying. And when the sun had long abandoned the autumn sky and the full moon cast its brilliance across the bloody battlefield, Zainab called upon the jinn in an elaborate, mystical ceremony designed to make her husband's belief in his own immortality become a reality. Warriors from each of the four corners of the Iberian Peninsula—Compostella, Barcelona, Silves and Almeria—huddled together in a cave adjacent to the battlefield. As per Zainab's instructions, each of the four cities sent one representative from each of their seven military ranks, from infantrymen armed with javelins and pikes to generals charged with leading them into battle. With their faces unrecognizable after being splashed with the blood of their enemies, they stood and watched Yusuf, himself painted in his own blood, lead the ceremony with his sorceress wife by his side.

Taking a dagger from one of the slain French knights, Yusuf etched into the blade a triangle, the universal shape for the attainment of desired goals and dreams as well as the symbolic representation of one of the four elements: fire; the essence of the jinn. He also etched into the blade the name of Allah, from whom all good things come. Again, following the instructions of his wife, Yusuf sedated a young Christian soldier taken prisoner at the end of the battle and laid him out on a makeshift altar in the cave. He placed a disk of chainmail with a hole cut from its center over the heart of the victim and chanted a series of incantations purported to excite and arouse the members of the jinn. He raised the dagger over his head and drove it through the hole in the chainmail, killing the prisoner instantly. Those in attendance were invited to taste of the young soldier's life force as it bubbled up from the wound.

In the years that followed, Yusuf refined his ceremony, using precision instruments made to his wife's exact specifications by his most skilled craftsmen. It was a ceremony he repeated at the same time every year, engaging in battle the day after the full moon closest to the autumnal equinox, fully confident of his complete and total victory. One after the other, year after year, Yusuf absorbed another of the Moorish kingdoms: Granada, Malaga, Cordova, Carmona. Yusuf soon came to understand that those who witnessed the ceremony, like himself, were impervious to the ravages of war. However, unlike Yusuf, the others were not immortal. When the eldest witness to the original ceremony, Al-Mu'tamid ben 'Abbad, died the following year, Zainab instructed Yusuf to replace the dead general with an infantryman from the battlefield, a stranger eager to please the head of the conquering army. This code of succession became part of the annual ceremony and it was this continual supply of participants, Zainab told her husband, and the reawakening of their souls through the introduction of Islam, that pleased the jinn and fueled her husband's immortality. And she warned him that if this continuity were to ever be broken, the jinn would consume him, making him remain with them in their realm for all eternity.

The glorious reign of Yusuf ibn Tashufin lasted more than three decades. Thirteen kings in Africa and Europe acknowledged him as their overlord. When there was war, Yusuf was an unrivalled warrior. When there was peace, he was exceedingly merciful. Every Friday Yusuf ibn Tashufin's name was proclaimed from tens of thousands of mosques throughout his empire as the people rejoiced in his majesty.

In those three decades he rekindled the fires of his immortality twenty-nine times: the first in the cave at Zalacca as well as twenty-eight sacrificial ceremonies that followed. And through the rules of succession established by his wife, there was no one left alive from his first ceremony, all having died one by one, year after year. It was then that Yusuf vanished, never to be heard from again. Some historians claim he died at the age of a hundred and eight, still looking in death as full of life as when he defeated Alphonso VI. Others claim he lives on as others continue the sacrificial ceremonies in his stead, thus perpetuating his immortality. Still others believe he joined the jinn in their unseen realm between that of the angels and that of men.

It was the Dark Ages and the spoken word was art, entertainment, law and religion. Each generation passed its traditions on to those who would follow in their words and in their deeds. And so it was for the Altered, the name by which the small group of twenty-eight participants referred to themselves, handing down from mouth to ear and hand to eye the mystic ceremony begun in a cavern somewhere in the Spanish countryside.

Though the spoken word ruled the day, the written word ruled the future. And Yusuf, understanding the significance of what was to be, meticulously transcribed all that had happened.

PART FOUR

The Ceremony

CHAPTER 22

Through the years, the dynamics of the group had shifted in subtle ways, so subtle as to be nearly imperceptible to its participants. Masks of secrecy replaced masks of blood. Social linkage between members replaced military rankings. Individual motives replaced the group's initial goals of victory in battle. A change in name marked also these shifts, a conscious effort to perpetuate members of the Commuters, what the Altered now called themselves, through an ever-changing, constantly evolving societal landscape.

The ceremony's purpose, however, remained unchanged: an imperviousness to the ravages of war.

This year, the group gathered at Gambel's, awaiting the impending ritual. They assembled in small clusters and idly chatted. Every half-minute or so another member came through the door and crossed the large dance floor on his or her way to the covered bar top. And with every half-minute, Sarah the Egyptian made introductions to the newest member, as was the established protocol, each time indicating that Jean Louise Finch preferred to be called Scout.

Upon being introduced to Scout, Samuel Clemens exclaimed, "How delightful. That, my dear, is someone who dwarfs even my over-inflated importance." Looking her up and down, Mr. Clemens continued, "And your attire is well-suited for the purpose. I loved the book. And the movie." He gnawed on his unlit cigar, thought and then spoke again. "A little tidbit of trivia for you, Scout. Mary Badham, the girl who played you in the movie, was also in the final episode of The Twilight Zone. Did you know that?"

"No I didn't," Scout replied.

"By no means could it be considered an exceptional episode but, like every Twilight Zone, the pre- and post-narration was memorable. It was about a brother and sister neglected by their constantly bickering parents. They escape this unpleasantness by diving into their swimming pool and emerging in a strange and marvelous world populated by disenfranchised children and presided over by a benevolent matriarch named Aunt T.

"If I recall properly, the opening narration went something like ...," and taking his cigar between his fingers and posing as if he were Hal Holbrook portraying himself on stage, Mr. Clemens launched into a soliloquy: "'A swimming pool not unlike any other pool, a structure built of tile and cement and money, a backyard toy for the affluent, wet entertainment for the well-to-do. But to Jeb and Sport Sharewood ...,'" putting his hand to the side of his mouth and whispering aside, "Mary Badham played Sport, you know. 'But to Jeb and Sport Sharewood, this pool holds mysteries not dreamed of by the building contractor, not guaranteed in any sales brochure. For this pool has a secret exit that leads to a never-never land, a place designed for junior citizens who need a long voyage away from reality, into the bottomless regions of ... the Twilight Zone.'"

The small crowd swooned and uttered words of appreciation. Some even applauded.

Sarah the Egyptian chimed in. "My, my, isn't that apropos, Mr. Clemens?"

"Well I'll be," Mr. Clemens chuckled. "I guess it is. How 'bout that? Ms. Scout, when you're done making proper acquaintance with the remaining members, I'll see you with tonight's other emcees."

There were five emcees in all: Members to Commute. This ceremony, Lord Spencerton's ceremony, like all the others before it, moved everyone up the membership ladder. As Lord Spencerton ascended from a Sophomore to one of the Beta Seven, Helios the sun god filled his vacancy as he transitioned from a Freshman to a Sophomore. This, in turn, opened up a spot in the Freshmen sub-group for Scout. Similarly, Lord Spencerton's ascension bumped David Reynolds, proprietor of Gambel's nightclub and the man behind the Samuel Clemens disguise, from the Beta Seven to the Alpha Seven. Mitchell Treadwell, known to all as Emperor Trajan, was *the* emcee of the evening, the Matriculating Commuter. With his membership responsibilities completed, he was graduating out of the Alpha Seven and out of the Commuters entirely.

Each emcee was responsible for a portion of the ceremony. The longest-tenured member, Emperor Trajan, was simply to preside over the ceremony, his twenty-ninth and final. The longest tenured Beta Seven was to secure a private location for the ceremony: Gambel's, the nightclub owned by Mark Twain's impersonator. Lord Spencerton, commuting from the bottom half of the group to the top half, from spectator to perpetrator, was officially casting off who he was in order to become that which he most wanted to be: a wealthy nobleman. He was to commit the most selfish act of barbarism to which the remaining members were to celebrate. The seventh-year Freshman, Helios, was to provide the victim of Lord Spencerton's selfish and barbarous act, while the hitchhiker, the newest member, was to dispose of the victim with the aid of his or her sponsor.

That's the way it had been since the group's inception. At least that's what they had all been told.

The room quieted a bit when Helios came through the entryway and onto the dance floor, still hauling the weighty bundle of rags on his shoulders. Many of the members marveled at the sight of Helios' cloak shimmering and hovering effortlessly beneath the load. When he reached the far side of the dance floor, several members helped transport the body from Helios' shoulders to the top of the bar. They poked and prodded the body until it was positioned in a manner befitting the ceremony and stepped back. Just then, the Alphas, Betas, Sophomores and Freshmen, distant acquaintances tethered by a string of handshakes, began to slowly but noticeably split off into their respective groups.

Emperor Trajan gathered with the other Alphas. In his time, he had seen twenty-eight other life vessels; all of them carved by the hand of a Commuter. He looked at the human form in rags lying on the counter and remembered driving the knife into his victim some fifteen years prior. He remembered the soft squishiness of its flesh under the knife as it pierced the skin just below the sternum. He remembered mimicking the others who had gone before him, rotating his wrist to get the knife blade under the boney material and puncturing the heart. He remembered the salty smell of the blood as it soaked into the rags before pooling and streaming onto the ground. He remembered watching in horror as the Slipperman fumbled his way through last year's ceremonial procedure, gouging the victim haphazardly several times before finally delivering the fatal blow. Standing there, staring, Trajan remembered them all.

The others stood staring as well, awaiting the arrival of the final few members. Most found it comforting that the body was always wrapped in rags, concealed. It allowed them to think of the body as an "it" rather than a "him" or "her," an already dead mummy rather than a living, breathing, sentient being whose life was about to be extinguished for the sole purpose of the perpetrator proving to have the will to commit murder.

It had never occurred to any current member or to any of the nearly one thousand previous members that the "thing" that lay before them could possibly be someone they knew, someone they loved, someone they had procreated.

CHAPTER 23

The doorbell chimed. She was startled a bit by the interruption and glanced at the cable box to see that time had slipped away. It read 11:56. Prudy actually felt relaxed, considerably more so than when she had called her sister. Mitchell had put her mind at rest with plausible answers to most of her concerns and she was content to believe that her son was a schemer and not the victim of some horrible misdeed.

She calmly strode through the formal entryway to the front door. Expecting to be embarrassed for being silly and jumping to conclusions, she opened the door to find her sister flanked by two men in suits. Behind them, another man, in uniform, like her sister, was talking on the radio in the squad car parked in front of another vehicle in their driveway.

"Hey, Prudy," Connie started. Then pointing to the officer to her left, "This is Detective Brown and ..." She pointed to the man on her right and looked blankly at his face.

"Detective Watts, ma'am," the other man offered.

Connie continued. "They're from Korova City, the 1st Division police department from downtown. Can we come in?"

Dumbfounded, Prudy asked, "What's going on, Connie?"

Connie asked again, "Can we come in?"

Prudy swung the door open wide and all three visitors stepped into the large entryway. The two men looked around as though they needed a moment to take in the room's opulence.

"You said it was probably nothing."

"Usually it is. But when I got to the parking lot, your car was still there and we found his keys about twenty feet away." She held them up for her sister to see.

"Oh, God!" Prudy staggered backward, fumbling with her right hand for one of the winged chairs that graced the room. Finding it, she sat down.

"We also found some blood on the ground near the keys."

At this, Prudy put her elbows on her knees, put her face into her hands and began to cry.

Connie jumped on her quickly. "You can't cry, Prudy. You need to be strong and answer these detectives' questions. You need to be as unemotional as possible so you can give them every piece of information you can remember. Crying is only going to make it harder to get to the bottom of all this."

Prudy only cried harder.

Her sister came at her more forcefully, grabbed her shoulders and shook her. "Prudy, stop crying. I need you. Davis needs you."

Prudy looked up and wiped the tears from her eyes with her sleeve. Somewhere deep inside the house, the deep, rich chimes of a grandfather clock announced it was midnight.

CHAPTER 24

The murmur of each conversation from the four distinct groups was low, but amassed in the echoing vastness of the club they became an amplified din. Members listened intently to one another until Emperor Trajan stepped forward from the crowd. "Good evening ladies and gentlemen. Tonight, we are gathered together once more to further our positions within the group, as well as once again establish for ourselves the boundaries of societal mores.

"This is my twenty-ninth and final ceremony, but you will continue on just as all those who have come before us. I believe Sarah the Egyptian has properly introduced our newest member, Miss Jean Louise Finch. She prefers to be called Scout, and when I first heard the chosen identity I thought it a magnificent choice. In time, many of you will come to know the back-story and motives behind the selection of that particular identity, but for now," and extending his hand toward the newest member, "let us all simply welcome Scout into the fold."

The troupe of characters applauded. Those closest to her shook her hand and, as she made her way to the front of the group, those that could reach patted her on the back. Scout, in appreciation, smiled through the mask and waved thanks for the gracious welcoming before taking her position beside Emperor Trajan.

"Tradition has lost its cachet," he began, launching into the preordained portion of the ceremony. "Today, speed and convenience are what drives innovation and makes billionaires of those who allow the average consumer to do less and less faster and cheaper. The near instantaneousness of the web has usurped television news, which itself usurped radio, the usurper of the printed word which, thanks in great part to Johan Guttenberg, ultimately usurped the spoken word, the very foundation on which all civilization was built.

"From the Egyptians to the Romans to all of Western Europe and Columbus' new world, the spoken word passed tradition from one generation to the next. It was education, entertainment and social morality all rolled into one as group elders retold to their descendants the stories told to them by their ancestors, adding to it and omitting from it particular nuances so as to better reflect the character of the storytellers and the times in which they lived.

"Tradition has lost its cachet, which is perhaps why it is so strongly adhered to by the members of this group. Members will hear many new stories told, but the story you are charged to remember is the one of the man who started it all: Yusuf ibn Tashufin. You've heard his story. It's been told and retold every year for centuries. It is a story which typifies why each and every one of us originally sought membership. It is story of triumph, rising from relative obscurity to become one of the most powerful and influential people of his time and region."

Mitchell felt his audience hang on his words, especially the newest member with whom he made eye contact as often as possible as he retold the story that had been handed down for a millennia.

"Yusuf ibn Tashufin was asked to help the Moors maintain their Islamic rule over Spain. And on a cold October morning, Yusuf, approaching eighty years of age, took on the mighty Christian army in Zalacca outnumbered five to one. But through superior strategy and the sheer willingness to overcome, he defeated the Christians who wavered, broke and fled the battlefield. It was a sweet victory won by an old man: a man with dedication, perseverance and, above all, the knowledge that he could do whatever he had to do, whenever he had to do it in order to become that which he most desired to be."

Mitchell took a break, both for effect and to allow for a proper segue.

"It was in surviving that battle that Yusuf came to believe he was immortal. His wife, Zainab, orchestrated an elaborate ceremony designed to charm the spirits in his favor to provide him with the immortality he believed he already possessed.

"In the ceremony, his warriors covered their faces with the blood of their enemies which we emulate today when we don our masks. They drank from a cup, the life force that spilled forth which we also emulate. And in that ceremony, Yusuf ibn Tashufin became that which he most desired to be: an immortal warrior. As were those who joined him in that ceremony, all of them immortal. His ceremony exchanged a life for a life. We are here today to continue that tradition."

Trajan continued, "Scout, as a hitchhiker ascending into the Freshman class, you will be given the responsibility of disposing of the empty life vessel at the conclusion of the ceremony. Are you ready, willing and able to perform this task?"

"I am," she replied.

"Please tell us a little bit about what you hope to get out of your membership here."

The woman dressed as a 1950's tomboy cleared her throat. Then, facing all the masks in the crowd, she began, "Umm, I'm not very good at standing up in front of a crowd. And, I'm kind of, you know, on the shy side and I've noticed that, because I am that way, umm, things pass me by. So, what I hope to get out of this is, umm, to become more confident."

Trajan felt sorry for her. He listened to her speak, knowing she was becoming more and more self-conscious as she went on. Like he had done nearly thirty years earlier, she babbled. He guessed that she was probably thinking about all the self-help books she'd read, as evidenced by her narration.

"I want to empower myself with the knowledge that I can do whatever I set out to do; that I am responsible for making my future happen."

She was visibly sweating. Her speech had quickened and her voice became crackly as she spiraled downward, unable to stop the cacophony of words from coming out of her mouth. "I want to establish my core essence and incorporate a manageable paradigm that will effectively bring about my most desirous essenceness."

Sensing her downward spiral, Trajan interrupted. "My dear Scout, you're nervous. We all were at our first ceremony. You have much on your mind and in your heart. Let me just recap what I've heard. You are here for many of the same reasons we all are: to find the path to our most brilliant destiny."

Trajan's words as well as his tone seemed to calm her. He went on.

"My most sincere wish is that the path which you start down tonight helps you find that most brilliant destiny. May you fully understand that what we do here deepens our understanding of ourselves and provides us with the confidence and self-assuredness required to make whatever is physically possible a reality."

Trajan jolted Scout out of her hypnotic gaze by placing his hand on her hip and gently nudging her aside. As she followed his lead and returned to the location she had vacated prior to joining Trajan up front, the eldest member quickly reflected upon his oration. In the blink of an eye he remembered climbing the company ladder, step-by-step, to his current lofty peak. He remembered the difficulties he faced and overcame when confronted by his wife's alcoholism as well as his own selflessness in helping her through it. He remembered tucking his boys in at night knowing he had raised them in a safe and loving environment. And he remembered the faces of those he touched every Christmas at the domestic abuse shelter when he dressed as Santa Claus to hand out books and toys to the children, and shoes and clothes to their mothers.

Then, he collected his thoughts and proceeded. "Each of us, in our own time, has taken or will take the life of another human being. It is not an easy thing to do and it is not something we do without considerable reflection. We do this not to appease our God or a god; we aren't a zealous religious cult performing human sacrifices to gain power or wealth or security. I contend we are a societal cult. Through commuting, we don't merely travel between Point A and Point B; we question what is taboo. We obliterate the status quo and decide for ourselves what we can and cannot do. We perform a task so unsavory and distasteful so as to know that we can, if necessary, do whatever it takes to achieve what our minds have conceived and believed. We do it to become invincible in body, mind and spirit."

He paused again, this time for effect rather than reflection. He looked out at the eyeholes of the masks that stared back at him, through the windows of their souls, and delivered the same message that had been given *to* every member of the group *by* every member of the group since the Dark Ages. "Tradition has lost its cachet," he reiterated. "But here, we embrace it, adding to and omitting from the oral history of our membership which has been passed down to us by our predecessors. And thus, through commuting, we become that which we most desire to be: immortal.

"Throughout my membership, I have been inextricably linked to several members who have had a part in the ceremonies I played a role. Of course I am speaking of tonight's pentarchy of emcees. Scout, who you just heard from, Lord Spencerton, who we will hear from later, yours truly, and two other gentlemen. Tonight, we will ascend together."

CHAPTER 25

"The next emcee I would like to introduce has always been a charming, affable and humorous gentleman, much like his chosen identity's namesake. I was responsible for setting up the location of his commuting ceremony; I extinguished the life of the victim he provided and, I procured the first body he watched eviscerated. He was responsible for obtaining this enormous venue for the evening as his duty for commuting from a Beta to an Alpha. Ladies and gentlemen, it's my pleasure to present Mister Samuel Clemens for a few words. Although, we all know it will more than likely be more than just a few words."

Laughter and a brief and quiet round of applause arose as Mr. Clemens slowly made his way through the small group standing between him and Trajan.

Turning toward Trajan, Mr. Clemens replied, "Emperor Trajan, are you calling me a blow hard?"

"Not at all, Mr. Clemens. I merely know just how much you enjoy hearing yourself speak and how humorous you believe yourself to be."

When the brief laughter died, Mr. Clemens stared out as if to say something and paused. He let the silence hang for just a moment, and then followed in the beautiful drawl that members had come to know not as mimicry, but his own affectation. "Ladies. Gentlemen. Please join me in thanking our own Emperor Trajan for his efforts thus far this evening."

There was a small applause that Trajan acknowledged with the nod of his head and a simple hand gesture.

Mr. Clemens proceeded. "I have come to learn a thing or two about Emperor Trajan," he started. "The historical figure, of course, not the gentleman who stands before us. As many of us know and all others will come to realize, the person behind the mask offers little insight for those here. It is our chosen identities that offer a glimpse into each and every member. And this person here has chosen Marcus Ulpius Nerva Traianus, second of the so-called five good emperors.

"Emperor Trajan, as he was called, ruled during the period known as the Pax Romana, 'the Roman peace,' particularly notable for its relatively peaceful method of succession. Under Trajan's rule, the empire reached its greatest territorial extent. He was strong, but ruled with moderation and compassion as well, freeing many people who had been unjustly imprisoned by his predecessors and returning a great deal of private property that had been confiscated prior to his reign. As an army general he conquered Dacia while having other realms bestowed upon him, such as Nabatea, which is now portions of Jordan and Saudi Arabia."

Mr. Clemens again let the air grow deep with silence before proceeding with his southern vigor. "These are not myths to be squabbled over, but facts to be remembered and celebrated. And my dear friends, I submit to you that the man you see before you is indeed that which he most desired to be. A true leader who has helped each member of this loosely affiliated menagerie of souls effectively ascend to their apices.

"If the moderation and compassion he shows us all here is any indication of his conduct and demeanor outside our little assemblage, I have little doubt that his family adores and cherishes him, that his bosses and subordinates benefit greatly from his wisdom and leadership, and, most importantly, that he has found within himself that person whom he wanted to become when he joined up with this cast of characters some thirty years ago."

Again, he paused.

"Immortality. What does it mean? Plato, da Vinci and Shakespeare are immortally remembered. But Yusuf ibn Tashufin is immortal. Ever living." And with his hands spread out, he said, "We are impervious to the ravages of war. Immortal during our time as a Commuter. Emperor Trajan, on behalf of those here today who you have touched as well as those who have matriculated out of this commuting commune, I humbly offer my thanks and gratitude. You have taught me through your exemplary deportment what it means to be a member. And I hope I, the Alphas who I join tonight, the Betas who I leave, all the Sophomores and Freshmen, can, as you have these many years, continue the excellence established by our predecessors.

"As you leave us, I wish you unimagined happiness for the rest of your days."

As was often the case when Mr. Clemens spoke, people began cheering, moved by his sentiment, passion and the embodiment of his costume. And as the tempered din dissipated, Mr. Clemens slowly strode over to Trajan, placed his hand on his shoulder and said, "You, sir, *are* one of the 'good emperors.' You will be sorely missed."

Trajan shook Mr. Clemens' hand. "Thank you Mr. Clemens for those kind words. You're a tough act to follow."

"As are you, sir," Mr. Clemens responded.

"Again, thank you. But we must move on."

* * *

Waiting for silence and stillness, Mitchell stared out beyond the members. "Helios," he boomed. "He rides his chariot, he shines upon men and deathless gods, and piercingly he gazes with his eyes from his golden helmet. Bright rays beam dazzlingly from him and his bright locks streaming from the temples of his head gracefully enclose his far-seen face. A rich, fine-spun garment glows upon his body and flutters in the wind and stallions carry him. Then, when he has stayed his golden-yoked chariot and horses, he rests there upon the highest point of heaven until he marvelously drives them down again through heaven to Okeanos.

"That was *Homeric Hymn #31 to Helios*. It projects an image of elegant constancy and regal stature, of warmth and radiance and of new beginnings. A fitting image for our ceremony."

Mitchell extended his hand, motioning toward Helios, the golden figure hovering between the Freshmen and the Sophomores. "Helios, as a Freshman commuting into the Sophomore class, you were given the responsibility of obtaining the life vessel that lies before us," he said motioning toward the bandage-wrapped figure on the bar. "Please come forward and share with us the details of your undertaking so that we may all understand the commitment Lord Spencerton makes this evening."

Helios floated effortlessly through the thin crowd until he stood before the body, the body he had brought wrapped as a mummy. Mitchell watched Helios, with his back to the other members, stare down at the overlapping swatches of cotton that covered the eyes. Then, he turned and faced the group.

"This was not a good person," Helios began. "This was a prostitute, a degenerate, a stain on society. He is no one I know, though I know many people like him. He was filled with self-loathing and self-doubt, confused by what he was and what he thought he should be. He sold himself as a plaything for other men to use like a toy. He disregarded himself and invited others to disregard him as well. He had no higher opinion of himself than his solicitors had for the condom wrapper they'd leave on the floor, if they were smart enough to use one, or the dirty towels that hung in the hotel rooms, if they were civil enough to use them."

Helios turned and looked directly at Scout. "He stood on the corner of High Ridge Road and Summit Avenue in Highland waiting for someone to pay him to satisfy his lust." He had told her where to leave the empty life vessel after they were done

Mitchell watched Scout take out a pen and write what he assumed were the street names on her hand. Her responsibility as the hitchhiker was to dispose of the body at the same location from which it had been taken. This was established long ago by Yusuf's wife and the group's other founding members as a way of expressing that all that had been taken was the life force within, not the vessel it occupied.

Beneath the guise of Trajan, Mitchell Treadwell heard these street names and established where they were in relation to where he lived. He associated them with the theater in which his son worked. Mitchell's mind drifted away from the soliloquy Helios was giving and fell into a snap-of-the-finger thought chain. It started with a movie he had seen at the theater, the actor in the movie, the actor's face on a magazine in the bookstore newsstand, the last book he bought at the store, the strange character in the book that reminded him of Helios and continued with Mitchell focusing on the peculiarity of Helios himself.

Before becoming a member, a prospective hitchhiker must receive the majority of support of the three senior-most groups in order to be accepted as one of them. Every hitchhiker in Mitchell's twenty-eight years had received the support of at least eighteen of the twenty-one members with only a scant few dissenting opinions. Helios, however, received ten dissenting votes, the absolute maximum, including five from the Alpha Seven.

Mitchell thought Helios was odd. The younger man seemed to be yearning to join the group for all the wrong reasons. He did not seem to want to become that which he most desired to be, but rather become more so what he already was. Mitchell quickly surmised that not enough members had paid attention during the induction meetings to see this slight, yet compelling nuance. Mitchell mulled this over in his mind and let it give way to the inertia of the situation. Helios was a member, Mitchell was matriculating out and there was nothing he could do to change any of it.

* * *

"... and after I shut the door behind him I struck him at the base of his skull with my brass knuckles," Andy, dressed in a golden gown, continued, demonstrating the blow by embedding his fist in the palm of his other hand. Some in the crowd gasped, but most, especially the Freshmen, listened silently, intently, as they did every ceremony. Andy, as was expected of a matriculating Freshman, explained how he had obtained the life vessel. It was necessary to provide all Freshmen with the parameters of what would be expected of them when it was their turn to commute as well as the knowledge of successful best practices.

"He fell to his knees and then to the floor without so much as a whimper. I checked to make sure he was otherwise unharmed, gagged him, bound him and placed him in a large steamer trunk I had brought to the room earlier in the day along with a large dolly.

"I wheeled him out of that unclean room," he said with disgust. "Down the elevator and into the U-Haul van I rented from across town with cash. Finally, I took him to a special place I have where I could prepare him properly."

He let a pregnant pause wash over the audience before stating, "That was last week."

There was no hard-and-fast rule regarding when a body was to be obtained, though, to a member, everyone did it either the day of the ceremony or the night before. When the concept of Andy obtaining the victim and keeping it somewhere for a week had time to sink deep into the minds of his audience, there was an uneasy stirring. Andy ate it up.

"My intentions were not malicious," he explained. "We all remember the difficulty experienced by the Slipperman at last year's ceremony. I was intent on ensuring that would not happen to Lord Spencerton. I was acting on his behalf, not my own, I assure you. But, how could he ensure no bloody mess, you may be wondering. I am longing to tell you just that."

Andy could tell the audience was entranced, staring into the deep darkness of his mesh-masked hood. As he had experienced previously, the ceremony took on an almost dreamlike quality: a blur of words and images and emotions melded together in an unidentifiable haze of surrealism. Now, he, Andy, this shimmering figure of the sun god stood before the crowd and meticulously explained exactly what he had done during the previous week. And he did so with utter delight.

"It's simple, really. So simple I wonder if our commuting forbearers didn't implement this in their time. They're called hirudo medicinalis. Leeches."

The deafening silence of the shocked audience aroused Andy. It was the exact reaction he anticipated. He consumed it and began his lecture.

"Etymologically from the old English word 'loece,' to heal, they were used medicinally as far back as 1500 B.C. by the Egyptians. There is even a resurgence in their use today to help patients recovering from various surgeries.

"Advocated as an effective tool for bloodletting by Hippocrates, the father of medicine, and Galen, the personal court physician to Marcus Aurelius, these misunderstood and wrongly reviled hermaphroditic annelids are a true wonder to behold. While famous for sucking blood, it is their pharmacologically active salivary secretions that really deserve our recognition and, quite frankly, our admiration.

"Their three jaws and hundreds of teeth saw into living tissue, yet their bites usually go undetected. That's because of the natural anesthetic present in their saliva. An anticoagulant, a vasodilator and an enzyme called hyaluronidase, all present in their saliva as well, work in unison to allow a wound to remain open for up to forty-eight hours with the possibility of draining as much as one-hundred fifty milliliters of blood, or about five fluid ounces. That's the wound. The leech itself can only ingest about five to ten milliliters of blood in one feeding."

Andy leaned out toward the crowd as if he were an actor on stage giving a soliloquy to stage left, "As a side note, Roman ingenuity found a way around that. They induced continuous blood loss by cutting off their tails."

Then, once again standing upright and addressing the entire audience, he continued. "During the last seven years, I have witnessed a disturbing amount of blood needlessly spilled. For the last week, I've used a handful of leeches to remove a good amount of this victim's blood; blood that has spurted, splashed or streamed its way into the fabric of our identities. Literally," waving his arm in front of his cloak like a game show hostess, "And figuratively.

"Tonight, you will see the simple beauty of this easy, inexpensive, painless and very practical solution to a very real problem. I hope those I am commuting from will take this knowledge and put it to proper use moving forward."

He knew deep down his audience would be unreceptive to his suggestion, that it might even repulse many. He also knew that once the ceremony was over and the benefits of bloodletting a victim before the ceremony was experienced by these attendees, his efforts would be vindicated and, perhaps, emulated. He pressed on.

"As I said before, this was not a good person, a prostitute selling his soul, and not even to the highest bidder, but to anyone with a few measly sheets of paper, ultimately worthless in the grand scheme of all things."

Turning toward Scout again, Andy went on, "The corner of High Ridge Road and Summit Avenue is a breeding ground for societal disease. It is a place where individuals go and become infected. I am sterilizing this corner for society's sake and for our sake. And tonight, I add this life vessel, this carrier of diseases, to the institution of social justice."

* * *

Mitchell watched Helios glide back to his station between the Freshmen he was leaving and the Sophomores he was joining, unable to find the words to continue the ceremony. For nearly three decades he had listened to Freshmen-turned-Sophomores retell their stories with physical difficulty due to their moral dilemma of perpetrating such a senseless and arbitrary act against another human being. If it wasn't in their voices, the anguish was always visible in their eyes as they peered at their audiences through the holes in their masks. This group, this membership, this "social cult," as he had described it moments earlier, was about defying social mores, expanding personal limits and empowerment in order to gain invulnerability. Helios described his ordeal while savoring every detail.

Mitchell was appalled and more than a little concerned for the future of the group.

He recalled his own disturbing ordeal, when he took a day off from work, rented a car and drove nearly five hours away into the desolate, pristine old-growth forests near Mt. Marcy, the place his father took him hiking as a boy. He almost passed out sitting in the enclosed car soaking a rag with chloroform, but he capped the bottle, threw the rag into a plastic baggy and quickly rolled down the window to limit the haze in his mind. In hindsight, his serendipitous light-headedness was probably beneficial to his overall success.

Mitchell surveyed the trailhead, waiting for the unfortunate soul who was at the wrong place at the wrong time. It was a long wait, longer than any he had experienced before or since. Several times he thought of driving around to find a hitchhiker or someone simply walking along the road but he remained steadfast, resisting the urge to leave, confident someone would emerge from the woods. It was a lone backpacker, a young man in his early twenties with long hair and a scraggly beard, who exited the trailhead and stood at the trail's map and information board.

Mitchell eased out of his car and strode to the board with his hand in the open baggy in his jacket pocket, wondering if the man thought it strange that someone in a desolate parking area would get out of his car the very moment he appeared from the woods. The backpacker's soft, unconcerned smile as he turned and watched Mitchell approach indicated he never gave it a moment's thought.

"How's the trail today?"

"Not bad; a little slippery up top, but under the forest canopy it's nice and soft."

"I'm only here for a short stretch of the legs; quick commune with Mother Nature before heading back to work."

The hairy man didn't respond. He only read the board more intently.

"You waiting for someone?" he forced, hearing his own desperate tone.

Still transfixed on the board, the hairy man said nothing.

Mitchell's heart raced and he felt a bead of sweat run down the center of his back. The backpacker's non-response sent him into a panic. Reactively, he pulled his hand out of his pocket and tried to place the rag over the backpacker's nose and mouth, but the backpacker moved quickly out of the way.

"Hey, buddy, what are you doing?"

Mitchell wordlessly lunged at the confused backpacker again who, weighed down by his gear, teetered as he shifted his body to avoid the chloroform-soaked rag. As Mitchell recoiled after missing the second time, his arm forced the teetering man to stumble. His hiking boots caught a smooth rock, slick with dampness, and he faltered. The man took one more step backwards but could not regain his balance, falling to the ground with his metal cup chiming against the trailhead's gravel. Mitchell jumped on him immediately, placed both hands over the backpacker's face, locked his elbows and shifted all his weight forward. It was over in seconds.

Retelling his story of acquisition as part of Richard Plantagenet's ceremony twenty-some-odd years ago, Mitchell stressed the importance of remaining calm. He imagined Helios remained calm throughout the week-long torment of his victim. And while it was never stated or implied how one was supposed to prepare the victim for the ceremony, Mitchell felt Yusuf ibn Tashufin would in no way approve of Helios' tactics.

Mitchell would later come to find out just how right he was.

CHAPTER 26

When the clock's peal subsided after indicating it was half past the hour, Connie was kneeling on the floor next to Prudy trying to coax her sister into some semblance of control. Officer Jenkins had joined the assemblage but added nothing of substance to the discussion since arriving. "There you go, Prudy. Nice and easy. These detectives will only be here another few minutes and then I'll stay with you and we'll talk some more."

Detective Brown leaped at the opening, "Actually, we're done here, officer," nodding for Connie to meet them outside. He continued talking, this time to Prudy. "As mentioned, your sister gave us most of the information we need before we got here." Then, handing Prudy a couple of business cards, "But, if you can have your husband call us as soon as he comes home. We have just about everything we need."

Connie rubbed Prudy's hand vigorously and stood up to follow the detectives out the front door, with Officer Jenkins following behind them. Connie had noticed her sister's uneasiness the past thirty minutes had forced her further and further into the large wing-backed chair until she all but impaled herself against the upholstery. Out of her eye, Connie saw Prudy's other son, Lowell, who had begun listening to the conversation from the top of the elegant stairway but, by the time the police finally left, had scooted nearly all the way to the bottom, making it an easy few steps to assume Connie's place next to his mother when Connie vacated it.

"Mom?" Connie heard Lowell mew. "Sorry if I was a jerk earlier. I didn't know anything about what Davis was—"

"Shhhh," she heard her sister say before leaving.

Connie went outside to finalize a few remaining details and, upon her return, yelled "Okay," to the other officers from the door frame. "And Jenkins, don't be a jackass about it." She smiled and closed the door behind her.

Seeing the look of discomfort on her sister's face, Connie added, "Sorry about that. My partner is not very in tune with other people and sometimes it rubs off on me."

"Lowell, you should probably get some rest," Prudy said.

Before Lowell could say anything, Connie jumped in. "Your mom's right. I know you want to help and be supportive, and that's great. But I got a few things to talk to your mother about and she's going to be needing your support tomorrow when I'm not here."

The boy looked lost.

"Seriously, get your ass up there before I cuff you to the headboard."

He smiled, turned and, without a word, headed up the stairs.

"As for you, Prudence, where's your favorite place to just sit and relax?"

Staring out into nothing, Prudy said, "In the over-stuffed chairs in the den. It's where I do most of my thinking."

"Well, I'll be talking and you'll be mostly listening, hopefully not too much thinking. But let's get you down there with something to drink. Maybe you can change into something more comfortable while I make tea. Then I'll fill you in on some of the more important details."

"Details?" Prudy asked. "About what? There's more? What aren't you telling me?"

Pressing her fingers to Prudy's lips, Connie whispered, "Not a word until you're relaxed and in one of those chairs. You hear me?"

In addition to tea to soothe her sister's nerves, Connie assembled an entire tea set with cream, sugar and lemon, along with a plate of cookies while Prudy changed into her pajamas, slippers and robe. Connie placed the tea set down on the ottoman and poured the Earl Grey into two of the tea cups she found in the cupboard; the good tea cups their mother used for company.

When Prudy finally joined her, she looked no more relaxed or comfortable than before.

"Come on over and fix your tea."

Prudy obliged, sidestepping a few of the boys' loose items scattered on the floor. Connie grabbed Mitchell's heavy leather recliner and hefted it closer to the ottoman so that the two women were facing each other.

Delicately depositing two sugar cubes into her coffee, Prudy said, "Constance, I've done everything you asked and I am as relaxed as I possibly can be. Tell me whatever it is that you think is going to upset me more than I already am."

Connie stirred her tea, took a sip and set the cup back on the tray. She took a deep breath and sighed, "Okay. I was really hoping to talk to both you and Mitchell so I wouldn't have to say this twice, but …."

And Connie proceeded to tell Prudy all she knew about Davis's abduction, the High-Sum street corner being a hot spot for prostitution, about the other abductions, and the two dead bodies found in dumpsters. When she came to the final few details, she noticed Prudy was limp. Connie was uncertain whether her sister was even listening. Or, if she was listening, uncertain whether her sister comprehended what was being said. Connie decided to check before pressing on.

"Prudy? Did you hear what I said?"

A low, steady voice uttered, "I heard you. They think the boys were killed. Murdered. And now you're judging whether to tell me something even more horrific."

"Do you think you can handle hearing something more horrific?"

"Descending plateaus doesn't work for me. I need to be at rock bottom before I can climb up and out."

Connie moved forward. "Well, the boys found in the dumpsters … evidence points to leeches, hundreds of them, from head to toe."

CHAPTER 27

The fact that all the members were looking about at one another indicated to Mitchell that they were as disturbed as he was by the picture painted by Helios' soliloquy. After a long and awkward silence, Mitchell finally gathered his thoughts and approached the bar in front of the small clusters of characters.

"Thank you, Helios, for providing us with your insights." Then, trying to alleviate the nagging notions of unpleasantness in the back of his own mind, he added, "Let us hope your efforts provide the desired results."

A voice in the crowd came low and sure, "They will."

Mitchell watched as everyone slowly turned to Helios like a compass needle.

Mitchell tried to redirect the mood of the crowd to respectful reflection and genuine thankfulness. "Fellow Commuters," he bellowed. "Let us now focus on the true matter at hand: the celebration of the self.

"I've witnessed twenty-eight separate and distinct ceremonies. The first, as Scout will come to realize, was somewhat awkward and difficult, if not unpleasant, to endure. As a Freshman, I grew in my understanding of the strength and power we each hold within ourselves. As an entering Sophomore, when I had a hand in the ceremony, selecting and obtaining the life vessel, I purposefully wielded that strength and power for the betterment of myself and the furthering of my hopes and dreams. For seven years as a Sophomore I watched and waited for my turn, to fully understand what it is to command the ultimate power: striking down and ending the life of another human being.

"I vividly recall the intoxication of its anticipation, a year's worth of build-up between ceremonies to contemplate and consider all its ramifications. Not just on my life, but on the life I was to take, on his or her friends and family, on the social and spiritual implications of my actions. I had a year to doubt my own fortitude to perform such an act.

"It has been a year since we have gathered together as a group to celebrate the power of the self when the Slipperman showed his mettle. Our Lord Spencerton has waited a year to do as so many before him have done and what so many after him will do as well.

"It is customary for the matriculating senior member of the group to research the characters participating in his or her final ceremony. It's a tradition as old as any we practice here and it is one that I hope continues to be practiced for as long as this membership exists.

"No one who has read the novel or seen the movie *To Kill a Mockingbird* could possibly forget the loveable, impetuous tomboy Scout. Greek mythology buffs no doubt know of Helios the sun god. Most everyone breathing knows of the author Mark Twain, if not the philosopher and humorist Samuel Clemens. Mr. Clemens went into great detail highlighting my selected persona, Trajan. However, I am a bit embarrassed to admit that I was unable to find any references to our next and final emcee.

"I remember Lord Spencerton's previous two ceremonies as a Member to Commute as a hitchhiker and as an incoming Sophomore. Neither of the matriculating emcees was able to provide much insight into his chosen character, so I don't feel so bad. The gentleman himself offered little insight, if memory serves, mentioning only that he was a tobacco merchant during the 1600's. I think it essential for all members to learn about each other's selected character as it provides insight into the person behind the mask. Therefore, I wish to yield the floor to Lord Spencerton at this time and let him tell us about his persona. Lord Spencerton."

A soft applause filled the air. It seemed to Mitchell that it was as much in acknowledgement of Lord Spencerton as in appreciation for removing the vile images Helios had planted in their minds.

* * *

As Willie Spence strode toward the bar, the magnitude of what he was expected to do welled in him a moment, turning in his gut. Living on the hard edges of the dark, urban underground, he had killed a number of people in his lifetime. But this was different, somehow. This was a ritualistic killing, not some street war or business deal gone wrong. This was calculated and precise. Methodical. These were the same emotions that touched him when he had abducted his victim for Samuel Clemens' ceremony.

He had been seven years younger and quite a bit rougher around the edges when the responsibilities of a commuting Freshman fell to him. He'd already heard seven very different ways to obtain a life vessel for the ceremony and used that knowledge to target his victim. The experience, like all experiences, was completely his own.

A girl from the neighborhood named Faith Underhill was dating Winston Johnson, a boy from a different neighborhood. He was mediocre in just about every way and, though he was never able to verbalize it, Willie Spence hated mediocrity. He certainly hated Winston.

He studied Winston's habits for weeks to find the right time and place to do what he knew he must. On the day of Mr. Clemens' ceremony, Willie Spence "coincidentally" bumped into the young man a few blocks from his girlfriend's apartment. He asked the boy for help changing a tire. When he opened the trunk, Willie Spence pulled out his gun and told the boy to climb in or die. The boy acquiesced. They drove to a vacant lot where Willie Spence stripped, bound and gagged the boy with tape and finally wrapped him with gauze. Then, Willie Spence beat and kicked the boy so badly that he welcomed death as an end to his misery.

"Ladies. Gentlemen. I am Lord Spencerton. I am an English nobleman and entrepreneurial businessman residing in the American colonies just outside of Jamestown, Virginia. A few years back, against the desires of King James the First, I drank smoke from the sweetened tobacco leaf introduced by John Rolfe and immediately saw its tremendous appeal and profit potential. I purchased vast tracts of land along the James River and beyond, on which I grow my product, literally worth its weight in gold, used as currency within the colonies and beyond.

"I provide that as background for my most infamous act. I was the first planter to purchase a slave." He paused to fully experience their reaction. There was little.

"It was early September, 1619, a year before the Pilgrims arrived at Plymouth, Massachusetts, on the Mayflower. And it was this singular action, my purchase of a slave, that set in motion the enslavement of approximately ten million Africans shipped to the new world to live and die in captivity.

"As you may have noticed, fellow Commuters, I am a person of color. I believe there are only a handful of members in the group of such distinction.

"Slavery, the subjugation of one person by another, has been around since the dawn of man. I have no illusions that if Lord Spencerton had not purchased a slave that those ten million poor souls could have been spared their hardship. If Lord Spencerton hadn't done it, someone else would have. And if it wasn't in Jamestown, it would have been in another settlement and, if not the U.S., then Brazil, the original destination of the appropriated ship from which Lord Spencerton bought his slave.

"I am well aware that it required a monumental shift in the status quo to bring an end to slavery, bringing me to the point of all of this.

"I know I'm not supposed to provide too much information about myself, but I was a very different person before becoming a member. I was a dealer. Hell, I was Slipperman's dealer, which is the only reason I'm even a member," he said with a small laugh. "Some of you may have suspected that of me, and whether it was suspected out of prejudice or informed judgment makes no difference. Here, together, we are all the same. Here, social classes do not exist. As far as my place in this group, I am the fifteenth member in a group of twenty-nine. And after tonight, I'll be the fourteenth and Trajan will leave. There's a purity of this system in that there is no luck or skill or knowledge needed to move up: just time. It doesn't matter what I know or who I know. I just have to exist and year after year I move up the proverbial ladder.

"And while that works well for this group, I don't live here. I live out there," pointing to the doors of the club.

"Lord Spencerton purchased one of my ancestors. Whether or not I'm a direct descendent of the man Lord Spencerton purchased is irrelevant. What is relevant is that I have had to suffer because of his actions that September day. And because of that, I am here to bring about a monumental shift in the status quo. I am here tonight to exact vengeance."

Willie Spence turned toward the figure lying motionless on the bar. Grabbing the arm resting across its chest, he unwrapped the bandages around its hand. The hand bore a peculiar marking in the webbed skin between the thumb and index finger. It appeared to be an odd, cursive "E" in some elegant, cryptic hand-written script. Willie Spence continued to expose more skin. When enough skin shone to make his point, he held up the arm and looked back at the group. The cotton gauze swung softly from the vessel's elbow.

"I am here as a black man to subjugate this white person. If that frightens the mostly white sensibilities in the audience, I do apologize. Growing up the way I did, where I did, I've already shown how far I will go to get ahead. However, this act, this ceremonial taking of a life, is different. Very different. Before, I did what I had to to survive. This," he said, holding the arm higher, "this is about immortality, an aura of impenetrability. I'm an important man in my neighborhood. I joined this group to become an important man, period. No qualifiers."

"Emperor Trajan said we aren't a religious cult sacrificing virgins to appease a god, but a societal cult tearing down the status quo. This is about sustaining the monumental shift in the status quo that began with the Emancipation Proclamation. That's why I'm here today and it's why I am going to take this fucker's life: to establish a new status quo. My status quo."

With that, he laid the half-exposed arm back across the body's chest and stepped back.

* * *

Mitchell sensed Lord Spencerton had finished and worked his way toward the front of the crowd. He thought a moment about apologizing for the sins of his ancestors but quickly decided against it as this was Lord Spencerton's ceremony, not his. Mitchell also decided Lord Spencerton more than likely wouldn't have accepted any kind of apology if offered and took a different tact.

"Thank you, Lord Spencerton. We each come here with our own agendas, looking to find something specific that cannot be found elsewhere. I came to find completeness and am delighted to report, as I prepare to leave you all, I found it. I hope you do, too.

"Now then, did you bring the tools?" Mitchell bellowed.

"I did," Lord Spencerton replied, motioning to the boxes resting at the end of the bar where Doug the bartender had placed them a little more than an hour earlier.

"Have you touched them since the night of the Slipperman's ceremony?"

Lord Spencerton was walking to the far end of the bar, making his way to the hinged section to gain access to the bartender's galley. "I cleaned everything that night a year ago and made all the proper adjustments. I haven't touched them since."

"Then, ladies and gentlemen," Mitchell announced with his hands raised high in the air, the folds of his toga sleeves sliding almost to his neck, "Let the ceremony begin."

CHAPTER 28

All eyes were fixed on the ornately clad figure behind the bar with his back to the crowd, opening a series of boxes. From the first small shoebox, Willie Spence extracted an oddly shaped piece of metal. It was hollow, like a tube, and had two curves extending from a central straight piece. One of the curves was long and shallow which Willie Spence rotated to sit on the bottom like a typographical descender; the other curve turned in a half-circle at the top like a hook with a long leg that extended three or four inches below the lowest point of the shallow descending curve.

He spoke his prerequisite line in a solemn tone. "This pneumatica represents the twists and turns of life." He added, "The life that we take and the life that we live."

Willie Spence heard this first line fourteen times prior, yet never before did it resonate as clearly as it did this time. Never before did he bother to try to understand the words as more than rote blather of the ceremony—other people's ceremonies. He took his year of preparation with his sponsor, the Slipperman, very seriously, as all members do, trying to find meaning in the words he was to recite during his ceremony. He succeeded.

"What mad pursuit? What struggle to escape? She cannot fade, though thou hast not thy bliss. That leaves a heart high-sorrowful and cloyed. Will silent be; and not a soul to tell."

Willie Spence gently rested the object on the neck of the body. Then, bowing ever-so-slightly at the waist, "'Beauty is truth, truth beauty. That is all.' The truth I seek is vengeance, and when it is mine, it will indeed be beautiful."

He returned his attention to the boxes and extracted a very large, very plain, bronze ring. The hole was about two inches in diameter, while the bronze material surrounding the hole was about an inch thick. It looked like a very large, very thick bronze washer. On closer inspection, the exterior surface of the ring was flawlessly smooth and shiny. The flat surface and the interior of the ring were decidedly not so, being nicked and gouged extensively from its innumerable years of use.

Willie Spence showed the bronze ring to the crowd by holding it up and over the body. Then, reciting the same words of a thousand ceremonies that had come before, he said, "This ring represents the circle of life, life that continues unbroken with no beginning and no end."

Then, grasping the meaning he found in the words, he continued, "In religion, we have 'ashes to ashes, dust to dust.' Science states that 'for every action there is an equal and opposite reaction.' From where I come from, 'you get what you give.'

"Tonight I give death, something I will never know firsthand. Because that's the whole point of what we're doing here, right? Immortality? Of Yusuf ibn Tashufin and ourselves. We all want long, happy and fortunate lives, only our ideas of what that is depends on who we are. So, I hope to use what I learn about myself tonight to become that which I most desire to be: the personification of the American Dream, a rags-to-riches success story."

He placed the ring just above the sternum, immediately below the mummy's hands, which rested across its chest.

From the final shoe box, Willie Spence pulled out a bowl. This, too, was bronze, small and shallow, like a rounded section of melon cut in thirds.

"This cup represents our thirst for knowledge, knowledge of ourselves and of everyone with whom we have contact."

In his year of preparation, this was the line Willie Spence found most difficult to personally interpret. He had accomplished much in his life, albeit from a different side of the law than most of the others in the room occupied, yet he had a nagging sense about himself, about his lack of thirst for information. He had initially assumed it was his upbringing that placed him at his perceived disadvantage but had dismissed that line of thinking by recalling the success stories throughout his neighborhood. Additionally, in his line of work, people paid top dollar to obtain quality information concerning territorial infringements, new product supply, technological advantages. He eventually realized the thirst for knowledge had little to do with reading skills or education, it was about drive and desire. And it bothered him that he lacked the drive that this group so highly regarded.

"Ladies and gentlemen," he started, ashamed. "I don't thirst for knowledge like all those people from past ceremonies. There's a saying that goes, 'it's important to know what you don't know.' What I do know is that I'm not all that interested in learning. So for me, I guess I thirst for the desire to 'thirst for knowledge.'"

Behind his mask he felt his cheeks flush with embarrassment as he turned his back to the crowd. He focused once again on the boxes.

From the first of the two large boxes he extracted a mask, sleek and featureless. He bent low behind the bar so no one could see him remove his extravagant, green floppy hat and plush, purple hooded mask before affixing the mask to his face. He stood, turned toward the crowd and placed his hat and hood at the victim's feet in one smooth motion. The juxtaposition of the simple, muted mask atop his audaciously dressed, brilliantly hued body was ridiculous, but no more so than for the

Slipperman or any of the others who had adorned the ceremonial mask. It was originally a beautiful, rich ivory porcelain, but through the years it was splashed with enough blood and subjected to enough dirt and grime that it now had a mottled sand tone.

"With this mask, I join my predecessors in ridding myself of myself."

He again turned his back to the crowd and extracted from the final box a long, steel dagger. Lacking anything remotely decorative, the dagger, like the mask, was utilitarian. Its sole purpose, to cut flesh, was instantly recognizable. The handle, perfectly cylindrical, like a roll of quarters, ran unobstructed to the pommel at the end, a simple flat disk only slightly larger than the handle itself, like five silver dollars forged together.

The crossguard, running oddly perpendicular to the blade, was a triangular bar extending out approximately two inches beyond both the handle and blade. It appeared as though the triangular bar mysteriously hovered above the handle, its base the precise width as the handle's diameter. The blade, about an inch wide and only six inches long, protruded from the top of the crossguard, each side of its symmetrical double-edged sharpness glinting as it caught the night club's dim illumination.

Though he had no knowledge of blacksmithing, Lord Spencerton took a moment to appreciate the extraordinary craftsmanship necessary to create such a weapon from a single piece of metal.

He clenched the dagger with both hands and raised it over his head. "With this blade, I join my predecessors in taking this life so that I may be that which I desire: immortal."

Then, Willie Spence drove the dagger down. The blade, running parallel to the length of the body, centered inside the bronze ring and disappeared beneath the mummy's bandages with tremendous force. A metallic ping rang out as the thin, leading edge of the triangular crossguard crashed against the brass ring, stopping the dagger's downward thrust. Lord Spencerton then drove the handle down like a lever against the top of the victim's belly, bringing reason to the perpendicularity of the crossguard: to allow the blade to sweep through the chest cavity, gashing all three layers of the heart wall and penetrating either of the lower valves.

The mummy's bandages absorbed the thick red liquid as it navigated past the steely blade and into the open air. When Willie Spence stood upright and slowly extracted the blade, the stain slowly crept in all directions across the victim's chest. It spread quickly at first, but then all but stopped as he inserted the shallow curve of the pneumatica into the fresh, clean wound, presumably directing the shallow-curved end of the device directly into the heart.

As he reached for the cup, he sucked on the end of the hook-like curve pointing toward him. Two, three, four draws before the salty liquid touched his tongue. He swung the pneumatica's long leg downward, behind the body, out of the audience's sightlines, siphoning blood directly from the heart and into the cup. It flowed like warm syrup, slowly but continuously. A thin, indented line marked the inside of the cup and when the line was covered, Willie Spence swung the long leg of the pneumatica up to stop the flow. He then pulled the pneumatica out completely and allowed what little blood flowed from the wound to soak into the bandages.

The ceremony was in stark contrast to the previous year's fiasco when the Slipperman had botched the insertion of the knife, first missing the bronze ring completely and then inserting the knife rotated ninety degrees so the crossguard ran parallel to the body. When he had swept the blade through the chest cavity, it had nicked several organs, tainting the blood with other fluids so when the Commuters drank from the cup, it was not only unpleasant, but nauseatingly vile.

This ceremony was clean and neat. The body was perfectly still throughout the ceremony. Even as its chest was penetrated by the dagger, the only movement was a reaction to the force of the blow. The blood was regulated perfectly, flowing enough to fill the cup, but not so much as to make a mess on the bar. Willie Spence stood and looked at Helios, who seemed to be beaming as brightly as a sun god behind his mask.

Willie Spence struggled to pass the cup of blood over the empty life vessel to Trajan, who stood on the other side of the bar in front of the crowd. Taking hold of the cup, Trajan then turned to the crowd and raised it in front of his face.

"I join my predecessors in taking this life so that I may be that which I desire: immortal," he muttered in a low and respectful tone. He shifted his mask slightly and sipped the cup's contents. The crowd was deadly silent so even those farthest away could hear his nearly inaudible words.

When he finished, Trajan moved to his far right where the remaining Alpha Seven stood awaiting his arrival. He handed the cup to the next member in line Conall Cernach, the great Celtic warrior. Conall Cernach clasped the cup surely and whispered to himself, "I join my predecessors in taking this life so that I may be that which I desire: immortal." He adjusted his mask and sipped the blood. From his hands the cup moved from member to member down the ranks, each whispering the same line and taking a small sip before passing it along. The cup made its way to the final Alpha member, Melusina, the two-tailed mermaid, who followed protocol and passed it to Trajan who had made his way through the small row of Alpha members to receive the cup in its due time. Trajan walked back to the front and handed the cup to Samuel Clemens.

Mr. Clemens, ascending from the Betas to the Alphas, turned to the crowd and, like Trajan, hoisted the cup in front of his face. "I join my predecessors in taking this life so that I may be that which I desire: immortal."

Again, the process continued, from Samuel Clemens to Tu-whakaheke-toto, the Maori god of war, and on through the Beta Seven to the Slipperman who, despite his bulbous costume's interference, took a long draw from the cup. When he was done, he passed the cup to Trajan who was standing in the very middle of the crowd. As he moved toward the bar, he stretched out his arms so that when his torso met the bar rail he was fully extended across the empty vessel. Willie Spence took the cup, looked into it and saw, to his surprise, that very little had been consumed. He assumed that most had merely moistened their lips with the crimson liquid and had not taken a full sip as he expected.

Then, he, too, raised the cup and repeated his own words. "I join my predecessors in taking this life so that I may be that which I desire: immortal." He let the warm liquid wash over his teeth and tongue before swallowing.

As was the ritual, in an exaggerated motion, Lord Spencerton tilted the cup until it was nearly upside down and emptied it into his mouth. The salty liquid was colder than when he had siphoned it from the corpse, and with a somewhat thicker mouth-feel. He thought that it must have been from coagulation and the idea made him shiver with disgust, nearly forcing his gag reflex into effect. He brought the cup back in front of his face and then placed it on the bar.

He assembled the pneumatica, the ring and the dagger on the bar near the cup at the head of the body. He grabbed his hat and mask from where he had left them, bent down behind the bar and switched masks, placing the modeled porcelain mask with the other items when he stood back up. The crowd was already dispersing when he turned from placing the various ceremonial devices on the bar next to their empty boxes.

As Willie Spence made his way around to the front of the bar, a woman, known to the membership as Marie Laveau, was already collecting the items to prepare them for another year's storage. He knew it was his responsibility to help her through her preparatory period, to fully appreciate the taking of another person's life, just as the Slipperman had done for him. He also knew her heart beat faster with every item she touched, just as his had a year earlier.

CHAPTER 29

A hushed contentment fell upon the audience, having witnessed Lord Spencerton taking the life from its vessel. The climactic release of tension transformed the group from individual anticipatory gawkers standing on the edge of suspense to a single organism of many sated participants coming down from an adrenaline high. The deed was done and all that was left was for someone to clean up the spilled fluids, to dispose of the body, and for all others to depart.

As was customary, Lord Spencerton, the ceremony's most important participant, the Commuter, joined the Alphas and the Betas, who had secluded themselves from the other two groups. Each member took an opportunity to shake his hand and congratulate him on his ascension. He responded cordially as he made his way from one end of the group to the other.

Mitchell was last and when his turn came to comment, the rest of the members listened intently. "Lord Spencerton, first off, how'd it taste?"

The group chuckled.

"I was surprised that it was as warm as it was. And a lot less salty than I thought it was gonna be. But when it came back the second time, damn, that was not what I was expecting at all."

The group chuckled again until Mitchell interjected.

"Thank you all for attending this evening. It truly was a marvelous ceremony. But, the other emcees and I, as well as our immediate descendants, need to make certain the rest of the evening goes as it should."

Each of the four groups congregated in small huddles. Mitchell broke away from the Alphas and stood in the center of the room's massive dance floor.

Mitchell called to the Freshman circle to get the attention of the two youngest Commuters, Sarah the Egyptian and Scout as well as the eldest freshman member. Then, turning to the other groups in turn, he called for youngest and oldest Sophomores, Betas and Alphas. Each of the called members gracefully exited his or her small circle of comrades and proceeded to where Mitchell and the others awaited their arrival.

"So, Scout," Mitchell started, "What did you think?"

"I'm still a little bit freaked out, y'know?" Her speech was crisp and clipped. "It was one of those things where you don't think it's real until it's actually happening right in front of your eyes and you can't help but be mesmerized by it all."

Mitchell and the other members nodded knowingly. Mitchell recalled his first ceremony and understood the surge of whatever it was flowing through the young woman's mind.

"I mean, holy shit, right?" Then pointing at Lord Spencerton, she went on. "This guy's up there talking about the injustices of slavery and then 'Bam' there's a knife handle sticking up out of that thing's chest. I mean, wow!"

The others in the group looked out of their masks with smiles in their eyes in appreciation of her enthusiasm. Standing in a circle more reminiscent of a football huddle than a cocktail party, Mitchell fixed his eyes on the babbling woman and continued. "As you know, Scout, the night's not quite over for you." Then, nodding toward Sarah the Egyptian, he went on, "It's not over for you or your sponsor."

Scout replied, "I know, we have to bring the body, I mean the vessel back to, oh man, where was it?" Then looking at her hand, "High Ridge Road and Summit Avenue."

"Yes, High-Sum," Mitchell repeated slowly with a hint of disapproval in his voice. He hoped tons of disapproval could be seen in his eyes which were intent on searing a hole through Helios' masked hood. "It seems Mr. Helios elected conscience over convenience when selecting tonight's vessel from a high-traffic area."

Turning his attention back to Scout and Sarah, "That means, ladies, both of you are going to need to be exceedingly careful. And be patient. There is no reason to be in a hurry. You'll need to push back your fear and apprehension and clear your mind so as to act rationally and responsibly."

Returning to his ceremonial responsibilities, he continued. "Sarah the Egyptian, Jean Louise Finch is now your understudy. It is your responsibility to help her find the meaning of these annual acts. You must pass on not just the words and the deeds, but the personal and societal ramifications of each. Use what you have learned these past two years to help Scout on her journey toward ascension. Can you be trusted to do so?"

Sarah nodded confidently. "Yes. Definitely."

"Scout, you're responsible for recruiting a new hitchhiker. Presumably, you've already begun?"

"I have," she answered.

"And your guidelines?"

"I have two: age and association. The person I sponsor must be no more than five years older than I am and no younger than twenty-one. And the person I sponsor must be from a different social setting than the person who sponsored me."

"And why is that?" Mitchell interrupted.

"To ensure the thinnest thread of connectivity between Commuters."

"Are you prepared to do these things?"

"I am."

Had either of the two Commuters seen Mitchell's face, they would have recognized his overwhelming approval. Then he turned and addressed the next pair of members.

"And make sure you scrub that ink off your hand before you go to bed," Conall Cernach added. Mitchell Treadwell knew the man behind the costume as Michael O'Donahue, a certified public accountant and his personal tax advisor as well as the father of one of Davis's coworkers.

"Helios," Mitchell continued, "You are now Beowulf's mentor. I commend you on your preparatory initiative. Your use of leeches, while disturbing," he shook his head to remove the mental image, "was extremely effective in limiting the unpleasantness that accompanied last year's ceremony. However, the location you selected to garner tonight's guest of honor leaves much to be desired.

"It is your responsibility to help Beowulf find the meaning of these annual acts. You must pass on not just the words and the deeds, but the personal and societal ramifications of each. Use what you have learned these past eight years to help Beowulf on his journey toward ascension. Can you be trusted to do so?"

"You know I can," he replied flatly.

"And Beowulf, you're responsible for obtaining next year's guest of honor. Presumably, you've already begun preparations?"

"I have," he answered.

"And your guidelines?"

"I have two: association and action. The life vessel I obtain must be a complete and total stranger; an arbitrary selection at the outset that slowly becomes an analyzed, calculated and premeditated target."

Mitchell again interrupted the recitation. "And why is that?"

"To protect the group from external analysis and to strengthen myself by removing any traces of personal motive."

"Go on."

"I must also take action to properly prepare the body for the ceremony."

"Are you prepared to do these things?"

"I am."

Turning to Lord Spencerton, Mitchell pressed on with his duties as the Matriculating Commuter. "Lord Spencerton, I could see true understanding in the deliberateness of your actions and the depth of your words that you have committed fully to this group. Marie Laveau is now your understudy. It is your responsibility to help her understand, just as you do today, the meaning of these annual acts. You must pass on not just the words and the deeds, but the personal and societal ramifications of each. Use what you have learned these past fifteen years to help Ms. Laveau on her journey toward ascension. Can you be trusted to do so?"

The long plume in Lord Spencerton's hat slowly waved as he nodded. "Yes."

"Marie Laveau." Mitchell had always thought her too timid to excel as a member and he wanted to ensure she was truly prepared for the tremendous undertaking to which she was about to commit. "You are ascending from a Sophomore to a Beta and in doing so you will be obligated to take a life, simply to show that you can. This is the essence of what membership in this group represents.

"You are responsible for extinguishing the life force of next year's guest of honor. Have you begun reflecting upon your tasks?"

"I have," she whispered.

"And your guidelines?"

"I have two: action and abandonment. I will be solely responsible for the act of extinguishing the life of the person brought before me. I will also abandon who I am and from that moment forward become Marie Laveau, not just as a member of this small group, but as a member of the world community. I will become that which I most desire to be: immortal."

"And why must you abandon who you are?"

"In order to become impervious to the ravages of war, I must start at the beginning; the beginning of Marie Laveau."

"Are you prepared to do these things?"

"I am."

"It scares the hell out of me that what you desire most is to become Marie Laveau," Mitchell added, letting out a quick giggle. "But I suppose even the Voodoo Queen of New Orleans has her own attraction."

Mitchell then faced Samuel Clemens and asked if he was prepared to guide his protégé, to which the man affirmed in his southern drawl.

"Tu-whakaheke-toto, you are ascending from a Beta to an Alpha and in doing so you must find a venue for the ceremony. Have you begun preliminary investigation into location options?"

"I've already found and secured a place," he answered.

"Excellent. And this locale conforms to our guidelines?"

"Absolutely. Abandonment and appropriateness. It is both secluded and secure, and it offers more than enough space without being conspicuous. I'm sure Mr. Clemens will find it more than adequate."

"I'm sure it will be fine," Mr. Clemens said.

"I'm sure it will be as well," Mitchell confirmed.

Then he took a moment to collect his thoughts. The memories of the group, horrific and macabre as they were, filled his mind. But rather than be repulsed, his heart warmed. No more meetings. No more obligations. He had disposed of the body twenty-eight years ago, abducted that backpacker and prepared him for ceremony twenty-one years ago, drunk the blood of his victim fourteen years ago, and secured the place of Mr. Clemens' commuting seven years ago. He was ready to leave. He had more wealth and success and possessed greater social status than when he arrived. That was the reason he told himself he had joined in the first place: to provide for his family, and more than merely adequately but substantially. But it was the thrill of surpassing his father, to do something not even he could do, acquire immortality, that was the real reason he joined. Natalie Belling knew that was what he was looking for as surely as he did.

The time for Mitchell to cease his membership had arrived. It was now up to Conall Cernach, Mitchell's tax lawyer, to oversee the group for a year, when he, too, would complete his membership and matriculate out.

Was it worth it? he asked himself. Was enabling, if not directly participating, in the death of twenty-nine innocent people worth the comfort and stability he and his family took for granted each and every day?

His wife had been a helpless alcoholic for years. How had being a Commuter made that any better? Would Prudy have died that night when she fell on the broken glass had he not sought membership some twenty years before it happened? How had these years of late night meetings and monthly excursions affected his marriage? And had that contributed to his wife's alcoholism? Was his career success due to the externalization of power he had displayed nearly fifteen years ago, was it hard work and dedication, or the simple fact that his father owned the company? How had his immortality benefited him in any way?

He forced himself not to dwell on these complex and conflicting issues. He was done. It was up to Michael O'Donahue, known to this group of murderers, kidnappers, co-conspirators and felonious abettors as Conall Cernach, a heroic warrior of the Ulaid in the Ulster Cycle of Irish mythology.

Mitchell looked at his tax preparer in full regalia and felt sick. How many cocktail parties had the two of them ignored their hidden comradeship only to engage in the banal trivia of triple exempt bonds? Beneath the mask, the dirty sackcloth and leather leggings was a man he had sponsored for membership. At that very moment, Mitchell hated him. Moreover, he hated himself for pulling his tax attorney into the squalor of humanity he wanted so desperately to rise above. And most of all, he hated his sponsor, Natalie Belling, for recruiting him into the Commuters.

Natalie took on the persona of Dors Venabili, an attractive university-level history teacher nicknamed "The Tiger Woman." The guilt of her crimes as a Commuter and their contradiction to her profession as Lieutenant Governor caused such internal turmoil, Natalie often confided in Mitchell about the Commuters outside the boundaries set by the group's founder.

She had worked diligently to right her wrongs, working through the Governor's office to introduce victim's rights legislation. And when that didn't extinguish the gnarled filth she felt churning in her heart, she had established a charitable foundation for the families of murder victims, an attempt to ease the pain she felt she caused at least one group of individuals every year in early autumn.

He contemplated her fate. She was found dead of a stroke the morning after her final ceremony. Irony? Coincidence? Karma, perhaps? Or was it simply her time to go? Mitchell wasn't sure. No one could be. Immortality, as it was explained in the ceremony, only existed while one was a member. Invulnerability to death and impenetrability to its cold grip where all anyone could know. As deliverers of death, Commuters had no control of the great beyond, knowing only that someday it would be their time. Apparently, immortality had its limits.

He stood in his place and hated Natalie Belling for so many things. He hated her for getting off easy and dying immediately upon matriculating, rather than having to face the years of guilt that surely awaited him. He hated her most of all for seeing in him his desire to step beyond his father's shadow and providing him with the means to do so. It took all of his will to suppress the disgust and loathing he felt for her, for himself, and for everyone in the bar, but he continued on with his final duties as a Matriculating Commuter.

"Conall Cernach is now the senior ranking member of the Commuters. I hope the excellence he demonstrates in his guidance and leadership is surpassed only by those who follow him."

Mitchell shook Conall's hand and watched as the others in the circle did the same. Once Conall Cernach had shaken hands with everyone in the circle, he turned back to Mitchell.

"Ah," Mitchell said, surprised that everyone was looking to him for more dialog. "I guess this is my cue." He cleared his throat. "I suppose I should leave you with some bit of wisdom, but I'm sorry to say I have very little to offer."

He turned from the group and took a few strides toward the door. Unexpectedly, he turned back to the group and paused. Then he looked at Conall. "Finding meaning has absolutely nothing to do with understanding."

He stood there looking back at them through his clear plastic mask, creating the slightest of awkward moments. He turned again from the group and, with his head down, he walked the entire distance to the exit watching his sandaled feet scuff across the dance floor.

CHAPTER 30

The man behind the Conall Cernach mask watched Trajan unceremoniously slip out the door. The man who had once been his frat brother, who had sponsored him for membership almost thirty years ago, who had explained to him what was expected of him at each stage of ascension through the Commuters, was now gone.

Lord Spencerton broke the silence. "Finding meaning has absolutely nothing to do with understanding. What the fuck is that supposed to mean?"

"I don't know," chimed Michael O'Donahue, "But I hope by this time next year I do." He turned to the small group huddled on the dance floor and quickly attended to his remaining responsibilities. "So, let's wrap this up. Sarah and Scout, you go get the vessel ready to be moved. Marie, you pack up the instruments and I'll get everyone else moving out the door."

The huddle broke as each member, save the three ladies, shuffled back to their corresponding group of seven. Sarah the Egyptian and Scout grabbed the plastic shopping bags they had brought with them and went to the front of the bar and sat on the floor. They each pulled out a pair of thin latex gloves and a bright orange plastic rain suit folded down to the size of a small purse. After putting on their raingear, they took out another shopping bag, slipped it over a foot and secured it with a rubber band at the ankle. They each put the first bag, the one in which they carried everything, on the other foot, secured it with another rubber band, stood and stared at the lifeless figure wrapped in gauze.

"Ladies and gentlemen," Michael O'Donahue shouted. "Thank you all for making tonight's ceremony another successful one. I'd like to ask that you please leave in order of seniority allowing sufficient time for everyone to get to their vehicle, change out of character and leave the parking lot. Henry the Fifth will be followed by Titus Oates and so on down the membership hierarchy."

Henry the Fifth walked toward the exit as Michael turned to the women behind him and took note of their progress. They had already removed the gauze and wrapped the body in a plastic drop cloth that came folded even smaller than their rain gear.

"You ladies need a hand?" he asked.

"I think we can handle this," Sarah the Egyptian stated confidently. "Thanks."

Michael stood and watched the Alpha Seven slowly dissolve as one by one they made their way across the large dance floor and out the door.

After Melusina left, Samuel Clemens, the newest Alpha Seven member, approached him.

"The owner said to just shut the front door on the way out and he'd lock up after we'd all gone. I told him we'd be done before two. I'll come back to clean up and meet him here."

Michael nodded, "I'll clean the bar and the surrounding area before leaving." He looked at his watch, which read 12:51. Ignoring the man in the linen suit as he strode away, Michael turned again to watch the two women behind him deal with the lifeless body.

He recalled his own trepidation and squeamishness at touching the dead body at his first ceremony. Michael was astonished at how deliberately and unwaveringly these two genuinely graceful women went about preparing the body like seasoned morticians. They used large, red rubber bands of various diameters, which Scout had in her denim pockets, to hold the plastic drop cloth secure around the body. The dark crimson liquid smeared wherever it came in contact with the clear plastic, particularly across the chest, but a second layer wrapped neatly atop the first ensured no blood escaped the bindings.

When all the other members had left, save he and Marie Laveau, the two women responsible for disposing of the body turned to the plastic-wrapped package on the bar top.

Scout took charge. "Okay, let's carry him on our shoulders. Hunch down and we can just about roll him off the bar. I'll take this end," she said grabbing the vessel's shoulders. "Sarah, you know where the car is, so why don't you take the feet and lead the way. Conall, would you please give the body a shove when we're all ready?"

As they both moved their shoulders to the bar and prepared for the weight, Michael made his way around to the other side of the bar.

"Everyone ready?" Scout asked.

When they answered yes, Scout asked Michael to push. The body slid off the edge of the bar and, after an initial wavering, the two women stood up, wrapped their arms around their portion of the body and proceeded across the dance floor. Michael hurried from behind the bar to the entrance and swung the door open just as they arrived. Marie Laveau followed behind, her arms hefting the five boxes containing the ceremonial implements.

"See you next year," Michael called. He waited for a response but none came. He watched the two women with the load on their shoulders disappear beyond the bright lights of the parking lot.

* * *

Sometime around 2:00 a.m., the owner of Gambel's, the man every Commuter knew as Mark Twain, left the chill of the night air and reentered the empty dance club. He walked across the wide expanse of the floor and made his way to the back side of the bar. He opened the plain, plastic shopping bag with all the various items Marie Laveau, Voodoo Queen of New Orleans, was told to bring and leave. First, he retrieved the latex gloves from the bag and pulled them on. Then, he retrieved the foaming disinfectant cleanser, sprayed the tarp that covered the bar, quickly folded the tarp in on itself so that the foaming cleanser was in the absolute middle of the bunched up fabric and set the tarp on the floor. Then, he sprayed the bar top and wiped it down.

He pulled off his gloves and placed them, along with the foam cleanser, in the plastic bag. He tucked the tarp under his arm and traversed the dance floor one last time. At the door, he turned to force it open with his back end and let it swing closed on its own as he headed to the lone car in the parking lot.

PART FIVE

The Aftermath

CHAPTER 31

Diane drove her black, two-door coupe through the near-empty city streets on her way to the hidden niches of intersecting alleyways near the corner Helios considered a breeding ground for societal disease. Her car was a nondescript Honda Civic she bought "gently used" from an ad in the Sunday paper. She felt when she bought it that she had overpaid for what she was getting but in the three years she owned it, it had never once given her a moment of trouble, making it worth every penny, in her mind.

The two women inside the vehicle were both in their street clothes, having changed in the parking lot once their cargo was properly stowed in the back. The garb for Diane's character, Sarah the Egyptian, rested in the back seat, each article of its assemblage folded neatly and placed in a sturdy brown grocery bag with handles. Her mask sat atop the bag and vibrated against a small wooden box. Inside the box were all the elements of the Scout costume her passenger had meticulously packed while in Gambel's parking lot.

Diane drove calmly but not too conservatively. She once heard that police cars patrolling for DWI's pulled people over for driving conspicuously slow on the assumption that everyone drives faster than the speed limit except those who are impaired, particularly by alcohol. Twenty miles further west, Summit Avenue still had farmland nestled up to the shoulder of the asphalt. However, the section of Summit that passed through Highland was a thick, four-lane corridor through urban sprawl. Its intersection with the north-south-running High Ridge Road brought city congestion to the otherwise free-flowing traffic grid.

These women were driving eastbound toward the intersection. Street lights and the mingling clientele from several all-night shops made disposing of the body a considerable challenge. Both of them seemed to have picked up on the ire in Trajan's voice when he reminded them to be careful. His ire quickly grew into their own when they both saw the flashing lights from the police cars on the north side of the next block at High-Sum corner.

"What is this?" Therese said.

"Stay calm. We're just a couple gals out on the town."

"At two in the morning? On a Tuesday?"

"Look around," Diane stated simply while looking at the handfuls of cars traveling in all directions. "We're not the only ones out here."

"Well, we're certainly the only ones with a corpse in the trunk."

Diane let loose with a Cheshire cat smile. "How can you be so sure?"

Therese stared back at her, a perplexing look on her face.

Diane felt empowered. There was no sign on the roof telling people there was a body in the back. From the outside looking in, their vehicle was as plain and ordinary as any other. Diane felt a warm ball of growing self-assurance well beneath her sternum.

The light changed and they crossed High Ridge with the other night travelers. Half a block past the intersection a police car sat in the entrance of an alleyway. From the glimpse they were able to steal from Diane's half-rolled-down window there must have been a dozen people, most of them police officers, milling about the parking lot lit up by blinding spotlights beaming down from high on their stanchions. The low but audible hum of generators and the intermediate traffic thwarted their attempts to hear anything as they passed.

"What now?" Theresa asked.

The two of them drove on in silence as Diane turned right at the end of the block.

"Okay," Therese offered. "We do exactly what we came to do, and we do it rationally and responsibly like Trajan said. Remember? We need to push back our fear and apprehension. We have to clear our minds. We just have to be calm and everything will be fine."

"Therese, I don't think this is what he was talking about."

"This is exactly what he was talking about, Diane," Therese said. "These are the kinds of things I've never been able to handle. I'd always run away. It's why I joined the Commuters. I don't want to run anymore, Diane. We can handle this."

Diane took her eyes off the road for just a second but it was more than enough time to see the focused determination in her passenger's eyes. At the end of the next block, she took another right.

"Okay, what now?"

"Look, Highland's not that big. Every cop in town was probably in that alley and those that weren't are either at home, at the station, or on patrol miles away. Take another right up here onto High Ridge."

"And drive toward the cops?" Diane shouted.

"Yes. We'll just pull into the alley on the left and dump the body back there. They'll be a full block and a couple thousand tons of brick and cement away. It's perfect."

Diane shook her head as she turned onto High Ridge Road. "Uh-huh, perfect. You've been to one ceremony and you think you're some kind of queen of the world."

"No, not the queen. But maybe a dame or a lady, something with a title. I'm telling you, Diane, this is perfect."

Diane could almost see the adrenaline coursing through Therese's system. Her passenger's foot tapped the floorboard like a happy dog's tail and her head snapped around in all directions to soak in as much of the scene as possible. It appeared to Diane that for the first time ever, Therese had overridden her flight instinct and stayed her ground.

Pulling across the wide expanse of the street into the alley just a half block south and a half block west of where the police car sat with its lights flashing, Diane had to be careful to avoid the unusually high volume of pedestrians flowing from the alleyway behind them. She thought about Trajan's comments. Yes, they were pushing back their fear and apprehension, but at the moment the rationality and responsibility of their plan was highly suspect.

"I don't know about this, Therese."

"Are you kiddin' me? This is perfect. Look, there's a line of dumpsters right over there. We park, check out the scene and go about our business like it's no big deal."

"What about all these people? Where are they all coming from?"

"A bar. A party. There're hundreds of possibilities. All I know is I have never felt so right about anything in my whole life."

Diane didn't know Therese especially well, but from what she did know, this seemed out of character, reckless and impulsive. They were co-workers who, until a little more than a year ago, didn't even know the other existed. Then one day in the cafeteria, Diane noticed Therese reading *You Are the Answer*. It was one of the hundreds of self-help books she had also read before finding the Commuters. They struck up a conversation and discovered they'd both attended dozens of the same "Fulfillment" seminars and "Actualization" groups hoping to wake the dormant power broker they felt languished inside of themselves. Each program had its own slogan which was invariably a variation on a single theme: "Be the most wonderful you possible." And they all fell short of expectations, leaving them just a bit more desperate for an answer each time. It was during those conversations that Diane noticed Therese "looking for a ride," as it was called during Commuter initiation, and she began the slow process of exposing Therese to the possibility of joining.

It was Recruitment 101 and Diane took it as seriously as all those who had come before her because to recruit another was the single most important duty of every new member. Diane had been approached by her neighbor down the block—known to group members as Physiologus, the "smart, brave and beautiful" unicorn—a little more than two years ago under the same auspices. They called it picking up a hitchhiker, or finding someone who had neither the means nor the direction to get somewhere and offering what they sought, what everyone seeks: more.

Diane parked her Civic just behind a large, green dumpster that had both its left and right black lids flipped up and leaning against the block wall of the building. She extinguished the lights and the ignition. "Look," she finally said. "I'll sit here for a few minutes and let these people filter out, but I am not sitting here all night."

"Fine, fine. Fifteen minutes. If the alley isn't completely empty in fifteen minutes, we'll go a block or two further west. I just want to do what's expected of me—put the body back in the same place it was taken from."

Neither spoke for what seemed an hour to Diane, until Therese exploded. "God, this is incredible, isn't it? I'm, like, so totally wired right now."

"Really? I hadn't noticed."

"Don't you feel it? I mean, if not now, didn't you feel it last year? The clarity of thought, the singularity of focus, the complete understanding of what to do? This is incredible, just incredible."

The two women stared out the windshield and watched dozens of people escape into the night. Diane sat with her arms propped on the steering wheel wondering what could possibly have happened for so many people to be heading for their cars all at once at this very moment.

* * *

Michael Stevens was Hollywood's newest star. After five years of consistent and legitimate, yet unremarkable work, he found himself cast as the lead in the small, independent film *John Horse*. It was the story of the son of a slave and an Indian warrior who, along with four hundred other "Black Seminoles," hid deep in the swamps of Florida on Christmas day, 1837, preparing to face Colonel Zachary Taylor and a thousand U.S. soldiers in what would be the final major battle of the largest and bloodiest slave rebellion in U.S. history. The movie received critical acclaim, took home a roomful of hardware, and made Michael Stevens an instant star.

Faith Underhill stood in front of her seat watching the final credits of *Grey Matter* slowly scroll up the largest screen in the metropolitan area. Faith had gone online weeks prior to secure her ticket to the midnight show at the Ridgeway Theater, the very first screening of Michael Stevens' follow-up to *John Horse*. She was completely enamored with his striking features and soft spoken demeanor, not to mention his defiance of white oppression, and she wanted to see him in all his thirty-five foot glory before anyone could tell her what they thought of the movie or of his performance.

As they made their way out of the theater, most of the audience members complained that the movie skimped on the details that provided depth to the characters and were essential to the success of the graphic novel. Faith, on the other hand, thought it a great film. She didn't read too many books, let alone comic books or graphic novels, so she had nothing to which to compare it. Besides, she had all but ignored the plot. Instead, she focused on the soft lines of the face and the undulating inflections of the voice that made her feel like a schoolgirl pining for a member of the latest mass-produced R&B boy band.

She had no idea what she was looking for in the final credits, but stood there nonetheless, fixated on the studio caterer, the long list of songs used by permission, the cities' chambers of commerce that were offered the producers' many thanks. When the house lights came up and the curtains were drawn across the screen, she turned to grab her jacket and noticed she was the only person left in the theater.

On her way toward the front exit, she made a stop in the ladies room to dispense the large soda she had bought at the concession stand and consumed during the film. While sitting on the toilet seat, she rummaged for her car keys and discovered them missing. A sudden anxiety came over her. She clumsily grabbed a few squares of toilet tissue, wiped and redressed before running out of the stall and back into the theater. She tried to remember in which row she had sat during the movie and side-stepped toward the middle. She bent down to find her keys but to no avail. She strode one row forward over the rocking seats and inspected the floor there with similar results. She then strode two rows back, certain she was in the right vicinity and gave a gasp of relief when she heard the gentle jingle of keys when her hand swept over them.

"Everything okay, ma'am?" a young red-haired usher asked. He stood awkwardly in the wide aisle between the elevated seats where Faith was and the reclining orchestra seats that were so popular with the teenagers.

"Yeah. I'm fine. I dropped my keys, but I found them."

"Um, okay," he muttered.

She skittered past him and headed down the aisle. Then she suddenly stopped and pointed to the exit door in the front corner of the theater. "Can I go out that way to go to the lot behind Spanky's leather shop?"

"Yeah, sure. It's actually faster."

She passed by him and walked toward the exit. As she did so, she watched him lower his sightline and focus on the tight, rounded pockets of her jeans swing with her movements.

"Thank you," she said, startling him, as she pushed the metal bar to open the heavy door.

The tall, gangly boy's "G'night" was inaudible under the screeching creaks of the old hinges and Faith wished she had gone out the front door instead. But, as the cold night air hit her face, she pressed on and let the door swing back closed behind her. She grabbed her key ring in the palm of her hand and stuck two keys up between her fingers, one between her index and middle fingers, the other between her middle and ring fingers. She saw a woman in a movie do it to thwart an attack by two shady characters. It gave her a sense of security.

She walked quietly down the alley toward High Ridge Road, smelling the lingering odors left from the industrial garbage bins that lined the building walls.

* * *

Traffic on Club Road was meager but present. In that neighborhood, at that time of night, plenty of people needed to be somewhere else. Uncle Max had made his way from the apartment where he was staying to Lionel's Pawn Shop, a few blocks west of Salem's Lot, careful not to jingle the pair of coins in his pocket as he walked. When they did bang against each other, they gave a deep, resonant thud rather than the usual, tinny sound of today's coins. Uncle Max needed cash to get his car out of the impound lot and the coins were his only options.

He shuffled up to the shop's thick, reinforced glass window. The man on the other side of the window sat watching sports highlights on a small television

"'Scuse me," Uncle Max said. When the man showed no reaction, he said it louder.

The man turned. "Yeah?"

"I got some coins to sell?"

"Oh yeah? What kind of coins?"

"Old coins."

The man paused, as if debating with himself whether or not it was worth seeing what the old man was offering. He clicked the remote control and the TV turned off.

He approached the window from the opposite side. "Gold coins, you say."

"Yeah, they's gold. But more than that, they's old. Real old."

"Come on, Uncle Max. You're in here selling low-end electronics and costume jewelry and shit like that. Where's an old man like you get his hands on some gold coins?"

"I've had 'em a while. Usually don't need more than a few bucks at a time, so I held on to 'em."

"All right," the man said, "let me take a look. Meet me at the front door."

By the time Uncle Max had shuffled around the corner to the front of the building, the man was already there holding the door open, looking suspiciously to his left and right. "Come on, Uncle Max, hurry up."

Uncle Max was unceremoniously swept into the pawn shop as the man quickly locked the door. The man then grabbed a stool and placed it in front of the glass case displaying various coins and medallions. Then, he went around to the back side of the case, pulled out a black velvet cloth and laid it out on the glass top.

"So whadda'ya got?"

"You prob'ly need to call Lionel for these coins."

"Oh yeah? Why's that?"

"'Cause he gonna want 'em and they's worth more than you allowed to spend."

"Bullshit. Let me see 'em."

Uncle Max reached into his pocket, pulled out the coins and placed them on the cloth. They gleamed in the dim, overhead light of the shop. Identical in size, weight and depiction, each was boldly struck with deep, clear edges and neither showed any signs of wear.

The man behind the counter stared at them a long time before asking, "You mind if I touch 'em?"

"Go 'head."

The man picked up one of the coins, measured its general heft and then turned it over, revealing a similarly flawless back.

"You didn't steal these, did you, Uncle Max?"

"I ain't no thief," he said, indignant.

The man continued to stare at the coin in his hand, speaking to Uncle Max as if he were a ghost. "These gotta be worth a couple thousand dollars apiece."

"More'an'at, I s'pose. So, you gonna call Lionel?"

"He's gonna be pissed I got him out of bed," the man said reaching for the phone. "But he'll be even more pissed if I let you walk out the door with these."

* * *

"Seriously, where did all these people come from?" Diane asked.

"It's just past two in the morning. I'm sure a bar just closed."

"But look," Diane pointed. "There must be fifty people getting into their cars, and all of them are coming from the alley."

"What's it matter? They come in one big wave and then they all leave. That makes it even better for us."

"I know it's no big deal, I'm curious is all. Don't you ever get that? You see something that just seems odd and you can't let it go until you figure out why. Like a word you've seen a thousand times that looks like it's spelled wrong and you can't do anything else until you look it up in the dictionary."

Diane's co-worker stared back at her with a blank expression.

"Forget it."

They both watched the line of cars escape the alleyway. It grew smaller and smaller until there were only a few cars left in the lot and no one walking toward any of them.

"What do you think?" Therese whispered.

"This is your idea. I'm just here to help."

"True, but it's both our asses if we get caught."

Caught dumping a murder victim's body into a city dumpster. Was it worth the risk, this unspoken promise of a better life? The same thoughts Trajan had contemplated forty-five minutes prior where running through Diane's head, the only difference being a shift in perspective—Trajan looking back, Diane looking forward. A nervous warmth swelled inside her as each woman pulled on a new set of latex gloves.

"If it were up to me, we'd go somewhere else. But seeing as how you're so determined to do this thing here and now, this seems like as good a time as any."

Diane popped the hatchback and the women shot out of their doors, leaving them wide open for a quick and easy return to its comfortable familiarity.

Diane lifted the hatch. "You get the feet and pull them out, I'll get it up top."

The legs were fairly simple to pull out and the two of them were able to maneuver what Diane assumed was the victim's rear end onto the bumper, but the upper body was far more unwieldy and cumbersome than anticipated. The plastic tarp, hardened by the night's chill, crinkled and rustled as the body fell against the pavement just to the side of the nearest dumpster.

"Damn, this is heavy," Diane whispered. "Forget the legs and grab the thighs."

Therese moved up and did as she was told. The new position put the women in much closer proximity to one another than before and they found themselves fighting for workspace.

"Wait, let me get a good grip first."

Diane sat the body up, squatted behind it and wrapped her arms around the biceps and chest. She motioned to Therese to do her part. Therese squatted down low and slipped her arms around the thighs.

"On three," Therese said. "One. Two. Three."

They each lifted on cue, the body shifting as it rose. The women were able to steady it reasonably well as Therese hoisted the bulk of the weight up onto her shoulder. They shuffled a few steps toward the dumpster, grunting as they did. Therese raised her elbow to clear the dumpster's front lip and, when she did, leaned against the cold steel box with her underarm. Diane struggled to lift the torso of the body high enough to get it over the lip, but when she did, she gave it a solid shove.

The plastic wrapped body teetered on the lip of the dumpster. Diane felt the force of gravity working against her until Therese gave it one last shove. That, along with Diane's twisting of the knees, sent the vessel over the edge. It dropped like a stone onto the bags of refuse piled inside.

* * *

Faith crossed the surprisingly busy street and continued down the alleyway toward her red Ford Focus. Two women further down the alley were struggling to throw away something very large, mostly red and wrapped in plastic. She could tell the item was heavy by the women's movements. When they were finally able to get the item over the edge of the dumpster, the two women shut the plastic dumpster lids and circled back to either side of the car. The woman getting into the passenger door, which opened into the alley, pulled off a pair of latex gloves and she crumpled into the car's front seat.

Faith sensed something odd. Two women. Two in the morning. Both car doors wide open. A large, heavy thing wrapped in plastic. Latex gloves. Her mind tried to make sense of it all in an instant as the doors closed and the car pulled away. She instinctively looked at the license plate.

She remembered a game her grandmother had taught her as a way to be as safe as could be expected in the unsafe neighborhood in which she grew up. When the two walked together, through a department store, or a grocery store, or a parking lot, or even a playground, her grandmother would ask, "What if someone robbed that department store. What would you tell the police if they asked you what you saw?"

As she grew older, her answers grew in greater detail. "A man in a brown coat and black pants," when she was seven grew to, "An unshaven black man a little less than six feet tall wearing a dirty, brown corduroy jacket with fleece lining and black pants with a sharp crease and cuffed bottoms," when she was twelve. It was, as she came to realize later, her grandmother's way of ensuring she pay attention to her surroundings. *Luck favors the prepared mind* was one of her grandmother's favorite sayings.

Working in the insurance company taught her that bad things happen to everyone. Listening to her grandmother and playing those kinds of games taught her that most bad things can be avoided by simply seeing the first sign of trouble and getting the hell out of its way.

"Two white women, the one on the passenger side wearing a blue flannel shirt and jeans, the one driving wearing a long-sleeve white t-shirt and blue sweat pants, both with brown hair, threw something big, red and heavy wrapped in plastic into the dumpster," she looked at her watch, "at about two-fifteen in the morning. They got into a black Honda Civic, license plate number 655-321. It went out the west exit and turned north."

Then, as a memory aid, another of her grandmother's games, she repeated the number out loud five times: "Six, double five, three, two, one. Six, double five, three, two, one. Six, double five, three, two, one. Six, double five, three, two, one. Six, double five, three, two, one."

She avoided the dumpster and continued to her red Ford Focus. If trouble came looking for her, she could provide a proper answer regarding what happened that night in the parking lot behind Spanky's leather shop.

But she didn't dare go looking for trouble. She quickly walked past the garbage bin, got in her car and drove home.

CHAPTER 32

When Mitchell finally made it home, he was greeted by his panic-stricken wife.

"You said he'd be home by now," Prudy screamed. "You said he'd be fine. You said everything would be fine."

Mitchell barged past his wife and into the house, confused and unbelieving. His wife's sister, in her police uniform, sat in the den waiting to tell him what she'd already told his wife. Those thirty minutes he spent listening to Connie were exhausting. If not for the clock chiming in every fifteen minutes, he would have thought time didn't proceed. He concentrated on every word Connie offered so as to slot them into the complex matrix he had created in his mind. He compared and contrasted the evidence the police offered with what he remembered from the soliloquy Helios had given to the Commuters. Had Helios thought his son was a "stain on society" simply standing there on the corner of High-Sum, the "breeding ground for societal disease?" Had he been the Matriculating Commuter and watched as the life of his own son was taken? Had the cup from which he sipped contained the blood of his own blood?

This final thought caught in Mitchell's mind. He began to sweat and his lips grew moist with saliva. His stomach clenched. He thought about excusing himself but before he could utter a word, he vomited, mostly on the tea set tray, but also on the ottoman on which it rested and the carpet all around it.

"Oh, God," Prudy gasped, clutching her face.

Mitchell ran from the den and knelt before the toilet, heaving heavily from the depths of his bowels until there was nothing left in him. Even empty, his body's reflexes continued convulsing while offering no more substance. A physical manifestation of his soul, he thought to himself. After a few moments, the convulsions stopped. Mitchell stood before the bathroom vanity, filled with self-loathing by the mere sight of the murderous man staring back at him. He tried to cleanse his conscience by washing his face and swishing with mouthwash before rejoining his wife and his sister-in-law in the den.

Connie was on her hands and knees wiping up his stomach's previous contents while his wife sat, almost fetal, in her chair. He got down on one knee and said softly into Connie's ear, "We have to get down to that corner, Connie."

"There's nothing we can do down there. The police—"

"You and me," he whispered forcibly, "Right now."

He looked into her eyes and knew she understood. He was going with or without her.

"What about Prudy?" she asked.

He instantly stood up. "Prudy. Connie and I are heading down to the parking lot to see if there's something the police missed. You stay here in case anyone calls, all right?"

Prudy sat still and said nothing. Mitchell felt guilty leaving her in such a sorrowful condition, but he had more important things on his mind than the fragile emotional state of his wife.

"C'mon," he urged, walking briskly out the door, forcing Connie to abandon her carpet cleaning efforts and chase after him.

He escaped into the garage with his sister-in-law trailing behind him. He opened the passenger door and collected his Trajan costume, throwing it into the vacant leg-space behind the front passenger seat. Connie had barely shut her car door before Mitchell backed his BMW into the driveway and punched the automatic door opener.

"What's going on, Mitch?"

There was only one person Mitchell allowed to call him Mitch and that was Connie. From everyone else's lips, the name sounded like "bitch" with an M in front of it. Coming from Connie, on the other hand, it sounded pleasant and friendly, even chummy.

"Connie," he started, trying to find the best way to explain his actions. He paused a very long time at the end of the driveway before pulling out. "I need you to help me find Davis."

"I will, Mitch. The police are—"

"Not the police, Connie. You and me."

"I'm gonna ask again, Mitchell, what's going on?"

If the tone in her voice didn't tell him she was losing patience, the fact that she called him by his full first name did. "I think I know what happened to Davis and I need you to figure out a way to help me find him without involving the police."

"You do realize that I am the police, right?"

"I mean the other police."

She studied him closely. "Did you have anything to do with this?"

He pulled up to a stop sign and stared directly into her eyes. "No. But, I can't tell you anything more until you give me your word that what I say stays between us. It doesn't get filed in any report. It's not leaked to some detective working the case. You don't tell Prudy or the kids. It's just you and me, the two of us, working this thing through."

* * *

It's just you and me, the two of us, working this thing through.

Connie had heard her brother-in-law say those exact same words almost twenty years earlier. They sat in the den, Connie and Mitchell, sharing a bottle of surprisingly strong wine Mitchell had brought back from a business trip to France. Her sister, pregnant with Lowell, nipped modestly at her shallow pour—her alcoholism wouldn't show itself for a dozen years—before exiting the room to make dinner. Connie eased into her chair as the alcohol slowly took effect. They talked in fits and spurts about the weather, Mitchell's sightseeing exploits in Paris, her evolving career aspirations in law enforcement. That led Connie to talk about one of her supervisors, a Sergeant Cohoe.

"You know, like the salmon. So this fish-faced bastard tells me that, as a woman, if I ever want to make detective, I gotta screw my way up the ranks."

"Is that true? Is that the only way to get a promotion?"

"Well ... no. There are plenty of woman who make it on merit. Plenty. But I personally know of at least four lieutenants who got there by ...," she looked to see that Prudy was out of earshot, "shining the brass pole."

Mitchell didn't smile as she had expected. He just leaned in and asked, "And this Cohoe?"

"What about him?"

"Is he looking for you to ... you know."

She laughed. "In his dreams."

He persisted. "Is he bothering you?"

She hesitated.

"Because if he's bothering you, I know a lot of people."

"Oh, Jesus, Mitch. The last thing I need is for you to fight my battles for me."

"No, no, nothing like that. I wouldn't bother going through regular channels. There are other ways to get things done."

Amused to see her conservative brother-in-law offer up some kind of clandestine scheme to fix what she considered only a minor problem she egged him on. "Oh yeah? What other ways?"

"It's just you and me, Connie, the two of us, working this thing through, right?"

"Working what through?"

Mitchell was deep in thought, and didn't hear her.

"Working what through, Mitchell?"

He visibly snapped out of his trance. "What? Oh, nothing. Forget it. I just thought I could help, but if you want me to stay out of it—"

"I do."

"Consider me out."

Two weeks later, an anonymous tip to Korova City Internal Affairs led to the arrest of Sergeant Cohoe. Boxes and boxes of child pornography were found in his basement. He was subsequently tried and sentenced to seven years in prison where he was killed six months later by another inmate.

It's just you and me, the two of us, working this thing through.

For whatever reason, she could never fully understand why those words stuck in her mind. Yet they did, and it frightened her to hear them again.

* * *

Connie hesitated. "Sure, okay. You and me, the two of us, working this thing through."

Mitchell stared at her even more intently. She gave him a curious look that he couldn't quite decipher. He looked around to make sure there were no cars, forgetting it was nearly 2:30 in the morning, and drove on through the intersection.

"I belong to this club. We have these parties once in a while."

"You belong to a sex club?"

"It's not a sex club. Jeez, Connie. Will you let me talk?" He took this moment to develop a plausible alternative. "It's more of a, umm, support group. We gather around and help each other find our bliss, crap like that. I haven't told anyone because I'm supposed to be this powerful businessman and I don't want people thinking I'm weak."

He looked over to see if she believed him. The look in her eyes suggested she didn't.

"So tonight, this guy in the group tells me he's sick and tired of certain elements of society, particularly young, male prostitutes, and he says he wishes they would just go away."

"I don't see why you just don't tell the police all this."

"No!" It came out much too harshly. "No. You and me, remember?

"Yeah, but—"

"You and me, Connie. You gave me your word and I'm holding you to it. Now let me finish. So, this guy, he said if it were up to him, he'd take care of it himself."

"You got a name?"

Helios the sun god was all he could think of. "No, we don't address each other by name. That's one of the reasons I like this particular group."

"Then how do you talk to each other?"

"Everyone uses a pseudonym. You know what that is?"

"I'm a police officer, Mitch, not a high school dropout."

"Of course you are, of course, my apologies. I'm out of sorts, here."

Then, thinking back on the evening, he remembered something that he had thought about years ago when he first joined the Commuters, that everyone drove their own cars to the ceremonies. If anyone really wanted to know the other members' identities, all anyone needed to do was run the license plates of all the vehicles that sat in the otherwise empty parking lot, field or gravel road leading to the ceremony.

Mitchell tried to remember the vehicles he saw that evening. He remembered Arwen, the elven queen, coming out of a Pontiac Solaris. But no other vehicle registered other than the one closest to the doorway. Logically, since it was Helios' responsibility to bring the victim, Mitchell presumed he would have parked closest to the door.

"I think he drives a green car, though. And it has a dinged up headlight."

"Make and model?"

"I don't know. It looked cheap, though. Domestic. That should narrow the focus a little, shouldn't it?"

"If he filed an insurance claim, maybe."

"How many can there be? Seriously? Twenty? Twenty-five?"

"I'll check it out. But don't get your hopes up. There are probably a lot more of them than you think. Hell, I rang one up tonight in the middle of Salem's Lot," she said as she wrote notes. "Anything else you can remember?"

Helios' disturbing ramblings filled his mind as he drove. *A stain on society; the dirty towels that hung in the hotel rooms; gagged him, bound him; took him to a special place I have where I could prepare him; that was last week; hirudo medicinalis; a handful of leeches.*

Mitchell's seat belt dug deep into his left shoulder as he slammed on the brakes and brought the car to a complete stop. His body was hurled back when the car's suspension recoiled from its forward momentum. He looked over at his passenger. On her face was the look of a woman completely lost in a foreign moment.

"What the fuck, Mitch?"

"It wasn't him," he mouthed.

"Who wasn't him?"

He tilted his head slightly, still wearing his smile. "Never mind."

He realized, at the very least, he hadn't drunk his son's blood. Helios said he needed a week to prepare his vessel for the ceremony. That minute detail gave him overwhelming comfort because it also meant that his son was probably still alive at Helios's "special place," wherever that might be. He pressed the accelerator and continued on toward Highland's High-Sum corner.

"Never mind? Mitch, you're not being straight with me. Stop screwing around and tell me what is going on."

He tried to sell his sister-in-law on the idea that he was on the level but she wasn't buying. Mitchell knew that during the course of a regular shift, his sister-in-law heard more lies than truths and was probably able to detect which was which as easily as he could.

"You're full of shit. Mitch. You know it and I know it. And if it wasn't for those city detectives who saw you drive off, I'd think you just might have had something to do with all of this."

"God, Connie, you know how much I love those boys. You know I'd never do anything to hurt Davis, to hurt either of them. Or Prudy."

"Yeah, but you're acting all weird on me, Mitch. Rest assured, if you had anything to do with Davis going missing I'll personally fuck you up. Understand?"

"Fine," he dismissed. "I'm a liar and I'm acting weird, but I didn't have anything to do with whatever happened to my boy. I know you know that. If we can both agree on that then you can take me off your suspect list, we can get on the same page and move forward."

They drove the next few minutes listening to the purr of the engine and the hum of the tires against the asphalt. Fairly certain his son was not the vessel on the bar at the ceremony, Mitchell concluded he didn't need to find the body. He knew it would be found soon enough if Sarah the Egyptian and Scout performed their requisite task. He figured that miraculously finding the body somewhere within a one block radius of the High-Sum corner would only add to his sister-in-law's well-placed suspicions.

He set his immediate goals on talking to the city detectives. From what Connie said to him in the den, he needed to discover just how close they were to the Commuters and steer them in a different direction if at all possible. Mitchell knew, as all Commuters eventually came to realize, that no matter how thin their thread of connectivity, there was still a thread, and it linked all members to one another—past, present and future. More importantly, Mitchell came to realize that the group is only as strong as the weakest link in the chain. If one member were to fall under the suspicion of the police for any one of the multitude of crimes they as a group committed, then all members were just a series of interrogations away from suspicion and possible reprisal. No matter how meticulous and careful they were in selecting and abducting their victims, selecting and securing the locations, preparing and disposing of the bodies, one slip and down the hole they all fell. Mitchell might have matriculated out of participation, but he was not completely out. No one ever was unless, like Natalie Belling, once the aura of immortality was gone you became an empty vessel.

They drove the lighted streets of downtown Highland to the corner of Summit Avenue and High Ridge Road. The banks of lights at the crime scene flooded the entrance of the alleyway and spilled out into the street. Mitchell wondered if it was like this when Sarah the Egyptian and Scout had driven there to complete their duties. Unable to turn into the alleyway directly, due to the median in the road, Connie directed him to turn left a block early and then right, to approach the parking lot from the other side.

Several media vans were double parked in the street, so Mitchell drove a ways up and found street parking. As they approached the lot entrance, Mitchell did his best to keep his face hidden from the media. But this was the night shift, he thought, the second and sometimes third-tier on-air talent. They were mostly young and inexperienced, far more familiar with pop-culture's sports and entertainment stars than with local business leaders. However, Mitchell felt *better safe than sorry* was the proper course of action and continued to hide his face.

After just a few words from Connie, one of the officers on crowd control allowed the two into the inner sanctum of the crime scene. As they walked, she explained, "If we're going to play outside the lines, here, Mitch, you gotta let me do all the talking. And do what you can to answer any direct questions with simple, truthful answers. Anything you need to lie about, don't look around and fumble for an answer, just say 'I'm not sure.' Got it?"

"Got it."

"You know you're a terrible liar, don't you Mitch?" It seemed to Mitchell an attempt to lighten the mood. "How can you be such a successful businessman and not be able to lie?"

If only you knew how long and how well I've been lying to everyone, he thought to himself. Aloud, he said, "Well, my clients—"

"Whoa, whoa, whoa. That was a joke," she said abruptly. "God, you have got to lighten up. Just keep your eyes and ears open … and your mouth shut."

He took her words to heart and simply nodded.

The parking lot was hot with activity. The crime scene unit from the Highland police department was taking photos and collecting evidence and generally busying themselves with their various tasks. Mitchell looked around for the two Korova City detectives and was perplexed after searching for a few moments in vain.

Connie tapped one of the worker bees on the shoulder.

"Who's running this show?"

A woman wearing a CSU jacket scanning the ground a few feet away stood up. "I am."

She was small in stature, her jacket billowing around her torso like inflated muscles, yet her face was stern and her disposition imposing without being oppressive. She stood and continued her work examining the ground from her newer, heightened vantage point.

Mitchell followed as Connie walked over with her hand extended. "I'm Officer Wyszczyzewski. I called in the missing person. Do you know where detectives Brown and Watts are?"

"Who's this?" she asked pointing to Mitchell without looking at him.

"This is my ...," she stopped herself. "He's the missing boy's father."

"And you brought him here? Do you really think that's wise?"

"Actually, he brought me. He was rather determined to come down here and since I couldn't stop him I figured it best to accompany him and try to keep him out of the way."

"I see," she snapped, finally looking at Mitchell. Her disapproval of his presence was evident. "Another call came in." In an aside, she whispered to Connie, "A body was found in a dumpster kitty-corner from here." she said it very matter-of-factly, making a motion with her finger as if indicating that the two detectives had jumped over the buildings in between to get there. "Brown and Watts are over there."

Mitchell heard the whispered discussion but made no comment or reaction.

"Mitch, are you okay?"

"Yeah, fine. Let's find those detectives."

"I'm not sure it's such a good idea for you to go over there. Didn't you hear what she said? They found a body."

Believing what he did, Mitchell paused to locate and then articulate the proper response. "If it's Davis, I need to see him now. But I'm hoping it's not him."

Connie seemed to look past him as he spoke and a strange pall came over her face. "It wasn't him," she muttered. Then, looking directly into his eyes, "That's what you said in the car.'"

Again searching to articulate the proper response, "What? No, that was ..."

Her face gnarled and she pushed him hard. "Get back in the damned car."

Mitchell was pushed and nudged until they were outside the crime scene and walking to his car. Mitchell got in and turned the key as Connie made her way to the passenger side. Immediately upon shutting her door, she laid into him.

"How do you know that body in the dumpster isn't Davis?"

"I'm not sure, officer."

"Officer? I'll pull my revolver and beat your ass if you keep up this bullshit, you lying—"

"Connie."

"What? What, Mitchell? What else do you know? What else are you hiding?"

"I'm not hiding anything and I don't know anything more than what I already told you."

"Bullshit!"

"No, I'm serious. Okay, wait, this guy, from the group, he said if he were to do it, he would need to keep them a week to prepare them. The boys you told me about. They were all taken on a Tuesday and then one week later their bodies were found, right? That's what you said. So if that's the pattern—"

"Then we've got a week to find Davis," Connie finished, nearly dumbstruck.

He turned and looked at her sternly, "I need you to help me find him, Connie."

She looked at him for a very long time, squinting her eyes to study his face before replying. "You are not making this easy. Let's get over there. And remember, you keep your lying mouth shut."

CHAPTER 33

Having already escorted his boss to the bank drop box around the corner and ensured all exit doors were securely shut, Chad O'Donahue, the most senior member of the theater's ushers, made his way into the alleyway behind the theater a little after 2:30 a.m. It had been a long day. He looked forward to climbing into bed for a few hours of sleep before inevitably having to wake up, shower, eat and get to his nine o'clock psych class. He took a long draw of Sprite from the straw extending out of his McDonald's cup. The cup was left over from his dinner but its contents were relatively fresh from the theater's soda machine. He crossed High Ridge Road and continued to the parking lot behind Spanky's leather shop, emptying his cup along the way.

He pushed up the flimsy lid of one of the dumpsters that lined the alley to throw his cup away and glimpsed inside just long enough to see his cup careen off of what looked like someone's hand. The lid came down soft but quick as Chad took another step before the image he thought he saw fully registered. He stopped, turned and lifted the lid upright, resting it against the building wall. A pale, naked boy wrapped in a clear sheet of plastic rested atop several black twist-tie garbage bags.

At first, Chad didn't know if it was real or not. The two or three layers of plastic created a frosted effect that made the face, with its eyes and mouth closed, appear oddly distorted and unreal. It wasn't until Chad noticed the dark brown streaks on the inside portion of the plastic and the deep, dark wound on the body's chest that he understood what he was seeing.

He took a few steps back and dialed 911 on his cell.

In the alley about one block southeast from where Prudy's car was being dusted for fingerprints by the Highland police department's crime scene unit, a pair of Highland police officers responded to the call. Upon initial discussions with Chad and the verification of his assertions, they quickly secured the area. Detectives Brown and Watts soon followed, relegating the Highland police officers to bouncers and denying access to all other vehicles and individuals.

Anticipating the discovery of the body, Brown had already alerted a team of crime scene detectives from D1 that they might be asked to overstep their boundaries somewhere within the metro area sometime that morning. But not even Detective Brown believed he would be calling them in while it was still dark. He wanted fresh blood and this was fresher than he ever dreamed.

Brown questioned the red-haired boy who had called it in. He questioned the boy for quite a while, hoping to find some bit of information that could further his investigation immediately rather than having to wait for his CSU team to run their tests and report their findings. His tired mind and worn out body, reinvigorated once more with a boost of adrenaline and a steady flow of coffee, made him terse and edgy.

"So let's go over this again. You were just walking by and then what?"

Chad, apparently tired and edgy himself, repeated his story. "I threw my cup in and when I did, I saw it land on something that looked like a person. I double checked, saw the kid and dialed 911."

Unhappy that this rendition contained no new details, Brown lashed out. "So you make it a habit of throwing your garbage away on top of murder victims?"

The young man stood there confused, as if deciding whether or not the question was rhetorically sarcastic or seriously investigative. Before Chad could answer, Brown turned and walked toward the dumpster.

Watts walked over to the boy and said, "Don't worry about him, champ. He's just tired."

"So am I. Look, I called it in, I did my civic duty. Can I leave now?"

Watts handed him a business card. "Wait here. Which one's your car?"

The only way out was through the plastic yellow police tape which extended far beyond the dumpster due to a lack of vertical markers on which to tie off the tape. Chad pointed to a black pick-up truck parked against one of the far buildings.

Watts paused and looked back over his shoulder at his partner. "Hang on, kid. Let me see if I can't get you on your way."

Watts walked back to an angry Brown. A noise caught Brown's attention and he turned. He saw two people making their way past the officers and yellow tape at the alley's entrance. The first person was the city cop he met earlier, the other was a man he had never seen before.

"Mr. Treadwell?" Chad said quietly.

Mitchell replied, "Chad? Are you okay?"

Mitchell walked past Connie and over to the boy who simply nodded and said, "Just tired, really. It's been a long day, these cops won't let me leave and I gotta get up in," he checked his phone for the time, "holy shit, it's almost three-thirty." Then, looking at Mitchell he added, "Sorry about the language, sir."

Mitchell brushed his hand through the air as if to indicate it was no big deal. Then he pulled out a business card and feverishly wrote something on the back. Handing the card to Chad, Mitchell asked, "What are you doing here?"

"I closed tonight. I was throwing something away in a dumpster and found a dead body. I called 911. That's it. That's all I know. Now they won't let me leave. I got class tomorrow at nine."

"You found the body? Who was it?"

Chad looked confused. "I don't know. Some kid. I've seen him before, though. A couple times. I think he's a runaway or something, living on the streets."

"What the fuck are you doing?" Brown yelled from twenty feet away as he approached. Then turning to Connie, "Officer Whiskey Chef-ski, why are you allowing this person to interrupt my investigation? And why are you here?"

"This is Mitchell Treadwell, detective. My brother-in-law and the father of the missing boy. Maybe you could be a bit more accommodating?"

Chad shot a quick look at Mitchell. "Davis is missing?"

Detective Brown wedged himself between Mitchell and Chad. "You know the missing boy?" he asked Chad.

"Well, yeah. Davis and me work together. At the theater." Then looking past the detective, he said to Mitchell, "He came in tonight to watch a movie."

"To *watch* a movie?" asked Mitchell.

Chad gave a confused look to the detective who positioned his head directly between him and Mitchell Treadwell. "Yeah. *The Charger*, the early show. He left right when it was over."

"That part I know," Mitchell answered. "I actually saw him outside at about nine-thirty. Detectives, Chad here was just wond—"

"You can go," Brown barked, apparently making sure everyone in the area knew it was his decision to let the boy leave.

"Chad, you get some rest," Mitchell said, flagging Chad with a "call-me" gesture, his hand up to his ear with his thumb and pinkie extended.

Brown turned to Mitchell but too late to see the gesture.

Chad stuck his hands in his pocket quickly as he walked over to the officers by the alley entrance. Moments later, Chad made his way to his truck and ultimately out of the alleyway.

CHAPTER 34

"Mr. Treadwell, I'd rather not do this right here or right now, but I don't seem to have a choice. Do you mind if we ask you a few questions?"

Mitchell, a few inches taller than the policeman standing before him, purposely took a position so he could stare down at Brown. "Not at all. That's partly why we came over here."

"Partly?" Brown took a few steps back.

Mitchell, smiling on the inside, stared at the detective blankly. "Yes, partly."

"And the other reasons for your presence here?"

"To see if the boy in the dumpster was my son."

"I see." Brown paused a long while. "You seem very calm for someone potentially identifying his son's body."

"I was panicky earlier, but then Chad told me it wasn't Davis and it passed."

Mitchell wanted to say more and the look on the detective's face seemed to be pleading him to do so. *You know you're a terrible liar, don't you Mitch? Just keep your eyes and ears open and your mouth shut.* Connie's advice took hold just before Mitchell was about to launch into his alibi, an elaborate tapestry of half-truths and pure fiction he had started working on the moment he went into the bathroom to clean himself up. Instead, he said nothing.

They stood, staring face-to-face waiting for the other to speak first. Brown flinched.

"Did your wife tell you we questioned her this evening?"

"Yes."

"Can you tell me where you were this evening after you left your wife at home?"

You know you're a terrible liar, don't you Mitch?

"I was with my accountant."

"Your wife said you were going to the office."

"Yes. That's what I told her."

"So, you lied to your wife?"

"Yes."

"And you met your accountant at midnight on a Tuesday evening?"

"We had some very pressing issues."

"Pressing issues, I see."

Brown looked at Watts in an obvious manner that showed everyone in the alley his disbelief. He then looked at Connie.

"Officer Whiskey Chef-ski, what do you think about your brother-in-law meeting his accountant at midnight on a Tuesday to discuss pressing issues?"

Connie responded quickly. "His family's loaded. I think accountants meet rich people whenever rich people schedule the appointment."

Brown smiled wryly at her and returned his gaze on Mitchell who was also smiling.

"This accountant, what's his name?"

"Michael O'Donahue."

"O'Donahue? Isn't that the usher's name?"

"Yes. His father is my accountant."

"Well, isn't that a coincidence?"

"Not really," Mitchell snipped.

Mitchell thought Brown was taken aback by the comment, but the detective seemed to regain control of himself quickly. "Getting back to your wife, what else did she tell you?"

"Not much, really. Connie, Officer Wyszczyzewski, did most of the talking."

Again, Brown seemed to wait for more to come. His wait was in vain. Mitchell wasn't saying anything superfluous to this man.

"Okay, what did Officer Wyszczyzewski tell you?"

Mitchell recited his experience in the den in bullet points, giving only facts, no opinions. The only thing he omitted was the fact that he vomited.

"Does your son often lie to you about his comings and goings?"

Mitchell recognized the technique. Brown was asking him questions to elicit responses requiring an emotional foundation. He responded calmly, "You'd have to ask him that."

"Were you surprised to learn that your son was a prostitute?"

"You told my wife and Officer Wyszczyzewski that Davis was only on the corner for a few minutes and that I was the first and only car that approached him. My surprise is in your assertion that he *was* a prostitute."

Mitchell feigned indignation and pressed Brown for answers to the questions he had. "The Highland police are scouring the parking lot where my son was abducted for evidence they hope will lead to my son's return. Why aren't you doing the same? Why aren't you helping to find my son?"

A broad smile crept across Brown's face as he said, "I am, Mr. Treadwell. I'm questioning you."

Brown returned to writing in his notebook when Mitchell's ringtone chimed.

"Excuse me," Mitchell said turning away from the small group. He looked down at the phone and turned back, "I have to take this."

* * *

Brown pretended to ignore Mitchell and continued to write in his notebook, wondering who might be calling him at 3:45 in the morning.

"Your brother-in-law is hiding something."

"Is he?" Connie asked in a sarcastic tone.

"You know you can't keep him out of trouble, don't you officer?"

Brown stopped writing and looked over his notebook to evaluate Connie's reaction to the question.

"Look," she started, leaning close to Brown and speaking softly, "he treats my sister really well and he loves his kids. I'm certain he had nothing to do with Davis going missing."

"But you see it in his body language and hear it in his voice, don't you? He's hiding something."

"Maybe. I don't know. I told him straight out if he had anything to do with this that I'd take him down myself. And I would, too." Connie looked at Mitchell hunched over talking on the phone and Brown followed her eyes. "When he said his alibi was his accountant, I thought maybe he was hooked into an embezzlement scheme or something like that. But he's got more money than God. And besides that, he's a pretty straight arrow. I just don't see what—"

"Don't you worry about that, officer. If he's hiding something, I'll find out what it is. And when I do and if it has anything to do your nephew's disappearance, I'll let you wrap the steel around his wrists."

Brown watched as she continued her blank stare at Mitchell. Then he followed up with, "But you know, this confrontational attitude you seem to be showing isn't reflecting well on you. If I'm going to keep you in the loop, I need the same professional courtesy."

When she said nothing, he prodded again. "Blood may be thicker than water, officer, but a prison cell is no place for a policewoman."

Connie turned to face Brown. She had no discernible expression that Brown could see. "I know you're just doing your job, detective, but I'm on Davis's side here, no one else's. If I know anything that I think will help you find him, I'll tell you. And if I think telling you something I've discovered hinders your ability to find him, I won't. Simple as that. And if you think for a minute your threats, idle or otherwise, hold any influence over me, please be assured, they do not. I'm more frightened of warm mayonnaise."

* * *

When Mitchell pulled the phone from his ear and snapped it closed, Brown and Connie were both turned toward him. He noticed them quickly turn away so that he wouldn't think they were interested in his comings and goings. Brown reinforced the illusion of their disinterest with a loud, "So that's about all we got on the body."

To Mitchell, Brown continued. "Mr. Treadwell, I hope everything is okay."

"Yes, detective, thank you."

"And who might be calling you at this time of night?"

"I have many colleagues in Asia and Europe who call at reasonable hours. Reasonable for them, at least," he laughed. "Now, detective, if you're through, do you mind if I ask you some questions about the investigation?"

Connie's head snapped at Mitchell. He saw her strained face seeming to beg him to keep his mouth shut. He noticed Brown, too, catching the look Connie gave him.

Brown smiled and said, "You can ask, but I may not be at liberty to reveal some of the facts to you. You understand, of course?"

"Of course," Mitchell said quickly, fully expecting the detective to lie to him at every turn. "Connie told me that there were two other boys abducted and found?"

"Yes," Brown replied. Mitchell assumed he was implementing the strategy of answering only the question asked.

"Did you and Detective Watts handle the investigation of those other cases?"

"No we did not."

"This body," he said pointing to the dumpster, "Might it be a third?"

"We don't know that yet."

"And Davis, you think he's the fourth?"

"As I said, it hasn't been determined whether this boy," Brown pointed his pen over his shoulder in the direction of the dumpster, "is connected to the first two. Nor do we know whether your son's apparent abduction is connected to the first two or this one."

"Do you *think* they are connected?"

"There are several commonalities that make it a possibility and we're not ruling it out as yet," Brown answered.

"What makes you think the first two cases are connected?"

Brown paused. "I'm not sure I understand the question, Mr. Treadwell."

Mitchell Treadwell knew his name held the ear of everyone worth anything in the city, including Brown's bosses' bosses. He dug in further.

"Sure you do, detective. I'm asking you what evidence connects the first two cases that may or may not be present in the latter two cases."

"You sound like a defense attorney, Mr. Treadwell. I thought you were a businessman." Brown forced a laugh as he said it.

"I am a businessman, detective," Mitchell said, gaining control of the discussion. "Much like you, I review facts as they become available, make conclusions based on those facts and act on those conclusions until otherwise dissuaded by other, contradictory facts. Upon what facts are you concluding that the first two cases are connected and these other two are not?"

"I'm sorry, Mr. Treadwell, but that's confidential information."

"Fine. Keep it confidential. But please tell me, at first blush, is the same connective evidence that was present in the first two cases present in this case?" He again pointed to the dumpster.

"As I mentioned, there are similarities."

"And my son's case?"

"We're not sure, yet."

"Is it because you need a dead body?"

Brown's face went white. "I'm sorry?"

"Is your confidential connective evidence found during the investigation of the abduction or the investigation of the dead body?"

"Uhhh."

"Since you are here and not at the location where my son was abducted, I'll assume it's the latter. Is it only these cases or are there others?"

"This particular investigation is focused solely on these three, possibly four incidents."

"So there are enough similarities between the first two bodies and the third to link them together."

"That's not what I said," Brown stammered. "That was a simple slip-up."

"Okay. But I take it by your previous response, 'This particular investigation is focused solely on these three, possibly four incidents', that there is another investigation focused on other incidents?"

"Of course. The police are involved with hundreds of investigations at any given time."

Mitchell hammered away, wanting to know just how much Brown knew about the Commuters. "Are you, detective, involved with another investigation focused on other incidents of a similar nature?"

Though Brown tried to play it off as nothing more than an annoyance, Mitchell's question turned the detective's face tense. "That's enough, Mr. Treadwell," Brown said smiling. "I've been extremely cooperative and answered all the questions I'm prepared to answer at this time. If you want any more information about your son's case, I recommend you contact the primary detectives."

"Not you, detective?"

"No. Although I may contact you for additional information, you should contact the Highland Police Department."

"So the Highland police are in charge of my son's abduction and you're in charge of this long string of dead bodies."

Brown blanched. "I'm not at liberty to say."

"Thank you, detective." Then turning to his sister-in-law, "Connie, I think we should leave the detectives to their business."

"Don't you want to know about the body?" Connie asked Mitchell.

Mitchell looked at both Connie and Brown. "Do you think I should? Chad said it's not Davis, so …"

"Trust me, this is barbaric stuff you have no need knowing about," Brown answered. "But I do have one more question for you, Mr. Treadwell. I asked your sister-in-law if she thought you were hiding something. She thinks maybe you are. I'm curious, why do you think she wouldn't offer you complete absolution?"

Mitchell answered unflinchingly, "You'd have to ask her, detective."

"I did."

"And?" Mitchell coaxed.

"She thought embezzlement."

Mitchell smiled and looked at Connie.

She shouted at Brown, "And then I told you that it was ridiculous."

Mitchell kept his eyes on Brown, his smile unwavering. "Come on, Connie, let's get out of here."

"You will be making yourself available to the police for further questioning, won't you, Mr. Treadwell? Or should I be contacting your lawyer?" Brown called out.

Mitchell turned and saw that Brown hadn't even waited for a reply. He simply scribbled in his notebook and returned to his partner who had been overseeing the CSU further down the alleyway. Only a single media unit had made it to this particular crime scene and they were not prepared to capture footage of Mitchell Treadwell and his sister-in-law cop leaving the alley, nor was the on-camera talent prepared to chase after them for a story. The pair escaped with little notice.

CHAPTER 35

"Mitchell, don't listen to—"

"Connie," he interrupted. "Quiet. In the car."

The two of them walked quickly to his car parked just outside the perimeter sealed off by the police. Connie was trying to work the various conflicting and incongruous details into a plausible explanation. She looked at Mitchell and assumed he was doing the same. However, working from very different starting points, their pictures of the same landscape were undoubtedly quite different, she thought.

They got into the car and both began speaking as soon as their doors were shut, making it impossible for either to understand the other. Mitchell held up his hand and said, "Stop." He took a deep breath, "Whatever you said to Brown, I don't care. It's not important. And if in fact you told him I was embezzling money from my firm, you've done us both a huge favor. I'm not and it will be a big waste of his time to investigate.

"We're going to see Chad O'Donahue, the boy who found the body. He says a woman left right before he did and that she might have seen whatever it was that happened in the alley."

"When did you …?" Connie started, but stopped when she put two and two together. "The phone call." Then she shook her head, "This is a dangerous game you're playing, Mitch. You really pissed off Detective Brown. Don't you think we should let the detectives do the detective work?"

"No, I don't. Davis is already in trouble, right? The police are only interested in finding his killer. I want my son back. Alive."

"The police always want a double win every time they can get one. They want to save Davis just as much as they want to catch your support group freak."

"Perhaps that's the police's stance. But Detective Brown has more on his mind than finding Davis." The car eased away from the curb. "Brown and his partner were watching the corner. What do they call it? A stakeout? How did a couple of city detectives know the two boys' cases were related? The boys were from very different backgrounds. You said they were dumped in two different parts of the metro area. The only thing they had in common was the place from which they were taken, the same M.O."

Connie smiled and quipped, "You've been watching too much TV."

"Seriously, though, think about it. Brown and his partner were at that corner, not the Highland police. If anyone was going to figure it out, it would have been the Highland police because the boys were taken from the High-Sum corner. But it was two Korova City detectives who knew something was going on before anyone else did. Why?"

Connie mulled this over. "Soooo, what? You think Brown and Watts are involved?"

"No," he paused. "Expediency is the critical issue. We need to find ...." He stopped. "I think Brown and Watts ...." He stopped again. Connie looked at him and wondered what could possibly be going on inside his head. "I think those two have their own agenda and Davis is just a footnote on it. That's why we need to stay one step ahead of them."

Connie laughed, "I'm not sure you understand the way things work."

"I don't give a rat's ass how things work. All I care about is getting Davis back, and I know that's what you care about, too. You and me, Connie. That's what we agreed on. You and me. And we have got to find him quick."

"A week, right?"

His eyes locked on hers. "No, now."

She looked at her notebook in her lap and chuckled. "That's ridiculous. You said we had a week."

"You don't think the FBI is going to be interested in the abduction of my son? Homeless prostitutes are one thing, but the media loves a story about the affluent facing adversity. This is a ransom note away from being on every news outlet in America. I'd be surprised if Federal agents weren't already at the house with Prudy."

"Oh, God," Connie said. "We gotta get back to her."

"No," Mitchell barked. "We have to find Davis. Lowell will take care of Prudy. We have got to focus on getting Davis back."

"Prudy will crumble without one of us there."

"I don't think so. And I don't think the FBI are involved. At least not yet. But even putting all that aside, Prudy will be worse if we don't find her baby."

"Jesus H, Mitchell. What is going on here?"

"I'm paying the price for success, Connie. Karmic retribution, that's what's going on."

She wanted to call her partner to get his opinion because she was certain he'd tell her to follow procedures. She wanted to scream at her brother-in-law and tell him that it was wrong—all of it. She wanted to call her sister to assure her that things were going well. She pulled out her phone and dialed the first six digits waiting to press the seventh.

"Don't call Prudy, Connie. She needs rest more than support."

Connie canceled the call and slouched in her seat, looking out the windshield as they drove through the lighted streets of Highland on their way to visit a material witness that Brown and Watts thought unimportant.

CHAPTER 36

It was still dark out when Mitchell and Connie pulled up to an unkempt bungalow a few blocks north of the city's prestigious Jesuit university campus. Mitchell grabbed two of the three large cups of coffee from the gray cardboard carrier that Connie placed on the hood of his car. Connie pulled the final cup from the carrier's friction-grip and followed Mitchell up the cracked cement stairs leading to the poorly maintained front porch. When they reached the top of the stairs, Mitchell stepped back to allow Connie to move ahead and knock with her free hand. The screens on the exterior door were missing.

"Lovely," she smirked and rapped on the door.

The door opened immediately. It was Chad O'Donahue. He looked at Mitchell and then at Connie. Then he looked over his shoulder back into the house, closed the door and quickly returned with a zippered sweat jacket in his hand.

"We should probably talk out here," Chad said pushing the screen door aside. "One of my roommates, he's on the couch."

"Coffee," Mitchell offered.

"No, thanks. I actually have delusions of sleeping sometime tonight. Look, I don't know what more I can tell you that I didn't already tell Officer Brown."

"Detective Brown," Connie corrected.

"Sure, whatever."

"Look, Chad," Mitchell began, "you said you saw someone leave the theater after everyone else."

"Yeah, a black chick. I mean, an African-American woman." He looked at both Mitchell and Connie, apparently to see if they were offended. He continued. "She stuck around while the credits for *Grey Matter* rolled and then came back to find her keys."

Connie's mind raced. A black woman seeing the midnight show of *Grey Matter*. "What did she look like?"

"I don't know, it was kinda dark. The lights weren't fully on yet, but she wasn't too short or tall. Her hair though." He shook his head and chuckled to himself.

"What about it?" Connie pressed.

"The back was pulled real tight to her head, I mean real tight, but the front was like a stiff plastic plate or something that swooped down in front of her face. It looked ridiculous. Why do black chicks think that's attractive?"

Connie looked at him questioningly.

"I-I-I mean African-American woman," he corrected himself again and rubbed his shoulders trying to keep warm. "She was wearing a red sweater and a pair of cheap knock-off jeans with a big leather patch on them. B-L-Z, I think." Then he added with an overbearing machismo, "She had a nice ass. What was I supposed to do, not look? If they got it, they flaunt it, and this chick had it in spades."

Chad had an amused look on his face, but it was quickly lost when his eyes looked into Connie's. He stammered to regain some semblance of decorum. "Um, anyway, that's about all I remember of the woman. Oh, and she was driving a Ford."

At this, Connie stood in utter disbelief. "How do you know that?" she asked while writing.

"Her keychain had a big blue Ford thing on it."

"Did you tell all of this to the detectives?" Mitchell wondered.

"Yeah, everything except the patch on her jeans and the Ford key chain thing. I just remembered those things." Then reverting back to the overbearing machismo, he added, "And about her ass."

Connie quietly wrote in her pad. The red-haired boy had just described the same woman from the Salem's Lot accident. She thought detective work couldn't be this easy, this coincidental.

Mitchell interrupted her train of thought. "Officer, do you need anything else of Mr. O'Donahue, here."

"No," she replied, still writing.

"Chad, thank you," Mitchell offered as the boy quickly escaped out of the cold and into the house. "Call your father and tell him to call me later."

"Okay."

"And, if Detectives Brown or Watts come back with some more questions, don't lie to them. You're more than welcome to tell them that we were here and about her jeans and the Ford thing on that woman's keychain."

"Got it, Mr. Treadwell. I hope this helps find Davis."

"Me, too, Chad. Thank you."

* * *

Mitchell strode down the steps and around the car. Connie was already in her seat, quietly staring at the notebook in her lap.

Mitchell spoke through the open window. "What's up?"

"I don't know," she struggled to say. "Something weird's going on."

Mitchell thought of prodding further but thought better of it. Instead, he got in, sat in his seat and waited for her to continue on her own. His wait was short.

"I was talking to Prudy earlier tonight. One's an accident, two's a coincidence, and three's a trend." Her voice was soft and distant as if she were talking in a trance. "We were talking about the abd ...," she paused and looked at Mitchell. She focused again on her notebook. "We were talking about the abduction of the boys. It's a saying we have at the station. It might be a principle of science for all I know, but still, one's an accident, two's a coincidence, and three's a trend.

"All night, little things kept hitting me. Something someone says, and I write it down. Something I see that's not quite right, and I make a mental note. It's not one big 'ah-ha' or a 'eureka', but small tiles that make up a mosaic."

Mitchell, against his better judgment, broke her stream of consciousness. "What are you talking about, Connie?"

"You said at these meetings everyone has a nickname."

"Yeah."

"What's the nickname of this guy who said he was going to get rid of male prostitutes?"

Mitchell cringed visibly and he saw that Connie caught it out of the corner of her eye. Hers was a question that went to the very heart of the Commuters. The identities of its members, or more precisely, the unknown identities of its members, were sacrosanct. Even knowing for the past two-plus hours he was no longer an official member, he was a Commuter bound by the rules and by-laws established a millennium ago by its founder.

His momentary apprehension to fulfill the contractual agreement he made with a group of relative strangers quickly gave way to the inherent nature of fatherhood.

"Helios. Why?"

She closed her eyes in disbelief, pursed her lips and shook her head slowly. "Damn."

"What? What is it?"

"I thought I had it all figured out," she said in disgust. "Who Chad's witness was. Who your group guy was— everything. But, that woulda been too easy, right? Nope, just another hunch that didn't pan out." She put on her seat belt. "Oh well. Take me back to the station. I think I know who this witness is, anyway."

CHAPTER 37

The clear, dark, night sky shone a thin layer of gray in its eastern rim as the sun, waiting for its time to rise and shine, sat well below the horizon. The hour, as told by either the clock or the sun, had little impact on the hustle and bustle of the police headquarters squad room.

Detective Lonnie Brown got up from his chair and navigated his way over to the large coffee urn that provided the liquid fuel he and his peers required to function properly. He slipped his large, insulated Jittery Joe's mug under the tap and filled it nearly to the top. The silk-screened logo was nearly indecipherable as more and more brushed metal shown through with each passing day. He secured the mug's plastic cap and returned to the chair in front of his desk.

He leaned way back, stretched out his legs, put his feet up and crossed them at his ankles, giving Watts only the soles of his shoes to look at. Brown stared at the thousands of holes in the acoustic ceiling tiles, watching them optically separate and move forward and backward as he shifted his focus nearer and farther than the two-dimensional plain of the ceiling. It was an old trick he played on himself. If he was ever stuck, he shifted perspectives and changed the way he looked at the situation. It allowed his subconscious to work through the details of a particularly difficult set of circumstances that the conscious part of his brain was unable to process properly.

"So, what's next, smokey?" Watts asked.

Brown answered, never taking his eyes off the dizzying ceiling. "Both kids were working the same corner the last time they were seen, each on a Tuesday night. A third vic is taken, a fourth vic is recovered. That doesn't fit my guy's pattern."

"Then what's with the ceiling?"

Brown spoke again as if he were in a trance. "I'm trying to see a new pattern."

"It's not a new pattern, Holmes. It's the same pattern with a new twist, that's all."

Brown swung his feet down and planted them firmly on the ground. "The Highland police have no idea about the prostitute, and the detectives in D3 have no idea about the Highland shop kid, right? If this is some coincidental nut job, fine, there's enough credit to go around on something like that. The brass can pin as many fucking medals on those other humps' chests as they want. But if this is my guy and they want to make this an interdepartmental thing …," he trailed off trying to fight off his anger.

Brown resumed his fully reclined position and stared.

Watts smirked. "Look, you ain't the only one with a new career waiting for him, tiger. While you retire to write your memoirs, I'm riding your coattails right up to Lieutenant Detective. If you think I'm gonna let a couple schlubbs from D3 take a millisecond of spotlight away from me, you're fuckin' nuts. Now, I realize that's not what you're thinking about staring at that ceiling, but that's where I'm coming from." Then he added, "Oh, and you're the one who made this an interdepartmental thing when you had me send your memo out on Friday, so don't start getting all bitch-soft on me."

Brown closed his eyes. "I'm just trying to figure out how these cases fit together and what Treadwell has to do with any of them. A couple months ago I excluded all the files that didn't synch up with a Harvest Moon. What if every one of them had the same pattern: one vic each week a few weeks prior."

"Are you asking me how this fits into your book? 'Cause I—"

"I'm not talking about my book," he shouted, slamming his fists down. The sound reverberated loudly from the desk's gray metal frame. "I'm talking about doing our jobs. How's it gonna look to the brass that I was … if *we* were so focused on the tree we didn't see the forest."

Brown's most pressing issue, the one that had him the most up-tight, had nothing to do with either of the two sets of cases they had uncovered. It was explaining what he and Watts were doing at the corner of High-Sum the very night the son of one of the most well-respected local business leaders was abducted and the dead body of an assumed prostitute showed up in accordance with his interdepartmental memo sent out just a few short days earlier. He needed an "in", but was unwilling to show his hand unless absolutely necessary.

From somewhere in the caverns of the First Division hallways came, "Brown. Watts. The Lieutenant wants to have a talk with you."

CHAPTER 38

"Hey, Whiskey, what're you doing here?" the third shift desk sergeant asked. "Aren't you second shift?"

It was the third time Connie had been asked those questions before making it to the door of the women's changing room in the stationhouse.

She replied for the third time, "I had some personal things I needed to get done last night and now I'm changing."

The booming voice followed with, "You're not using department—"

"All in the line of duty, Sarge."

Then, before going through the door, she called Mitchell over. She pointed to a fairly large, open space in the corner of the building furnished with one large, square table and eight chairs, "Over there is as good a place as any for you to wait. I'll be out in a couple minutes."

"Is there a television?"

"Yeah. Why?"

"I want to catch the news."

As his sister-in-law slipped away, Mitchell turned awkwardly, feeling more like a criminal than at any time during his tenure with the Commuters. He looked around and slowly made his way to the open space in the corner. He walked over to the television and turned it on, clicking to the local morning show, hoping not to see any of the crime scenes he had visited the previous night, official or otherwise. No mention had been made by the time Connie appeared a few minutes later in jeans and a sweatshirt.

"C'mon."

He followed her through the maze of hallways to the room where she had sat filling out the paperwork for the Salem's Lot accident some eight hours earlier. She guided him to her partner's desk and, pulling out the chair, all but ordered him to take a seat. He complied. The hard wooden chair squealed as he sat in it. She shuffled through a few wire baskets atop the long line of filing cabinets before pulling one file from the group and set it aside.

"That's Jenkins's," she explained. "Now I gotta find mine."

Mitchell pretended to be interested but he was fixated on how he could best handle his encounter with either Scout or Sarah the Egyptian when the time came; more precisely, how he might approach them without his sister-in-law. From those two, it was a few handshakes and intimidating discussions up the Freshmen ladder to Helios, the man who had his son.

He heard her voice in his head, *You and me, Mitchell. That's what you said.*

She pulled a second file from a different wire bin and set it down in front of Mitchell.

"Look through that and see if anything sticks out or doesn't make sense."

"I'm not going to get arrested for impersonating a police officer, am I?"

"Hell, you sit there long enough you might get promoted."

Mitchell remembered hearing Connie say over and over that most of her fellow officers didn't have the common sense or street smarts necessary to make quality police men and women. For the sake of his son, he hoped she did.

He pored over the case file he was given and extracted the three or four pertinent pieces of information needed to contact Faith Underhill, the woman Connie believed Chad O'Donahue was describing as the last person to leave the theater.

Connie scoured through her partner's file. Mitchell assumed she was doing the same thing, extracting pertinent pieces of information to contact Andrew K. Walker, the owner of a domestic, recently damaged, green sedan.

And then something disheartening struck him. Before him sat a file that Connie had just pulled. The fact that she was able to so quickly find a file matching his vague description of the vehicle he remembered parked in from of Gambel's severely lowered his expectations of there being any relevant connection. He went through the motions nonetheless, hoping something might come of it.

He closed the folder and pushed it to the corner of the desk closest to the wire baskets and filing cabinets from which Connie had retrieved it. After tearing the sheet of paper from the pad he had written on, Mitchell offered, "So, you thought you had it all figured out, huh?"

"Yeah. Hunches. More times than not they don't pan out."

"What hunch?"

"Did you see the guy's license plate?"

"No."

He pulled the file from Connie's outstretched hand.

"See? You're guy's name is Helium?"

"Helios," he corrected her.

"Check out the vanity plates."

He looked intently at the police report. In the space next to *Lis.* # on the report form was typed P-H-A-E-T-O-N.

"With all the coincidences that kept coming up, when I asked you the nickname of the guy in your group, I thought for sure you were going to say 'Fay-ton' or however you pronounce it."

Mitchell sat there confused for only a second. Then, it all came rushing into focus, thundering over him like hooves of a stampede. The name Phaeton had been cited several times while he researched the matriculating Commuters' chosen identities for his remarks during the evening's ceremony. Mitchell now knew that Andrew K. Walker, the driver of a green Saturn SCV2, was Helios.

"Connie?" he blurted out.

You know you're a terrible liar, don't you Mitch? Her words ran through his head. He tried to stay calm, to leave Connie with the impression that this was another dead end. But it was no use. Unlike her peers, Connie possessed both the common sense and the street smarts necessary to make a quality policewoman.

She grinned widely. "'Fay-ton' means something, huh?" The grin grew to an ear-to-ear smile, "I knew it. Tell me."

"Tell you what?"

"Tell me how Phaeton fits into all this."

Mitchell was already several steps ahead and couldn't be bothered retelling the whole story, "It's all part of the Greek mythology surrounding Helios," he said, flustered. "We don't have time for this. I need to do some research, see what turns up."

Connie looked at him strangely. "Research? Screw that. Let's go grab the son-of-a-bitch and haul his ass in here. We got guys—"

"No." He looked past her eyes, straight into her soul and whispered, slowly and softly, "No cops."

"Damn it, Mitchell."

"Look, if I summarize the Phaeton saga, will you stop trying to bring someone else into this? We can't do this dance every time something comes up."

Connie shook her head.

Without any acknowledgement from Connie, Mitchell began hastily explaining, "Helios was the immortal sun god. He had a son, Phaeton, by a moral woman who married the King of Ethiopia. So, the boy grows up, gets teased by his friends for being a bastard child and asks his mom who is father is. When she tells him he is the son of Helios, the boy runs off to the sun god's eastern palace. Helios has a palace in the east and one in the west and he travels between them across the sky each day.

"So the boy enters the palace and confronts his father. They share an emotional embrace and Helios is so moved he tells his son he can have anything he wants. Phaeton asks to ride the chariot. Helios tells his son that not even Zeus can handle his horses and that the boy should ask for something else, but the boy wants to show his friends he's not a bastard child, he's the son of the sun god.

"You with me so far?" Mitchell interrupted, looking at Connie for cognition.

"Don't worry about me, just keep going."

Mitchell continued his rapid-fire summary. "Okay, so morning comes and Phaeton, against his father's pleas, takes the reins of the horses and ascends into the sky. Then, all hell breaks loose. The horses bolt. They take the sun chariot up away from the earth and the people freeze. Then the horses run too close to the earth, scorching the African continent, creating deserts and darkening the skin of its people.

"Gaea, or Mother Earth, tells Zeus what's going on and she asks him to put an end to the senseless destruction caused by the runaway chariot. Zeus chases after the runaway vehicle on his war eagle and hurls a thunderbolt at the chariot to make it stop. The thunderbolt hits Phaeton in the head and he falls to earth, into a river actually, and he dies.

"Helios regains control of his horses and brings his chariot to rest in the stables of his western palace. The next day, Helios is too grief-stricken to ride across the sky. However, the fires lit by his son burn brightly across all the lands. And, in a final act of sorrow, Helios names one of the horses in his stable Phaeton in honor of his fallen son."

Mitchell looked at his sister-in-law. She appeared to want more.

"That's it," he said.

She had a questioning look on her face, "So he ..."

Mitchell broke in slowly and softly, "So, no police, right?"

She stood up and walked between two other desks to look out the window. "You're putting me in a bad spot here, Mitch."

"I know. And when this whole thing pans out and we get Davis back, and we *will* get him back, I promise to come completely clean with you. But until then, we have got to keep this just between us. Understand?"

"Fine"

Mitchell's cell phone rang. He looked down and then back at Connie.

"All right, good. Now, I'm sorry, but I have to take this."

As he stood, the chair let out a high-pitched sigh and he nonchalantly picked up the piece of paper on which he had transferred the file information. He paced back to a corner of the space near the file cabinets and huddled there with a finger of his free hand plugging his off-ear, occasionally bringing his hand down to read elements of the paper.

Mitchell finished his call and looked at Connie standing by the window. If the ancient Greeks were right, four fiery steeds of the sun god were yoked to his golden chariot and just beginning to stamp their way across the clear, lightening sky.

"Okay, where's a computer I can work on."

She continued to stare off into the dawn. He reached over and shook her shoulder, unexpectedly startling her.

"I'm sorry," he said, "I didn't mean to scare you."

"No problem. I was just thinking about how much trouble you're getting me into here by not allowing me to go through the regular channels. Your unwillingness to share these secrets of yours might very well prevent the police from getting Davis back faster and under the proper authority. And just a reminder, standing here in my street clothes, I'm still a member of the police force and, as such, am obligated to work within the guidelines set forth by the department. I'll be honest, the more I think about 'you and me,'" she said in a mocking tone, "the less appealing it becomes."

"I'm sorry about startling you and I'm sorry about putting you in a bind, but it can't be helped at the moment. Now, a computer?"

"Use mine."

"Is there someplace more isolated? I don't want anyone to recognize me."

"You're a businessman, not a celebrity. You're not even a politician. No one's gonna know you from Adam." When he continued to wait, she said, "There's a small room with a computer on the next floor up we can use."

She led the way down the hall to a staircase and headed up. "What're you looking for anyway? All we need is an address, right?"

"As you so plainly pointed out, I'm not a celebrity, I'm a businessman. I've never moved on a deal until I've covered every angle I could think of before entering negotiations. This Helios, he's no power broker, but he's sharp, intelligent. And I think he might be a bit unstable."

"A bit?" She stopped in her tracks and turned to face Mitchell. "He's killing young boys, Mitch. He's keeping them alive for a week while leeches suck their blood, stabbing them in the heart and leaving them naked in dumpsters. I think that qualifies as more than just a bit unstable, don't you?"

"Depends," he said simply. Then, as they continued through the stationhouse hallways, he said, "More people have done worse things and weren't found insane. In most states, they use a person's understanding of right and wrong as the basis for determining sane or insane. Most serial killers know what's right and what's wrong, but either choose or are compelled to do what's wrong. Dahmer, Haskins, Wuornos, Bundy; they were all found guilty, but not insane."

A shiver ran down his spine when he considered Davis being held by a man so easily associated with the world's worst and most vile killers.

"Sometimes you scare me, Mitch. Greek mythology. Serial killers. You know way to much about way too many things. Way too many creepy things."

* * *

Mitchell was always a bookworm, reading ravenously about whatever topic piqued his curiosity at any given moment. During his first few years with the Commuters, Mitchell had compulsively sought out information about serial killers in an attempt to differentiate himself from the names he had just rattled off. Thankfully, he was successful. As he came to understand the various classifications of his criminal brethren, he accepted himself as a garden variety murderer who killed a single victim to gain power, no different than the immediate forefathers and descendents of his selected persona, Emperor Trajan. As his mind slowly justified his actions as an ignoble means to a noble end, his research and the knowledge he gained from it provided surprising comfort. They also provided him with a solid basis for understanding Helios to a degree: a multiple murderer, a mission-oriented serial killer.

Mitchell was stunned to discover during his earliest days as a Commuter that homicide is a relatively easy crime for the police to solve. It's usually a crime of personal relationships and short, intense emotions or an unintended consequence of other crimes. If it's the former, the murderer usually makes little effort to conceal the crime and often confesses quickly. And if there is no apparent suspect, the police run through a list of family, friends and acquaintances, search for possible motives and focus on the most likely perpetrator, usually ending up focused on the guilty party. If the crime of murder is an unintended consequence of other crimes, the murderer is usually a local criminal of whom the police are already aware and all they require is enough evidence to prosecute.

These assumptions, with which any law enforcement officer naturally approaches a single murder, are the precise barriers to catching a serial murderer. Serial murderers are much more difficult to detect and apprehend as they rarely know their victims, seeking types of individuals or particular circumstances rather than any easily detectable link to their victims. This lack of association with their victims not only helps them escape suspicion, it also makes the act of killing them easier due to the inherent objectivity: the killer sees their victims only as targets, objects, and not human beings. The Commuters call them life vessels.

The mission-oriented serial killer, the category into which Mitchell believed Helios fell, targets a specific group of people who the killer believes is unworthy of life and without whom the world would be a better place. They are not compelled to murder because they hear voices or see visions but to cleanse society. Helios made his intentions quite obvious during the ceremony and it is what Mitchell had keyed on during the disturbing soliloquy delivered some six hours earlier.

In all his years as a member, Mitchell always marveled at the Commuters' founder for devising a systematic process of murder that completely defied the advances of criminology a millennia after the group's purported beginnings. It was impossible to profile a Commuter because the victims are the main focus in determining the psycho-social background of the perpetrator and each year a new victim was selected with a completely different set of circumstances, leaving only a minute thread of a pattern for investigators to follow. The focal point of any possible investigation, the killer, was a moving target and didn't fit any of the definitions of a serial killer established by psychologists or profilers.

Each ceremony was as unique an incident as a snowflake, with four complete strangers called upon to provide only a portion of the crime—a secure location to conduct the ceremony, the physical act of plunging the knife into the victim's heart, the selection and ultimate abduction of the victim, and the disposal of the body—all with no discernible linkage; a pattern of unpredictability. That is, until Helios.

"I didn't mean to freak you out, Connie. I happen to read a lot. Anyway, knowledge is power and we've got an hour or so before we can drop in on Mr. Andrew K. Walker at home, so I figured the best way to spend our time would be to do some poking around?

"You can access police records and things of that nature, right?"

"In the line of duty, yes."

"Then, in the line of duty, why don't you see what you can drum up on this guy while I search on-line and see if something turns up in the papers or blogs."

PART SIX

A New Day

CHAPTER 39

The buzz of morning rush hour was still far away and only the occasional distant car alarm interrupted the soft crinkling of colorful leaves rustling in the autumn wind. The sky was brightening with the promise of a new day when another interruption pulled slowly up to the curb in front of the multi-unit building. Moments later there was a knock at the door.

Winston, the splotchy black and white Boston Terrier, raised his head from his forepaws and growled, low and rolling. The woman, at whose feet Winston curled himself up every night, was sound asleep in her flannel pajamas, which she had removed from her storage unit in the building's basement only a few nights earlier in response to the unseasonably cold weather.

Hearing *knock, knock, knock*, Winston barked once and bolted upright. He barked again and continued his low rolling growl.

"Stop it, Winston," Faith mumbled.

The dog sprang from the bed and rushed to the door, continuing his menacing growl. Faith slowly rolled out of bed, her eyes still shut. Had they been open she would have seen her dog staring at the doorknob, prancing back and forth and continuously licking its nose between growls. She felt her way, as if blind, through the small apartment to the front door, knelt beside her dog and patted his head.

"Good boy, Winston. Now, sit."

The dog sat immediately, twitching temperamentally at having to remain in one spot.

Then another *knock, knock, knock,* and the dog uncoiled and snapped off two quick barks before reverting back to his prancing growl.

"Sit, Winston! Quiet!"

The dog obeyed both commands as best it could, trembling and growling.

She peered through the spyhole in the door. In her hallway stood a stout, fairly distinguished-looking white man in his mid-fifties. He was dressed in a gray jogging suit with his hands behind his back looking nervously left, then right, then down the stairs.

"Who is it?" she asked.

He stared back at her through the spyhole. "Miss Underhill? I was asked to speak with you about the traffic accident you witnessed yesterday."

"Accident?"

"Yes ma'am."

She pulled away from the door and began unlocking it, then stopped. "Couldn't this wait until later? You woke me up and—"

"Miss Underhill," he whispered at the crack between the door and the jamb. "I apologize for the inconvenience, but this is a, um, delicate situation that I've been asked to take care of as soon as possible. The other man involved in the accident is dead and the police are initiating a murder investigation. I'm afraid it can't wait until later, ma'am."

"Let me see your badge."

"I'm not a policeman, ma'am. I'm a private investigator making an inquiry regarding the accident."

"Not to be impolite, but what is so important that it can't wait until later?"

"Miss Underhill. As I said, I am here regarding the accident, the one in which Mr. Sledge was involved."

"Uh-huh," she nodded.

"I was asked to go over with you some of your statements to the police and, based on your cooperation, determine if you are eligible for a cash settlement."

"A cash settlement? I was just a witness."

"Again, this is a delicate situation, one I'd rather not discuss through the door."

Had the man outside her door appeared the slightest bit more threatening, she would never have considered letting him in. As it was, she acquiesced, reminding herself of her grandmother's efforts to teach her to be safe. She wanted to cooperate in any way she could, so she convinced herself it would be okay, but to be careful. "Just a minute."

She went into her room to put on her robe and slippers. When she returned, Winston sniffed at the space below the door and growled. Faith peeked through the spyhole one last time to ensure the man outside was doing nothing peculiar. He stood facing the door looking around as he had before.

She moved the dog back behind her with her foot and whispered, "Scram, Winston," while unlocking the door. An uneasiness swirled in her stomach as she opened the door to the stranger. He entered, walked immediately to the dog, bent down and scratched the soft part behind his head where his ears attached.

"So, you're the little guy making all that noise, eh?"

Winston lowered his head, rolled on his back and exposed his underside. The man obliged and scratched the dog's belly roughly. Faith walked into the small living space and leaned against the back of her favorite overstuffed chair.

The man looked up. "Do you mind if I sit down?"

She motioned to the matching overstuffed chair and the man sat. Winston followed, getting up on his hind legs and pawing at the man's hands hoping for more attention.

"Down, Winston," Faith stated firmly.

"Winston, what a wonderful name."

"And your name? May I ask what your name is?"

"My name, Ms. Underhill, is unimportant."

Faith was suddenly struck with fear. The man's presence in her apartment contradicted all of her grandmother's life lessons. She suddenly grew uncomfortable and stood up.

"It's important to me. Tell me who you are or get the hell out of my apartment," she said, standing up and pointing to the door.

He immediately worked to rebuild a common ground. "My apologies, Ms. Underhill. I didn't mean to upset you. My name is Conall Cernach."

The uneasiness remained in her belly and showed visibly on her face and in her mannerisms.

"I represent a very interested third party: that's someone unrelated to the situation."

"I know what third party means, Mr. Cernach," she replied, "and I'm starting to think—"

"Excellent, you know what a third party is," he responded before she could make it to the door, catching her a bit off guard. "That makes my job one step easier. As I mentioned, this third party would like to know a few things."

"About the accident?"

"Yes, let's start with the accident."

A gentle smile crept across the man's stony façade as he continued in a soothing tone. "By the look on your face, I'm guessing you're frightened at the idea of someone showing up at the crack of dawn, unannounced, and telling you that he wants to know about a few hours of your life in greater detail. I assure you, Ms. Underhill, I am not a stalker or a madman. I am a businessman. I am here to make a deal with you."

His soothing tones successfully disarmed her. "What do you mean 'a deal'?"

"A deal. A trade. A situation in which both parties come out ahead. I get something from you and in return, you get something from me."

"What do you want from me?" she asked, walking back toward her chair.

"I want information and in exchange, I'm authorized to pay you in cash for that information."

"You're going to give me money for telling you what happened in Salem's Lot?"

"Yes," he stated simply. "Among other things."

She pondered this for a moment and sat. "And how much are you going to pay me?"

"That all depends on what you tell me. At the very least, I'll give you a hundred dollars for waking you up at such a horrendous hour. If what you tell me is of value to this third party, then I will pay you a thousand dollars."

"A thousand dollars? Just to tell you what happened?" she asked, sinking her fingers deep into the cushioned arms and plying her body deeper and deeper into the chair back.

"That's it."

She'd only been awake for a few minutes but she'd completed enough tension and release exercises to last the most grueling thirty-minute workout.

"This isn't illegal, is it? I work in the insurance industry and—"

"I'm not a lawyer, Ms. Underhill, but I don't think someone telling someone else about her evening could be considered illegal. Hell, if you want, you can call the police as soon as we're done and tell them the exact same thing you tell me. Or you can choose not to tell me anything. That's up to you. However, the third party I mentioned earlier, they would like to know what you saw and heard and, as I said, are willing to pay you for this inconvenience."

She instantly thought about the handful of purchases she had put off to get her car tuned up and wondered just how many of those purchases a thousand dollars would cover. She hesitated, and then slowly gave one bit of information at a time.

"It happened so quickly," she started. But like a river that breaks a dike, once she started, the information flowed easily. She recounted what she had told the police some ten hours earlier with details omitted and others embellished due to the fallibility of human memory. When she was done, another gentle smile crept across the man's face as he tried to move the conversation in another direction.

"Very good, Ms. Underhill. That's fine. Now, can you speak a little about what you did after the accident?"

"After?"

"Yes. Did you go out somewhere, maybe to dinner? Or a movie?"

She was at a movie. How could he have known? Was it a lucky guess? She was frozen with fear, unable to speak or move. The image of the two women struggling in front of the dumpster flashed as six, double five, three, two, one, echoed in her head.

"Did you do anything of that nature after the accident?"

She regained some composure and rose quickly from her chair, hoping the move away from him and out of his sight might help her stay calm. "I need some water. Would you like some?"

"No, thank you."

She spoke nervously from the kitchen area, which in the small apartment, was not very far from the living area. "I'm sorry, but I fail to see how that has anything to do with the accident."

"Of course. Of course. The information I'm hoping to obtain from you relates to another accident. I'm investigating on behalf of the family of a hit-and-run victim and somehow your name popped up."

"How could that be?" she resisted.

"I'm not completely sure. I was told to ask you about the accident yesterday and then your whereabouts late last night."

"You think I was the hit-and-run driver? You can check my car."

"Ms. Underhill, I don't think you're a hit-an-run driver and I don't need to check your car. But like I said, your name popped up and I was asked to gather some information."

Confusion replaced her fear and she wanted more than anything to make this person sitting before her understand that she had absolutely nothing to do with a hit-and-run accident the night before. She also wanted him to go away, but not until after she got whatever money he might have for her. "Well, let's see. I got my car at about eight."

"Actually, if I can steer the conversation a bit, I'm hoping you're going to tell me you were here, asleep in your bed, at about two last night."

Faith's eyes exploded wide. "No. I was at a late movie."

"Can anyone verify that?"

"Sure. I bought the ticket on-line. And, I left my keys in the theater, the Ridgeway Theater, and an usher there helped me find them." Her voice was panicky and she was racing to tell her story.

The man's gentle smile came again as he reached down in front of him to scratch the belly of the dog, which lay out of his owner's sight lines. "And after the movie, Ms. Underhill?"

"I left the theater and walked through the alley to my car. It was around two-fifteen. I checked my watch. I crossed the street to the next alley behind Spanky's leather shop. I don't shop there, I just parked there because it's free and close to the theater. So I'm walking to my car and I see something at the end of the alley."

"What?" he pressed.

"I think it was two women with brown hair. They were behind a black Honda Civic trying to throw something big and awkward into the dumpster. After they finally got it in the dumpster, they got back in their car, went out the far exit and turned north."

She took a long sip of water from her glass.

"All that from such a quick glance?"

"The whole thing seemed so odd, you know? So I made myself remember as many of the details as I could. Oh! The license plate number of the car was six, double five, three, two, one."

"What did you do then?" he said still attending to the dog.

"From there, I just got in my car and drove home. I fell asleep and was sleeping when you knocked."

The man continued to work Winston, turning over his shoulder to speak to Faith. "That's quite a memory you have."

"I got that from my grandmother. She used to make us do all these memory exercises when we were little."

Faith had no time to react when the man stood up and lunged at her. She let out a tiny, high-pitched yelp before his left hand found her neck and forced her head against the upper cabinets next to the immaculate kitchen sink. His forefinger ran along her jawbone and his thumb pressed up under her chin, exposing the soft brown skin of her throat. The latex gloves, which he donned while pretending to pet the dog, crackled with his every movement. Her arms and legs flailed wildly, trying desperately to escape his grasp, occasionally striking him or banging the doors of the cabinets.

He thrust the small, thin blade of the bulky Swiss Army knife, the one he kept in his car's glove compartment, into the vulnerable and exposed area of her neck. With the initial puncture, blood sprayed everywhere; on him, on her and to his left. The man held tight the knife and forcibly pulled the blade a few inches down her neck and her blood escaped more quickly, pulsing like bubbly lava down her shoulder, pooling on the counter behind her and the floor below her. He pulled the knife out and let her go. She teetered a bit before gravity had its way with her and contorted her body into an awkward pile of bones and flesh. Her life had long faded from her face, her eyes vacantly staring off under the chair in which her guest had sat and petted her dog. He stood and saw where she looked, wondering if she ever saw Winston lying lifeless in a pool of his own blood.

The man folded the knife and slipped it into the front left pocket of his jogging suit pants. He pulled off the top of his jogging suit and wiped his face with the soft lining inside, noting the brown streaks of blood. He tore off his gloves inside-out and placed them in the right front pocket of the jogging pants. A second pair of gloves and a large, black plastic kitchen garbage bag came from the khaki pants he wore beneath the jogging suit pants. He put on the gloves and took off the outer pants, placing everything into the garbage bag.

The pool of her blood grew and narrowed and crawled across the tile floor toward the apartment's front door like a shimmering stream of crimson mercury. The man ran to the bathroom, grabbed a towel from the hook and spread it out to block the red river's progress. He stood on the clean part of the towel and scanned the room to see if he had missed anything. Noting no flaws in his execution, he removed the last bit of clothing and pushed them deep into the garbage bag. Then he turned and exited the apartment.

The musty scent that hung in the hallway was a welcome distraction from the carnage he left on the other side of the door, which he locked and pulled behind him. His heart pounded as he quickly descended the stairs, loping two-at-a-time down to the ground floor with the clunky garbage bag in hand.

On that Wednesday morning, not a single person was walking the neighborhood to witness the well-dressed white man carrying a plastic garbage bag in his latex-gloved hands. No one was there to see him hastily exit the building and run to his silver Mercedes Benz S-Class sedan which stuck out among the other vehicles that were dispersed up and down both sides of the street in various stages of designed obsolescence.

A local bakery's delivery truck roared past the Mercedes Benz just after the man pulled the driver's side door shut. He took off the gloves, hastily placed them in the bag and turned the key. The engine roared to life. He shifted into drive, pulled a u-turn in the middle of the block and headed back toward Club Road.

Michael O'Donahue, a certified public accountant and the personal tax advisor to Mitchell Treadwell, made just one stop on his way home. Behind one of the large, gourmet grocery stores that catered to the distinguished tastes of the affluent, he threw the black plastic bag into the dumpster. He stared at it for a long while, Mitchell's words ringing in his head: *May you fully understand that what we do here deepens our understanding of ourselves and provides us with the confidence and self-assuredness required to make whatever is physically possible a reality.*

He had always known he possessed the physical ability to take another human being's life, but until that morning he had never known he had the mental ability to actually do it, at least not outside the insulated security of the Commuter's ancient ceremony.

Michael turned to face the rising sun. A tear glinted in its brilliant rays as his eyes reddened. He slumped back into his car and drove through the streets in which his children and their friends played, crying as he drove. Both he and his vehicle remained idle in the garage for several minutes, cooling down from the morning's exhausting excursion. After collecting his composure and wiping the tears from his face, he entered his home feeling sorrow in his soul for what he had done. The feeling would grow for weeks and ultimately consume him.

CHAPTER 40

Mitchell's BMW wound its way through the suburban streets west of the city on its way to the Walker residence. He and Connie had just grabbed a bite to eat at the Century Diner: a small, retro 1950's stainless steel prefab classic, complete with the black and white checkerboard tile floor and Formica counter tops. His face was drawn and expressionless. He hadn't said a word to his passenger since they left the diner. He hoped she assumed his distraction was due to a lack of sleep combined with the emotional drain of dealing with a missing child. He hoped even more that she'd never find out what exactly was bothering him.

"So what'd you find out about Walker?" she finally asked.

Deep in the *Bugle Gazette* archives, Mitchell had found a news item in which the author exploited an unremarkable, yet tragic death to make a point about the injustices of society. The story went on to describe how the political and legislative machines in metropolises across the nation are ill-equipped to address the struggles of the typical middle class family who rely on these governmental institutions to level the playing field for all citizens. It was formulaic daily newspaper pap, quickly absorbed and easily forgotten by hundreds of thousands of subscribers. However, buried under the author's fill-in-the-blank rants were significant, relevant facts about the man beneath Helios' halo which shed a great deal of light on the chosen persona and the motives for his recent actions, far more information than Mitchell wanted to share with his sister-in-law cop.

"What?"

"What'd you find out about Walker?" she asked again.

"Not much."

Mitchell could feel Connie's eyes on him, almost willing him to continue speaking. He didn't. She finally said, "What does 'not much' mean?"

"I found his parent's obituaries and that's about it."

"That's more than I found. As far as the state is concerned, he's clean. Hell, Jenkins told me yesterday the guy was going on and on about never having been in an accident or getting a ticket."

"Hmm," he grunted.

Mitchell sat in the driver's seat going over snippets of imaginary conversations with Mr. Walker trying to determine the best tactics to elicit the important information that would lead him to his son. He was skeptical that his six college credits of introductory psychology thirty-five years ago, his better-than-average understanding of serial killers, and the tidbits of information he had gleaned from the *Bugle Gazette* article were going to be enough to get his boy back. But as the houses in the subdivisions grew less extravagant, he was determined to try.

Then, the anger he felt during the ceremony toward his fellow Commuters, and Natalie Belling in particular, returned. She died the day after matriculating out of the Commuters. Then, one day after his final ceremony, his youngest child was being violated by a lunatic.

Beneath the calm, expressionless façade Connie saw staring out the windshield, Mitchell was seething at the karmic irony. He wondered if tragedy befell all former members of the group. And, if so, what form they would have taken through the ages. The black plague came immediately to mind. And war and the great famine. All of them were plausible deaths for individuals who convinced themselves of being immortal only to realize too late that it was all a lie.

Natalie Belling went to sleep and never woke up: the preferred method of death for those who ponder the subject for curiosity's sake. She got off easy, he thought. Was it because she tried to make up for her misdeeds while she was still a member of the group? Establishing a foundation for the families of murder victims?

He reverted to the awe he felt at the founder's development of an enigmatic murder machine that stumped the authorities a thousand years after its creation. He suddenly realized that the cunning went even deeper. Not only did the Commuters go undetected by the police and the general public but, because members were a handshake removed from each successive member, the matriculating Commuter possessed the knowledge of only his or her sponsor's demise and nothing else, leaving no pattern for the next member to reconstruct.

And what about Michael O'Donahue? Should Mitchell inform the man he had sponsored almost thirty years ago of what could possibly lay ahead? Would his accountant figure it out on his own, or would it take a tragedy on the day after his final ceremony for it to come together in his mind? Would he ever put two and two together? Was Mitchell to die saving his son, leaving no one to warn his accountant?

Connie had mentioned the axiom *one's an accident, two's a coincidence and three's a trend*. Geologists use triangulation to find the locations of Earthquakes. Owls use it to hunt without moonlight or when prey is hidden by bushes. Bad things happen in three.

Was all this just a coincidence? Natalie Belling's death and Davis's disappearance? Were they not some kind of karmic payback?

There was no third point of reference to make a solid conclusion one way or the other. It was his guilt drawing a conclusion and influencing his decisions. And therein lay the utter genius of the Commuters: there would never be a third point of reference.

As he drove on and the streets rolled by, this line of thinking made him further wonder if there was any point in his trying to stop the inevitable. The Harvest Moon took Natalie last year — its eye for an eye. Mitchell's ticket was all but punched. The knowledge that his actions were causing the unimaginable suffering of his son was obvious restitution for his behavior the last three decades. Or was this just a precursor? Was he to suffer the loss of his son's life as well? He reasoned that dumping the body after his first ceremony and stuffing the backpacker into the trunk of his car were cause enough for his son's torture. Plunging the dagger through the brass ring would be paid for with Davis's life. Possibly his own. Possibly both.

He pushed past the guilt, focused entirely on his son, and finally engaged his passenger. "We're going to get him back."

His voice was imbued with reassurance.

"Damn straight," Connie cheered and slapped his knee.

CHAPTER 41

The neighborhood was quiet and lifeless in the early morning sun when they pulled into the driveway of Andy Walker's unsightly suburban home at 42 Simsbury Road. He pulled in behind the damaged chariot that sat outside the garage. Its license plate, P-H-A-E-T-O-N, seemed as big as a billboard. No lights shone through any of the shaded windows, leading him to believe everyone was still asleep.

He turned to Connie and waited for her to look back at him. "What are the chances I can go in there and talk to this guy by myself?"

"Zero. Why?"

"Well, you're a cop. If he recognizes you from yesterday, he's not going to incriminate himself or say anything helpful with you there."

"Hey, this was your call, Mitch. 'You and me,' remember?"

"Sure, but this is about getting Davis back and —"

"Is that what this is about?" she snarled. "Getting Davis back? You'd never know it from where I'm standing. You've been lying to me all night long, Mitch, and holding back information at every step."

He shot her a look as if she had just called him a murderer.

"Don't give me that, 'What? Me?' crap. This stupid club of yours and whatever you found out about Walker's parents, you've kept it all to yourself. But when it came to, 'Hey, Connie, what can you dig up?' I gave you everything I had. Now you want me to forget all about that and just let you waltz right in there solo so you can give each other some secret handshake and chat over a cup of coffee about the whereabouts of my nephew.

"I got two words for that, Mitch: No-Fucking-Way!

"My ass is on the line here. I'm breaking procedures left and right. I'm withholding evidence from a city homicide detective, for Christ's sake. You're all but certain the guy in there abducted Davis and, hello, that doesn't set off any alarms in that thick head of yours? And the way you've been acting all night, I could be aiding and abetting a felon, for all I know."

Her face was more flush than usual, sweat beads were forming on her forehead and she was breathing heavily. "So don't you think for a millisecond that I'm gonna let you set one foot in that house without me. These were your rules, Mitch. You live with them."

Mitchell smiled disarmingly before exiting the car. "Fine," was all he said.

The walkway up to the front of the house was a slow, arching curve to a deep, wide cement slab at the middle of the house covered by a wide dormer. Mitchell was half-way to the door when he stopped and watched Connie, leaning against the green Saturn, looking into the rear tire well.

"What are you doing?" he asked.

"Just a little detective work. I was checking to see if the guy's been off road, lately."

"Has he?"

"There's no mud, but he's got a couple pieces of gravel wedged in the tires' treads."

"What's that mean?"

"I don't know. Maybe nothing."

As she approached him in the middle of the sidewalk, he asked, "You got your gun and cuffs?"

"Of course," she stated, opening her jacket to show him.

"Wait here. I got some pepper spray in the car."

Connie watched him jog the few steps it took for him to reach the passenger side door of the vehicle and open it.

"That's probably not going to be necessary," she said.

He sat in the seat rummaging around. Connie looked back at the house. She was taking in what he had already seen when they first drove up: chipping paint, stains on the gutters, a crooked house number on one of the posts flanking the stoop. She turned again when she heard Mitchell shut the door and watched as he briskly walked back toward her with his hands behind his back.

"Don't you think you'd be less conspicuous if you put the pepper spray in your pocket?" she asked as he moved closer.

Mitchell quickly swung around behind Connie and grabbed her right wrist with his right hand and pulled it up into the middle of her back. "I'm so sorry," he whispered in her ear. He swung his left hand around and pressed the back of her head firmly against his chest while covering her nose and mouth with a damp cloth. He swung his left leg in front of hers and pushed with his entire weight so they both fell hard into the tall grass of the yard. His handkerchief momentarily slipped from her face, but he quickly replaced it and after just a few more seconds felt her resistance slowly subside.

When she was motionless, he pulled his handkerchief away from her face and saw blood on it. He rolled is wife's sister over on her back and saw that she had a bloody nose. He looked around to see if anyone saw them tumble together and noting no one in the vicinity, Mitchell reached under her body and picked her up, grunting as he did so.

She was heavier than he had expected, though he was able to carry her to his car and eventually, awkwardly, set her in the trunk. He threw the chloroform-soaked handkerchief in as well, pulled her handcuffs from their belted case, and secured her wrists behind her back. Then, he removed her gun from its holster and slipped it into the pocket of his jacket. Before leaving her, he pulled an old restaurant napkin from the pocket of the passenger door, wiped the blood from her upper lip and mouth, twisted one of its corners into a point and stuffed it up her bloody nostril. "Sorry," was all he said as he shut the trunk and strode up the curved sidewalk.

He rang the bell and waited what seemed longer than the actual thirty seconds it was before ringing the bell again. Another thirty seconds passed and there was still no answer. He opened the storm door and raised his hand up to knock when the interior door swung open.

CHAPTER 42

Andy, wrapped in a towel and dripping water on the floor, stood before a man he had never seen before. "Please don't make any more noise. My wife is … not feeling well."

"My apologies, Lord Helios," the man said calmly.

"Excuse me?" Andy replied.

"Lord Helios," the man said in a softer tone, apparently complying with Andy's earlier request. "I am Emperor Trajan. I was hoping to have a few short words with you regarding the Commuters."

Andy stood in the doorway dumbstruck. One of the most revered aspects of the group was anonymity yet here was a man claiming to be Emperor Trajan, the recently matriculated ex-member, calling him by his assumed persona. He responded slowly.

"I'm sorry, who are you?"

"You know me as Trajan."

A confused look overcame Andy's face. "Did you say I know you?"

"Yes, Helios. I'm Trajan."

Confusion gave way to an uncomfortable smile. "You must have me mixed up with someone else, sir. My name's not Helios and I don't know any … Trajan, was it?"

"I understand this might seem confusing to you, but one of my responsibilities as a matriculating Alpha is to review and grade the performances of the other emcees and offer suggestions for improvement."

The uncomfortable smile completely left Andy, leaving only a blank expression.

"Would you like to put on some clothes?" the man asked.

Andy looked down and was genuinely surprised that he was in nothing but a towel. Embarrassed, he shuffled backwards through the entryway.

"Please, come in, take a seat and," he lifted his finger to his lips, "shhhhh."

As Andy disappeared into the recesses of the house, he heard the front door shut. The thick scent of bleach hung in the air and Andy hoped it would either be missed or ignored. Andy knew the place was not ready for guests. The living room to the left of the entryway was tidy, but far from clean. Dust had settled visibly on the entire sectional sofa pushed against the back wall of the space. The lone recliner facing the television, awkwardly positioned in the middle of the sitting area, was the only thing that remained dust-free.

Andy threw on a pair of navy sweat pants and a grey sweatshirt. The towel he wrapped around his waist to answer the door he hung around his shoulders. He stepped into the living space and stood, wondering what to do next. He extended his arm to this man calling himself Trajan and softly said, "Please, sit."

The man headed back to the dusty sectional and stopped. He motioned to the recliner and asked, "Do you mind if I sit here?"

"Not at all." Andy stood drying his hair with the towel. "I apologize if I seem, ah, rude, but, how do you know me?"

"Let me cut to the chase, Mr. Walker. I'm not here to give you a report card or anything of the sort. Quite simply, I believe you have my son."

Andy peered out from beneath his towel, "What?"

The man inched to the edge of the chair and whispered, "Every Tuesday for the past few weeks you have been picking up young male prostitutes from the corner of High Ridge Road and Summit Avenue, abducting them and keeping them somewhere to use as test subjects for your leeches experiment. I echo my comments of last night. I applaud your thoroughness and your initiative with the leeches. Last night's ceremony was exceedingly clean, particularly in comparison with last year's Slipperman fiasco."

Andy forced back the smile he felt from the glowing adulation of his achievement.

"Last night's victim, whom you tattooed with the number '3' in the webbing of his thumb and forefinger," and the man pointed to the same spot on his own hand, "he was to be your final victim. However, with your experiment complete and your responsibilities to the group fulfilled, you abducted another young boy last night standing on that same corner. That boy is my son, Davis. I have been trying to track you down for the better part of the night in an attempt to get him back. I have employed the assistance of the police, at arm's length, of course, but I'm afraid I will not be able to keep them at bay for much longer."

Andy stood peering out of the towel listening to every word with disbelief. Skeptical that another member would ever break the code of anonymity, let alone include the police in anything having to do with the Commuters, Andy chose his words very carefully so as not to attach himself to anything Mitchell was implying. "You contacted the police?"

"As I mentioned, at arm's length. Let's just say I have someone on the force that I trust greatly."

Andy remained silent.

"Did you know your previous abductions have caught the attention of a couple of Korova City detectives? It seems these two detectives have connected the dots, so to speak, and they are hot on your trail for last night's victim as well as the abduction of my son. I think they've also established a link between the Harvest Moon and the victims of Commuter ceremonies. All because of you," the man said, his voice growing louder. "They were ready and waiting at High-Sum for a victim to show up this morning. They have a potential witness that puts Scout and Sarah the Egyptian in the alley where a young boy was found less than thirty minutes after he was disposed: the same high traffic location from which you took him last week."

The man's voice grew even louder, "In fact, the police were standing on the High-Sum corner last night waiting for you to grab a victim. And if I can find you, Mr. Walker, I'll bet dollars to donuts that these two detectives can find you, too. Do you understand the repercussions of this, Mr. Walker? They are about to close in on the Commuters, an organization that has remained effectively cloaked to the general public for almost a thousand years, all because of some repressed anger which you need to unleash on reasonable facsimiles of the young boy you hold responsible for the death of your son."

A disturbing frown crept across Andy's face. "What did you just say?"

"Eight years ago, your wife's parents were babysitting your son, Franklin. They were bringing him home from the ice cream parlor when a black Lincoln Continental t-boned their Hyundai Sonata. The driver of the Lincoln had picked up a young boy, a young red-headed boy and paid him to, um," the man paused, seemingly struggling to find a word or phrase, "use his mouth on him while he drove around. Everyone involved in that accident died except for the young boy who was a prostitute, a degenerate, a stain on society. And since he was a minor and he wasn't driving, you had no legal recourse to hold him accountable for contributing to the events of that evening."

Tears were streaming down Andy's expressionless face as he listened to the man who called himself Trajan recount the death of his son which was the crystallizing event that led Andy to seek out the support he could only find in the Commuters. His wife had never been able to recover and she had laid in bed for years, hopelessly depressed, unable to reconnect with the outside world in any meaningful way.

"You don't know what you're talking about," Andy spat through his clenched teeth.

"I know enough," the man said. "I know you are angry and I know you are trying to make these other boys you pick up atone for what happened to your son and that you blame them for taking away Franklin. I also know that you think my son is a prostitute because he was on that same street corner last night. I assure you, Mr. Walker, Davis is a hard working young man, an usher at the nearby theater. He was simply people-watching, not soliciting prostitution. You've taken the wrong boy from a place … how did you say it? 'Where people become infected?' You are punishing him under false pretenses."

A long pause hung in the air. The chaste image of his baby boy washed over Andy. In his mind he saw the tiny casket in the huge hole in the ground, little fingers wrapped around his thumb, a smile sparkling with drool. Then, through tearful eyes, he looked down at the man sitting in his recliner. He said nothing.

"I'm begging you, Mr. Walker, please don't take my son away. Spare me the pain and agony you and your family suffered. Take me to him now. I want nothing more than to get Davis back home and into his mother's arms."

Andy wiped the salty wetness from his eyes and the shiny tracks from his cheeks with the towel. He looked at the floor for a very long time before answering.

"I'm sorry your son is missing, Mr. Trajan, but I don't think I can help you."

The man sitting in the recliner shook his head as if to clear a haze from inside it and said, "Excuse me?"

In the same monotone in which he had delivered his soliloquy to the group of masked strangers, Andy Walker apathetically pronounced, "Yes, I lost my son in a car accident eight years ago. It was quite tragic. Not a day goes by that I don't think about him. It's taken a great toll on my wife as well. But as for these other things—tattoos, prostitutes, stains, leeches—I have no idea where that's coming from or why you are telling me about them. I wasn't at High-Sum last night. Last night and the last couple of Tuesdays I've spent right here in that chair watching television. I don't know any Davis or Scout or Sarah. To be honest, I don't know you, Mr. Trajan. And I don't know what to make of all of this, but I do know you're frightening me. So much so that I think I would like you to leave before I call the police."

Andy walked to the front door and opened it, standing behind it waiting silently for the man sitting on his recliner to leave.

"Mr. Walker—" the man pleaded.

"Please leave, Mr. Trajan. Now!"

CHAPTER 43

Mitchell sat in the chair in utter disbelief. His thoroughness in presenting the pertinent facts, their logical progression and the sincere plea for his son's life had come forth in better fashion than he could have possibly hoped. Yet, before him stood the man who had taken his son and most assuredly subjected him to a number of unspeakable horrors, denying any culpability or even knowledge of what Mitchell accepted as infallible truths. He reexamined the few words Andy had spoken during their conversation and could not find any sense in them.

"Do not make me ask you again," Andy said still holding the front door open.

Mitchell stood and he said, "Or what? You're going to call the police?" Mitchell audibly scoffed at the notion, knowing full well the police were already on the premises, knocked out, handcuffed and locked in the trunk of his car.

"Could you please keep it down? My wife—"

"No, Mr. Walker. No, I can't keep it down," Mitchell proclaimed.

He reached into his pocket and pulled out the weapon it concealed. He raised the barrel level to the ground and pointed it at Andy Walker's sternum. Andy watched, unfazed. The gun seemed much heavier than Mitchell expected but also felt much softer and more comfortable in his hand.

"Now you listen to me, you sick bastard," he growled. "You are going to take me to my son and you are going to let me take him home."

"I can't give you what I don't have, Mr. Trajan," Andy smirked.

"Really? Then I guess I'll have to put a bullet in your wife," he said flatly and motioned toward the hallway.

"No," Andy shouted, darting from behind the front door to place the entirety of his bulk in the middle of the hallway.

Mitchell stopped and reset the pistol's sights back on Andy's sternum. "I've been involved in twenty-nine separate murders, Mr. Walker. Remember? One more isn't going to make much of a difference, now, is it? That's the whole point of the Commuters: to provide you with the knowledge that you can do whatever you have to do, whenever you have to do it."

"You have no idea what it means to 'do what you have to do.' You have no idea what being a *Commuter* is."

"I'm getting my son back from you, Mr. Walker, and I'm prepared to do whatever I have to do in order to make that happen."

"Are you? Are you prepared to die for him?"

"Yes."

The immediacy of Mitchell's response seemed to take Andy off guard, but he stayed on the attack.

"Are you prepared to die for me?"

A puzzling look crossed Mitchell's face. "What?"

"Are you prepared to die for me?" Andy shouted. Then calmly, "If you're right, then I'm the only person in this whole wide world who knows where your son is. So, in that scenario, if I die, then so does your son."

Andy broke from his position in the middle of the hallway and sauntered toward Mitchell. Then, like a faux-magician, he swept his hands back and forth in front of the gun and plugged the barrel with his pinky finger.

"You hold no sway, Emperor," he mocked. He removed his finger, walked into the living room and jumped into the air, swinging his legs out and landing hard in the recliner.

"There's your wife. Are you prepared to let her die rather than give me my son?"

Andy let out a few forced chuckles. "You said the whole point of the Commuters was to provide members with the knowledge that they could do whatever they had to to get what they wanted. Well, mission accomplished. I know exactly what I can do. Do you?"

"Do I what?"

"Do you know what it means to be impervious to the ravages of war? To be impenetrable from death?" He paused. "I do, Mr. Trajan. Racked with sadness over my son's death, I've brought myself to the threshold of death's door on more than one occasion only to fall short each time. Do you know just how far you could go before reining it in? Just how much the human body can withstand and still not give in to death? Do you know the depths of depravity you can administer? What quantity and quality of pain you can deliver unto others before their minds call it quits and force them to black out so as not to endure any more?"

Mitchell's mind raced, looking for an edge. He all but forgot about the gun and his arm relaxed at his side. The gun nestled in his hand and rubbed against his pant leg when he shifted his weight. The unpleasant bleach odor was stronger where he stood but he paid little attention to it. He was solely focused on trying to find the "sway" Andy had mentioned—the idea, threat or proposition that would entice this madman to release his son.

"The point of the Commuters is imparting knowledge of oneself."

"Knowledge?" Andy offered from the recliner. "Please. The only knowledge this imparts is the knowledge of how to kill without being detected."

"It seems to me, with the cops staking out your favorite corner, you haven't learned a damned thing. It also seems to me you haven't looked deep enough," Mitchell accused.

Andy smiled. "What's the phrase? Ah, yes, 'become that which you most desire.' The way *you* throw the phrase around, it means nothing. The Commuters rely on their newest members to revert back to their sheepish ways, following instead of leading, slowly slipping into the soft, comfortable pattern of behavior, or misbehavior as the case may be, established by some mysterious man so long ago no one can remember when. It's a slow immersion into complacency reinforced by a generally accepted mob mentality. It's not knowledge, it's programming."

Andy wistfully grinned and let his head roll on his shoulders as if he were working out a kink. "Granted, it got me through the tough years, those first few years following the death of my boy. But like anything else—narcotics, sex, religion—it gets old fast and eventually you need more and more to get the same feeling of satisfaction."

He paused and stared off into the corner of the room. "'That which I most desire to be,'" he mumbled.

Mitchell watched Andy's eyes glaze, as if the insane man before him was letting the concept swirl around his mind like a fine wine enveloping his tongue. Then, once he had completely swallowed the thought, Andy snapped back to the moment.

"To answer your question. Yes. I am prepared to let my wife die rather than give you your son. But truth be told, I really don't think she'd mind. Maybe you should go ask her."

An uneasiness filled Mitchell and he instinctively set the gun again on his host.

Andy cocked his head to one side and groused, "This again? I thought we were past idle threats. You can't shoot me, Trajan, and we both know it." Then he motioned with his hand as if shooing a fly, "Now go ask my precious Chastity what she thinks about you killing her."

Mitchell turned, looked at the light spilling in from the open doors off the hallway and then back at Andy who was lost in thought and completely unconcerned with what Mitchell did. He took a few steps to the first door, the bathroom, and peered in. His eyes and nostrils burned from the bleach. Seeing nothing inside, he shut the door.

Past the bathroom were two more open doors. Mitchell edged down the hallway's left wall and peered into the room on the right. In it he saw the vertical bars of a crib in the foreground, what he determined was a make-shift changing table made with pillows atop a painted dresser and toys scattered about. The room looked as if no one had set foot in it in years.

He moved to the other side of the hall and peered in the other open door. The room was much darker than the nursery, the sun trying to make its way past the drawn shades. Mitchell inched closer, seeing more and more of the bed as he moved. He leaned against the jamb and took in the whole of the scene.

On the bed, nestled atop what was surely an enormous blood stain in the bedding, was a woman's naked, dismembered body. The torso lay in the middle of the bed with its arms and legs, severed, placed in their approximate corresponding location. The woman's detached head was placed where it would have been had it not been cleaved, but it faced downward, one-hundred eight degrees in opposition of the torso.

He crept back into the breathable air of the living room to find Andy still sitting in the same position in the recliner.

"She died early this morning. Actually, she died eight years ago when we buried our boy. It just took her this long to realize it."

The subsequent pause was long, but not uncomfortable. Andy looked up and into Mitchell's eyes and said, "But that's not what this is about Mr. Trajan. This isn't about my wife or my son. You seem to be a smart man. You tell me what this is all about."

Without missing a beat, Mitchell said, "Power."

"That goes without saying." Then Andy's face brightened, "Hey, I'll tell you what. You tell me what this is all about and I'll give you back your son. How's that sound?"

Entranced by their intense discussions and the disturbing death chamber that was the Walkers' master bedroom, Mitchell had nearly forgotten about his son; forgotten about the sole reason he was standing in Andy Walker's living room. The mention of Davis' release brought a re-engaging excitement Mitchell had to consciously curb. Mitchell didn't trust the disturbed man in the recliner. How could he trust this man with all that had happened and all that he had heard and seen since his arrival in Andy's house? Since Andy's arrival in the Commuters? But Mitchell figured he had no other choice. He had to play the game. He quietly hoped he was up to the challenge.

"Okay, Helios. You got a deal."

Pensively, deliberately, Mitchell gave the impression he was thinking hard before offering, "I go back to knowledge of oneself."

"Aaaaaan." sounding like a game show buzzer. "Wrong."

Mitchell gently pounced, "No, I don't think I am. You were right. This is about the knowledge of killing without being detected."

It wasn't until the words came out of his mouth that he fully understood what he was saying. The idea was perfectly clear in Mitchell's mind, just as it must have been in the mind of Yusuf, the Commuters' founder. Andy had become that which Yusuf most desired him to be:

someone who could kill without remorse. And the more he thought about it, the more Mitchell knew Andy was absolutely right. Yusuf ibn Tashufin was creating followers, not leaders; cowards hidden behind masks killing without cause or justification all in a misguided attempt to climb an imaginary status ladder the have-nots had created, with each rung representing an invented milestone to track their own ascension.

"I don't know why I didn't see it earlier," Mitchell confessed softly to himself.

Andy sat in his chair with an eerie grin. "What are you talking about?"

"You. Me. The Commuters. 'Become that which you most desire to be.' But you don't. You don't become what you want. You become that which *they* want you to be. An invincible killer. This whole time I thought I was doing all this for myself, for my family. But here I am, a thousand years after its creation doing exactly what they wanted me to do, what they required me to do.

"And you," pointing the muzzle of the gun at Andy, "you're their crowning achievement."

Andy squirmed a bit in his chair. "Huh?"

"It was just a matter of time, I suppose?"

Mitchell subtly glided the gun back into his jacket pocket. He wanted there to be no coercion in Andy's mind. He needed Andy to feel relaxed and thinking clearly, of his own accord.

Fidgeting in his recliner, Andy asked, "What was?"

"You. Andy Walker. It was just a matter of time before someone like you made it through the process."

"What do you mean 'someone like me?'"

"You're obviously insane, Andy, or haven't you figured that out yet?"

"What?"

Mitchell counted one on his unencumbered hands, "Your wife is dead, yet her disembodied corpse is lying in your house; in your *bed*." He counted two and added, "You prey on young male prostitutes. C'mon, that is classic transference."

Andy was getting visibly annoyed.

"I'll bet your father was physically abusive and you tortured the neighborhood pets whenever you had the chance. And then there's the other thing," counting three on his hand.

"What other thing?" Andy yelled.

"Bed wetting." Mitchell chuckled.

Andy stood and, pushing his face inches away from Mitchell's, screamed, "Shut the fuck up. You don't know me. You don't know my father. You don't know what the fuck you're talking about."

Mitchell smiled back through the screams and shouts. He walked toward the front door and hammered away at him again. "Is that so? You are so classically insane, Andy. I know things about you that you don't even know about yourself, and I've only been talking to you for fifteen minutes."

Collecting himself, Andy sat back in the chair. "It's all a ploy, Trajan. A scam. In the unlikely event that these policemen you spoke of catch up to me, I need a Plan B. Insanity is my Plan B."

"Well, I must commend you on your efforts," he offered with more than a touch of sarcasm. "It shouldn't be too hard for an insane person to convince twelve rational jurors you are in fact insane. If I were you, though, I'd worry about the prosecution's army of psychiatrists. If it's a ploy, they'll see it for what it is."

"I'm not insane."

"I beg to differ. A sane man would have seen the benefits of releasing Davis."

"Davis?"

"Yes, my son, Davis. The boy you think is a prostitute."

A droll smile crept across Andy's face. "Nice try, Trajan."

"I'm diagnosing you from the little pieces I remember from Psych 101 in college. Tell me, why covet *that* boy? By now you've figured out he's not a prostitute, so why not give him back? Hell, you and I both know who that prostitute was in the car that killed your son. *He's* the one you should really be punishing. A sane man scheming to beat a murder conviction would realize Davis is the chink in the armor. This whole transference thing … it's sad, really."

Andy sprang to attention. "What do you mean we both know who that boy was?"

Mitchell looked at him, confused. "Excuse me?"

"You said we both know who that prostitute was. How could you possibly know that?"

Mitchell smiled. He found his sway.

"I'm a fairly well-connected businessman in this city, Andy. Very few things happen, things of such importance, without my knowledge. I am, excuse me, I *was*, very good friends with Natalie Belling. She died last year. I assume you know who she is?"

"Sure. She was one of the few people who actually gave a shit when Franklin died. She was a consultant for our attorney."

"She was a passionate woman," Mitchell stated. "She was dedicated to the cause of victim's rights. Ironic that a victim's rights advocate would come to the aid of a murderer. Wouldn't you agree, Andy? But I digress.

"Did you know she was a Commuter? Yeah, my sponsor, the Tiger Lady. She and I had lunch on several occasions when she told me all about that case." Mitchell looked at Andy from the corners of his eyes. "*Your* case. I later came to find out that the son of another acquaintance of mine was the young boy in that car."

"You know the boy who killed Franklin?"

"You don't?" Mitchell prodded.

Andy sat there and said nothing, staring at Mitchell.

Connie's words came drumming in Mitchell's ears, *You're a terrible liar*. Luckily, thankfully, everything he was saying to Andy was true. He frowned and offered, "I guess since he was a minor, they kept everything anonymous. But weren't you at the trial? Didn't your attorney address him by name?"

"There was no trial," Andy bemoaned. "It was a plea bargain. And since Belling was involved, the prosecution argued that his client was a victim of statutory rape and required some kind of added protection, using Belling's work for victim's rights against her. That bastard lawyer got it so his name was never put in any of the public records. They called that red-headed kid Defendant, like it was his name."

Mitchell could almost see the dendrites flashing in Andy's mind as he mulled over the possibility of discovering the name of the boy responsible for his son's death.

Then, in a melodious tone, Mitchell asked, "So, then, Andy, do I hold any 'sway' now?"

Andy's head snapped up and looked directly at Mitchell. His eyes narrowed as he growled, "Are you playing me? Is that what this is? How do I know you're telling me the truth?"

"You are a far better liar than I am, Andy. But I'm a far better judge of character than you are. You had no intention of letting my son go, even if I was able to win your little game. But then, I knew that. I just needed you to understand that you can never assume you know all the angles.

"That said, let me ask you, what's it going to cost you to find out if I am telling you the truth or not? You can snatch up another young prostitute off the streets tomorrow and transfer all your hatred and loathing into him rather than Davis. Although, with the police hot on your trail, I highly recommend you find another street corner.

"The question simply is, can you afford to let this opportunity, the chance to find out who was in that car, to find out who killed your boy, slip away? And that is something only you can answer."

Mitchell stood, watching Andy mull over the idea, weighing the pluses and minuses to accepting Mitchell's proposal

After a long internal deliberation, Andy said, "Okay, Trajan. You got a deal. What now?"

CHAPTER 44

The sun was streaming between the vertical slats of the Venetian blinds which hung across the sliding glass door between the den and the expansive deck overlooking the pool and the meticulously groomed backyard. It blinded her before she even opened her eyes, which she instinctively did. They teared as she shielded her face. She quickly sprang upright on the overstuffed couch, sinking into the lavishly plush, velvety, chocolate-colored fabric.

Prudy wondered what time it was. She checked her cell phone, white-knuckle-clutched in her fist while she slept, first to see the time, 7:42, and second to see if her husband had returned any of the thousands of messages she had left him before nodding off. She knew he hadn't even before verifying that fact. Her ringer was on, full volume, and she slept lightly. But those details had little to do with her assurance he hadn't called.

She knew her husband well. She knew he wouldn't listen to more than the first few seconds of any one of her calls. She knew it before placing each one, but hoped somehow the set of extreme circumstances in which they found themselves would make a difference. She also knew that no set of circumstances would make a difference.

She wasn't alone in the house. Lowell had stayed the night rather than returning to his college dorm. She figured he probably wished he hadn't stayed. How much can any woman expect her son to comfort and console her the way she wants her husband to? The way Prudy *needed* Mitchell to?

Sitting there she noticed a faded wet spot on the carpet, the remains of all the cleaning efforts to remove her husband's vomit. She stared at it, hoping it wouldn't stain. Great big sobs burst forth when she processed why she was worried about a spot on the carpet when her son was being tortured by a maniac. Then, just as quickly, she stopped bawling.

"Get a hold of yourself, Prudence," she whispered. "You are going to make it through this."

She wiped the tears from her eyes and put on what she considered a brave face, a face that no third party evaluation would have considered brave. She stood up and walked into the kitchen, the phone still clutched in her fingers like a fish in an eagle's talons. She looked at the phone again to see the time, 7:44, and placed it down on the granite counter top, stretching, flexing and rubbing her sore fingers.

She turned and opened the refrigerator. A clear plastic pitcher of orange juice sat on the top shelf. Dressed in her pajamas and robe, she remembered how, at one time in her life, a screwdriver would have been the sensible way to calm her nerves. But she immediately replaced that thought with an overwhelming desire to create the world's fluffiest omelet. She extracted all the ingredients from the fridge and surrounding hardwood cabinets to do so.

She hadn't yet added the yolks back into the whipped egg whites when the phone on the wall between the den and the kitchen rang. She instinctively reached for her cell phone, but when the hard line rang again, she changed directions and lifted the handset from the cradle.

"Hello?" she asked in a shaky voice.

"Mrs. Treadwell, this is Detective Brown. From last night."

"Yes?"

She heard him stammer and then say, "Um, yes, Mrs. Treadwell, I've been trying to get a hold of your husband for some time and it seems he is not taking any calls. Would he be there, ma'am?"

"Mitchell? No. He's not home at the moment and I'm not at all sure when to expect him."

"Do you know how I might get a hold of him?"

"I've come to learn, Detective, that unless you're an important business client, you'll have to wait for him to get back to you."

"When I met with him last night, his phone rang. Did he speak with you at all after he and your sister drove here?"

"No." Her shakiness was steadied by anger. She was sent to voice mail each time she called. "I tried calling him several times during the night, but, no, I never spoke with him."

"How is it you called and didn't get through yet someone else did?"

Prudy sighed heavily. "I don't know."

"Do you know who might have been calling him around three or three-thirty in the morning, Mrs. Treadwell?"

"Other than me? I have no idea. Probably some foreign investor."

"Okay. Thank you for your time, ma'am. And if you do speak with your husband, please have him call me immediately."

"No offense, detective, but if he's not calling me, he's not calling you."

"I understand. Could you please pass along the message anyway? Thanks."

Prudy hung up the phone on the wall and immediately picked up her cell phone, pushing the redial button. She listened to three rings before her husband's recorded voice politely told her that her call was important to him and asked her to leave him a message.

Calmly, yet still with the anger in her voice that Detective Brown had stirred, she complied. "Mitchell, this is your wife. I have been waiting for you to return my calls with any information you can possibly offer.

Please call me. If you need another reason to call home other than having a wife worried half to death, I have a message for you from Detective Brown." And as hard as she tried not to sound desperate, she ended with, "Oh, God, Mitchell, please call me."

* * *

The sun was streaming between the horizontal slats of the vinyl mini-blinds poorly attached to the wood frame of the large window that overlooked the yellow grass and scattered trash of the low-rise apartment's courtyard. It would have blinded him had he not been sleeping with one of the lumpy cushions over his head. He slowly rolled over and opened his eyes, noting how much later in the morning the sun was rising compared to the long days of late June and early July. He swung his legs over the edge of the battered and broken couch and sat up, slumping into the permanent, deep indentation that made sleeping on it unpleasant.

Uncle Max wondered what time it was. He checked his phone, first to see the time, seven-forty three, second to see if he had any calls requiring his attention, he had none, and third to call someone, anyone who owed him a favor and could give him a ride to the impound lot.

He was ready to call Faith, but once he determined she'd already done enough for him, he reconsidered and ran through the list of individuals who were in the red on his mental ledger of favors. The name Willie Spence came immediately to mind, but knowing how late he was up the previous night, a call this early would not be well received, not to mention the fact that Willie Spence would not want to be anywhere near that impound lot; not after being responsible for opening a hole in the fence big enough for a man to squeeze through.

He knew plenty of other people willing to do a favor for an old man in need. He scrolled through his phone list and pushed send.

"Hello?" the voice on the other end answered.

"Sweetheart, this here's your Uncle Max. How you doin', girl?"

"Uncle Max," she sang sweetly. "Wha'choo got goin'?"

"You know me. I got somethin' goin' all the time," he said and chuckled. "But the thing is I'm in need of a little help this morning. My car, you know Goldilocks, well, she was towed to the impound lot and I was hoping maybe you could give me a ride to the police station to clear up some fiduciary discrepancies, f'ya'no'wa'mean."

"Uh," she thought a moment, "Where you at?"

"I could meet you at Salem's Lot in twenty minutes, if that works for you?"

"Yeah, I guess that'll work. I see you in twenty minutes."

"Ain't you somethin' sweet? You too good to an old man like me."

"Anything for my Uncle Max."

He hung up the phone and stared at it a while before getting up off the couch. He dropped it onto the leather-bound ledger and made his way into the bathroom for his morning constitutional. He wanted to be sure he took his ledger with him.

* * *

The bustle of campus life was in its earliest stages, meaning there were plenty of bikes and pedestrians, but few motor vehicles and little noise, making for ideal sleeping conditions. The morning sun, on the other hand, easily shined through the thin, tattered drapes that hung on the large expanse of glass looking out over the crumbling cement porch. The sun's rays filled the front room with such brilliant light that it made it nearly impossible to stay asleep. He felt something hard and pointy jabbing his ribs and wondered what he was sleeping on. In a flash he pieced together the bits of information available to him and determined the discomfort was the elbow of the boy that lay beside him.

Slipping off the well-worn leather couch, obtained from his parent's basement, Chad rolled onto the floor, sat up, leaned back against the bulky piece of furniture and rubbed his eyes. He was still extremely tired. All that time talking to the detectives as well as Mr. Treadwell had thrown his circadian rhythm completely off. He was in a bit of a haze when the hand attached to the pointy elbow landed on his shoulder.

"Are you getting up?" the deep, sleepy voice asked.

"I can't sleep, so I guess I might as well," Chad answered.

"Are you going to take a shower?"

"I don't know. Why? Do I smell?"

"No. I was just wondering if you wanted company."

Chad thought about the offer. "You remember the last time?"

"I'll be more careful," the other boy said sheepishly. "I promise."

Chad, wearing the same clothes he had worn home from work, leaned to one side so he could pull his cell phone from his pocket to check the time, 7:44.

"I got a while before class," he accepted playfully.

Then, as he leaned back again to replace the phone in his pocket, it rang. He looked at the text screen: Unknown Cell Number.

"Don't answer it," pleaded the boy, still lying on the couch.

Chad answered it anyway.

"Hello?"

"Is Chad there?" the caller asked in a soft monotone.

"Speaking," he replied cheerfully.

"I know this may seem a bit out-of-the-blue, but were you arrested for solicitation eight years ago after being involved in a fatal car accident?"

His heart nearly stopped.

All legal records of the incident were expunged when he turned eighteen. His family had gone to great lengths to ensure less than a handful of people in the world knew anything about it.

"Ah, I think you have the wrong number," he stammered.

"No. No, I'm quite certain I have the right number. Thank you, Chad. I'll be seeing you. Soon."

Chad listened in horror as the call disconnected.

* * *

The morning sun was completely blotted out by the thick drapes that hung in the north facing window. There was very little chance he would have awoken any time before noon if not for the constant ringing in his ears. As he crept out of the foggy unconsciousness left by the one-too-many beers he consumed at the afterhours bar that catered to cops getting off their shifts at bar time, the ringing in his ears gelled and solidified as the recognizable ring tone of his cell.

With each passing note, the ring tone became clearer until he scrounged around for his jacket. It lay on the floor in front of the couch with the rest of his clothes, save his white boxers. He chose to sleep on the couch because he knew he'd had too much to drink and didn't want to wake his wife by fumbling around in the dark.

His hand came across what he determined was the jacket's collar, pulled it toward him and held it up high in the air while the other hand groped for the pocket concealing his phone. Once found, he reached in, pulled it out and answered.

"H'low."

"Jenkins, get your ass out of bed. I need your help. I'm handcuffed and riding in the trunk of a car, I'm pretty sure it's my brother-in-law's car: a black BMW 760Li. The last thing I remember —"

"Whoa, whoa, whoa," he said sitting up. "Who is this?"

"It's your partner, you jackass."

"You're handcuffed?"

"I was able to swing the cuffs down around my feet so now they're in front of me."

"You're in the trunk of someone's car?"

"Shut your mouth and listen!" Connie growled slowly. "Get your ass out of bed, grab a pen and write this down."

Jenkins rolled onto the floor and walked toward the kitchen to find the pad of paper he knew was there. The kitchen lights blinded him momentarily when he turned them on but he shielded his eyes and prepared to take notes.

"Okay, shoot," he said, still tired and groggy.

"I'm in the trunk of a black beamer, a 760Li, license plate number, damn, I have no idea what the license plate number is. I'm not moving now, but I was knocked out. My last known location was 42 Simsbury Road in Highland. You got my cell phone frequency, right? I need you to follow my signal if I'm not at the address I gave you."

"I'll have to dig that frequency out of the files at work."

"I don't give a rat's ass what you have to do, just get here. Quick. Oh, and Jenkins?"

"Yeah."

"I need you to keep this completely to yourself. Don't tell anyone, don't call anyone, don't go to anyone for help."

"Why not?"

She paused. "He's got my weapon," she admitted. "So I need your back up, too."

"I met your brother-in-law. You couldn't take him?"

"It wasn't a wrestling match. He jumped me and put something over my face. That's not the point. Focus Jenkins. This is all somehow related to my nephew's disappearance and, while I might have to arrest my brother-in-law when this is all said and done, I also need you, someone on the outside, keeping an eye on me as well as the bad guys. Got it?"

"Yeah, sure," he chuckled. "I should be able to get out there—"

"Make it quick. And you better have stopped laughing by the time you get here. Don't call me unless you can see the car and if you can see the car, don't call unless no one's around to hear the phone ring. Got it?"

"Whatever," and Jenkins pressed end.

CHAPTER 45

The bleach still burned in Mitchell's nostrils when he stepped out of the front door of the house with his son's captor. Fresh air had never smelled so fine.

"I'll follow you," Mitchell said, digging into his pocket for the keys.

"Is that necessary?"

Mitchell kept walking and, without turning around said, "Absolutely."

"I assumed we'd be riding together?"

"You were mistaken."

"And why's that?" Andy asked.

"I told you I'm a better than average judge of character and you, Mr. Helios, I'm sorry to say, I do not trust."

"Really?"

Mitchell stopped and peered over the top of his vehicle. "The only reason you're doing any of this is to find out who that red-headed boy was. I have no reason to hide it from you other than to use it as, how did you put it, 'sway.' Until I have Davis safe and sound in my car and am driving away from you forever, that information is mine and mine alone. You, on the other hand, are, as we speak, trying to figure out a way to obtain that information without letting Davis go. I know that because I have spent my entire professional career weeding out those I can trust from those I can't. And you I cannot trust.

"It's why I only told you his first name and why I had my phone service dial his number. And, it is why we're taking different vehicles to the location where you are holding my son."

Andy smiled. "You think you got me all figured out, don't you?"

"Not at all, Mr. Helios. But as I like to say, I know a thing or two about a thing or two. I'm merely doing everything I can to ensure I get my son back."

Andy scoffed and walked to his car door. Mitchell slid into his front seat confident that he had played his hand as well as possible, chalking up his success to his due diligence at the police station. He shut the door and brought the German-engineered driving machine to life.

"Mitchell," Connie yelled from the trunk. "Get me out of here."

It startled Mitchell. He hadn't expected his sister-in-law to recover so quickly, hoping to spend the entire car ride plotting his next strategy.

"I'm sorry, Connie, but I can't do that. Not just yet."

"You have no idea what you're doing, Mitch."

The word 'Mitch' grated on him as soon as it hit his ears, but then that was why she said it the way she did.

Connie continued to chatter as the car backed out of the driveway, "This is going to end bad for you, for me, for everyone involved, including Davis unless you get me out of here. Right fuckin' now."

"Connie, I am truly sorry for, um, the way things developed."

"Developed. You knocked me out, cuffed me and stuffed me in the trunk of your car. That's not a development, that's kidnapping. And a police officer, no less. Do you realize that puts you in line for the death penalty?"

"Interesting you would bring that up. I'm pretty sure I'm going to die today. I have recently come to accept this as a consequence of my actions the past thirty years. But as long as I get Davis back, alive and in one piece, I don't care. And as far as I'm concerned, what I'm doing right now, including kidnapping a police officer, is my last, best chance to get Davis back."

Mitchell, having already backed out, watched as Andy eased out onto the street. The green Saturn made its way up the picturesque hill that Mitchell found somewhat comforting as he followed.

"Mitchell, I swear to God—"

"Look, Connie, I'm a fairly savvy businessman used to dealing with irrational people. If you had been in that house, a cop and all the baggage that comes with being a cop, good and bad, I can guarantee you we'd still be in there and getting nowhere."

"Mitchell."

"Instead, we are currently on our way to pick up Davis."

"Mitchell!"

"I need to concentrate on what I'm going to do next, Connie. I can't have this conversation with you. Suffice to say, when we are back at my house, comforting both Davis and Prudy ..." He paused. "Damn. I'll bet she's called a million times. When we get back to my house, you can do whatever you want to me: arrest me, beat me, kill me, I don't care. But until then, I need to think."

"Mitchell."

"If you keep on talking, I'm going to have to pull over and knock you out again, Connie. I really don't want to do that, but I will."

"Let me out, Mitch."

He didn't answer.

"Mitchell."

Mitchell still didn't answer. He considered stopping and placing the rag over Connie's face again to stop her from prattling on and on but thought Andy might find it suspicious. He followed the green Saturn for nearly an hour driving to the absolute opposite side of the city before pulling into the parking lot of the 777 East Hope Street building. It was an unattractive, even ominous-looking stone building with very little to offer passersby other than a viable reason to continue on. The Saturn nestled under a maple sapling. Mitchell pulled up next to it and watched the driver meticulously remove his sunglasses and then his driving gloves. Mitchell noticed Andy looking at the gloves as if they were some kind of rare and exotic treasure.

Mitchell's car was standing still with the engine cut. Connie's voice, which had been adequately drowned out in transit, was quite audible and sounded very annoyed.

"Where are we?"

"We're up in the North Bend area. Now please shut up. If he knows I've got someone in the trunk, we'll never get Davis back. Don't make me use the rag again."

"If you don't let me out—"

"Shut up. He's getting out of his car."

Andy placed the gloves between the seats, got out, walked around his car and leaned on Mitchell's door, obviously waiting for him to roll down the window.

"Is this the place?" Mitchell asked as the pane lowered.

"No. But I have to go in there to get a few things. I'll only be five minutes or so."

"Are we close?"

"Why? You have somewhere to be?"

Mitchell contemplated making a wisecrack and thought better of it. "I need gas."

"There's a station right up the street."

"Thanks," he said while lowering his head to find the button for the electric window. Mitchell started to zip up the window when Andy latched his fingers to the top of it, appearing to want to say something. When Mitchell stopped raising it, Andy paused then, changing his mind, said, "Never mind. You'll be back." With that, Andy retreated and walked to the front door.

Mitchell turned the key and brought the vehicle back to life. He backed up and pulled out of the parking lot in the direction Andy indicated with the nod of his head.

"You know you can't trust that psycho," came from deep in the back of the car.

"Of course I know that, Connie."

"Hey, I am very uncomfortable back here, Mitch." Her voice was calm. "Let me out at the gas station and let's talk about all this."

"I can't, Connie. Look, I know you're a cop. I know I've put you in a bad spot. I know you're going to kick my ass when I finally do let you out of there. But I can't do it yet, not until I have Davis back. You will only be a distraction in negotiations. I can't."

"Negotiation? What is this, some world peace summit. That bastard kidnapped your son and you're treating him like royalty or something."

"Until I have Davis back, he's the king of my realm, Connie."

"You're going to let that psycho walk all over you and—"

"Look, Connie. I have information he wants. He has Davis. It's a simple transaction."

"Yeah, with a psychopath, Mitchell. How stupid are you?"

"Connie, I'll ask you one last time to please shut your mouth."

She continued, undeterred, ranting and raving to the point of distraction. Mitchell pulled into the gas station and, rather than pull up next to the pumps, he backed into the furthest parking space from the station's door. Connie's voice instantly became louder when he popped the trunk, but only momentarily. Mitchell raced back and smothered her face with the chloroform-soaked cloth again. Connie, her hands bound by her handcuffs, mustered little resistance.

CHAPTER 46

After reuniting with Andy in the parking lot of his office, Mitchell drove into the heart of the city, not the beating heart of the downtown business district that Mitchell all but owned and operated, but rather the central-most bowels of the city where the industrial concentration of factories, warehouses, transmission shops and metal scrap yards co-mingled. It was rare that Mitchell ever found himself in that particular part of the city, but it reminded him what it meant to be a hard worker. Here he saw the laborers who drove their double wheel pickups, punched their time cards, and paid their union dues. Downtown he saw those who merely leveraged that hard work into profits.

Mitchell was a smart businessman and whenever he found himself in the area, he paid close attention to every detail of his surroundings so as to ensure he never forgot for whom he worked. He looked for buildings with broken windows and put a mental note next to the executives he knew from that organization. He did the same with crumbled cement driveways, rusted façades and other exterior blemishes, knowing full well that an organization that allowed its physical assets to deteriorate had very little understanding of long-term business success. Mitchell also knew the executives associated with those run-down buildings were ultimately destined for failure.

As he followed the green Saturn past the police impound lot, he was curiously impressed with its cleanliness and general appearance. Even the razor wire, while ominous and imposing, gleamed brightly in the early morning sun and thus reflected well on the department as a whole, but on the facility management team in particular.

Standing at the gate was an older, dark-skinned gentleman whom Mitchell recognized. It was Uncle Max, a well-known character and pseudo community leader from the inner city whose connections within the political machine were surprisingly deep and well-rooted. While his personal demeanor and physical appearance would never indicate his true stature within the community, there wasn't a social program press conference or a ceremonial grand opening of an urban youth center ever missed by the pepper-haired elder statesman.

The old man's eyes narrowed and his brow furrowed as he watched the dented green Saturn pass by. They then glared at Mitchell's unblemished BMW which, in that part of town, stood out from the American-made sedans, trucks and SUVs. Mitchell tossed a half-felt wave at the man waiting for the fenced gate to roll away, but Uncle Max had lost interest and engaged in some unheard conversation with a man on the other side of the barrier. The old man was waving a few sheets of paper in the air and didn't notice Mitchell's attempt at cordiality.

After turning just past the impound lot, he followed the green Saturn past a transmission shop and up the short gravel driveway of a large, apparently abandoned building. Both he and Andy got out of their cars simultaneously and stood watching one another.

"Is this it?" Mitchell asked.

Not even acknowledging Mitchell's question, Andy calmly stated, "Take your gun out of your jacket pocket and leave it on the seat of your car."

Mitchell replied immediately, "No," and shook his head ever-so-slightly.

"Excuse me?"

"You heard me, I said no. I'm not going in there with you. I don't trust you, remember?"

Andy smiled and leaned back against the trunk of his car. "And how do you recommend we resolve this impasse?"

"We both want what the other has, Andy. It's a very simple transaction. You go in there, get my boy and bring him out. While you're in there, I'll write down every last detail about ...," and remembering a cop was the trunk, sedated or otherwise, he chose his words carefully, "the person we discussed earlier. As soon as Davis is sitting in my front seat and I'm backing out of this driveway, I'll crumple up the note and throw it out my window."

"My, my, my, you put a lot of thought into this."

Mitchell said nothing.

"This plan of yours requires an awful lot of trust on my part, Mr. Trajan."

"I'm a businessman, Andy, and an honest businessman at that. In fact, my sister-in-law, she's a cop by the way, she wonders how I can make a living being so honest. The fact is, dishonest businessmen have no chance of repeat sales. And while I hope to never see you again, no offense intended —"

"None taken," Andy smiled and nodded.

"A leopard can't change his spots. I'm a bad liar. I'm hoping that your trust in me has grown in the short while we've spent together today and that you can see past your own distrust of people to do what has to be done ... for both our benefit."

"But I so wanted to show you my little play pen."

"Life is full of disappointments. Now please stop stalling and go get my son."

Andy headed toward the door jingling his keys and said, "It's going to take a while. I have a few things to … undo. Are you sure I can't interest you in—"

"Thank you, no. The faster we do this, the faster I can help my son recover from whatever horrors you've put him through and the faster you can administer whatever forms of justice that mind of yours can concoct on someone else."

Andy smiled, apparently pleased with Mitchell for knowing what was on his mind. He unlocked the door and passed through without any further discussion. When the door closed, Mitchell took a deep breath and audibly exhaled.

"You awake in there, Connie?"

Connie's voice came from the trunk, slow and dopey. "Like you care."

He placed both hands on the roof of his car, just above the door seam, looked down at the millions of little grey stones and said, "I told you Connie, this isn't about you. This is about getting Davis back. You think this is easy? You think I'm enjoying this? I'm not. For Christ's sake, Connie."

Mitchell heard the heavy thump of a car door slam and looked behind him.

"Connie, eh? Iz-at wha-cha call your car?"

Mitchell gasped and reflexively turned around. "Uncle Max?" he said, watching the old man walk toward him. "What are you doing here?"

"Yeah, I call my little beauty Goldie," he said, pointing at the vintage Dodge Dart parked just beyond the gravel driveway. "Like Goldilocks. She ain't much to look at now, but man do she run smooth, like the silky fur of a nubile young vixen." He snickered.

Mitchell was dumbstruck.

"Anyways, Mr. Treadwell, I got myself into a little fender bender yesterday and had my car impounded over there. I saw you drive by and wondered just like you, 'What's he doing here?' So I thought I'd say hello."

"Hello," was all Mitchell could muster.

Uncle Max fixed his eyes on the green Saturn, "Well I'll be God damned if that ain't the dumb-ass that hit my car yesterday. You know this guy?"

"Um," he stammered, "He's a recent acquaintance, I guess."

Mitchell was becoming increasingly agitated. He looked around to see if there were any other unexpected surprises with which he had to contend. Helios was unstable at best and Mitchell had done everything he could to keep the madman focused and in check. In all negotiations, a good businessman eliminates as many variables as possible so that all parties can focus on the three or four most important issues, come to an agreement and move forward. Uncle Max's arrival was a variable fraught with negative implications beyond Mitchell's grasp and therefore beyond his control. He surmised he had to eliminate the variable. And quickly.

"Uncle Max, let me be perfectly honest with you," Mitchell began as Uncle Max walked to the front of the Saturn to verify it was indeed crushed. "I'm brokering an extremely important and extremely sensitive deal at the moment. Is there another time we can—"

"He's the newest Sophomore, eh?"

Mitchell was caught again by surprise, this time by the content of the dialog rather than the timing. "I'm sorry. What?"

"I asked you, the senior member of the Alpha Seven, the Matriculating Commuter, if the fuckhead driving this here piece of shit moved up from a Freshman to a Sophomore last night."

Mitchell flashed to earlier that morning when he had barged in on Andy Walker and spouted centuries-old secrets as if they were taught in seventh grade social studies classes. Mitchell, placing himself in Andy's shoes momentarily, found the discussion initially disorienting, but the idea grew into normality and quickly made sense. Then, once his head grabbed hold of the idea, he smiled and responded carefully.

"I don't think this is the forum for this particular discussion, Uncle Max. How about—"

"He's the same fuckhead who killed those couple of boys the past few weeks, ain't he?"

If his knowledge of the Commuters unsettled Mitchell, then Uncle Max's knowledge of the tangential murders perpetrated by Andy left him stunned; his mouth hung open and nearly unusable. "Uhhhh ..."

"Dammit," he shouted. "He's screwed everything up. There were safeguards in place designed to eliminate this exact thing from happening."

Thoroughly annoyed, Uncle Max rubbed the long, faded scar on his forehead, the one he'd received so long ago. He stared at the front driver side of the green car, then at Mitchell and huffed, "A'ight, then. C'mon. Get that foolish blank look off your face and let's go talk to that dumbass."

The gentle old man said nothing more and walked toward the building, disappearing into the same door Andy Walker had passed through only moments before. Mitchell found himself ignoring every warning sign his mind was setting off and following the dark-skinned, pepper-haired old man into the building, certain he was walking to his own death. The door made a loud thud as it closed behind him.

"Mitchell?" Connie mumbled.

There was no answer.

CHAPTER 47

After their very long and mostly unfruitful night at the crime scene, detectives Brown and Watts were exhausted. They had both anticipated a "eureka" moment—when a crucial piece of evidence cuts through the ambiguity of an investigation to provide clarity and a singular focal point. When it never came, they felt dejected and frustrated, knowing all along that those moments are happened upon, found unexpectedly, and can't be created or constructed.

Their "discussion" with their lieutenant was equally exhausting and frustrating. They stood silent, absorbing the verbal attacks. They knew defending what they did as well as what they didn't do would only result in a longer "discussion" and lead to no possible good end. They left the station and drove once again to the corner at High-Sum hoping to find something, anything that might make the entire evening worth the effort. Aside from Brown's call to Mrs. Treadwell, the drive over was quiet.

They sat in Jittery Joe's sipping their coffees and exchanging various theories and hypotheses. It was a routine exercise they hoped would uncover a hidden gem. When it, too, left them further exhausted, dejected and frustrated, they agreed to stop talking about the case until they had a chance to get some sleep. But with designer coffees coursing through their systems, neither one could stop.

"Look, hombre. The sun's up, I'm all juiced up on caffeine and I don't feel much like sleeping. What can we do between now and when the M.E.'s report comes out?"

"Not much."

"What about Treadwell's alibi, his accountant? O'Connor or O'Reilly."

"You want to interview him right now?"

Brown was less inclined to do anything more than talk about the case. Actually doing something required a clearer mind than he currently possessed. He didn't want to miss unintended body language or a slipped word due to his own inattentiveness.

"C'mon," Watts pressed. "I'll bet the guy doesn't live more than a ten-minute drive from Treadwell's place, which is only a few minutes from here."

Without waiting for a response, Watts was on his cell phone. Brown, taking the cue from his partner, flipped through the pages of his notebook. "Michael O'Donahue," Brown sighed.

There were three Michael O'Donahues in the Korova City greater metropolitan area, but as Watts had suspected, one lived close by in

Highland. They pulled up to a very large, very imposing Colonial home, approximately five minutes from both Jittery Joe's and the Treadwell residence. The moniker 'M. & C. O'Donahue' rose above the top of the gray, metal mailbox like the dorsal fin of a marlin. Unlike the Treadwell's very formal semi-circle driveway, the O'Donahues' drive was purely functional, going straight back along the side of the house and extending into the back yard to an expansive garage with six bays.

"A car freak," Watts said.

"If you're gonna spend it on something …," Brown replied.

Watts parked the vehicle close to the front of the house near the mouth of the slate pathway leading to a massive portico. When they arrived at the front door, Watts leaned in, pressed the doorbell button and eased back to stand next to Brown. They watched as the door slowly creaked open. A man, smiling too-wide for the time of day, appeared in his robe and slippers. His hair was wet and slicked back, the thin waves of a comb's teeth still noticeable.

"Good morning. I'm Detective Brown of the Korova City Police Department and this is my partner Detective Watts. We were hoping to speak with a Michael O'Donahue."

The smile ran away from his face. "That'd be me. Is this about Davis Treadwell?"

"Sadly, yes it is."

"Come in, please."

Michael led his guests into a sitting room just off the entryway. They all sat.

"Can I get you gentlemen anything? Coffee, juice, something to eat, maybe?"

"No, thank you," they both replied.

Brown continued, "What do you know about Davis's disappearance?"

"Not much," Michael offered. "I was with Mitchell for maybe three hours last night, for business. We must have started around eleven-thirty or so. Then later I talked to him and he told me of the situation."

"You called him?" Brown asked.

"The first time, yes, I did. I believe he said he was with the police at the time. Something about an alley and a body in a dumpster. Dreadful stuff. I can't even imagine what he's experiencing."

"What was so urgent that you needed to speak to Mr. Treadwell at time of night?"

"I'm sorry. I'm not at liberty to discuss that," he replied.

"Last I checked there's no such thing as accountant/client privilege," Watts remarked sarcastically.

"Probably not, but as Mr. Treadwell's tax attorney …," Michael said, looking annoyingly at Watts, "I think the courts will back me up."

"Do you know Mrs. Treadwell had tried to call numerous times last night?"

"No."

"Yet yours was the call he took? At three-thirty in the morning?"

"Apparently."

"Why do you think that is?"

"Mr. Treadwell is an international businessman and money never sleeps. Sometimes three-thirty in the morning is the only time people on the other end of the call are available."

"His son is abducted, his wife is at home worried sick and yet yours is the call he takes."

Michael didn't answer the repeated question implied by the statement.

Brown took a different tact. "You spoke to him more than once?"

"Yes, the second time he was with his sister-in-law at the police station." Just then, his own cell phone rang. He looked down at the display and then at the detectives. "Excuse me, gentlemen."

He stood up and walked into an adjoining room. The conversation was short, but he came back very disturbed. "I'm very sorry, gentlemen, but I'm going to have to ask you to leave."

"We have several more questions," Brown said.

"Which I will be more than happy to answer for you later in the day. I must attend to an urgent matter, one of a personal nature, so I really must ask you to leave."

Brown, pulling a card from his wallet, said, "Here's my card if—"

"Yes, yes, Detective …," glancing at the piece of heavy stock paper, "Brown. I will call you this afternoon."

He led the two men through the entryway and briskly opened the door.

"And if you have any further contact with Mr. Treadwell, please let him know we are trying to contact him as well. It's very important."

Michael O'Donahue didn't say a word. And when the detectives were just barely beyond the door jamb he slammed the door.

"I wonder who was on the other side of *that* call?" Brown said as the two men walked back to their car.

* * *

Michael watched the detectives through a side window. When they were in their car, he scrolled through his address book and pressed enter.

"You bastard," he blasted into the phone as he paced the front entryway. "How dare you. How fucking dare you."

"Calm down," came back at him in a whisper. The sentiment only infuriated him further.

"Calm down? Calm down? Chad just called. You know what he said? He said someone called him and asked if he was a prostitute. A God-damned prostitute, Mitchell. He was asked if he was in the car when that boy died. Those records were sealed, for Christ's sake. Sealed. Specifically so he wouldn't have to put up with this bullshit. And you are the only person outside of this family—"

"Look, I'm taking care of everything as we speak. I can't talk now, but in about an hour, I'll call you back and explain everything."

"You're God-damned right you'll call me back," he screamed. "After what I did for you this morning, you're God-damned right you'll call me back." But the call ended well before he finished and his final words went unheard.

CHAPTER 48

The onboard computer in his unmarked police vehicle, which he had signed out of the station earlier that morning, was locked onto Officer Wyszczyzewski's cell phone's registered GPS frequency, leading him to a side street adjacent to the city's central impound lot. He pulled up behind an oddly familiar bronze car parked on the side of the road, odd until he remembered it had been impounded the previous night and towed to the nearby lot, making its presence there somewhat understandable. In the gravel driveway sat another oddly familiar vehicle and Jenkins could find no plausible explanation for its presence: a green, dented Saturn with the vanity plate P-H-A-E-T-O-N. Behind it sat a BMW, presumably the one with Connie still locked in its trunk.

He pulled out his phone, scrolled through the speed dial and pressed send.

"Hello?" she whispered.

"Hey, it's Jenkins."

"Where have you—"

"Where've I been? Yeah, nice talking to you, too. Look, do you want to sit here and chit-chat or do you want me to get you out of there?"

"Yeah, yeah, yeah. Is anyone around?"

"Did you or did you not specifically tell me not to call you until no one was around?"

"Okay, get up here, pop the trunk and get me out of here."

"But, you didn't say please," he chided. He hung up before she could respond.

Looking about as he walked, Jenkins tried to keep the crunching sound of gravel to a minimum as he approached the driver side door of the black sedan. The door opened easily and quietly. His hand moved down to the base of the seat and pulled the release lever for the trunk, which also opened easily and quietly. He walked back to the trunk and laughed when he saw his bloodied partner staring back at him.

"Stop laughing or I'll kick your ass."

"Well if that's going to be your attitude," he joked, swinging his key ring as he held the odd-shaped handcuff key, "then I may have to rethink uncuffing you."

"C'mon, Jenkins, cut the crap. My nephew's inside with some psycho."

Jenkins turned the key to her shackles. "So what's the plan?"

"You got your extra pistol, right?"

"Ask and you shall receive."

He pulled a Smith & Wesson Model 10 service revolver from out of his jacket pocket and handed it to her once she had climbed out of her temporary cell.

"I'm pretty sure there are only four people in there. Mitchell and Davis are on our side. Well, for the most part, anyway. The other two are the two men involved in the—"

"In the accident in the Lot last night, right? I knew it. Why are they both here?"

"Your guy, Andrew Walker, he's the psycho who took Davis, the boy Detective Brown and Watts were looking for last night at High-Sum. He's the guy we want. The old man, I have no idea how he's involved. Or even if he's involved. Not yet, anyway."

His partner was looking at him dead in the eyes as she continued. "This is the big time, Jenkins. This ain't no beat cop crap, this is high-level, award-winning, get-your-picture-in-the-paper-shaking-hands-with-the-mayor stuff, here. We're gonna go in there and see what we can see, hear what we can hear. But remember, no bullets if it can be avoided. At least half the people in there are good guys."

"Right."

"You ready?"

Jenkins was poised to make a break for the door from behind the black sedan when he heard himself ask, "Shouldn't we call for back-up?"

He watched Connie's face slowly relax as she slumped against the car's bumper and sat down. It was a question he had to ask, if not for her than for himself. She sat there a while and looked at everything around her, everything but him. Finally, their eyes met.

"Yeah," she said sadly. "We probably should. If this goes bad, it could get really, really bad."

"This is your call, Whiskey."

She looked off into the distance, "I made a deal with my brother-in-law."

"The same one who doped you up and stuffed you in the trunk of his car?"

"Look, just because he's a lying, back-stabbing bastard whose ass I'm gonna kick from here to hell and back doesn't factor. My integrity is just about the only thing I have that's entirely mine and I don't go back on my word."

She looked back down and away from him. "Besides, I don't want to share this, Jenkins."

While her eyes were staring at the ground around her feet, she knew he was smiling.

"But every fiber of my being tells me we should get back-up."

They sat behind the vehicle, silent.

"How about this," Jenkins offered, "We call it in and go right away. By the time anyone gets here, we'll be hip deep in whatever it is that's going on."

She wedged herself against the trunk of the car. "I can't believe he stuffed me in his fucking trunk."

CHAPTER 49

After ending the call from his irate tax attorney, Mitchell turned his phone off and slipped it into his coat pocket. When he heard it clink against his sister-in-law's pistol, he pulled the phone back out and dropped it in his pants pocket.

"I hope Helios didn't hear my phone ring."

"Don't matter much if he did," the old man replied. "Besides, with all the clattering of those chains, I'd be surprised if he could hear anything else."

The vacant factory was a picture postcard of urban blight. Large panels of wood covered vast expanses of broken window panes. Small, irregular black circles on the floor suggested small fires. The dank smell of urine and feces punctuated the air, leaving little doubt that the factory had at one time been home to squatters.

The older, pepper-haired gentleman navigated the space, moving comfortably, deliberately through the debris toward a door on the opposite side of the vast floor from where they entered. Mitchell followed him cautiously, like a boy trying to keep up with his older brother in a haunted house attraction at the local church fair. He bent low and moved on the balls of his feet with short, quick, intermittent strides, always turning his head from side to side to ensure nothing caught him unaware. He noted the faint clanging of metal on metal he wouldn't have been able to place if Uncle Max hadn't mentioned the clattering of chains.

When they reached a door on the opposite side of the factory floor, Uncle Max stopped and looked into Mitchell's eyes. "I knows this may not be the best time to ask you, but are you planning on killing this dumb-ass piece of shit?"

"Excuse me?" Mitchell replied.

"I've had a long time to think about things, Mr. Treadwell. I'm a tired old man who's lived a long life, some lives being longer than others, if you know what I'm saying?" Uncle Max snickered. "Anyways, things being what they is and you with that gun in your pocket, I need to know what you're thinking."

"I'm sorry, but ..." He trailed off.

Mitchell had nothing left to say. He had initially intended on killing Andy Walker in his unkempt home if Andy didn't agree to let his boy go. But now that Andy seemed to be cooperating, Mitchell no longer saw the need and the thought of killing him was as foreign to him as standing in the middle of a filthy, rundown, shell-of-a-building in the city's industrial district with an old black man who he barely knew.

"No, Uncle Max. I'm not planning on killing anyone. I've seen enough death over the course of the last three decades to last me a lifetime."

"That's good," he muttered. "Yeah, that's good. You're smart. I always thought that about you." Then the old man added, "I'm ready to give up the ghost, too, if need be. All this technology and national security concerns of who is who is making it damn-near impossible to continue the way I have. But no sense throwing it all away if there ain't no need, right?" Then he leaned in close to Mitchell. "The thing is, if you killed this dumb-ass piece of shit, and I can't say as I'd blame you if you wanted to, but if you did, well, you break the chain, is all, and then I'm done anyway."

"The chain?" Mitchell asked, entirely engaged with Uncle Max's eyes. "What chain?"

Uncle Max let out a soft snicker. "And I just got done saying how smart you was. What chain? The Commuters, son."

Mitchell was dumbstruck.

Uncle Max spoke softly, "C'mon, Mr. Treadwell, you know what I'm talking about."

In an instant, staring into those gray, ageless eyes, Mitchell understood it all. "Well I'll be God damned."

The old man snickered, "Well, that has yet to be seen." He snickered again. He placed his hand on the door knob but didn't turn it. "But as long as you're okay with that piece of shit walking on out of here, then you might as well give me that thing in your pocket for safe keeping."

Without hesitation, Mitchell reached into his pocket and pulled out Connie's service revolver. He stared at it for a split second before giving it over to the pepper-haired man. Mitchell watched the gleaming metal disappear into the man's pants pocket and returned his eyes to those of his most unlikely companion.

"Now, let's go get your boy."

CHAPTER 50

The two of them crept down the stairs, their soft steps muffled by the clanging and jingling of metal as well as the other indecipherable noises that grew louder with each descending footstep. They followed the din down a wide, dimly lit cement hallway. At the end of the hallway was a gnarled wooden door jamb from which no door hung, and probably hadn't for quite some time. The blue haze and gentle buzz of an ancient fluorescent fixture spilled out of the doorway as the two men crept closer and the stale odor of an outhouse became more and more pronounced. Gone were the loud banging and clanging of chains and in their place were the soft clinking and chinking of small metal instruments.

They stood in the doorway, Mitchell absorbing everything in front of him. It was a large, vacant space with no windows, only the same cement block walls and floors they had followed down the stairs. Off to their left, in the middle of the room, sat a box made entirely of plywood: about four feet long, two feet high and two feet deep. Affixed to each corner was a five-foot length of chain looped onto a karabiner which itself was looped onto a stretch of chain that disappeared into the ceiling. Without having to bear the full weight and contents of the box, the chains rested in a soft, gentle curve, juxtaposed with the hard edges of the plywood container.

Off to the right, but again in the middle of the room, was a long stainless steel counter. Mitchell thought it might have once been used in a cafeteria kitchen. It sat on a rudimentary base constructed of four-by-four posts and was covered with dozens of baby food jars, each filled almost to the top with a clear liquid. On the counter lay a teenage boy wearing only his soiled underwear and strips of tape across his eyes and mouth. His body was covered by what initially appeared to be glossy brown splotches of mud. In an instant Mitchell knew what they were. In front of the counter stood Andy, with his back to the two men, methodically scraping the skin next to the leeches in what looked like an attempt to remove them.

Mitchell and Uncle Max were several steps into the room by the time the entire experience collectively caused Mitchell to mutter, "Oh, my dear Lord."

Andy, startled, promptly turned around. He positioned the metal scraping instrument in his hand against the boy's neck and in a panicked voice he shouted, "Don't come any closer or I'll kill him."

Uncle Max said, "No need for that, now. We's only here to help."

"Who's this?" Andy asked Mitchell, his panic still wholly apparent. Then, after a moment of studying the old man, it appeared to Mitchell that Andy recognized the old man. He eased his position and lowered the instrument, using it as a pointer as he spoke. "Hey, you're the old man who banged up my car last night."

"That's what you say," the old man snickered. "I say you hit me. But you're right, that's how you know me. At least that's how you know me now."

Mitchell listened to the old man speak. He noticed the affectation of dropping letters and syllables and stringing together word fractions into meaningful mumbles had eroded. In their place were the clear utterances of a well-spoken man. Mitchell also felt his rage, which had grown inside of him the moment he walked through the doorway, slowly disappear as the old man spoke.

The two men edged closer and closer to Andy and his captive.

"Who knows," Uncle Max continued, "Maybe in a couple years, when you got a little closer to holding that dagger in your hand and were *fully prepared* to participate in that portion of the ceremony, you might have gotten to know me in a very different manner, quite possibly in the same manner as your Emperor Trajan here knows me as a civic leader and warrior, a champion of the downtrodden. What do you think, Mr. Trajan?"

Caught off guard, Mitchell capitulated, "Yeah, sure, Uncle Max."

The old man pleaded, "No, Trajan, not Uncle Max. Let's try that again."

Mitchell caught on to what the old man expected of him, "I'm sorry, you're right." Then turning to Andy, Mitchell made the introductions, "Helios, considering our discussion from earlier this morning, you of all people should be delighted with this. May I introduce to you the Sultan of Africa and Conqueror of the Champions of Christendom, Yusuf ibn Tashufin."

A crooked smile grew on Andy's face. "Yeah, right."

Mitchell replied, "In the seven ceremonies you've attended, what have you learned about the Commuters' founder?"

"Well, he wasn't some shriveled up old black guy, that's for sure."

"Really? He's the Sultan of Africa, leader of the Almoravides from the Moorish dynasty. Of course he's going to be a black man. And he was eighty years old when he defeated Alphonso VI. That's when Zainab initiated the first ceremony." Then Mitchell looked at the old man, "Right?"

Yusuf ignored Mitchell's wavering belief and locked eyes with Andy, "These boys you kill, Helios, they're not part of your training. It's got to stop."

The old man stepped toward Andy who brandished the scalpel he was using to remove the leeches from Davis's body when they first walked in.

"It will," Mitchell interrupted.

Yusuf paid no attention to Mitchell. He focused on Andy who stepped back, away from the approaching figure.

"He's right," Andy muttered. "We have a deal, Trajan and me. I give him back his son and he gives me ...."

"Gives you what?" Yusuf asked. "Someone else to kill? Before you've completed your training? You don't get it, and it's going to cost everyone everything." He paused. "This isn't about revenge, Helios, it's about sacrifice."

"Well, duh," Andy mocked. "That's what we do every ceremony."

"Not a human sacrifice, shit-for-brains, personal sacrifice. The ceremonies, the nearly one thousand ceremonies through the years are about each member giving up a little piece of himself or herself, slicing off a tiny piece of the moral fiber that makes us all good people."

Yusuf, ignoring the extended scalpel, put his face right up to Andy's. "Each and every day people peek into the dark corners of humanity, never getting too close. Through this ceremony, we don't just peek into these corners, we shine a spotlight into them and immerse ourselves in the distasteful pinnacle of doing wrong—the taking of a life.

"Everyone thinks today's society pushes that line between right and wrong so much that it gets harder and harder to see it. But that's nothing new. It simply amazes me how each generation thinks these atrocities of society—incest and pedophilia and rape and genocide—are some kind of new problem that they have to fix. I'm here to tell you it was going on before my time and it will sure as shit be going on when I'm gone. There's just a lot more people than there were a thousand years ago. Add to that the instantaneous nature of the media and you got yourself a whole heap of dirty laundry that will never come clean. No, people haven't changed that much. The difference is, now you simply notice more of the nasty bits."

The old man laughed at that final thought, a hearty, resounding laugh that Mitchell felt was as odd and anachronistic and its source. The old man continued.

"Today, people are too apathetic. Or too self-absorbed. I'm not sure which. Either way, they don't understand or they don't care how one person can impact an entire community. They forget or they ignore their responsibilities to their neighbors and because of that, people like you slip through the cracks."

Yusuf poked Andy's chest with his forefinger. "You know what I'm talking about, don't you? People like you who don't find doing wrong distasteful. People like you who relish it. And in the end, that's what's going to bring down the little thirty-person society my Zainab and I began a thousand years ago."

It was then that Mitchell realized both men were drifting further into the darkness and away from the makeshift table on which Davis lay motionless.

"You are so full of shit, old man. Do you honestly expect me to believe you're a thousand years old?"

The old man took two steps back, pulled the gun from his pocket and directed it at Andy. "You can believe whatever you want to believe. But know this, you are going to die today."

When Andy looked around and finally recognized where he was in relation to everything else in the room, Yusuf smiled at the terror shining on Andy's face. "Now you understand what the rest of us feel when we stand up there and drive that knife into that innocent victim. I tried to stem the tide yesterday, to nullify the ceremony. Unfortunately, I underestimated the resolve of our distinguished Lord Spencerton, not to mention your fucked up psychosis."

"What are you talking about?" Andy questioned.

"The accident. I was trying to keep you from grabbing another boy."

Andy looked at Yusuf and smiled even wider, "So the accident wasn't my fault."

"Dammit," Yusuf exploded. "That's exactly what I'm talking about, you self-centered piece of shit. I should just end you right now and get this over with."

Panic filled Andy's eyes. "O God, you can't," he blubbered.

Yusuf stepped back. "Of course I can't. You're impervious and impenetrable, remember? Besides, I'm not about to do a damn thing until it's time." Then he turned to Mitchell, "Get your boy off that table and go."

Mitchell stammered in confusion.

"Now," the old man shouted.

Mitchell was completely absorbed in the conversation between the other two men and hadn't realized he could have picked up his son at any time during the previous few minutes. He eased over to the table and slipped his arms under his seemingly lifeless son.

"We had a deal, Trajan," Andy pleaded from behind the old man.

"My word is my bond," Mitchell answered with the heft of his son fully in his arms. "When I get outside I'll write down everything I know about our mutual friend, I'll crumple up the piece of paper and throw it out my window as I'm driving away."

Yusuf stepped further away from Andy and clumsily took out a leather bound book from the back of his waistband. He wedged the book between Mitchell's left elbow and his body while saying, "Maybe you could use this to write it on."

When the book was firmly tucked under his arm, Mitchell, still cradling his son, walked toward the doorway. He suddenly stopped just inside the doorless frame and asked, "What about you? What about the Commuters?"

He snickered. Then, reverting back to his slurry, Uncle Max way of speaking, he said "We's all had a pretty good run, huh? But all good things must come to an end. Even this."

"What are you talking about, old man?" Andy blurted.

Yusuf sneered and his tone got mean, more urban, "Never you mind 'bout'dat."

Mitchell hung his head and thought about all those centuries of ceremonies. In a thin and pale voice he asked, "What about me? I mean, the day after her final ceremony, Natalie Belling died of a stroke. What's going to happen to me? Has all this with my son been penance enough for my actions?"

A long, toothy smile stretched across the old man's face. "It ain't about you, no more. It's about who it's about," he stated. "For the Tiger Lady it was all about her. You still walking and talking, so you's okay, at least for now," he snickered. "My guess is you'll find what you's looking for as soon as you gets your boy safe and have some quiet time with that there book. You trust ol' Uncle Max and get on. You and your boy gonna be safe, at least for a couple years. Now go on, I got this."

Mitchell digested the old man's comments, standing motionless for what seemed an eternity in the large, dark and dank space. *The great abyss,* he thought. The great unknown beyond death. The moment passed in an instant and he moved toward the doorway. The two men he left behind continued to speak, Andy Walker raising his voice on occasion, but Mitchell's understanding of their words was nullified by his own deep thoughts of relief and triumph.

Once beyond the door jamb and with the stairs just a few feet away, he noticed to his left Connie scurrying against the wall, crouching down with her gun clutched between her hands in front of her chest. Her eyes darted back and forth in an attempt to tell Mitchell to keep moving, which he did with only the slightest hesitation. As he continued walking, he turned his head to his right and saw another police officer, Jenkins, if he remembered correctly, already against the wall on the other side of the door with his gun drawn and locked against his chest. Mitchell saw Connie and her partner but paid no attention to them as they prepared to assess the situation in the other room. Mitchell kept walking toward the stairs deep in thought. He understood. Fully. Not just his sister-in-law's pantomimed desire for him to get her nephew out of the building and out of harm's way, but all of it: the message in Uncle Max's last few comments and why he had reverted back to his slurry urban speech patterns.

Mitchell's feet carefully trod each step. Standing at the landing, he struggled to turn the doorknob while clutching his son's body draped across his arms like Michelangelo's *Pieta* while simultaneously pressing the book tucked under his left elbow to his side. He managed to open the door and, with it swung wide, he made his way through, being careful not to hit any part of his son against the jamb. He crossed the debris-strewn floor to the building's entrance and backed out the building's front door into the mid-morning sun.

Hundreds of noises blended into one loud rustle before Mitchell stopped in his tracks. Before him were several uniformed officers shouting and pointing their weapons at him. Stunned, Mitchell barely noticed one of them breaking from the pack toward him, also shouting, but at the others, not at him. He heard, "It's okay, it's okay, lower your weapons," but its meaning didn't immediately register.

Detective Brown ran over and helped Mitchell carry the boy over to the BMW.

"What's going on in there?" Brown asked.

Mitchell answered dispassionately while opening the passenger door, "I think it's all coming to an end."

"What is?" Brown asked.

"Everything."

Brown tried to further engage. "How many people are in there? Do they have any weapons? Did you see any police officers in there?"

"Excuse me, detective, I'm taking my son to the hospital."

"Hospital? You got to stay here and tell me what's happening."

Mitchell, unfazed by the intrusive questioning, simply went about nestling his son in the seat comfortably, slipping the leather-bound book under the front passenger seat, shutting the door and walking around to the other side of the car.

"The old man's in charge, now. I'll be at St. Joe's if you need me."

Mitchell slung himself into the driver's seat. He could almost feel Detective Brown watching as Mitchell feverishly scanned his phone's screen and scribbled something down on a scrap of paper. Brown shouted and motioned to the officers to let the black sedan pass. Watts, who was standing with a small group of uniformed officers, repeated the commands and walked to the mouth of the driveway to direct traffic. When he was done writing, Mitchell backed out of the gravel driveway, carefully avoiding the police cars that lined the city street in front of and behind Uncle Max's bronze Dodge Dart. Halfway down the block, Mitchell rolled down his window and threw out a small, crumpled-up piece of paper. He rolled the window back up, turned at the end of the block and disappeared behind the chain-link fence topped by razor wire that ran along the length of the police impound lot.

* * *

Brown had watched the vehicle back out of the driveway until it passed behind the Dart that he knew from his days growing up in Salem's Lot. That's when he figured it out. The 'old man' Mitchell had referred to had to have been Uncle Max. Having come late, Brown was annoyed he hadn't recognized the vehicle earlier.

He turned around and, noticing there was only one other vehicle in the area that wasn't part of the Korova City Police fleet, walked along the passenger side of the green Saturn and peered inside. He was surprised by how clean it was inside, immaculate. He noted the sunglasses and gloves neatly placed between the front seats. And that's when he noticed, in the passenger's seat, a small wooden frame with a picture of a crying newborn boy. He was wearing a blue, striped cap and was wrapped in a matching blanket.

His focus on the photo was broken by a single gunshot which echoed from deep within the building. He spun on his heel and stared at the front door of the warehouse as more shots quickly followed. All of the police officers instinctively ducked down behind their vehicles as if they were in the immediate line of fire. Then a small team of officers wearing bullet-proof vests and helmets sprung from their places and raced to the door, disappearing one by one into the building. Detective Brown followed them and let the door swing closed behind him.

CHAPTER 51

Before Mitchell had escaped through the entryway, Andy shouted, "You can't do this."

To this, Yusuf replied, "Of course I can."

Just the two of them remained when the rest of the conversation unfolded.

"Not you, old man," Andy shouted. "I was talking to—"

"Just because you wants something don't mean you gets it, you dumb-ass piece of shit. Now you and me, we gonna have a little discussion. And I want you to listen carefully to everything I says. You got that?"

The manner in which the words touched Andy's ears sedated him like a tranquilizer dart. "Yeah, sure. What do you want to talk about?"

"I want to talk about what you did to them boys."

"What boys?"

"That boy whose daddy just took him out of here. And those boys before that."

"What about them?"

"Why do you kill them?"

"Well, as you saw," he smiled with great pleasure, "I didn't kill that one, and, assuming you are a thousand years old, you already know that the boy last night—"

"Tell me about the ones you *did* kill," Uncle Max interrupted before Andy could finish.

"Trial runs."

"Trial runs? You mean for the real thing? Last night?"

"I had to make sure there wasn't too much blood. So, to reduce the blood volume, I had leeches sucking on them night and day. The Slipperman—"

"Too much blood?" Uncle Max shouted, purposely interrupting again. "So there wouldn't be a big a mess to clean up afterward, is that right?"

"For someone who's supposedly so goddamned old and wise, you ask some pretty stupid questions."

"I just want to understand why you killed those boys and did all those horrible things."

"Are you kidding me? That kid? All he's got is a couple bite marks from the leeches."

"All that kid's got is a lifetime of doctors to help him deal with the pain and suffering you put him through for your own enjoyment. And those other boys? It wasn't enough to torture them, you had to kill them? For your own enjoyment, too, I'll bet."

"I had to make sure everything was perfect for the ceremony. So, yeah, I had to kill them. But then, something unexpected happened."

"You got hooked, didn't you, din'choo?"

A mysterious aura grew about Andy's face, "Yes. I got hooked. But not on the killing. That was just the dotting of the "i's" and crossing of the "t's". In high school English I remember it was called the dénouement: the cluttered wrap-up after the intense climax. And let me tell you, the climax was good, every time. But it wasn't the killing. No, I got hooked on the anticipation, the preparation. It was like sex, you know? You spend all that time working up to it, the teasing and taunting, the flirting and the foreplay. Hell, prepping those boys for the ceremony, paying attention to the very last detail was even better than a climax, you know, getting him ready for death. Getting yourself ready for ..." His voice trailed away.

Andy closed his eyes, tilted his head back ever so slightly and smiled widely. Blood engorged him, making a bulge in his pants that even Uncle Max could see if he cared to look. Andy moved his hand to adjust the growing discomfort when Uncle Max shouted.

"Open your eyes."

Andy opened his eyes, slowly, keeping the soft, wide smile on his face.

"Smile all you want to, 'cause now you gonna die for what you done."

"Police," both Connie and Jenkins shouted and they bolted into the room with their guns leveled. Connie's gun on Uncle Max, Jenkins's on Andy.

"Drop the weapons," Connie yelled.

The smile instantly vanished from Andy's face, but Uncle Max's resolve was steady. He merely squinted, holding his gaze on Andy's eyes and the gun in his hands on Andy's sternum.

"Officers," Uncle Max whispered, "This man is a public menace who needs to be brought to justice."

"And he will. That's why we're here. Just put the gun down."

"I seen the way the justice system in this town works. A black man holds a gun on a white man. Any lawyer worth his salt will get the charges thrown out."

"Maybe if we weren't cops. But we are, and we can testify to what we heard, verify it wasn't coerced and put his ass behind bars forever."

"That same lawyer gonna say anything what come out of his mouth was coerced, with a gun pointed at his heart, and therefore inadmissible."

"You don't know that."

"Yes I do. All too well. And what about them boys he killed? He might be behind bars forever, but they's *dead* forever."

"Killing this man won't bring them back."

A toothy grin crept across the old man's face. "Maybe not, but I'll be damned if he don't pay for what he done."

Desperate, Andy shouted, "Shoot him. What are you waiting for?"

Jenkins replied clearly and sternly, "Keep your mouth shut, you sick bastard, or I will drop you."

"Uncle Max. It's Uncle Max, right? You remember me from yesterday?" Connie prodded.

"You the one who impounded my car."

Connie stammered, "Um, yes, but I was just doing my job. Which is what I'm doing right now, Uncle Max. I'm doing my job. It is my job to catch the bad guys and put them where they belong."

"'A'ight, but this one here belongs in hell, young lady. You gonna put him there?"

"Well, that's not really for you or I to decide, now is it, Uncle Max?"

Andy watched as Uncle Max took his eyes off him for the first time since pulling the gun from his pocket. Instead, the old man looked over his shoulder, looked at Connie and said, "I disagree."

With that, Uncle Max turned back to Andy, lobbed the gun underhanded to him and said "Catch." Andy caught it cleanly. Instinctively and in one continuous motion, he positioned the gun's handle into the palm of his hand, stuck his finger through the trigger guard, leveled the gun on Uncle Max and fired. The lone shot echoed like a cannon in the large, empty room. It was soon lost and overwhelmed by the thundering sounds of multiple gunshots.

Andy felt the first bullet hit its mark, penetrating the core of his upper torso. He let out a scream that dimmed with each subsequent bullet that tore at his flesh and everything went black.

* * *

Andy fell to the floor in a heap. Uncle Max stood in place, fighting gravity every inch of the way down until he, too, was laying in a heap on the cold, cement floor.

Connie saw Jenkins run toward Andy while she ran to Uncle Max. The old man was gasping for air, his breaths labored and gurgling with the blood she knew was flowing into and out of his punctured lung.

"How does it feel officer?" Uncle Max whispered.

"How does what feel?" Connie asked.

"Your decision to send him to hell?"

"That wasn't my decision. That was the decision he made when he pulled the trigger."

The old man snickered, "Yeah, you keep telling yourself that."

She quietly shushed him and laid him out flat on the floor, applying pressure with both her hands to the bloody wound in his chest.

She turned to her partner who was crouched beside them watching. "Jenkins, get a wagon here. Now." Jenkins disappeared.

"Where's Detective Brown?" the old man asked Connie. "I thought for sure he'd be here."

As if on cue, Connie looked up and saw Brown hurry through the doorway. He took half a step to assess the situation and, once he'd done so, jogged on to the old man lying on the floor.

"Ahhhh, shit," Brown muttered. "What happened?"

Connie looked over at the dead man on the floor and then back at Brown. "That one's a suicide by cop, with a little help from this old fellow, here."

"What do you mean a little help?" Brown asked.

"I tried to convince the old man to put the gun down but he threw it to this Walker guy who caught it and shot the old man. Then we shot Walker. He gave us no choice."

"You always gots choices," Uncle Max whispered, the gurgling blood making up more of the sound coming from his lips than before.

His words and their sentiment made Connie angry. Who was he to question her? It was a righteous shoot—text book. She pushed away the thoughts Uncle Max's words brought about and continued to apply steady pressure to the wound.

Detective Brown got down on one knee and grabbed one of the old man's hands. It was a tender moment, palpable despite the surrounding noise and chaos in the room.

"You know him?" Connie asked.

Brown kept his eyes locked on the old man and smiled. "Who don't know Uncle Max? If you grow up in Salem's Lot, you better know your Uncle Max or you ain't never gonna make anything outta yourself. Ain't that right?"

The old man smiled back.

"Don't worry," said Brown. "You gonna be just fine."

"That's okay, boy," he wheezed with Connie's hands pressed against his chest. "I think I done enough good so as to balance off all the bad I done." He strained to breathe deeply. "Plus, you got your man."

"Actually, you got him," Brown chuckled. Then, looking at Connie, "Did he …," nodding his head at Andy Walker, "say anything about killing those boys?"

"Hell yeah. He went on and on about how he got off torturing and killing. No audio, but Jenkins and I will write up a report as soon as this guy gets in the ambulance. No problems, this guy's your killer."

"How many?" Brown asked.

"How many what?"

"How many boys did he talk about?"

"Two trial runs and the kid last night. That's three. Davis was apparently going to be number four. Hey, what about Davis? Did you see him outside?"

"Treadwell's taking him to the hospital. He should be fine."

Uncle Max, still looking up at Brown, gurgled, "You got your man."

Brown looked at him questioningly. "For these three, yeah, but not the other thirty-seven."

"Not him. Me," Uncle Max confessed.

"What are you talking about?"

"The wagon's here," Jenkins announced as he made his way back into the dark and dank room. "Stretcher's coming now."

"Hold it," Brown said.

Jenkins ignored him. "This old man fucked everything up."

"Hold it," Brown said louder.

"We had the situation under control when—"

"He knows," Connie explained. "He knows."

"Did you tell him?"

"Yes," she said, stopping her partner again. "I told him everything. Now shut up." Then she looked down at the old man's pale face and caressed his pepper hair.

"Shut up," Brown exploded. "Everyone!" Then he leaned in and pleaded with the dying man, "What do you mean 'you'?"

Uncle Max looked up and held Brown's eyes intently, "You got your man," he snickered, only the snicker was more than his failing lungs could handle. Uncle Max coughed a breath-full of blood into the air, covering both Connie and Brown with red speckles.

Connie kept her hands on Uncle Max's wound as the stretcher clanged down the stairs. She watched as a female EMT raced over to check Andy Walker. Detective Brown yelled from behind the handkerchief he was using to wipe the blood from his face, "Fuck him. Dead or not, fuck him. Get over here and save Uncle Max."

Connie was gently moved aside by the male EMT as he ripped open the old man's shirt to assess the damage. Connie sat and watched the paramedics work furiously, as if in a dream. She watched as one by one the other officers left the room when it became obvious the old man was beyond repair. She watched Brown cry and she began to cry, too. She wanted to justify her actions to the old man, to explain she had no choice but to shoot Andy.

"Sorry, guys," the female paramedic said. "Maybe if we got to him right after he got shot, but he was losing blood into his lungs faster than we could have pumped it out. He drowned."

"Drowned?" Brown laughed. He walked away into one of the dark corners of the room.

Connie sat and contemplated the absurdity of drowning in the basement of a decaying factory. Then, with her hands and clothes still cold and sticky with blood, she followed Brown into the darkness.

"So, what was all that about?" she asked.

"All what?"

"'You got your man' and 'the other thirty-seven?' You looked like you were going to shake out what little life he had left in him. Just wondering what was going on between the two of you there."

"Long story."

"Condense it."

Brown looked down at the floor and then up at Connie. "I've been trying to clear a bunch of open cases. I think he was telling me I could just pin them all on him. He's dead, so it don't matter much legally, but I could get all the glory."

"That's it?"

"He was a figurehead in the neighborhood, the only guy who gave a shit, you know? He helped anyone who asked for help 'cause he knew he could count on you to do him a favor when the time came."

"Maybe that time is now?"

"This ain't no favor. It's pissing on the good name of one of the only people ..." He trailed off with no signs of continuing.

"Maybe he is responsible for doing whatever it is he says he did, whatever those open cases are."

Brown was silent a moment. "Doubtful. But even so, what good does it do to put all these open cases on an old man that just helped save the son of one of Korova City's most powerful and respected businessmen?"

She thought a minute before offering one last salve for his pain, "Maybe he just wanted you to stop looking."

PART SEVEN

Impact Beyond Measure

CHAPTER 52

"Your son certainly has been through an awful lot the last little while, Mr. Treadwell," the doctor said. "Physically, the worst is behind him. We put in a couple stitches at the base of his skull, but nothing out of the ordinary there. We found traces of pancuronium bromide in his system, a kind of muscle immobilizer. Its effects should wear off quickly and pass completely without incident within a few weeks. And contrary to popular belief, leeches are extremely sanitary, so there's no worry about infection. The redness and swelling around the bite marks should subside within a few days and there should be minimal scarring."

"Any bad news?" Mitchell asked without making eye contact.

"Well, he's severely traumatized, which doesn't go away over night. We do have psychologists on staff."

"Thank you, no," he interrupted. Then, when the doctor looked at him questioningly, he continued, "We have an existing relationship with a therapist, is all I meant. I'll be sure he gets the help he needs. Is there anything else?"

"Not really. Should I be looking for something specific?"

"Because of the circumstances," he said in a low tone, "I was wondering if there were any signs of, um, sexual abuse."

"Ah," the doctor exclaimed much too loudly for Mitchell's comfort. "Initial examinations were negative." Then, quieter, "We have his blood and will contact you with those results, but I'm fairly confident there was no abuse. No sexual abuse, anyway."

"One other thing, the drugs that were administered, if it were a dirty needle shared with a male prostitute ..." Mitchell was unable to verbalize the rest of the thought.

"Yes, well," the doctor responded more subdued than previously, "We'll get those results in a few day. I'll be sure to contact you in regards to any possible developments on that front."

"Thank you, doctor. Please do. Can I see him?"

"Sure. Go right in. He's awake, but his motor skills are still deficient."

Mitchell stood outside the exam room feeling awkward for having had a hand in his son's ordeal. He put a huge smile on before pushing the door in, altering the smile to a tiny grin after rationalizing Davis would see through the façade.

Davis lay on the examination table draped in a surgical gown and attached to an I.V. The image, one of such helplessness and reliance, was reminiscent of Mitchell's memory of his son following his birth, swaddled in a non-descript hospital blanket and matching knitted cap. A sizable bruise, already a greenish-yellow, ran down the side of Davis's face, distorting his boyish features. Mitchell fought back the tears in his eyes, immediately walked over and hugged his son who only managed to lift his hands to stroke his father's waist.

"I am so sorry about all this, Davis."

"It's not your fault, dad."

A pang of guilt rode through him. "Maybe not, but still." He stepped back from the exam table and noticed traces of adhesive by Davis's temples, the bridge of his nose and along his cheeks. "Nobody should ever have to go through an ordeal like that. No one."

After a pregnant pause, Mitchell offered, "The doctor says you're going to be fine."

"Oh," Prudy yelped entering the room. "Oh, Davis!"

And like her husband, she immediately went to the exam table and hugged her baby boy, dropping a bag filled with his clothes.

"Mmmmmm," she cooed. "You scared your mother half to death, you know that?"

"Sorry, mom."

"No, no, son. I'm sorry. I shouldn't have said it like that. It's not your fault. It's just ...." She hugged him once more, letting him go and said, "And did I hear your father correctly, the doctors say you're going to be fine?"

"Not all the tests are back yet, but so far so good," Mitchell confirmed. "We need to schedule a few sessions with Dr. Goodrich to smooth out some of the rough edges, but other than that, Davis should be fine."

Prudy stood back and, looking at his face, she covered her mouth with her hands and began to cry. She then looked down at the swollen welts on her son's arms and legs, hugged her son and whispered, "I'm just so happy you're okay."

"Once I can move my arms and legs, the doctor said I can go home."

Panic flashed across her face as she pulled back, "He's paralyzed?"

"Relax," Mitchell consoled, jumping to her side and rubbing her shoulders. "He was given, ah, what did the doctor call it? A muscle immobilizer? Something like that. It should wear off very soon and then we can take him home."

Prudy buried her face in Mitchell's chest. He looked past her and gave Davis a mockingly stern look. Davis smiled and shrugged his shoulders.

CHAPTER 53

As Connie stepped up to the front door, the peal of the grandfather clock seemed almost never ending as it signaled noon, echoing in the expansive entryway. As it reached its final few notes it was joined by the elaborate chiming of the doorbell. Prudy opened the door and looked up and down at Connie.

"Hey," Connie said as she walked through the front door. "How is he? How are you?"

She moved to hug her sister but Prudy backed up and said, "No, no, no."

Connie wore the same clothes she had changed into at the station, only now they were stained with the blood of the men responsible for her nephew's abduction. She contemplated going home to change, for her sister's sake rather than for her own, but since it had been such a long day, she wanted to see her nephew before heading home and slipping into a hot bath.

"Sorry," she said sheepishly. "I forgot about … this." She took a few steps into the foyer and sat on the stairs. "So how are you?"

Prudy stepped back and sat in one of the chairs in the entryway. "Me, I'm fine. My nerves are all but shot, but nothing a little meditation and deep breathing can't fix."

"Medi-TA-tion, not medi-CA-tion, right?"

Prudy looked angrily at her sister but let the comment pass. "Davis is fine, too. He's upstairs in his room." She smiled. "He's so much like his father: tough as nails, hyper-resilient, and not a clue as to how his actions affect those around him."

"Speaking of Mitchell, is he around?"

"Sure. He's in the study. Do you want me to get him?"

"No, you do whatever you were doing before I showed up. He and I need a couple of minutes alone."

"Sounds serious."

"Not really," she lied. "I just need a few things for my report, is all."

She walked back through the entryway to the study on the other side. Mitchell was at his desk pouring over what looked like an antique book. As soon as Connie entered the room, she watched him nonchalantly close the book and stand up to greet her.

"Hey, Connie," he said. She recognized it as the same tone he used to greet party guests he wished hadn't shown up. He stretched out his arms as if to give her a hug. Connie stopped short and swiftly thrust the palm of her hand just below his sternum, hitting her mark. Mitchell crumpled to the ground, gasping for air.

"You stuffed me in your trunk, you lying bastard. 'You and me, Connie. You and me.'"

Mitchell tried to reply, but he just flailed about, panicky, writhing on the floor.

Connie crouched down and looked into his eyes, "And don't you dare say you're sorry, because then I'll have to start, I don't know, breaking your kneecaps or something."

Mitchell finally inhaled, making a loud, sucking sound that marked the end of his spasm. "I had to," he whispered.

"Bullshit."

"I had to, Connie," he said, finally able to put some force behind the words. "I told you, he wasn't going to talk to a cop and you were determined to come into the house."

"You knew he was crazy and you went in there by yourself? You left me outside and went into that factory with some defenseless old man. Have you got some kind of death wish? Jesus, Mitch. You're smarter than that."

"I did what I had to do to get my boy back, Connie. And that old man was not defenseless. He could charm the rattle off a diamondback."

Mitchell crawled across the floor and sat, propping himself against his desk. Connie stayed crouched where she was.

"I did what I had to, Connie. I'm sorry I cut you out of it."

"No, you are *not* sorry. Everything worked out in the end and now you want me to be good ol' Connie again. But that's not the way it works. This was a trust thing, Mitch, and I can't trust you anymore."

She stood up in the middle of the room and crossed her arms. "Besides, I told you I was going to break your kneecap if you said you were sorry, and a relationship just can't be patched together after one person breaks the others kneecap. Which one is it gonna be, your left or your right?"

"My golf game is in the crapper, so maybe you should crack the right one and we'll see if I can hit the ball straight after rehab," Mitchell said.

They said nothing for a while. Connie thought about Mitchell carrying her nephew up the stairs and out of the dank basement. She hoped Mitchell was thinking about how terrible he felt betraying her trust but knew he wasn't. She stood and strode over to where he sat on the floor.

"I'm too tired to break your kneecaps," she said, offering him her hand, which he took. She pulled him to his feet and mockingly dusted him off.

"I'm gonna see how the kid's doing and then go home," she said walking away. She stopped, turned, pointed a finger at him and said, "This isn't over, Mitch. I'm gonna catch hell since it was my weapon that killed Uncle Max. And I am not pulling any punches. You *will* be charged with something for what you did to me. I suppose with your connections you'll get it knocked down to some crappy misdemeanor and do community service, but it would serve you right to do time. Serious, hard time."

Mitchell shrugged. "If it'll make it easier on you, I'll take whatever blame you want to heap on me."

"No," she said simply. "I tried it your way, Mitch. Remember? 'You and me' didn't work out that well."

Then something clicked. "Hey, do you remember that night, maybe twenty years ago, when we drank a bottle of wine together and I told you about a sergeant in my department harassing me?"

"Sergeant Cohoe, right?"

"Yeah, Sergeant Cohoe. Did I ever tell you what happened to him?"

"No," was all he said.

"A couple weeks after our little chat, he was arrested for having tons of child pornography in his basement."

Mitchell, unaffected, walked around his desk and sat in his chair. "Hmm."

"Hmm? That's all you got? You planted those pictures in his basement, didn't you?"

"Now, why would I do that?"

"Because you think you're some knight in shining armor saving this not-so-little damsel in distress. That was the first time I heard you say 'It's just you and me, the two of us, working this thing through.' You remember that?"

"No, I don't remember that. And let me clear the air. I didn't 'plant,'" he said, making air-quotes, "anything in that man's basement."

"Well, then, you had someone else do it. Either way, it doesn't matter." Then, in a sad tone, she added, "It's never going to be the same with us, Mitch. And along with everything else, that is completely your fault."

As she walked toward the foyer she watched him open the heavy, leather-bound ledger. She wanted to ask about it, but thought better of it and continued out the door. She moved through the foyer, up the stairs and through the labyrinthine corridors until she found her youngest nephew's door. Davis was lying on his bed staring at the ceiling.

She knocked lightly and stood in the open frame, "Hey, buddy. How you feeling?"

"Pretty good, I guess."

"C'mon. You can do better than that."

Quick on the comeback, he sat up, smiled widely and said, "I'm doing swell, Aunt Connie."

She laughed. "That's more like it," she said and sat next to him on the bed. "Hey, I need to talk to you about a few things. You got some time?"

"Mom said I could go to the police station tomorrow after school."

"Yeah, that's fine, I'll be there when they take your statement. But I was hoping to talk to you kind of off the record. You mind?"

"Sure. What do you want to know?"

"When your dad walked into the room with that old man, you were conscious, right? You could hear everything that was going on, couldn't you?"

"Yeah. I couldn't see or move, though. Listening was all I *could* do."

"Do me a favor, tell me everything you can remember about the conversation that was going on before your dad carried you out of there."

CHAPTER 54

Detectives Brown and Watts sat at their desks. Watts had just put the finishing touches on his report while Brown sat staring at the thirty-seven open files strewn in front of him. Watts stood up and walked behind Brown, looking over his shoulder at the file folders of various thicknesses. The two of them stared at the files not knowing how to properly segue into a conversation about them. Watts made the first feeble attempt.

"Soooooo, what? You think Uncle Max killed all these people?"

Brown stared intently as if he hadn't heard his partner. "No," he finally said, exhausted. "No, I do not think Uncle Max killed all these people."

The silent staring resumed for a long while. Then Watts grabbed hold of Brown's chair and pulled him away from his desk. The chair screeched as it was dragged across the floor.

"What are you doing?" Brown asked.

Ignoring his partner, Watts carefully closed the top-most file, ensuring all the corresponding papers were safely tucked inside. As Brown complained again and again, Watts placed the file on his own desk and proceeded to do the same to the next top-most file, then the next and the next until Brown's desk sat empty and a tall, neat pile of folders sat squarely in the middle of Watts' desk.

Brown looked at them a moment and said, "Okay. Now what?"

Watts hoisted his rear end up onto Brown's empty desk and spoke, "Now? Now we go home and get some sleep, champ. We come back tomorrow to a huge fanfare for having closed three murder cases, four if you include his wife, plus the safe return of a young boy to his exceedingly affluent family. Then, when the lights die down and the cameras are all turned off, we go about our business of solving crimes and catching bad guys."

"Go about our business? What about my book?"

"Man, fuck your book. Wrap it up now or wait another Harvest Moon, I don't care."

"Shhhh," Brown pleaded.

"Don't shush me," Watts exclaimed. "You seriously think anyone else in here gives a rat's ass about those files?" he said, pointing to the neat pile on his desk. "You know as well as I do that the lieutenant don't want to hear about it. Unless you can link Walker or Uncle Max to all of these cases, hell, unless you can link 'em to even *one* of these cases, you ain't got shit. So until that happens, we're done. We bask in the limelight for a few days and move on."

Watts walked around to his own desk and sat, pouring through the few hand-written messages next to his phone.

"Until next year, of course," Watts offered with a sly grin.

* * *

At that moment, in Brown's old stomping grounds of Division 3, a 911 call was being placed to report that a woman and her dog had both been stabbed to death.

CHAPTER 55

Mitchell sat in his study engrossed in the book Uncle Max had slipped under his arm nearly a month earlier. It was a hand-written ledger with some thirty rows running fully across each two-page spread. And from the very moment he opened it, he knew what it was: the Commuters' accounts payable. The first handful of spreads was filled with beautiful and intricate calligraphic entries. He would come to find out later that they were written in Hassaniya Arabic, the ancient language of the Moors. Following the Arabic pages were several spreads written in Archaic Portuguese, followed by another handful of pages in Modern Portuguese. Only the last few spreads were written in English.

In these final spreads, the first columns were filled with the names he reflexively associated with the worst of human behavior. They were the ceremonial names of the Commuters. It was headed with the word Identification. In the five center columns were dates ranging from early September to early October. They were headed with the words Disposal, Acquisition, Ascension, Provision and Matriculation. A cursory inspection of the dates revealed no obvious linkage. However, a deeper look showed a stair-step pattern as each date entered into one column was repeated in the next column seven lines above it, then again in the next column another seven lines up, then again and again and again.

The final spread's stair-step pattern was even more pronounced than the others due to its incompleteness, Only the first row in the spread, Marcus Ulpius Nerva Traianus, had all its columns filled while the seven bottom rows had only the first column filled. Mitchell's fingers rubbed the dried ink in the first column of Jean Louise Finch's row which bore the date of his son's abduction. The same date was written as the final entry in each column seven rows apart. This final entry was a stinging reminder of his involvement in his son's ordeal.

Turning back a page, he reaffirmed another of the ledger's patterns. The first row on every spread was carried over from the last row from the previous spread. Even on those pages he couldn't read, the pattern was evident.

He knew some of the names entered into the Identification column from high school history lessons nearly forgotten or from books he had once read, but most of the names were foreign to him. The dates, on the other hand, he knew what they represented, even those that predated his membership and even his birth. Every one represented the date when a family had been instantly shattered by the violent, seemingly senseless death of a loved one.

The next-to-last column on each spread bore the heading Payment. "Payment," Mitchell whispered in disgust.

He surmised that most of the entries in that column were the actual names of each member—Jeremy Matthews, Kurt Williams, Michael Tucker, Christine Hathaway—because the next column, the one furthest to the right and headed Relationship, was filled with the word "self" in nearly every row.

He read the entry immediately above his own on the next-to-last spread: "Dors Venabili." Under Payment, the name listed was "Natalie Belling" and under Relationship, it read "self," like all the others on the page. The first time he read it he instantly understood what Uncle Max meant when he told Mitchell he would find what he was looking for if he read the book. His understanding came further into focus when he read the last two entries in his own row. In them, in the same hand that wrote all the other entries, were written "Yusuf ibn Tashufin " under Payment and two Greek letters under Relationship: "A" and "Ω".

The first few times he studied the book he cried when he read his row of entries. He cried in horror of what he had done. Then he cried in thanksgiving that his death and the death of his son, his eye-for-an-eye karmic penances, were avoided. He cried in gratitude that the man responsible for creating the Commuters had sacrificed his own immortality. But as the days passed and he read deeper into the book, he cried less and less. His horror, his thankfulness and his gratitude were replaced with a burning inquisitiveness into some of the book's most unsettling peculiarities.

Two pages before the end of the book was an entry that puzzled Mitchell to no end. It wasn't the dates that he found mystifying, as they followed the same seven-year stair-step pattern as all the other entries in the book. It was the entry in the Identification column of the next-to-last row: Yusuf ibn Tashufin. The entries in the final two columns added intrigue to his confusion as the Payment column listed the name "Michael Tyrone Sledge, Jr." and in the next space, in the Relationship column, was written the word "son."

Based on what he inferred from studying the ledger for nearly a month, Mitchell figured Michael Tyrone Sledge, Sr., assuming the name Yusuf ibn Tashufin , matriculated out of the Commuters the year before Mitchell joined. Reports and news coverage of the entire incident involving Davis verified that Uncle Max, the man who had died from a fatal gunshot wound in the basement of an abandoned factory, was in fact named Michael Tyrone Sledge. A quick check into public records verified that a Michael Tyrone Sledge, Jr., died of pneumonia on the same day listed in Yusuf's Matriculation column.

What Mitchell found most intriguing was that in all thirty entries within the Relationship column between Yusuf ibn Tashufin and Marcus Ulpius Nerva Traianus was the word "self." By Mitchell's estimation, that meant everyone in the Commuters who had ever known of Yusuf was dead, reminiscent of the mysterious disappearance of the group's founder nearly a thousand years earlier.

He flipped back and forth between pages looking for answers. Had Mitchell met the immortal Originator of the Commuters or the bereaved father of a dead son? And if the man who died in the basement of that factory was just a former Commuter named Michael Tyrone Sledge, of no more importance than any other member, then where did he get the book? And how did he know so much about the current Commuters? About Andy? He turned these and other conundrums over and over in his mind for hours on end, trying to make the pieces fit. They never did.

* * *

Mitchell sat at his desk thinking and rubbing his forehead when something suddenly came into his peripheral vision. He jumped.

"My apologies, Mr. Treadwell. I didn't mean to frighten you."

"Detective Brown," he exclaimed.

"Your wife let me in."

"I didn't even hear the doorbell," Mitchell responded.

"You were probably engrossed in that book."

"Yes, that must be it," Mitchell replied slowly, shutting the ledger.

Brown looked down at the desk. "Speaking of which, that looks very much like the book I saw under your arm the day you carried Davis out of that factory basement. Did the old man give it to you?"

You are a terrible liar, Mitch, rang in his head. "As a matter of fact, he did," Mitchell acknowledged. "Are you interested in book collecting?"

"No. But your wife tells me you spend almost all your time sitting in here reading that thing. Mind if I take a look?"

"Do you have a warrant?"

Brown looked at Mitchell, not suspiciously as Mitchell had expected, but longingly, with pain and confusion in his eyes. "Those entries, they looked like dates."

Growing tense and uncomfortable, Mitchell said, "Is there something I can help you with, detective?"

Brown stared at the floor. "Did you know I'm writing a book? It's based on a stack of open murder cases that me and my partner gathered over the years."

Mitchell felt panicky, but tried desperately not to show it.

"It's about a serial killer," Brown continued, "who kills one victim each year on the night of the Harvest Moon. That's the full moon closest to the autumnal equinox."

"Really?" Mitchell noted an uncharacteristic lack of focus in the man standing before him.

"Yeah. Because it was so bright, farmers used to harvest late at night." He paused. "With his dying breath Uncle Max told me he was the serial killer, the one from my open cases. With all those dates in the book, I'm wondering if that might not be a log of his murders."

"You think Uncle Max was a serial killer?"

A defeated look appeared on Brown's face. "I don't know what to think anymore." Then he added, "But if he *was* the serial killer, Mr. Treadwell, I can get a search warrant to obtain that book as evidence in an ongoing investigation."

"You tell me when you'd like to execute that search, Detective Brown, and I'll be sure to have my lawyers present," Mitchell fired back.

"You know, it's funny, you bringing up your lawyer. I replay that evening over and over again in my mind the night your son was abducted. Every time I tried contacting you that night, you never answered your phone. Instead, you were following up on a lead. Your sister-in-law told me you were pulling leads out of your ass all night long."

Mitchell blurted out, "Are you suggesting I had something to do with my son's abduction?"

"No, not at all." He paused. "However, it's curious that a month later, your alibi for the night your son was abducted, your lawyer, Mr. O'Donahue, kills himself."

Mitchell could feel his eyes grow wider. "What are you talking about?"

"Oh, of course. You couldn't possibly have heard yet?" Then, sounding sincere, Brown said, "I'm sorry to be the one to break this to you, but he died last night. He was found earlier this morning."

Tears came quickly to Mitchell's eyes. "Oh, God. What about Cathy, his wife? She's not the one who found him, is she?"

"No, she's fine. She's a bit distraught, obviously, but she didn't find the body. No, he broke into a bakery and hung himself."

"A bakery?" Mitchell replied much too forcefully. Then he added softly, "Where?"

"In Cedarberg. Why? What's it matter?"

"I don't know."

Mitchell would cry a couple days later reading the obituary that explained the building in which his tax attorney was found was the site of Conall Cernach's ceremony, where the Commuter he had recruited and sponsored ascended from a Sophomore to a Beta member by wearing an ancient mask and plunging an ancient double-edged dagger through the hole of an ancient brass disk into the heart of a complete stranger.

Brown pulled a folded-up piece of paper from his pocket. "He left this on the counter. It's a suicide note."

Mitchell grabbed the photocopied paper from the detective's hands. He instantly recognized the handwriting as Michael O'Donahue's, with everything written in capital letters. The first half of the note professed his never-ending love for his family. But it was the final two lines that struck Mitchell like a thunderbolt.

TRAJAN, SHAME ON YOU FOR RECRUITING ME.
FAITH IS NO MORE AND THAT IS ON YOUR HEAD.

Mitchell calmly took a moment to absorb the note in its entirety. His initial panic subsided when he realized everything was written in capital letters, giving no indication that the word "FAITH" was a proper noun.

"Trajan. Does that mean anything to you?"

Mitchell cleared his throat. "Should it?"

Brown smiled, "Answering a question with a question, eh? That might work in the business world, Mr. Treadwell, but the police view it as avoidance, if not bad manners." A moment of silence passed and Brown said, "I looked it up on the internet. Trajan was a Roman emperor." He looked at his notebook, "His full name was Marcus Ulpius Nerva Traianus." He looked back at Mitchell.

He wanted to confess, explain everything, that his death or the death of his son had been miraculously avoided by the generous gesture of an old man. He had yet to determine if it was the bereft father of a dead son or a thousand-year-old African emir, but at that moment it was inconsequential. He wanted to unburden himself by letting the world know about the Commuters, about the ceremony and the line of succession, about what he had done as one of its members. Mitchell looked at the note atop the closed ledger, shaking his head in disgust and disbelief as if the book itself was the tell-tale heart beating on his desk.

Suddenly, a burning sensation arose in his chest and he consciously resisted the urge to say anything. Mitchell expected to hear more threats and accusations, but Brown gently took the note, folded it up and placed it in his pocket without saying a word.

The two remained silent, deep in thought before Brown, nearly pleading, said, "I need you to help me make sense of it all, Mr. Treadwell. When he died, Uncle Max, he said, 'You got your man.' I'd been collecting evidence for two years and I have this novel written except for the end. I was hoping … no, I was banking on catching this bastard to validate that he was your prototypical serial killer: white, middle-class, emotionally and physically abused as a child. And then *he* said *that* to me and it was like everything I knew to be true was shattered. And then I remembered the book, the one he carried around with him everywhere he went. And that you had it coming out of the factory the day he died. I need to know what's in it. I need to know why."

Mitchell leaned back in his chair and looked about the room. "You're not the only one looking for answers in this whole mess, detective," Mitchell began. "It was eating me up inside, too. I was wondering why an old man who I hardly knew would walk into that basement and allow me to walk out. To die for me. For my son. I've been studying this book since Uncle Max gave it to me and I still don't understand it all, but I do understand one thing: Uncle Max was an immortal hero. Not just to me and my son, but to thousands of people, like you, who were richer for knowing him."

The two were again enveloped in silence.

"So, you're not going to let me see the book without a warrant?"

Mitchell shook his head. "It's hard to explain. It's personally relevant to me. But, let me assure you, there is absolutely nothing in this book that is going to help you put your issues to rest. It is not a murder log."

The lie slid off Mitchell's tongue without effort and seemed to pass by the ever-attentive detective as if it were the gospel truth. Mitchell heard in his voice the same soothing tones Uncle Max had used to mollify Andy during their confrontation. A warmth grew inside him as he saw in the detective's face the relinquishing of his pursuit. Mitchell forced back a malevolent smile.

"And the note?" the detective asked.

Mitchell felt empowered by the acceptance of his previous lie and so he continued, "Well, the only thing that comes to mind is I told Michael about a support group I belonged to. I even invited him to sit in on one of our sessions, but he said no and that was that."

"'Faith is no more and that is on your head'?"

Mitchell shrugged. "I have no idea what that means." The warm surge returned to Mitchell's mid-section and it felt good as he watched Brown accept it without question. "I wish I could be more helpful, detective. Is there anything else?"

Brown looked him in the eyes and smiled. "Do you know any publishers looking for a great crime drama?"

This time, Mitchell let his wicked smile burst forth. "Networking is one thing I can help you with."

He stood up, shook the detective's hand and showed him out of the study, speaking to him as they walked. "I'll put you in contact with someone over at Korova Press, but all I can do is make the introduction. It'll be up to you to sell her on your writing."

"Thank you," Brown replied. "Oh, I forgot to ask, how's Davis?"

"He's fine. Thank you for your concern." He held the front door open wide with one arm and nearly shoved his visitor out with the other. "So, do you know how your book is going to end?"

"With a period. That's about all I know right now."

They both forced an uncomfortable smile.

"Well, good luck, detective. And have a nice day."

Detective Brown stepped off the porch and muttered, "Thanks. You, too."

Mitchell shut the door.

CHAPTER 56

It was nearly noon. It had been two years since Davis' abduction. Mitchell and his wife had moved their son into the dorms earlier that fall, leaving even more of the enormous house silent and empty. A brisk wind howled past the windows, dislodging a handful of leaves from their branches as Mitchell sat comfortably at his kitchen counter reading the day's massive *Bugle Gazette*. Several articles of personal significance caught his eye that morning. The *Business* section picked up a press release from his firm's marketing department highlighting a large refurbishment project set to break ground on the disheveled asphalt of Salem's Lot. The project was a joint effort between the city and the Treadwell Foundation that promised to generate hundreds of local jobs for the depressed area and bring renewed hope to a long-forgotten part of the inner city. The crown jewel of the project was the "Uncle Max" Community Center.

A particularly lengthy story that started on the front page and extended deep within the first section of the paper explained the rare astrological occurrence of the Harvest Moon falling squarely on the Autumnal Equinox, an anomaly that happens about once every three decades. As it happened, the previous night had seen just such an occurrence.

In the *Arts & Leisure* section was a scathing book review of a local author, a retired police detective. It was his debut novel, *a fictional thriller inspired by actual events*, if one believed the book's dust jacket. The review didn't give away many details of the plot, but the main concept was serendipitously tied to the lunar story from the front page. The gist of the novel was that a police detective, Detective Greene, was hunting down the Harvester, a serial killer who, one night a year when the moon was its brightest, felt compelled to stab a young boy through the heart and devour his genitalia. The plot was panned as "trite," the writing described as "amateurish" and the over-the-top passages detailing the victims' deaths vilified as "contemptible and abhorrent gore for gore's sake."

Yet another story highlighted the handful of Korova City police officers who had received their Detective shields, his sister-in-law Constance Wysczyzewski among them. The author of the story made a point of insinuating Officer Wysczyzewski's promotion was due in large part to her involvement in the Street Walker Killings, the name the *Bugle Gazette* had so cleverly given Andy Walker's depraved handiwork when the story first broke.

For weeks after his son's abduction, Mitchell and his family had been hounded by the media for details of their ordeal. Several publishers offered to pay handsomely for the story rights, but their offers fell on deaf ears. The Treadwells wished nothing more than to return to as normal a life as could be expected after such an intense and exhausting experience. Thankfully, the Street Walker Killings moved further and further away from the *Bugle Gazette's* front page as well as the local TV news' top-of-the-hour slots until it completely disappeared from mention. It had been the first time in more than a year he had read about the killings and he was pleased when he realized he wasn't crying.

Upon finishing his pleasure reading, Mitchell took up the arduous task of reading the obituaries: a habit he had begun upon the death of James Duncan, the brother-in-law of Michael O'Donahue. Mitchell had originally glanced through the obituaries just on the off chance that Conall Cernach's death was a harbinger of things to come. As it turned out, it was. Mitchell read that Duncan died from an apparent amphetamine overdose, his body found in another of the Commuter's ceremonial locations, a vacant field where Henry V's ceremony was held, the ceremony which occurred the year following Conall Cernach's. The obituary coincided with November's full moon and it gave Mitchell pause. Michael O'Donahue's suicide was one point of reference; James Duncan's suicide was a second, a coincidence. The following December's full moon had shone just before Christmas. Mitchell feverishly read the obituaries looking for a third instance to move his theory from a coincidence to a trend. He thumbed through the section looking for someone in their late forties to early fifties who had died somewhere that coincided with a ceremony location. He found the obituary of Titus Oates, the next member in the Commuter hierarchy and his third reference point.

First Conall Cernach. Then Henry V. And then Titus Oates. And the trend continued. The Alpha's were killing themselves, one by one and in succession, and Mitchell, a string of handshakes between him and them, was helpless to stop it. A few days after every full moon his theory was bolstered by the announcement that another Commuter had died in another of the Commuters' ceremonial locations, in a place Mitchell had stood, dressed in a bright white toga with a broad purple band and adorned by a large iron ring. He cried with each announcement.

When Mitchell read how Mr. David Michael Reynolds, an entrepreneurial nightclub owner and father of five, had shot himself in a graveyard where Samuel Clemens had dispensed death eight years prior, he had hoped the deaths would stop at the Alpha Seven and he could forget about it all. But the following month, a man drove his car into the building the Commuters had used for Tu-whakaheke-toto's ceremony and Mitchell knew the Betas would continue the disturbing onslaught.

Feeling helpless against the momentum of overwhelming mortality sweeping through his ex-compatriots, Mitchell made a ten thousand dollar posthumous donation to the Belling Foundation in the name of each member as his or her name appeared in the paper. It had been almost ten months since he made his last donation in the name of William Jerome Spence, whom Mitchell assumed was Lord Spencerton, the last member of the Betas. His death however, wasn't buried in the *Community* section of the paper with the hundreds of others recently deceased. Willie Spence's death was the lead story on every station's newscast for several days.

Willie Spence had entered a crowded nightclub just off of Club Road near Highway 101, stood in the middle of the dance floor and emptied a thirty-two-round clip from his IMI Micro-Uzi. He killed six and sent dozens of other unsuspecting patrons to the hospital. He then reloaded, dug the barrel into the center of his chest and pulled the trigger with his thumb. The short burst exploded through his heart, tearing it to shreds and killing him instantly.

But old habits die hard and on that brisk Sunday morning, Mitchell thumbed through the death notices thankful he was once again unable to find a write-up on a black woman in her mid- to late-thirties who might fit the profile of Marie Laveau. As the highest ascending Sophomore at the time of his matriculation out of the Commuters, she was the next logical member to take her own life, yet Mitchell was unable to find any mention of a suicide or a location he recognized in the obituaries following a full moon.

Mitchell assumed that Marie Laveau, the other Sophomores and all the Freshmen had been spared the fate of their senior members because they never had their own ceremony; had not performed the heinous act Mitchell so desperately wished he had never performed, the heinous act that separated dead members from what he considered the blissfully ignorant ones.

He was wrong.

Unbeknownst to Mitchell, Sharanda Randolph, known to the Commuters as Marie Laveau, had died twenty-eight days after Willie Spence took his own life. However, Sharanda didn't commit suicide and wasn't found in a locale he recognized. She died as the victim of a hit-and-run drunk driver, thereby avoiding Mitchell's notice. In fact, all the Sophomores and most of the Freshmen had already filled caskets in the same line of succession and following the same timetable as had been set by the group's senior members. They were listed in the same section of the paper that Mitchell read so intently, but their innocuous deaths went unnoticed. A car accident here. A slip-and-fall fatality there. Benign, unceremonious events that raised no red flags for Mitchell, but completed the circle of life, completed the membership requirements of the Commuters: Payment.

Mitchell folded the *Community* section and placed it on the pile of other sections stacked on the counter, straightening out the pile as he did so. He grabbed his coffee, walked out of the kitchen, through the living room and foyer, and eventually entered his study. Once there, he sat in the large, leather chair on casters, scooted in under the desk and turned on his banker's lamp, spreading light across the aged parchment bound inside the rich old book laid open in front of him. It had become his default place to spend idle time; reading it, studying it, researching portions of it online. In his two years of ownership, Mitchell had had the entire book translated, never giving any one archivist more than one spread at a time. He had innumerable purchase inquiries but he never accepted an offer. He could never put a price on his own redemption, not a financial price, anyway.

* * *

"Mitchell?" Prudy yelled, coming through the doorway between the kitchen and the garage. "I'm home."

Getting no response, she called louder, "Mitchell?"

Still nothing.

She slowly made her way to where she was all but certain her husband would be, where he always was whenever he was home. Her shoes clicked as she trod across the tile flooring of the entryway. She poked her head in the door, "Mitchell?"

The banker's lamp poured its light over the desk. Prudy recognized the book that lay open under the lamp and moved in to read it. It was a gift from her father to her husband, a thick and comprehensive leather-bound dictionary. She walked around the desk and sat in her husband's chair. The dictionary lay open on the desk. The definition for one of the words on the left page was forcibly scribbled out in ink. Though she recognized the fairly common word, she turned to the computer, wiggled the mouse to disrupt the screensaver and went about looking up the definition of the scratched-out word online.

The entry read:

com•mute
Pronunciation: kə-myōōt'
Function: verb
Inflected Form(s): com·mut·ed; com·mut·ing

Etymology: Middle English, from Latin commutare to change, exchange,
from com- + mutare to change--more at MUTABLE
transitive verb
1 a : CHANGE, ALTER
1 b : to give in exchange for another : EXCHANGE
2 : to convert (as a payment) into another form
3 : to change (a penalty) to another less severe
<commute a death sentence to life in prison>
4 : COMMUTATE
intransitive verb
1 : MAKE UP, COMPENSATE
2 : to pay in gross
3 : to travel back and forth regularly (as between a suburb and a city)
4 : to yield the same mathematical result regardless of order – used of two
elements undergoing an operation or of two operations on elements
- com·mut·able /-ˈmyü-tə-bəl/ adjective

"Hm," she muttered before quickly logging off. She got up and
wandered back into the kitchen, curious as to where her husband might
have gone.

About the Author

After a quarter century in the advertising industry, including twenty years writing award-winning copy for a number of agencies in and around Milwaukee, Patrick S. Lafferty is embarking upon a whole new career. He took his love for craft beer, developed a business plan, secured financing and is now the proud proprietor of a craft beer store in Wauwatosa, Wisconsin. He still dabbles as a copywriter on a freelance basis but spends what little free time he has writing short stories, screenplays and novels.

Outside of work, Patrick is the founding member of the Tosa Writers' Group and a long-time member of the Milwaukee Writer's Workshop (MWW) where, as the organization's Novel Group coordinator, he moderated critique sessions for more than twenty novels submitted by members, including three of his own novels. He's delivered his *You've Written a Novel. Now What?*, *Demystifying Royalties* and *Creative: The Noun, Not the Adjective* presentations to audiences at UW-Milwaukee's Osher Lifelong Learning Institute and WriteCamp Milwaukee. Learn more at patrickslafferty.com.

ALL THINGS THAT MATTER PRESS

FOR MORE INFORMATION ON TITLES AVAILABLE FROM
ALL THINGS THAT MATTER PRESS, GO TO
http://allthingsthatmatterpress.com
or contact us at
allthingsthatmatterpress@gmail.com

If you enjoyed this book, please post a review on Amazon.com and your favorite social media sites.

www.ingramcontent.com/pod-product-compliance
Lightning Source LLC
Chambersburg PA
CBHW052020020726
47501CB00004B/1155